A Day We Met In Lynbrook

K. Scott Fuchs

Published by K. Scott Fuchs, 2025.

This is a work of fiction. Similarities to real people, places, or events are entirely coincidental.

A DAY WE MET IN LYNBROOK

First edition. February 16, 2025.

Copyright © 2025 K. Scott Fuchs.

ISBN: 979-8230197973

Written by K. Scott Fuchs.

Table of Contents

A Day We Met In Lynbrook 1
Chapter 1 - Homecoming...2
Chapter 2 – Brothers and Sons 15
Chapter 3 – The Morning After 21
Chapter 4 - Melissa.. 29
Chapter 5 – A Chapter Not Named Like A Fall Out Boy Song 40
Chapter 6 – I Circled No Before You Could Say Yes 60
Chapter 7 – New Beginnings.. 71
Chapter 8 – The First Game 79
Chapter 9 – The Fair... 97
Chapter 10 – Orange Checkerboards and Smoke 114
Chapter 11 – Victory Formation 130
Chapter 12 – Holy Ghost... 136
Chapter 13 – Home Away from Home... 151
Chapter 14 – The Spawning of Progressions............................. 170
Chapter 15 – Work and Pain 177
Chapter 16 – Wash Out.. 187
Chapter 17 – Somewhere in Franklin Square 221
Chapter 18 – The Ice Shack 244
Chapter 19 – Flowers for a Funeral 256
Chapter 20 – Samantha Jayne Foxe 268
Chapter 21 - The Only One 278
Chapter 22 – xo Irish Southern Belle xo 292
Chapter 23 – It's All A Long Hello 297
Chapter 24 – The Day to Remember... 308
A Selection of Poems by K. Scott Fuchs.. 316

Dedicated to The Lord Jesus Christ for being there in the moments I needed Him most. This book took eighteen years to write and you guided from start to finish.

With special thanks to: Richard Caster, Juan Rodiguez, A.J. Maniscalco, Deanna Langdon, Marguerite Peugeot, my big brother Chozen, Michael Brunetta, Rebecca Anderson, Alexandre Desinor, Kenny Sargeant, Craig & Sarah Shaw, Big John, Tony Bolton, Kevin Kuchmak, and Martyn Robinson for telling me to give them nothing and take from them everything.

When you look back at your life over the years, you will identify moments where you say to yourself, "That's where it all went wrong". When I was seventeen, there was a point in my life where there was no hope for me either. There was a point in my life where everything seemed to be shadowed by fear and anxiety. Doubt was the only compass directing me on a path I would never be able to return home from. But then I met you and didn't realize you were always there guiding me.

Chapter 1 - Homecoming

I lived on Holmes Place in North Lynbrook, New York. The town was just five miles from the Queens/Nassau County border separating the City of New York from Long Island though geographically they were one and the same. That didn't make any difference though as Lynbrook was a world to itself.

The house I lived in was Ranch-styled on a quiet, dark, and secluded block, much like any other residential street in a suburban community, anywhere else. I enjoyed sitting out on the porch late into a hot summer night reading a book or listening to some music.

It was Friday, August 13th, 2004 my brother Michael, slowly stepped out of a taxi with a zipper bag in his hands which had many personal belongings. He was dressed in a midnight blue New York Yankees fitted hat along with a blue striped collared shirt. The buttons were undone showing his ivory white t-shirt beneath. Mike also wore matching blue baggy jeans and clean white sneakers. His chin strap and goatee were neatly kept.

My brother looked around took in the sounds of kids playing and dogs barking in the surrounding streets; it was as if it were a harmony to his ears. I quickly put down a glass of orange juice along with a copy of Machiavelli's *The Prince* taking a whiff of the aroma of grilled hamburger meat escaping from the windows. Mike walked up the brick path and I met him at the top of the steps, as he approached the bottom.

"Little brother." Mike smiled, I sprinted down and gave him a hug. My mother came out the door, relieved at the sight of him.

"Welcome home, Michael" she said softly with tears in her eyes.

"It's good to be home." Mike embraced our mother with a very tight grip. For all of us it seemed longer than a year when he was arrested on August 9th, 2003 for an assault and two other miscellaneous offenses. His life had been put on pause, returning to us exactly as we last saw him over a year ago.

Mike gazed around the kitchen, taking in the subtleties that seemed like luxuries compared to where he had spent the last year and six days.

"So, Core, how are the ladies treating you?" Mike scratched his head.

"They're okay, I guess"

"Ok?" He sat back. "Do you still have a crush on what's her name..." He kissed his teeth. "Um Mel, Melissa Paducah!" He chuckled, as I snapped at his remark.

"Ah sweetie, Melissa is a lovely girl. I know her mother, Teresa, we play Bingo at the Church on Wednesday nights."

"You play Bingo Mom?" Mike laughed. "Are you collecting Social Security now?"

"Michael Joseph Montgomery! I'm 39 years old, but I feel like I'm 100 raising you!"

Mike took a scoop of his *Hamburger Helper*, as our mom left the simmering pan on the stove and sat down to join us.

"You never know Ma, maybe you will make a second living off of it. Shit, I thought Monopoly was just a game until I applied the teachings."

"Watch your mouth." Mom shot Mike an icy glare, he looked down in a show of acknowledgement and respect. Though Mike always liked to be grand in his mannerisms, he knew Mom was the one who is in charge.

"The extra hundred dollars I won last week by the way is paying for this lovely meal we are eating tonight." My mom grabbed a fork full off her plate.

"Kool-Aid and Hamburger Helper" Mike wiped his mouth, "Top notch, Ma." He smiled and put his hand to her cheek with a gentleness.

"Well Corey, we are happy to have Mikey home. We do love his sense of humor, don't we?"

"I think we are going to have to feed him some biscuits and mashed potatoes tomorrow, cause I'm sure he's sick of jail meatloaf." I teased.

He slammed down his fork. "All of a sudden, you have some balls Corey?"

The doorbell rung and I got up from my seat to see who it was, waving my hands as I headed for the door.

"Yea, walk away." His fork clanged against his plate.

"Michael, quit your tough guy antics. If you don't stop it, I'm going to feed you soap for dinner." Soon the exchanges became muffled as I opened the door to see my best friend Ricky Moreno standing on my porch with a football in hand. Ricky was like me going into his senior year of high school, not knowing what was in store for him. Ricky and I played football together for three years. Unlike me who rode the bench, Ricky was one of the best running backs in the conference. He rushed for 1,187 yards as a Junior in eight regular season games. For those who don't follow the sport, that is quite the feat. As for me, I had no accolades, occasionally I'd get in the game for a few plays. Also, unlike me, Ricky had no problem with the ladies. But despite our differences, we were the best of friends.

"What's up bro?" I opened the door.

He shook my hand and gave me a quick embrace. "Not much man, how are you doing?" Ricky entered. "It smells good, what do you got going on?" Ricky strolled in to the kitchen wearing a white Florida Gators jersey and blue jeans.

"Some pasta and salad."

"Who's that?!" Mike called into the hall as Ricky walked into the kitchen.

"Oh, Ricardito! my Dominican cito. What's up fool, you still running from guys like me?!"

"Nah Mike, still running guys like you over" Ricky shook his hand, happy to see Mike like the rest of us.

"What's going with your sister?" Mike wiped his mouth. "I'm fresh out and looking for a new friend..."

"I don't think Joanna wouldn't consort with the likes of you." Ricky took a piece of bread from one of the dinner plates. "Ya weasel..." He bit into a piece of Italian bread, the stub breaking off in his teeth.

"Hello Ricky." My mom kissed him on the cheek. "Would you like some pasta?"

"Sure Mom, would love some, thank you."

"On a serious note Rick, hook my brother up with one of ya gal pals..." Mike waved his fork. "...This kid needs it."

"Well I just might be able to do that." Ricky took his first fork of Cheeseburger Mac *Hamburger Helper*.

"Oh really? Mike smirked "Who?".

Ricky finished chewing his food and made gestures with his hand. "Melissa" He took a sip of some Grape Kool-Aid.

"Melissa?"

He nodded and swallowed. "I thought that's what you wanted?"

"Well there you we go." He slapped my back. "Don't shit ya pants Corey."

Mom slapped down a bar of soap next to Mike's plate. When it came to girls, I was a nervous wreck. I was always afraid I'd say the wrong thing and I almost always clamed up in the presence of a beautiful woman. I venerated women to an absurd capacity, and yet it was too no avail. Nevertheless, I always prayed for a day I could be as "smooth as silk" with Melissa Paducah, a beauty of Italian descent that stood five-feet six inches with long flowing dark brown hair and green eyes.

After Ricky devoured his meal, he and I stood outside on the porch with Mike. Mike brought out a pack of Marlboro Red cigarettes and flipped a cigarette into his mouth. He reached into his pocket to grab a hold of his blue Zippo lighter with a flaming 8-ball design. Mike always called that his "lucky lighter".

"This may sound hypocritical but don't ever smoke Corey, no matter what the reason may be." He propped himself on the railing. "It's the worst thing you can do to yourself." His words muffled somewhat by his inhaling and exhaling of the smoke. "I'm not saying you shouldn't go out with girls and get shitty from time to time. But smoking can fuck up your football career. "His words were interrupted by a white 2001 Ford Thunderbird Supercharger rolling up to the curb. The sound system echoed through the still streets, *"7th Chamber"* by the Wu-Tang Clan reverberated from the subwoofers. The passenger door swung opened and out came our cousin Shawn screaming *Yo!* repeatedly with excitement.

Mike stood up to acknowledge him as he charged up the walk with his black t-shirt and gray sweatpants swaying with each step. Shawn had on a pair of black and grey Nikes to add to his look. Shawn kept it simple: crew cut and clean shaven. Despite his average height, he was a stocky dude. He had a way of being intimidating to others but still kept a boyish look to him with his red hair, freckled-fair skin, and baby blue eyes. My mother often referred to Shawn as the "third brother" because we have always been attached at the hip since we were young. He was after all only six months older than Mike.

"Welcome home brother, we missed you." Shawn hugged Mike.

"Happy to see you too Terror."

"Corey, what's up little bro?" Shawn looked up at me on the porch.

"What's up big brother, how are you?"

"Lovely, just gonna take our brother out for a night, to celebrate his release from the New York State Criminal Justice System. What are you up to tonight?"

"I..."

Mike interrupted. "Let him be, he's going to see a girly"

"You have a girlfriend, Corey? Shawn smirked and tipped his head at me. "Is she cute?"

"I'll tell ya about it later." Mike placed his hand on Shawn's shoulder.

"Well good luck then, little brother."

Mike and Shawn turned towards the car, making their way down the steps.

"Dem Rep, ya heard. Ghost is free!" The faint cheers of their running mates Marcus "Slick" Diaz and Jerome "Numerals" McDonald were heard from the backseat. Shawn gave Mike the honor of riding shotgun.

Ricky and I started our walk towards Greis Park, a recreational sprawl composed of baseball fields and basketball courts. The combination of twilight and streetlights recently powered on gave us just enough illumination to throw the football around as we walked. It was great, the simple activity of catching and throwing the ball, it took my mind out of the impending battle. I felt like the Spartans in the face of the Persian Empire. As my heartbeat raced from a nervous excitement, I couldn't help but also feel a sense of determination; the dream was becoming a reality.

"You going to handle ya business, right?" Ricky walked ahead with the football tucked tight against his sweatshirt.

"Yea man, I got it" I continued to look down at the crevices in the granite of the street. I was looking for little pebbles and stones to kick to quell my nerves. It was an ironic nervous comfort. I enjoyed my moments that led up to the moment. At the same time, I was filled with dread. A part of me wanted to fake sick and go home but then when I laid in my bed tonight, I'd think about what could have been. We only get one life and when my time came to go before The Lord, I wouldn't want to have any regrets.

I surged ahead of Ricky while he was practicing his juke moves and stiff arms in the middle of Horton Avenue. He himself was imagining being on a different battlefield: the football field.

"Woah, woah Corey, easy guy, chillax a bit." Ricky grabbed my shoulder and slowed me down.

"I'm good man" I shrugged off his hand.

"You see Corey, that's your problem right there, bro. You need to just chill out and not make this a big deal. It's just a girl."

"I am chill man, just let me be."

"Just do your thing and not worry about it, alright?" Ricky threw his hands out. "You know Foxy, right?"

"She was in my Chemistry class, last year, but I never really spoke to her."

"Well, I've been hitting that so I'll be busy with Samantha and you'll have plenty of time to do your thing with Melissa." He lectured with such confidence. As mentioned previously, Ricky had no problem with the ladies. He was smooth, he was sophisticated, and he was charming. Honestly, I could see any Hollywood bombshell eating out of his hand.

As we came to the traffic light at the intersection of Merrick Road and Horton Avenue, the light turned green and Ricky shouted from behind me.

"Hey Corey, give me a 10 and in!"

I smiled and ran across the crosswalk and cut in towards the fence, Ricky threw me the ball and I made the catch.

"Touchdown Gators!" Ricky ran across the street and slapped the street sign. I wasn't a Gator fan though; I have always been a faithful Miami Hurricanes fan. Needless to say, we sometimes we had disagreements over this pivotal subject.

I stopped, turned sharply, and pressed my two thumbs together while solely raising my index finger and middle finger, forming a U. Commonly Miami Hurricane players made this gesture when they sacked the quarterback or scored a touchdown.

"Please stop with that corny ass bullshit"

"Not my fault your goons blew a twenty-three-point lead last time you played us, right?" I flipped the football.

Ricky had skin in the game, he loved the Gators and they were very much a part of him as much as anything else.

"Ok Core, they're going to be on the baseball field." Ricky led the way as we passed by a firehouse on our left until we were met by a sign that said Horton Avenue Entrance. "They got a couple of treats for us."

"Beers?"

"You bet bro." He smirked as we walked in and passed the hockey rink on our way to the derelict backstop on the baseball field ahead of us.

Ricky and I traversed the baseball diamond past the pitcher's mound as we approached, I couldn't help but look up at the sky and admire the beauty. It was a clear night and the sky was filled with stars. It looked like a masterpiece painting that only a genius could create: only The Lord could create such a wonder. It's funny when you look up at the heavens, everything that is going on in your life seems so insignificant and simple.

We heard a whistle. Emerging from the darkness, accented by the field lamps was Samantha followed by Melissa. Samantha had her long auburn-colored hair tied in a bun and down her back. She wore a green tank-top with black leggings and white sneakers. Her eyes seamed to shimmer in the moonlight and her eyes sparkled as she walked over to Ricky with a childish smile and kissed him. Ricky grabbed a handful of her ample backside and pulled her in for a more engaged exchange. Melissa wore her hair down over her white tank top which was tucked into blue jeans. She wore sandals to complement her casual look.

"Well, I see that those two are busy." She quickly looked at Sam and Ricky making out. "I'll introduce myself them, I am Melissa."

I extended my hand and shook hers.
"Corey Montgomery." I stuttered.

"Oh snap, is your mom named Mary?"
"Yeah, why?" My nerves coursed with anxiety.
"My mom plays bingo over at the church with her sometimes. Your mom is a nice lady, I met her once or twice."
"Thanks, I'm sure your mom is nice too."
She laughed and approached me with a can of Keystone Ice beer.
"Want one?" She popped open her can and took a sip.
"Thanks." I took it and followed suit, hoping it would establish a ground level for us to converse from.
"My bad, my bad." Ricky gasped out of breath. "Sam, Melissa, this is my boy Corey..." He cupped his hand outwards. "...we play football together."
"A little late there." Melissa chuckled.

As Samantha and I made eye contact for the first time, I felt as if I was reunited with a long-lost friend. There was a haze between us which kept our eyes on each other, it was hard to describe in words, but once I put made eye contact with her it seemed impossible to pull it off her. A curiosity filled Samantha; her eyebrows raised for a brief moment as she extended her hand for me to shake.

"It's nice to meet you Corey, you can call me Sam."
"Or Foxy..." Melissa smirked.
"Either will do..." Sam fixed her hair that was thrown out of sorts by her and Ricky's vivacious hook-up session.
"It's a pleasure to meet you."

"I haven't really seen you around before." She squinted, fascinated by my very existence. Equally, there was something about her, something unique that made me believe she was someone who was going to become a very important part of my life, for some reason I also could not express.

"What position do you play?"

"Corey is a skilled Wide Receiver." Ricky put his hand around the back of my neck.

"Nah, I don't really play much"

"Stop." He dismissed my lack of confidence. "Go run a 15 and post."

"Uh it's dark out, Rick I won't see the ball."

"I'll hit you in the light, don't sweat it."

"I'm good bro."

"Quit being a wuss and show these lovely ladies your skills." Rick twirled the ball in his hand. Melissa continued to drink her beer and look up at me. I looked at her and then sprinted about fifteen yards and cut across the field. Ricky stepped back and threw me a great ball, the only problem was that it was a bit overthrown, so I had to stretch for it. For you football players out there, that means one thing: you have to dive. I leapt up in to the air and got one hand on it, brought it down, and still managed to keep my balance and land full stride. For some incredulous reason, I had made the best catch in my high school and pick-up game career up until that point, right then and there.

"Wow!" Sam raised her eyebrows.

"Yea, wow indeed!" Ricky lost his composure and appeared bewildered. "Where has this been?"

I walked back and tossed the ball to Ricky.

"If you make plays like that in practice, you're going to be a starter no question."

Sam put her arms around Ricky. Ricky turned quickly and started to kiss on her again, the two were consumed by each other and soon forgot we were there: it was the perfect opportunity.

"Hey do you want to go over the gazebo?" I asked Melissa.

"Good idea" She grabbed a few beers and we ventured toward the gazebo. Melissa led and I followed. Minutes later I was sat at one end of the bench and she on the other. Melissa placed a few beers on the bench and popped another open. I fixated on the scoreboard as my nerves began to catch up with me and I looked for a distraction.

For a few moments I wasn't thinking about what stood in front of me. I was focused on playing football. What if I could actually start? What if I could actually play? Our old coach was obsessed with winning. He had his few players that he always played and that was it. For the most part a lot of the kids like myself who gave their time and effort to the program were rewarded with nothing more than a position on a depth chart. However, this year, we had a new coach. And with that change came new possibilities.

"So, Corey, you play football but I never see you hanging around at the parties with your teammates."

"Well I just hang out with Ricky, that's pretty much it." I sipped my beer. "Or with my brother, if he's not locked up..."

"Who's your brother?" Melissa took another sip of a beer.

"His name is Mike."

"I don't know him. How old is he?"

"He'll be 20 in November."

She smirked "You certainly know how to keep your distance..."

The gesture caught me off guard.

"Well, I figure you have a boyfriend and I didn't want to be disrespectful."

"You're so cute." She smiled. "Well you're right I do have a boyfriend, but we are on a break right now." Melissa sipped on the can. "What about you Corey? You have a girlfriend?"

"Not at the moment."

"Why not?" She giggled.

"I don't know."

"Well don't worry I'm sure you'll meet a nice girl one day."

There was a voice inside my head that said tell her *"you never know it could be her"*. But I choked on the sentences. Instead, I stared out once again examining the luminescent hue of Foxy's long mane of hair.

"So, Melissa, who is your boyfriend?"

"His name is Matt, he's from Oceanside" She held her can of Natural Light.

"How long have you been going out with him?"

"About three months, but as mentioned we're on a break now."

"Why?" I covered my mouth. "I'm sorry, I didn't mean to be rude."

She laughed, "No it's okay. It was more his idea then mine. He felt we were moving too fast."

"Oh really? That's rough."

"Yea I really like him." Her face beamed with infatuation.

"Well, I might not know much about this type of stuff." I took a full swig of beer to numb out the nerves. "But uhh, if you ever need someone to talk to about this stuff. I know we just met and all, but I'm a good listener."

That was my boldest move of the evening and quite possibly my life up to that point: offering to be a friend to the girl.

"Thank you, that's really sweet of you."

Ricky and Sam walked into the gazebo to join us.

"Dukes, we have to get over to Katie's house, now." Foxy gasped.

"How could I forget?" Melissa got up and put her empty can down on the bench.

"Pleasure to meet you, Corey. I hope we talk more soon." When Samantha extended her hand towards me and our fingers touched, I couldn't forget the look in her eyes, blue and inviting as if there was a universe beneath them.

"Nice to meet you too, Samantha, I hope so as well." The anxiety left for a moment as we glanced at each other and shared a pleasant smile. Then she and Melissa exited the gazebo.

"Melissa..."

"Yeah?" She turned around.

"Don't you want to take my number? In case you ever wanted to talk, or maybe we can hang out one day at lunch during school or something." I breathed heavily under my sedated words.

"Yea no doubt." She handed me her Nokia phone. "Put it in there."

My eyes focused on the screen and making sure every stroke of the keypad was perfect so she had my number, I didn't want to miss the chance.

"Okay, give me a call if you need to talk or anything." I handed the phone back to her, nearly dropping it as my hand fidgeted.

She took the phone and pressed it twice, soon a message arrived at my phone as the cell phone flashed for a moment to acknowledge it.

"Thank you, there's mine."

"We'll see y'all later."

My eyes wandered to Foxy, the way she said y'all. It didn't sound like someone that was from around this neck of the woods.

"Peace out." Ricky waved his hand and watched as they walked for a moment, chugging his can before he wiped his mouth. "There ya go boy!" He rubbed my head and shoved me playfully. "There ya fucking go!"

Chapter 2 – Brothers and Sons

Ricky and I left the park through a hole in the fence, cutting through the drive-thru of a Wendy's before we emerged on Merrick Road, heading towards the center of town. Cars whizzed by as we wandered in no particular direction. Ricky pulled out his headphones which split in to two different earbuds.

"Shall we?"

I plucked at the gummy blue headphone and put it into my ear. Ricky opened up a blue Discman player and slid a CD into it, its reflection sparkling under a passing streetlight. *Pardon Me* by Incubus started to play.

As we crossed over Wilson Avenue, we looked in to the parking lot of Taco Bell to see Sniper's car parked in the lot. Sniper and Numeralz were standing by the car, taking drags of their Newports. Both men showed little emotion, stoic in their mannerisms and expression. The glass door flung open and Mike stormed out of the building snacking on a burrito with Shawn closely following. Mike launched his half-eaten burrito into the fence, beans and cheese exploding everywhere as he rang out a chorus of profanities.

"Let's go see what this is about" Ricky tapped my chest.

I plucked the earphone from my ear and nodded. We through our hands up to get their attention, they responded in kind. All were sitting on the hood of the Thunderbird with their backs to us. Numeralz was the first to notice entering the parking lot as we went around the bushes that lined the perimeter.

"It's Little Ghost!"

Mike turned around, his eyes watery and bloodshot.

"Everything alright big brother?"

"Nah, Corey, it's not alright." He swiped his brow. "I heard there is some Sovereigns runnin' around here looking for me."

"Alright well then maybe we should get you home. You know, Ricky, me, you, Shawn and the boys we can all play some N C Double A."

"Yea Ghost, fuck it lets grab some 40's and do that. Little Ghost has a good idea." Sniper's voice was filled with encouragement at the notion.

Mike glared at him, displeased with the suggestion.

"Yea, fuck it bro." Shawn put his hand on Mike's shoulder. "It's your first day home, we should hang out as a family. That's what we all are." Shawn looked around at all of us. "DEM REP!" He screamed, the other two threw up signs as a response to that.

"That's my point!" Mike turned to each person. "We are all a family and Lynbrook is our home. Fuck the Sovereigns, Fuck RVC and fuck Marion!"

"Listen if you want to ride, we got you." Sniper took a drag of his cigarette. "But we don't want you going back in the county, when you just got out."

"The reason why I was in jail is cause of this motherfucker." Mike pointed downward." I say we fuck these losers up!"

"Corey, you down?" Mike looked at me from the corner of his eye.

"Woah, woah Mike..." Shawn stepped in. "Why you getting your little brother involved?"

"He's grown ass man!" Mike looked at both Ricky and myself with ice in his eyes. "He can answer." He looked reminiscent of Alonzo Harris from Training Day, leaning against the hood of the car and sizing me up. "I know I don't need to ask him because I know where he is heart is at. But I just want to ask him because I want to hear it."

"I got you, bro." Though my reluctance was very much evident, I always stood shoulder to shoulder and behind Mike. He always had my back and always made sure no one ever picked on me or messed with me otherwise. I was blindly loyal to him, as he was to me.

"Hop in, little brother." Mike nodded and ushered me to the car. "Ricardito?"

Ricky followed me with a slack-jaw expression, perhaps a bit shocked that Mike would recklessly put myself and him by default in such a situation. But I knew how this all worked, Mike wouldn't let anything happen to us.

"It's straight..." I looked at him to reassure him. Numeralz opened the door and pulled up the seat so Ricky and I could get in. Shawn shook his head at Mike with disgust, as we jumped in last.

"What?!" Mike threw his hands out. "He has his brother's back, there isn't loyalty like that anymore."

"You missed the point, Ghost." Shawn retorted.

The car sped out of the parking lot on to the streets of Lynbrook. Sniper wheeled with one hand on the steering wheel and the other hand out the window with a lit cigarette. Mike sat up front on Shawn's cell phone. "It's a shame, Slick and Tripz had to bounce." He pressed the phone to his ear as he dialed old friends and acquaintances who were involved with Dem Rep before Mike was arrested. Their first engagement with him since his release, if they even knew that he was out was another call to arms. Surely, Mike would have gotten it by then, but he didn't.

Numeralz both sat by the windows, as Ricky and I were in the middle, squeezed together and flanked by Shawn on the other side, who wreaked of wet dog and sweat. The car made a turn on to Charles Street and to my horror we saw a group of ten to fifteen wearing black and white congregated in the parking lot of a Window factory which had been closed for the evening.

"There's that motherfucker right there." Mike glared out the window and looked back to us. "Alright well here is the game plan. There is six of us, they got about fifteen heads. I got some dudes coming from Valley Stream and I got a couple of the boys from back in the day down to ride. We'll drop the whips and post up a couple of blocks away, then we'll fuck these bitches up."

And just like that, the stage was set for an epic showdown between the Street Sovereigns and Dem Rep. In a matter of minutes, the cars were parked in a vacant lot on Peninsula Blvd. Tactically, this served as a convenient rendezvous point to make a swift exit undetected. The environment become more animated when Mike drew attention to himself as he called a sea of green bandanas to surround him. There must have been about twenty members of Dem Rep present. Many reminisced about moments shared years back as they puffed on their cigarettes. The majority were confident, unshaken at the prospect of what might happen. Ricky and I stood firm but we were shaking underneath the calm surface.

As we made a right on to Remsen Street, my adrenaline began to build even more with each step that we took. It was similar to the emotions of when I was walking to meet Melissa. Excited and nervous at the same time. I couldn't help but stare at the passing cars on Peninsula Blvd. The drivers and passengers likely unable to see us in the midst of the darkness and the trees that lined the road. They were unaware, driving home from work, driving to work or maybe driving just to get away. I was hoping I could get away too. I was thinking of Melissa, hoping that I'd get to see her again before school started. Hoping that she wouldn't read about me in the papers. Hoping the nice guy that she believed she met, didn't turn out to be a ruffian arrested for hanging out with a bunch of gangbangers. We followed Mike who led the way. Numeralz and Sniper to his right, myself and Ricky to his left. Eight more us. I could see the illumination of the streetlights of Merrick Road ahead.

We turned the corner swiftly and continued through the parking lot of the window factory. We halted as we intersected the group of Sovereigns. I looked around and counted the numbers, there were eight of them. All were bold and proud, audaciously clad in black, some rocking bandanas over their foreheads.

"Welcome home, Ghost." Emerging from the crowd was a tall and thin built male with earing in both his ears. He too wore a black bandana over his forehead accenting his flip-top cut. Dressed in similar regalia to Mike, the character wore baggy black sweatpants and a white t-shirt with a gold chain. His face drowned in smoke from a lit cigarette he puffed on.

"I've been waiting for you."

"Yea that's cause you a man-crush on me, we know Truck." Mike jeered.

The whole group broke out in laughter, myself included. As these two old foes sized each other up, I couldn't help but look across the street at these group of four girls looking on. There was a taller one, about 5'5, wearing a brown leather coat with silky black hair falling up on it, both of which glowed in the moonlight; she was absolutely breathtaking.

The best part of it was that she was staring right at me. I looked back at her and smiled; she did the same. Even though she was wearing blue jeans and brown boots, my imagination couldn't help but run wild with what it all looked like underneath.

"So, what are we going to do about this Ghost? You going to throw a sheet over your head and haunt our town?"

"Nah, here's what we going to do." Mike whistled and the other group of 10 led by Shawn emerged from the darkness and surrounded the invaders. The collective lost all their courage, it was clearly spelt across their face.

Shawn and Mike led the charge. Needless to say, it was tactical brilliance. I ran and in followed the crowd. Dem Rep got the upper hand quick as I saw Shawn throw their "Number 2" PJ in to a dumpster, followed by a flurry of kicks and stomps. Mike already had Truck on the floor and then smashed a bottle over Truck's head. His hair was soaked with blood and riddled with shards of glass. Truck covered up as a last-ditch attempt to absorb the punishment Mike was relentless to deal. As I surveyed the bedlam, I saw Ricky land a solid cross to one of the smaller adversaries. I hurried and picked up a baking pan that was laying on the ground next to me and made me way toward my brother, cousin and friend.

"Get him!" Three Sovereigns came rushing down the street from behind us. It seemed that they were planning an ambush of their own. I ran into the crowd, three brave men who tried to aid their fallen comrades were met by Numeralz, Slick, and Sniper. I was confused and I peered on looking to avoid any form of conflict. I tightly gripped the baking pan for what I thought would be a safe measure.

One of the fallen Sovereigns rose to their feet and charged at me. As a reflex, I smashed the baking pan over his head. The force of the impact caused the pan to bend to the contours of the adversary's skull. He fell to the ground immediately.

"That's what's up Corey!" Mike cheered and gave the retreat signal as we heard sirens approaching in the distance. There on the ground lay eleven severely beaten Sovereigns. The fight was over in less than five minutes, but there was enough carnage there to last for days. As the sirens rang in the distance, we sprinted back to the cars and scattered into the night before anyone could get a trace on us.

Chapter 3 – The Morning After

I woke up the next morning to the sun shining on my face as I was jostled from my sleep. When I opened my eyes, I saw my brother Mike standing over me dressed in a white New York Giants jersey and blue basketball shorts. Mike wore a cream New York Yankees fitted hat and his signature white sneakers. He stood at the foot of my bed with a football tucked in his hand.

"Good morning, little brother."

"What's up?" I yawned.

"I was thinking I could take us over to the Brookvale for breakfast..." Mike twirled the football. "And then we could throw the ball around to get you ready for the season."

"That's nice of you dude, but I got money saved up."

"Listen, Corey I ran that fool's pocket last night." He smirked. "He had three hundred bucks on him"

"What?!" I rose with alarm.

"Mike, you're going to get charged with robbery. Just let me spot us..." Mike placed his arm on my shoulder.

"How is he going to file a robbery charge, when I left his four bags of marijuana and his wallet with him?" Mike smiled from ear to ear. "Besides, I only have fifty bucks on me anyhow and it's not like his bills are marked, right?"

I was stunned; I am not supposed to support criminal behavior but I couldn't help but admire the tact and strategy.

"What time is it?"

"Time for you to get up." He chuckled. "Get whatever you want at the diner alright? It's my second day home, I just want to spend some time with my little brother that I missed a lot. The little brother that had my back last night and SMASHED A BAKING PAN over some kids head!"

"He charged at me what was I supposed to do?"

"You did what you had to do." Mike gave me a nod of respect. "And you had your brother's back." Mike got off the bed. "Grab a shower, get some clothes on, and let's go man, its ten-o-clock already." He threw the football up in the air and caught it as he walked down the hall. "In the county, we were up at 5:30 every day."

About forty minutes later Mike and I were on our way.

"Ah man, I'm starving. I can't wait to get some grub at the Brookvale, it's been too long." Mike's excitement was ripe.

"What are you going to get?"

"That's a good question, I was thinking about that the whole time we were walking. I'm thinking I'll get the deluxe eggs platter with the home fries, juice, coffee and a glass of chocolate milk to start."

"To start?" I raised my eyebrows.

"Listen Corey, I haven't had a good meal other than last night in a long time. I'm going to dine the fuck out bro." He threw the ball up. "So how, we looking this year?"

"I couldn't tell you since I was riding the bench all season last year."

"That's the problem right there, little brother, you're not even giving yourself a chance." He threw the ball to me and I caught it.

"Well, what's going to be different?" I tossed the ball back to him.

"Today is a new day, whatever changes you want to make in your life begin with you and end with you. You like that Melissa chick, Go get her!" He threw the ball to me again and threw his arms out. "You want to play football? Get to it and don't let no one else tell you it can't happen."

"With God all things are possible."

"We don't have to take it that far." Mike paused and shook his head at me. "I don't believe in Him."

"But Mike, I prayed for you..."

"Dude, stop!" He put his hands up. "When you are locked up in the pen and you have all day and night to reflect, you'll come to realize that God isn't there with you, you are on your own."

"And when you were away how did Mom and I cope?" My nose wrinkled. "We prayed." I raised my voice in response. "You may not see it now, but one day I pray you will. He was always there and will always be there."

"If you feel that passionate about it..." He laughed for a moment and rolled his eyes, as we continued on until we finally arrived at the Brookvale Diner. A local treasure to residents of Lynbrook, Malverne, and North Valley Stream. The best food you can eat in the area hands down.

We didn't speak again until the two of us were sat in a window booth after we had ordered our breakfasts.

"Look Corey, we'll just have to disagree about God. If you believe in him that's wonderful and I hope you're right. But I just don't see it, I'm sorry."

"I just pray you figure it out one day, He'll change your life. He can make zero in to a hundred and can make any loser a winner." I looked out the window and admired the blue sky and sunshine. "He transforms lives and people daily." I couldn't help but reflect on everything that has transpired over the past twenty-four hours as I took my first sip of Vanilla Coke, the bubbles cascaded into the back of my throat and relieved the scratchiness.

"Right, if I need a new car, I know who to go to." He teased as he took a sip of coffee, his eyes bulged with delight. "Damn that's good, it's not that mud shit in Nassau." He continued to sip. "Sorry." He wiped his mouth. "So, how did your date go with Melissa?"

"It wasn't a date."

"I know." He smirked and immersed himself in his coffee. "You get her number?"

"Actually, I did." I smiled.

"Nice!" Mike put out his fist for me to pound, I tapped it.

"You see Corey, things are looking up for you already." Mike looked out the window at The Trestle Billiards Hall as he held his coffee.

"Yeah, but she has a boyfriend."

Mike placed his cup down. "So what?"

"That means she's not interested."

"Yea Bullshit, Corey." Mike chuckled. "Women say that sometimes to gauge your interest and if that's not the case then who says she is faithful?"

"Yea but why would I want to date her, if she isn't?"

"You were always a wise man." He nodded and took another sip of coffee. "So, what did you say when she said she had a boyfriend?"

A woman in a white shirt and red bow tie arrived with her breakfasts, setting them both on the table.

"Thank you, Ma'am." Mike nodded.

"Thank you." I smiled at her, as well.

She spun her circular tray back in her hand and popped a bubble between her lips, as she walked away.

"Well she told me they were on a break but it was more him than her that wanted it." I grabbed the pepper and sprinkled some over my eggs. "And I said if you want to talk about it, I'm here." I passed the glass canister with a meniscus of black and white grains half-way up over to Mike."

"Okay…" He sprinkled some pepper on his eggs and swiped his hands once. "If she is on a break with him, it's for a reason and if he can't man up and appreciate what he has, then you can." Mike dug in to his home fries and wiped his mouth. "Let me tell you something Corey, sometimes in this world the things we want the most, we have to do what we have to do to get them. You can't always worry about the next guy because the next guy could be trying to take what could be yours." He threw his napkin down. "Your chance may never come if you wait in line."

"She is hooked on this other guy."

"Here is what you do." He reached for a bottle of ketchup and rolled some across his plate. "Call her up or text her and ask her if she wants to hang out and go get a..." Mike looked at his coffee cup. "Cup of coffee or something; nothing over the top."

"Wouldn't that make it obvious?"

"Well, yeah." He snickered. "But that's not the point. Sure, it shows intention but you can see if you really like her and where she stands with this guy."

"I'll give it a whirl." I cut my sausage.

"And don't be afraid to talk to other chicks Corey." Mike slammed his fork down as he emphasized this instruction. "Keeping your options open is a good thing." Mike ripped off a piece of toast and swam it through his egg yolk.

I smiled and thought about that girl I saw last night before everything went down.

"During the fight, I looked across the street and I saw these four girls watching the whole thing go down. And one of them was this really hot. She was like five-five, she had long black hair, it was really wavy and shiny and it went well with her leather coat."

"Wait a minute." Mike looked up at me with a sense of urgency "I didn't see that."

"Don't worry about it, they didn't seem interested."

"Ight, ight..." He wiped his mouth and settled. "So, she had a nice ass and a rocking' body?"

"She had nice hips."

"Ok well that's looking good then, if she has nice hips, she has a nice ass. Ass is important on a woman; it gives them shape." He looked over at the ketchup bottle again and admired the curvatures of the bottle. "And legs are good too. My old-girl she used to look amazing in a tank top and them velvet joggers that every girl is trying to have." Mike dipped a home fry into the puddle of ketchup on the left corner of his plate. "Find one like that."

"You have a great way to describe a woman..." I shook my head.

"I am not trying to objectify them; I am only speaking into the aesthetics..." He chewed on his toast.

I rolled my eyes. "I didn't know you had an ex-girlfriend, either..."

"Really?" Mike seemed visibly amazed that I couldn't recall this.

"It was back in the day when we were living in Rockville Centre." Mike stabbed into his sausage.

"What was her name?"

He shrugged his shoulders. "It doesn't matter now, she's gone."

"But what happened?"

"Damn, Corey are you a friggin detective?" He took a jam from the black holder on the end of table placed just in front of the menus and sugar jar. "I'd rather not get in to it." Mike looked away with a look of regret spelled across his face.

"Alright bro, if you ever want to tell me..."

"I know Corey, thanks." Mike put the half-crushed packet of orange marmalade on the table in front of me.

"Let's get out of here." Mike threw down his napkin and made his way to the counter to pay the check. I followed him out into the sunshine, nearly comatose from all the food we had ingested. There wasn't much said as we walked down the tree-lined street past Westwood Train Station.

"Shit Corey, I'm full. How about we run routes later?" Mike stopped to stretch his arms. "Why don't we go home and play some college football on the PlayStation as a warm up?"

"Yea, I'm stuffed too man, let's go."

"But I do love Westwood and it's a beautiful day." He paused and glanced around at the oak tree whose leaves danced over the breeze in the glowing green grass. "How about we stop for a sec and have a smoke?"

"Sure, but I don't smoke, remember?"

Mike pulled out a pack of Marlboros and offered me a cigarette.

"Take one." Mike ordered. "Let's get it out of the way. You have your first cigarette with me that way you don't try some skunk at some stupid party, alright?"

I took a cigarette and placed the filter tip between my lips.

"Don't make this a habit though." Mike pulled out his Zippo and lit my cigarette before lighting his after me.

He took his first drag and I followed, the smoke was coarse against my lungs and I nearly coughed but maintained my composure.

"So how did this whole thing get started with you and that Truck guy anyway?"

He spat then puffed again. "Come on Corey, you know that motherfucker snitched me out."

"Yeah but how do you go from being best friends with someone to just snitching them out?"

"Not everyone is like you little brother, some people have no heart; they have no balls." He flicked some ash from his cigarette. "They talk big when they playing *Grand Theft Auto* but when shit gets real, they fold. "

"Yea but Ricky is my best friend and I'd never rat him out, no matter what."

"And you should have change that." Mike pointed at me.

I nodded as I looked towards the parking lot of the Malverne side of Westwood. I gazed at the green of the trees and the pastoral field in the center of the park. My eyes ventured to the basketball court with chain link baskets hidden beneath several oak trees. The beauty of this simple train station made it an everyday hidden gem. Westwood was a cozy serene setting and I often found myself thinking most effectively here. Westwood was my piece of the Earth where I could go to get away from my problems. No matter what troubles stalked me, they had always lost my scent when I was there.

Chapter 4 - Melissa

I didn't wait long to text Melissa. The following morning, I reached out to her and to my delight she replied fairly quickly. My eyes were more glued to the screen of my cell phone, distracting me from a round of video games with my brother. Mike knew what was going on but didn't say anything, he just took advantage of the fact I wasn't on my game. Our game of college football dragged out for over an hour, when it should have been a quick thirty minutes due to my consistent pausing and sneaking off to the bathroom to check my phone. The conversation had momentum but then it stagnated, I was wired. My pulse was thread-like, my heart thumped awaiting the fix I would get when a new message came in from Melissa.

The cold water splashed over my face as I ran it over my buzzed hair. I wiped my cheeks and stepped out from the bathroom to find Ricky sitting in my place in the living room.

"Yo!" Ricky smirked; Mike joined him in an inquisitive smile. "Since you were taking so long, I hope you don't mind if I took over." His eyes shifted to the screen of the television. "Got to get a win for the old Orange and Blue." He shook out the sleeve of his blue Florida Gator jersey, the number 1 glistened in white.

"Please tell me when is the last time the Gators did shit?" Mike teased.

"1996" Ricky pressed the button and flicked the joystick of the PS2 controller.

"Do me a solid and don't fucking tell me how you always beat the Bulldogs because they suck. Georgia fans are a bunch of scoundrels."

"What's your problem with Dawg fans, Big Brother?" I chimed in.

"I think I can answer that one." Ricky chuckled and shook his head. "Damn cult." "So, Corey what's the deal, you getting with

Melissa?" Ricky paused the game and reclined against the couch. "Mike was telling me that you were obsessing over your phone."

"I was just texting her now, I'm about to ask her if she wants to chill."

"I thought, I taught this kid well." Mike chuckled and it prompted a scowl from me.

"No need, we're chillin with Foxy and Dukes later."

"Awesome." I turned my head towards my brother. "Do you want to come along?"

"I got to go take care of some shit with Shawn." Mike smirked. "But I'll offer you moral support with your girlfriend, if you need me."

Mike and Ricky both shared a laugh and slapped five. After a round robin of college football, the three of us finally headed in to town. We strolled on to Atlantic Avenue, the main drag of Lynbrook and central gathering place for many high school kids to wander about on a weekend evening. There was a movie theatre, a pizzeria, ice cream shop and an Italian restaurant to name a few of the local amenities. As we passed a canopied tunnel to the parking lot, Samantha sped out and attacked Ricky with a huge hug, jumping on him in the process. Samantha was wearing black bike shorts and a white tank top, her chiseled legs nestled under smooth fair skin. Her long auburn hair flew wild in her movements.

Even though Melissa was front and center in my mind, I found myself noticing Foxy more than before. She moved with a quiet grace—even in the midst of all this chaos—that made her stand out, I couldn't help it but think that Foxy was also extraordinarily attractive. She was a girl next door and it seemed as though she sold herself short, her lack of self-esteem was apparent in her very body language. Though Foxy was doing her best to fit in, she didn't. She was clearly a quiet girl that rolled with a loud crowd.

"Didn't know he got it like that." Mike pulled out a cigarette and lit it up. "Take notes, Core." He took his first drag. "Who is that?"

"Sam..." I watched her kiss Ricky. "Ricky's girlfriend."

"Thanks, I couldn't have figured that one out." He teased, turning back abruptly at as another car's speakers were blasting out *Move Ya Body* by Nina Sky, though we were in the middle of the walkway, the volume was loud enough from the street.

Down the path, Melissa waved at me with her beaming smile. Her skin glowed under a blue polo shirt with black jeans and white sneakers. The friend that accompanied came out sporting similar attire only wearing a red Lynbrook Cheerleading t-shirt instead. She had brown hair and green eyes accented by freckles, a bit shorter than both Sam and Melissa.

"You boys got champagne taste with beer money." Mike exhaled some smoke and continued with the gags. "Good for you guys." He patted my shoulder.

"This is our friend, Katie." Melissa opened her hands toward the direction of her companion.

"Nice to meet you." I put my hand around Mike's back. "This is my brother, Mike."

Mike nodded and flicked his cigarette. "I've heard a lot of great things."

Melissa bantered. "Oh yea, like what?"

Mike looked over at me and cracked a smile.

"I have heard things about you too." Katie's voice entered the conversation, bringing the light-hearted discourse to a halt. "Aren't you a felon?"

The discussion fell silent as all the parties awkwardly looked at passing cars.

"Depends on who you ask."

"Like who?" Katie raised her eyebrows.

"Doesn't matter, I heard you were a bit of a public disturbance." Mike countered with a wry smile, completely composed and confident.

"You're funny." Katie jeered.

"Hey Fox, did you meet Corey's brother?" Melissa adjusted the collar of her shirt.

"It seems, he is also quite the comedian." Katie stared hard at Mike.

"I am afraid, I haven't." Sam let go of Ricky's hand and extended her hand with a big smile across her face. Even when she wasn't trying, she exuded a grace and class that was all her own. "I am Samantha, it's a pleasure to meet you."

"The pleasure is all mine, gal." Mike took his hand and looked over at me for a moment and then back to her. "I detect an accent."

I thought I heard it the first time I met her but as afraid to inquire, Mike however was never afraid to speak what he thought.

"Are you from down south?"

"Tennessee actually." Sam nodded. "I was born in Ireland but spent my childhood there. I didn't come here until Middle School." She ran her hand through her hair once.

"You'll have to write that one down for me."

We all laughed, but Mike quickly raised his hands, he was concerned of offending her which took me by surprise. There was a gentleness from him, directed toward her. But her smile was gentle and her eyes were full of life, there was an innocence about her that hid in her smile.

Mike's usual swagger—hands jammed in his pockets; shoulders squared—softened as he met Foxy's gaze. She looked at him with open curiosity, her smile unafraid. For once, Mike hesitated, almost shyly, before offering her a lighthearted tease.

"Has my brother been alright with you, so far?"

"He seems very pleasant." Sam smiled before she directed her attention back to Ricky, her eyes were kind and filled with intrigue; a friendliness flowed from her that was genuine as if she was looking into your soul with a desire to know you as a person.

Mike cupped his hands in front of his mouth and leaned toward me "I like her, she's a sweet kid..." He appeared puzzled for a moment as he observed Foxy hanging her arm around Ricky's neck. "I don't know what she is doing with the Dominican Sensation." Mike whispered. "She's got it twisted." He gently put his hand on my chest. "If I was you." Mike pointed at Samantha covertly. "Forget about Melissa..."

"What are y'all two chatting about?" Sam batted her eyebrows.

"We wanted to know what's on the agenda for the evening?" Mike responded composed with a swiftness and smoothness.

"I don't know I was thinking we hang around here?" Melissa's eyes scanned the group.

"Fuck that, let's take a walk over to the gas station and get a few beers in."

"Sounds good to me." Melissa looked at me, giving my brother a nod of approval. "Katie?"

"Sure, I can kick it with thugalicious." Katie replied with a snide tone in her voice.

"Woah?" Mike about-faced. "Thugalicious, more like delicious, sweetheart."

"In your dreams." Katie crossed her arms.

"I'm sorry but I don't live there, I am afraid." Mike placed his arm around Katie, gently coaxing her to walk with him as he led the way. Despite her outward reluctance, she was charmed by him and didn't want to show it.

We crossed the larger town parking lot and under the train trestle. Melissa and I were in the front with Mike on my left and Katie on Mel's right; Sam and Ricky were far behind us. As we approached the illuminated signs for the gas station, Ricky and I saw three of our teammates hanging out with two cheerleaders.

"What's up Greenie" Ricky extended his hand to Marlon Green our starting wide receiver. He was tall and lanky, but he was a pure athlete. He wore a baggy white red t-shirt draped over sagging black jeans which matched the pick in his afro.

"Corey, what is going on?" Danny Russell our backup quarterback acknowledged me, a stocky boy with a short crop of blonde hair and beady brown eyes.

"You ready for the season, Rambo?" Brendan Adams, our all-conference quarterback embraced Ricky clad in a green letterman jacket.

"What up, Greenie; Danny; Brendan?" I greeted them all, Marlon was the least forthcoming of the bunch in response.

"Well, well, well if it isn't Smelly Melissa." One of the cheerleaders sullied the pleasantries.

"Listen bitch!" Melissa started to stride towards her pulling her fist back. I ran over and grabbed Melissa and took hold of her. Ricky ran to grab Foxy too, while Brendan and Danny made an effort to separate the two potential adversaries. All the while a chorus of "woahs" carried throughout the parking lot focusing anyone's attention who was nearby.

When the tension settled, we took note of the two adversaries who were Christina Caputo and Allison Partridge. Christina was Romanesque in her build and every bit confident in posture. She had long blonde hair trickling down her back and over her bust from her Lynbrook Cheerleading jacket. She was a captain of the squad, signified by the white "C" on the right sleeve of her black coat.

"You're lucky." Christina puckered her strawberry colored lips at Mel. "I'd beat up that pretty little face of yours."

"Tina, it's cool." Katie put her hand on Christina's shoulder. "I don't want this parking lot to be on the next episode of gangland." She shot a suggestive glare at Mike.

"What the fuck does that mean?" Mike cringed.

"I don't know where is ya flag at?" Katie continued to mock my brother.

"I don't know what your deal is, if this is your way of showing you have a crush on me, that's cool but just be real about it."

"Honey, please." Katie brushed her hair over her shoulder.

Christina stepped forward flaunting her denim short shorts, her long firm legs glistening in the moonlight. Both Ricky and I were both guilty of lustfully gazing at her. "Come on." Ricky pulled Mel away and I gently tugged on Foxy's arm as I escorted her away from Christina, Allison, and the guys. Mike flanked us from behind pointing at our teammates in an obnoxious fashion, asserting his dominance.

"Come by one day after practice one day, gorgeous. I'll be waiting for you." Christina beckoned Mike with a wink but she didn't know who she was talking to. While many may have been awe-struck or overwhelmed by the advances, Mike boldly paced up to Christina quickly, grabbed her and planted a passionate kiss on her while gently caressing her face. Her eyes shut as she was clearly overcome. When he pulled away, he whispered to her "Where should I meet you?"

"On the corner." Christina was now on the back-heel, no longer intentional in her response.

"Only appropriate." Mike chuckled and kissed her hand. Despite his innuendo, he charmed her some more by whispering things in her ear that caused her to grimace with ecstasy.

"I'll see you at three, Monday." Mike pulled out another cigarette and lit up his smoke effortlessly.

In the background I heard my teammates laughing at her statement about meeting Mike on the corner. Christina yelled "*Shut up*" at them.

"Damn, I can't wait to fuck that bitch." Mike exhaled some smoke, a grey cloud wafting into the clear night sky.

"Good luck with the infection." Sam came up beside him. "I'll get you some antibiotics."

I laughed and Foxy broke a smile.

"Hey Mike, can I bum a smoke?" Melissa drew to Mike's side.

"Sure." He pulled out his pack of Marlboros. "Under one condition though..."

"Okay..." Mel took a cigarette and giggled.

"Give my brother a kiss." Mike moved his head in my direction.

"Mike, it's cool." My voice rose from the tension. He was always straight to the point and sometimes it created awkward situations like this one. I didn't want blow it with Melissa because Mike couldn't help sparking mischief.

"Well I would, but I have a boyfriend."

"So what?" Mike smirked, though it was evident it was beginning to cause duress for Mel.

"Mike, let her be." I shot him a look, begging him to stop as he swirled his tongue in his mouth.

"Alright" Mike flicked his lighter and lit Melissa's cigarette courteously. "How about you, Ms. Spitfire?" Mike glanced at Katie.

"Oh, fuck no!"

Sam grabbed Katie and pulled her over to Mike. "Don't be shy now." Foxy came over to give me a pound, I gave her a pound explode.

"Nicely played."

"Mhmm." Sam batted her eyebrows as she reciprocated the gesture.

Mike flicked his cigarette, grabbed her, and planted another passionate kiss on Katie, this time. When he released her, she had the same reaction as Christina. She appeared in awe and was breathing heavy.

"Damn." She gazed at Mike "Can I have another?"

"Of course." Mike suavely responded before the two continued to trade tongues and swap spit.

"Let's leave them for a while, he'll be back."

"You sure?" Sam played along with the joke.

"You just let him be. He'll call when they are done." I put my arm around her back.

Samantha laughed. "We can have a gab about this under the wee arches over there."

"Wee?"

"As if you never heard it before." She flipped her hair and smiled with an effortless propriety.

"Truly, I can't say I have."

"You may hear it a lot then from me." Sam's tone of voice shifted to a playful one. "Sorry for that..." She bantered. "It means small by the way...."

"I know what it means..." I smiled. "Just nothing something you hear every day in an Old South accent."

"Old South?" Samantha feigned offense. "It's Tennessean". Her indignation quickly broke in a cheery and playful smile and I couldn't help but dig her spunk.

The four of us made our way across the parking lot and sat underneath the trestle awaiting Mike and Katie. Within minutes, Melissa and I were left alone again, as Foxy and Ricky spontaneously ran off and took a page out of Mike and Katie's book.

"So, would you really have kissed me or was that a cop out?"

"Not so shy, anymore are you?" Mel winked.

"My big brother encourages me to not be timid."

"That's cute, I wish I had a big brother like you do." Mel pressed the end of her cigarette against the granite of the trestle column.

"Do you have a brother then?"

"Yeah, but he just drinks and gets high all the time." Mel smiled at me. "But your brother loves you, it's easy to tell..." She glanced down. "With all things considered, my brother would pound Matt, if he knew about the shit he was doing." She stretched out her legs, the soles of her shoes rubbing against the granite. "Is there any girl that you like?"

"Yeah there is one, but I don't know." I looked down somewhat nervous that the truth would be unveiled. "I don't think she really likes me."

"Why not?"

"I think she likes some other guy." I replied with caution, a tremolo in my voice would reveal I was talking about her but it never crossed her mind.

"It's Foxy, isn't it?" Mel flicked her hair. "She isn't going to be with Ricky long, she is totally not his type."

I laughed at the irony of the remark, here we were conversing about romance and it was painfully obvious I was into her. And yet, she deferred to her best friend.

"If you two got to know each other, I think it would be unstoppable."

I looked one of the many concrete pillars that help up the train tracks above us, pondering how to respond to the remark. After all, Melissa was the girl I always wanted. Although her words were kind, they were like daggers ripping through my heart. They were words that left me unrequited and sentences that suggested I wasn't even a blip on the radar; I was utterly despaired.

"Shit, I need a beer." I looked away at the streetlight on the telephone pole across the lot. My throat became swollen with frustration, my eyes saturated with tears although I did not cry. Here six feet away from me, sat a woman who I thought the world of, and yet she may never know. And even if she did, it wouldn't matter. Melissa Paducah was stuck on some Oceanside heartthrob who probably only saw her as one thing. Beyond my lament of Melissa's relationship status, I rejoiced in making a new friend: Samantha Foxe. She was easy to speak to, conversation flowed naturally, and though I had just met her, I felt as if I had known her forever and that we were simply waiting to be reunited.

Chapter 5 – A Chapter Not Named Like A Fall Out Boy Song

Later that night, I was awoken to the vibrations of a bass system outside. I wiped my eyes, squinting in the darkness to see if I could read the time on the clock. I turned over and pressed the side button of the phone, the light from the screen piercing in the blackness of the room. It said 3:37 with a message icon. I flipped the phone and open, seeing a text from Samantha. *It was wonderful to get to know you this evening <3 Foxy.* I smiled, recollecting on our conversations which seemed to go off on tangents. We started discussing cheerleaders doing splits and what it's like for her to do them because they looked painful; or whether honey or gravy is better on biscuits, laughing several times in between. I knew there was more to her than the surface-level stuff, Samantha always appeared deep in thought like I often was.

I looked out the window and saw Mike exiting the White Thunderbird, stumbling in front of the glowing headlamps as he shut the car door before it sped off. I sent a text back *likewise, I hope to see you again soon.* I placed the phone back down upon the bed and waited for the door to creak open but it didn't. After five minutes, I went downstairs and walked out on to the porch. Mike was laying on the couch with one foot on and the other resting on the ground. He was on his side with one arm stretched over his head as he snored in a deep slumber. I didn't bother waking him as the alcohol wreaked off him and he was clearly passed out. I went back upstairs and fell right back asleep only to wake a few hours later.

It was about 7:15 AM and as I stepped out to a crisp beautiful August morning. There was a slight chill in the air and the sun had just breached the horizon. I looked at Mike who was still comatose on the couch. The sun shined on Mike's face and yet he still remained undisturbed.

"Is he still out?" Shawn's steps thundered across the lawn. In my focus on Mike lying on the couch, I didn't hear or see Shawn coming. His freckled arms escaped from beneath a Chicago Bulls jersey, the black lettering matching his "murdered-out" New York Mets fitted, denim shorts, and black-on-white adidas hi-tops. Shawn had thrown a white towel around his neck likely to dab the beads of sweat forming below his pale blue eyes.

I shrugged my shoulders.

"Yo!" Shawn put his hand against one of the columns that held up the overhang that canopied our porch. "You alive?!"

Mike opened his eyes, squinting finally at the sunlight, before sitting up and stretching for a moment.

"What happened to you last night, dude?"

"Well little brother, I ended up having some crazy sex on a playground with miss hot shot over there. Then I grabbed some beers, went to Shawn's house here and woke up here."

"Yo, you were fucked up man." Shawn chuckled.

"I don't know how I got back..."

"We drove you motherfucker." His laugh grew louder. "Little bro, I heard you making some progress with the ladies."

"Yeah, I guess." I muttered.

"Don't worry Core, you'll see it aint shit." Shawn let out a loose of roll of laughs and pounded Mike's fist with his own.

"I tell you one thing - I am going to rail your friend Christina over there." Mike waved his hand through the air as if he was smacking her butt as he let out a goofy laugh of his own.

"She aint my friend, so by all means..."

"I don't blame you; I'd go for that other chick..." Mike looked up, snapping his fingers. "What's her name?"

"Melissa?"

"Fuck that..." He shot me a look. "The southern one who was Irish..."

"Irish?" Shawn raised his eyebrows. "Like I am Irish...."

"No like she was born there, motherfucker...." Mike snickered. "You can hear a bit of Brogue in that Scarlet O' Hara dialect."

"You mean Foxy?"

He snapped his fingers again and pointed at me. "That's it." Mike shook his finger. "She's right up your alley man."

"She is with Ricky, you know..."

"That goofball can't handle a woman like that..." He chuckled and threw his hands together, his energy returned to him as he became lively, you wouldn't think he was nursing a hangover by any means. "Bro, let me tell you about this Christina chick." His eyes shot back to Shawn. "She is thick in all the right places! Like two biscuits with all that jelly in the back."

"Word?"

"Yes indeedy..." Mike reached into his pockets and shifted his fingers around. "Yo, you got a smoke?"

I couldn't help but be repulsed and amused at how Mike described Christina as if she were a Waffle House breakfast so nonchalantly.

"Depends..." Shawn tossed him a pack of Newports. "She got friends?"

"Man, you always asking that!"

"Give me a break Ghost, you're such a lucky opportunistic fuck with women. We can talk about previous exploits or we recent times that include that Persian chick at the pool hall, the girl last night, and now this Christina chick." His smile widened. "You've been out of the county for a sec and you already running through them."

"Yeah well, that's what I try to teach my brother here. When you see an opportunity, take it and own it." Mike looked up at me. "Right, little brother?"

"Yep..."

"He knows..." He nodded with approval.

"Speaking of women, have you spoke to Jessie, yet?"

Mike's smile evaporated; his eyes enlarged as he sternly gazed at Shawn. Clearly, the mention of the name hit a nerve and equally it seemed that it was something Mike didn't want me to know about, judging by his reaction.

"Don't worry about that." He waved his hand and turned his attention to me. "Listen, I got to talk to Terror out here for a minute about something. I'll meet you inside in a little bit."

"Yeah sure." I put my hand to Shawn's shoulder. "Later, Big Cuz."

"Peace, Core." Shawn patted my back as I passed.

Not much happened the rest of the day, as tomorrow was the first day of football practice. Mike was in and out, but I was immersed in my reading. I spent most of the day, stuck in the book *Justine*, a novel that took place around these parts a decade ago but the story was all the same: a crush. Kind of like, Melissa, with the same heartache and longing. I related to it but I thought that this would be different: this would somehow work out. Romance was like that for me, the notion of love conquering the odds was something that stirred me, you know like in *The Notebook*. Perhaps I could be a part of something like that one day, or perhaps I could write it. Mike went off to Valley Stream to hang out with the rest of his crew, desperately attempting to persuade me to go along, but I resisted, I had to keep reading and find more inspiration.

The next morning, I joined my teammates on the practice field beside Lynbrook Union High School. It was a clear and sunny day, we all stood waiting eagerly to meet our new Head Coach. He wasn't what we expected. He was young, dressed very casually wearing black basketball shorts and a red Georgia Bulldogs t-shirt. At first glance, one might think he was a player, not a high school football coach.

"Good morning gentlemen." His voice tingled with energy. "You guys can call me Coach Kenny, not sir, not mister, just coach, will do...." Coach held a clipboard at his side. "Before, we get into the fun stuff. Let's go over particulars. On this team, we take academics seriously." He took two steps closer. "If anyone wants to mess around in school, I can't take you seriously. If you can't stick out a forty-minute class which can affect the rest of your life, how can I trust you to play forty-eight minutes to win one game?" He smirked as he glanced down at his clipboard. "We don't do tough guy shit either. If anyone is getting into fights, trying to impress some girl by puffing out their muscles, or being disrespectful to any of your peers, elders, or teammates, a like. I will run your fucking ass all the way down to the Nautical Mile in Freeport."

A chorus of chuckles broke out at Coach's candor.

"Does anyone like it down there?" He scanned the crowd. "Show of hands..."

A few teammates boldly raised their hands.

"Good, you'll be staying there if you don't do things to our standard. That begins with your relationship with The Lord, your family, your studies, and this team...." He paused. "But I promise you, if you do that, everyone will play here..." He rubbed his chin. "Everyone will get a chance..."

A chance, that is all I ever wanted; an opportunity to show what I could do. I didn't hear that with our old coach, it was only about winning and ironically enough we didn't do that.

"...and we will succeed. What that success looks like is up to you..." Coach put his clipboard to his side. "Now, I look forward to getting to know each and every one of you. So, let me tell you a little about me. I am 26 years old and I played linebacker at South Side High School, just up the road in Rockville Centre..."

Rockville Centre, the neighboring town with the sordid history that moved my family here. It's where Mike was arrested and where my parents divorced, a place I wanted to keep tucked away in a dusty file cabinet hidden in the basement of my thoughts.

"...I went on to Nassau Community College for two years after that, I transferred to the University of Georgia." He pointed at the writing on his shirt with the Bulldog insignia centered among the words Bulldogs. "Are there any Gator fans here?"

Ricky bravely raised his hand with a smirk on his face.

"Take a lap."

"Seriously?" He retorted.

Coach nodded.

"That's because you guys can't beat us" Ricky bantered.

"Make it two then..." Coach didn't even flinch at the rebuttal; the entire team broke out in laughter as Ricky went for a jog.

"For the Dawgs, I was a safety but I had two NFL prospects playing ahead of me so that's how it goes sometimes. Nevertheless, I got my Master's Degree, came back here, and became a professor of sociology at Farmingdale. I joined the fire service just up the road there by Greis Park..."

The mention of the place brought me back to the night I met Melissa and the curious look that Foxy and I shared.

"...Ever Alert Engine 3 and I met my wife." He crossed his arms and broke a smile for a moment. "I was elected lieutenant by my company, had our first child, and now we are expecting our second..." Coach gazed ahead at Ricky who was at the far end of the field jogging. "I haven't been a head coach before, I spent years as a defensive coordinator in Floral Park, so we're all in this together, men..." He placed the clipboard down near to a white chalked line on the grass. "But if we stick together, who knows what we could do?" Coach smiled. "I'll be here for you guys every step of the way. My job is to help you and by doing that..." He moved his fingers in front of him. "We'll help each other."

Call it charisma or perhaps an ability to orate beautifully, but Coach Kenny captured my heart right then and there. He seemed accessible, he seemed real. I had just met him but I had felt like I had known him my entire life. Our previous coach was distant and focused solely on winning, ruling by force to instill fear and intimidate us into doing what he said. Coach Kenny was firm in establishing boundaries but I felt as though he was doing that for our best interest. He was a leader, but also a mentor. But then as we have seen and known, the best leaders are the ones that encourage; they are motivated by love; and they have a vision that enhances all those that surround them. That five-minute speech but Coach Kenny made more excited to be on this football field than it had the last three years, but still I wondered if I was nothing more than a glorified mascot? I didn't see the field much and even with all the musings offered by our new skipper, I still didn't believe that would change, at all. But maybe, I'd be proven wrong.

Chapter 6 – A Summer Afternoon

After practice, I was exhausted and found myself leaning against the cool brick wall of the high school's wing, just out of the reach of the sun's oppressive rays and just beyond the steps that led down to the locker room. The cheerleaders also had their first day of practice, some exited in pairs and trios while some left on their own. I counted each cheerleader up to nine until Christina appeared in a white tank top and black short shorts.

She noticed me and sauntered over, halting in front of me. Her long blonde hair tossed behind her briefly. "Hey..." The timbre of her voice was empty and timid.

"Hey..." I muttered.

"Where is your brother?"

"I don't know." I glanced over to the entrance gate and saw no sign of him. "But if he said he'd be here, he'll be here." I looked away at my playbook, uneased.

She placed her hand softly on my cheek and firmly caressed my face toward hers causing me to stare in to her beckoning brown eyes. "Well if he doesn't show, we can always go over this together." She put her hand over mine on the playbook and spoke in a breathy voice. "You are kind of cute..."

"Thanks..." The playbook shook in my hand. "You are not so bad yourself."

"Yo!" Mike yelled out as he stormed down the pedestrian path towards the two of us. He wore a grey t-shirt and a black fitted hat with matching black jeans and his signature white Nikes. "Which brother you want?"

"Your brother is hot." She flirted. "Sometimes you have to keep it in the family."

"I expected you to say something like it." Mike replied coy as he put his fist out to me to pound him. Without hesitation, he grabbed Christina by her shorts, groping her buttocks in the process and engaged in heavy kissing with her. I watched them for a moment and diverted my eyes away to Ricky walking hand-in-hand with Foxy towards us from the back of the school.

"Mmm, you really are delicious girl." Mike released the lip-lock.

"You're quite tasty yourself." Christina giggled.

"Little brother, what's mine is yours. I'd have a threesome with you and this lovely specimen right here, if you wanted." Mike offered with his arm around Christina. "We'll just close our eyes or something..."

"I guess that would be nice." I felt the heat rise in my cheeks.

"You're a virgin, aren't you?" She teased.

"That's none of your business." Mike plucked his arm away.

"There is a first time for everything, Corey. I'll truly be unforgettable." Christina shot me a salacious look.

"Yeah, I'm sure you would, cause everyone else can't remember your name, just the time and place, right?" Mike continued the verbal assault.

Christina scowled. "Says the pervert who didn't even graduate and is still hanging around a high school when he can be working or doing something meaningful with his life."

"Alright, if that's the way you feel about shit. I'm out." Mike about-faced. "Little brother, I'll see you later." He paced off and never looked back.

"Wait!" Christina pursued him and tried to grab his shoulder, but he shrugged her hands off, their confrontation taking each member beyond the front gate onto Union Avenue.

"What's up my brother from another mother?" Ricky shook my hand. "What was that all about?"

"Mike..." I rolled my eyes. "Need I say anymore?"

"No..." He chuckled and leaned up against the wall beside me.

"How was practice?" Samantha interjected.

"Pretty much the same thing, it always is. A whole bunch of nothing..." I rolled the playbook up in my hand. "How was cheerleading?"

"We were issued our uniforms and went over some basics." She struck a strand of her long auburn hair back, a green bow was fixed to the top of her hair, matching her golf shirt.

"So, what do you think of coach, Corey?" Ricky spat.

"I think he's cool but he was torching you about the Gators though." I chuckled.

"Yeah well, he best be careful. I'm an All-County Half Back and he needs me to fuel his offense."

"No need to fuss and bother." Foxy eyes met the both of us. "Just have fun guys, you only get football once."

"Yea and you're a cheerleader." Ricky spoke with condescension in his voice, a frown immediately formed on Foxy's face.

"Come on Rick, she's just trying to be supportive."

"Thanks Corey." Samantha crossed her arms.

"Do you even know how football works?" Rick continued to speak in a mocking tone.

"Perhaps, more than you..."

"You think you are Brainiac all of a sudden because you know the goal is try and score a touchdown?"

Foxy lightly smacked Ricky's arm as he laughed at his own joke.

"Does she even know that a touchdown is six points and an extra point is one and that six plus one equals seven?"

"I'm in Calculus, Ricardo." Samantha raised her voice, a tinge of Irish accent inflected in her otherwise heavy Old South drawl.

"Whatever you say..." Ricky simpered.

I looked across at Christina on the other side of the fence, leaning against it with a long frown.

"We're going to get out of here." Ricky moved off the wall and put his arm around Foxy. "What's your plan?"

"It looks like I got to clean up another one of Mike's messes." I kept my eyes on Christina who held her head low.

"I see..." Ricky turned to look at Christina propped against the fence. "She is sexy as hell I get that, but I don't know..."

"Wow, Ricky really?!" Samantha yelled. "I'm your girlfriend and you say right out in the open?!"

"I'm just giving him advice." Ricky hunched his shoulders. "You need to chill!"

"Sam's right." I raised my hand. "You shouldn't be saying shit like that."

Ricky raised his eyebrows and leaned back, unable to respond to my rebuke.

"She's a beautiful girl, Rick. Take good care of her."

Samantha looked at me from the side of her eye, a smile forming as she was touched by the remark.

"You trying to deal with her, she gets mad over every little thing." Ricky waved his hand and Sam's pout soon returned.

"Maybe, she's just sensitive." I put my hand on his shoulder.

"Like you, right?" Ricky joked.

"Why don't you take her to the shop and get her some flowers?" I tapped my playbook once again my hand. "I am sure, Foxy would appreciate that." I shot her a smile as I turned my back and made my way towards Christina.

"Bye, Corey!" Sam spoke at length. "Why can't you be more like your friend?" Resentment was in intermingled in her tone of voice, as their conversation soon faded into the chatter of schoolmates and sound of cars passing. Christina's eyes stalked me with every step that I grew closer. Finally, when I was near on the other side of the fence, I watched Ricky and Foxy head towards a car parked close to the front entrance of school, the two bickering every step of the way until they got into a blue Geo Metro.

"Hey..."

"Hey..." She replied as she looked away at the ground,

"Where did Mike go?"

"He left." She brushed her hair back and remained motionless standing against the fence. Although she was not showing her emotions, one could sense that she was hurting and embarrassed.

I was intimidated by Christina, her body was a masterpiece, every time I glanced at her I was breathless, feeling a warm and invigorating sensation consume my body. I never had sex before, but when I examined her my thoughts could not escape the notion of doing such things with her. It was different to Melissa. Sure, Mel had an amazing physique too, but Melissa pierced my heart with her eyes and captivated my soul with her smile. Christina made me intoxicated me with lust. I wanted to know what it was like to take a chance and do something I never thought I would do.

My heart was pumping through the ceiling, I was unsure of my approach, my strategy was simply to kiss her and see what happens.

"Maybe, I can be your company?"

We locked eyes for a minute until I gently placed my fingers on her face and caressed her cheeks. She moved in closer and placed her hand on my face as well. I closed my eyes and softly pecked her lips, she met mine. The kiss was sloppy but soon reined in when I tried again and she bit my lip, as she kissed me.

We continued to kiss, Christina grabbed my shoulder and gripped my shirt tight. She placed my hand on her breast, I squeezed it and moved in, kissing and biting her neck. She dug her nails in to my back and began to grunt. A euphoric feeling washed over me as our bodies pressed firmly together against the rusted chain link fence. I rubbed her legs and tactfully placed my hands on her glutes, pinching them as I picked her up and she wrapped her legs around me. I continued to kiss her neck, she breathed heavier as I made me way down her cheek to the top of her supple bust. She seized control of my head and rained kisses on my lips and then down my neck, filling me with a tingly sensation to the tips of my toes.

"Do you want to take a walk somewhere?" She slipped her hands over my crotch which showed how aroused I was.

"Oh, you're excited, aren't you?"

"Uh huh." I gasped. I was inexperienced with women and figured I didn't even know how to please a woman but I wanted more. I trusted I would be up to the task, if given the chance.

Christina took me by the hand and I followed her until we reached her house which was a few blocks away. The duration of travel must have been about five to ten minutes but the anticipation made the walk seem longer. We didn't say one word, we were too charged to speak. Not once, did I even clock where I was or where we were going. All I could remember was that it was around 3:30 PM, the sun was at its apex, hanging high in the summer sky. The streets were scorching and the air was thick with humidity. August in New York is like a sauna but the green glass and blue skies were tickled with cirrus clouds would make you think otherwise from inside an air-conditioned house.

When we entered Christina's house, I was met by a cool rush of air. Inside, the home was clad in mahogany toned wood paneling which accented the moldings and door frames, which gave the house a regal and elegant look.

"Let's go upstairs." She grabbed my hand, the door behind us slammed with a thud as our steps pounded up the carpeted spiral staircase. The door flung open to her bedroom and Christina shoved me from behind on the bed. My fall was halted by the plush pillow top of her mattress. Her room was painted with warm colors, an orchid shade. I didn't notice much more than the vibrant paint scheme as Christina nibbled on my earlobe. In abrupt fashion, I directed all of my attention to her and kissed her some more, touching and feeling her all over her body. She removed my shirt and I did the same gliding my fingers up her toned midsection to remove her tank-top. The process was gradual until we both were naked. I took a good look at Christina's body; it was a divine sculpture. The first time I ever saw a woman naked and in that brief moment I felt sorrow and sadness. I wanted to this to be special but here I was experiencing this for the first time with a girl I didn't know. My hormones got the best of me and consumed me when I felt her tight arms and smooth legs. Her abs were defined yet feminine and voluptuous breasts that fell onto my face. As I marveled in the sight, Christina plucked at my pants and pulled them off.

"Wait!" I shot up and she pushed me back down. "Don't we need protection?"

"Shh..." Christina sat her firm buttocks on my lap. "I am on birth control." She slithered forward and soon I felt her for the first time, the warmth wrapping around me like a glove as she thrusted her hips.

A DAY WE MET IN LYNBROOK 53

Our gyrations carried on for a few minutes until her sheets as she moaned loudly. I soon climaxed and found myself lying on the flat of my back with no energy to move. Finally, I had gone where my brother had been so many times before, crossing over a threshold that I thought I would never get to. But still I wondered if this was all that actually was? I wanted more than this.

I fell asleep for an hour until the buzzing of a saw from beyond the backyard woke me. "Damn..." I stretched out; soreness filled my body. "I never needed a smoke more in my life and I don't even smoke."

Christina rolled over and smiled at me, pulling the duvet over us. "I didn't take you for one who smoked." She kissed me again.

"So, when do your parents get home?" I pulled the duvet down, my stomach knotting at the thought of getting caught. "I really don't feel like moving yet."

"They are away overnight." She nuzzled up closer to me.

"So, you are going to be on your own?" I ran my hand over the small of her back.

"Why do you ask? Are you interested in staying?" She ran her lips over mine. "I can put on my cheerleading costume." Her lips drew close to my ear as she breathed into them. "Then we can have some fun again."

"I can't say no to that." I ran my fingers down her stomach and rubbed her, she clutched my shoulders. "But I don't know..."

Christina squinted at me.

"Do you want to go out somewhere?"

"Are you asking me out?" Christina's eyes brightened, surprised by the gesture.

"Well, yea..." I sat up. "We can talk and have some food or something. We might really hit it off."

She sat up and chuckled once, throwing her hair back.

"What is it?"

Christina shook her head. "No, I am just amazed. Most boys just think of me as a piece of meat and don't even care about anything else."

"But what do you think?"

She had fully sat up and looked down at me, deep in thought. I don't know where the question itself was difficult to answer or she was perplexed at the timing of the deeper discussion.

"I think I need to go to the bathroom." She turned and scampered out of the room, still fully naked. I reached over and grabbed my pants on the floor, reaching in the pocket to grab my phone. I saw that home had called and I knew it was Mike, given Mom was out at work late. I was eager to call as a part of me was dying to share the news with him. I always thought of myself as lesser to him in many ways and I guess, I wanted him to be proud of me. Our father wasn't around much since him and Mom divorced when I was younger, and in many ways, Mike was my role model. I called home; it rang a few times before the phone was picked up.

"Little brother." He greeted. "Are you coming home for dinner?"

"Not tonight..." A smile formed at my face.

"Where are you?"

I paused to answer the question, listening to hear if Christina was coming.

"It's a bit of a long story."

"What did you get laid or something?" He joked.

"Actually, yea..."

"I knew it!" His voice exclaimed with excitement. "I need details." His enthusiasm seeped through the speaker.

"Well when you took off on Christina, after football practice I went over to her to ask where you went. Then basically we went back to her house, her parents weren't home, and one thing lead to another."

"You lucky son of a bitch, you bag a dime like that you're first time!"

"I don't know why I didn't do this sooner." I chuckled.

"I'll leave you to it then. My man!" Mike hung up abruptly.

I slipped the phone back into my jean pockets and grabbed my boxers thrown on the floor. Christina entered the room, in full cheerleader outfit – a white vest with green and yellow piping, the words Lynbrook Owls embroidered across the chest. Below it she was wearing a green long sleeve shirt that was shiny, comprised of a stretchy material. The vest and top below cut off just before her waist. Her green skirt hung from her hips with her hair fully down her back.

"Ready for Round Two?" She threw her hands on her hips.

I slipped my boxers on and stood on the other side of the bed. "How could I not be?" I moved around the bed toward a map of Nassau County pinned to the wall. "And then we can go out, if you'd like…"

She looked at me with a wry smile. "What did you have in mind?"

"Let's close our eyes and see where our finger lands."

Christina joined me and stepped in front of me, my hand going around her stomach as my other locked with her hand. She grinded her butt against me as we came together. Our eyes shut and we circled our fingers together until it landed on a town at random: Floral Park.

"How ironic. Coach was there before he came here…" My eyes peered at the names of the streets in the Zinnia, Mayfair, Crocus, Elm, and Primrose for example. But that's not all I saw, I saw a story, I saw love, faith and kids like me going to school every day struggling to survive class. College applications and adolescent romances; hopes and dreams. Maybe there was a Corey Montgomery in Floral Park with an older brother who has been in and out of jail. He goes to school every day and plays football and at the end of the day he goes home with his girlfriend who he loves more than anything in the world. I romanticized the notion that he enjoys his days while he is still young with the world still in front of him.

When you drive through towns you gaze at traffic lights along with the familiar bars and building, some never stop and think that despite being a short drive away, you may as well be in another world. You are just a stranger in a foreign land. A village with a tale to tell. I wondered if there was someone like Melissa there...

"There is a really good Applebee's up there on Jericho Turnpike. We can take the car..." She turned her head toward me and our lips met again.

"Sounds good." I ran my hands up and down her stomach and chest. "How about we work an appetite then?"

She nodded and threw me back onto her bed, crawling across me as our lips volleyed. This time, our session lasted longer with far more passion and intensity compared to the first encounter. The nerves had left me and I enjoyed the moment, as minutes melted away in our rough intercourse.

Soon after we finished, Christina ran to grab a shower and I threw my clothes back on. The sun was setting, twilight was trickling in. I sat on the steps waiting for her until she descended the steps in a white dress that hugged her figure and tied around her neck.

"Wow." I got up off the steps. "You look amazing..."

"Well..." Christina blushed. "I've never been asked out before, so I wanted to make the effort."

"I look like a bum compared to you." I glanced down at my scuffed white T-shirt and gray basketball shorts.

"You look cute." Christina pecked my lips. "We can stop at yours on the way, if you want to grab some jeans, if you want..."

"I don't get it..." I leaned back and put my hand under my chin. "I don't understand why Melissa and Samantha have a beef with you."

Christina leaned against the bannister. "I never had any issue with Foxy. She's just blindly loyal to her friend." Her eyes flared with ire. "As for the other one, she blames me for snatching her boyfriend when meanwhile I liked him before they ever hooked up."

"It sounds complicated..."

"It isn't. Dave said he liked me, got with Melissa, and then came back at me..." Christina stepped down.

"But why would you even be interested in someone who does that?"

"We can't help who we like." Christina pressed her lips against mine. "Right?"

The image of Melissa entered my mind and I was reluctant to reciprocate the affection, maybe I was in the wrong place too, looking for answers in the wrong place.

"I suppose..." I feigned a smile.

"And your best friend is a man that seems to be the complete opposite of you..."

"If you get to know Rick, he's really nothing like what people think, at all."

"I can say the same for you." She put her hand on my shoulder. "You've always been this quiet brooding kid that isn't particularly popular and keeps to himself. But I like you, Corey; I feel like with you I don't have to be the hot girl that everyone wants to sleep with..." She smirked. "Though, we did make the most of it this afternoon..." Christina squeezed my butt as she slithered around me. "I'll go get the keys." She pressed her lips against my cheek as she darted off.

As I watched Christina walk down the dark hall, I thought about all the events of the day and how I could have never foreseen things unfolding as they had. She was the captain of the cheerleading squad and I was pretty much a nobody. The tale and the cast of characters within it had all the makings of a memorable romance. Many would fawn at the notion of having Christina Caputo on their arm by virtue of what it would do for one's reputation alone but still, it didn't feel right. I wanted this with Melissa and an emptiness washed over me in the pit of my stomach. If I kept this going, I would never get my shot at her and though conventional wisdom would dictate to forget about her, I couldn't. I had to finish what I started and not be detracted by anyone or anything, no matter how alluring the alternative may seem.

My phone started to ring, at first, I ignored it as I waited for Christina to come back. But as soon as the ringing stopped, it started again. I pulled out my phone and saw it was Foxy calling, for her to call several times like this clearly meant something was up. I peered through the stained-glass window on the door out into the night, thinking what could be going on out there.

"Is everything okay?" Christina returned with a black purse over her shoulder, keys in hand. "Are you going to answer that?" She glanced down at the phone.

"I can't do this..." I looked down at the marble tiles.

"Then don't answer it." She chuckled and stepped towards me.

I put my hand up to halt her.

"No, I can't do this..."

"Can't do what?"

"Us..." I pressed the tips of my fingers to my forehead. Foxy, Melissa, if I set foot out that door, I risked losing both of them forever and I simply was not willing to do that.

Christina backed away. "But a second ago, you wanted to go out and now you've changed your mind?"

My eyes moved upward to meet Christina's who sat across from me with a look of confusion and irritation in the shine of her irises.

"I can't."

The phone started to ring again, but I silenced it.

"I thought it would be a good idea but I realize that my heart is not in it and that wouldn't be good for either of us...."

"Is that so?" Her reply was smug. "Does your sudden change of heart have anything to do with that?" She glanced down at her phone. "All this time I thought you were different but in reality, you are just like every other scumbag that I have met previously."

"There's no reason to call me names."

"You are a scumbag." Her eyes were filled with resentment and bitterness.

"Will you let me at least explain?"

"No!" Her hand wrapped around my arm as she opened the door. "Take your player ass and get the fuck out of my house!" She shoved me on to the front step. "I'll be sure to let Melissa or Samantha or whoever else you are fucking, that you are nothing more than a two-timing fink!" She slammed the door in my face.

I looked out into the street, stunned. Just five minutes ago, there were two women in my life and now if Christina followed through on as she threatened, I'd be left with none. If Melissa caught wind of everything, that would be it, any possibility of a miracle in getting her would be gone before it ever started. Maybe, I should have kept my mouth shut and went to Floral Park with Christina. Perhaps, it could have turned into something unexpected. I could have found what I always wanted in the form of someone else. I was too stupid then to realize this because my mind and heart were set on Melissa, but though I be a villain to Christina, I knew I was doing what was right. I shouldn't give her half of a heart when she was willing to give me hers full. I just hoped that things would have a way of working themselves out and I wouldn't be punished for both my discretion and indiscretions which had the poorest of timing.

Chapter 6 – I Circled No Before You Could Say Yes

As I left Christina's house, I didn't look back, I didn't want to give her anymore opportunities to spew her venom at me or escalate this any further. What was I thinking? Could I fall into such a trap so easily over a girl who throws herself at me? Distance, I needed distance from the day both time and space, it will all blow over.

I turned the corner onto McKinley Avenue and looked into a lime Victorian house with lights illuminated, oblivious to the turmoil. I could see inside the windows, the house was pitched upon a hill and set back between two large oak trees. I observed a woman, middle-aged with a voluminous bob of dirty blonde hair hovering over a table, liking down to children sat eating dinner. The scene of domestic bliss was probably nothing to her, she didn't even realize I was out in the warm night watching her, wishing I was there in that moment; the street felt lonely like me.

My phone rang in my pocket again, it was Foxy. Did she already know? Has it already started? I couldn't avoid her though; she was my friend and likely in distress. Plus, if I couldn't trust her, who could I trust?

"Hey." I could hear Sam's gasps on the other end of the phone. "Sorry for missing your calls, I was just going to call you back." I paced down the street away from the house, perching under the shadow of a tree. "What's going on?

"Where are you?"

I looked around, surveying the quiet suburban street for anything that appeared out of place. It was just me, as I left it. "I am just heading home."

"Are you close? I need to talk to you..."

I gulped. "About what?"

"Ricky..."

I took a deep breath and composed myself, relieved for a moment that the rumors hadn't started to spread. "Sure, where are you at?"

"Near the library."

I put some extra pace in my steps, I was going to take the long way there to avoid passing by Christina's. "Give me ten minutes."

"Thank you." Relief filled her voice.

"Of course." A brief smile broke to my face. "I'll see you shortly."

The phone call ended and covertly, I circumnavigated the tree-lined streets until I emerged across the way from the Lynbrook library. Sam was already outside sitting on the steps, sick with despair. As I approached, Sam shot up, her hair trailing behind her as her orange Tennessee Volunteers jersey glistened in the night along with her black yoga pants.

"That's a nice jersey." I tried to lighten the mood with a compliment but Samantha's sulking didn't lift.

"Thanks, they are my favorite team." Her response was bereft of any kind of joy or energy, it was hollow and sorrowful.

"What's wrong?" I gave her a tight hug and embraced as her as she sobbed, Samantha nestled into my arms finding refuge from her woe.

"I am sorry, I know he's your best mate, but I didn't know who else to call."

" It's okay..." I rubbed her back. "I am glad you did; I am here to help."

"But since you are his friend, you can tell me where I went wrong."

"What do you mean?" I kept my hand gently on her shoulder.

"I saw the way he looked at Christina yesterday, it was like she was a five-star entrée at a steakhouse. He looks at me like I am a value-menu appetizer."

Despite her melancholy, Foxy had an uncanny way of integrating her wit in to the conversation.

I chuckled. "That's not funny but I appreciate the analogy."

Sam broke a smile for a moment, expressing some faint delight in my amusement at her remarks.

"Are you sure that you aren't imagining that?"

Foxy curled her lips.

"Samantha, if he doesn't see there is something special about you." I tightened my grip around her. "He's crazy."

"You're just saying that..." She struck back a stand of her loose hair and sniffled.

"Not at all." I wiped her tears away. "You got a wicked sense of humor, you're intelligent, charming, and you love football..." I had hoped the gag would cause Foxy to laugh a bit, she at least settled and broke a smile.

"He doesn't really talk about a lot; he just stuffs it." I ran my hand up her back. "It's hard to know where he stands most of the time but he is a great guy deep down."

"He talks to you, doesn't he?" The twang of her southern drawl emerged in her emotional state.

"Sam, we are best friends." I shrugged my shoulders. "If he didn't..." I opened my palm.

"Well, he doesn't talk to me, one iota." She dabbed her cheeks. "I am supposed to be his girlfriend." Her fingers pinched the bridge of her nose to stop any more tears from flowing. "When I first met him, he was so dashing and charming. He had this swagger about him and I just ate it up." Sam shrugged. "I swear Melissa and I are pals because we fall for it. Crawling back every bloody time." An Irish intonation meshed into her accent, like it did earlier in the day.

"I wish I knew what that was like..." I reflected on minutes ago, thinking perhaps that was the closest I'd ever get, sacrificing myself for Melissa unbeknownst to her.

"Don't say that..." She shook her head. "I'm sure one day you'll find the girl of your dreams and she won't even know what hit her."

"That's kind of you, I can say the same for you." I peered across the passage way to the high school next to the fire station, imagining a figure that may emerge from the darkness when no one was there. "So, where is he?"

"I don't know. I left him..."

"At his house?"

"No, like for good..." She replied firm, full of spirit, crossing her arms in a final act of defiance.

"Are you sure want to do that?"

"I am not taking his shit, anymore."

"Good for you..." I patted her shoulder. "You should stand up for yourself." I leaned in toward her.

"I thought you'd take his side." She smiled briefly.

"By default, I would, but he's in the wrong here." I ran my hand across her back once more. "May I share my thoughts on it?"

"The floor is yours." She replied demurely.

"Do whatever is best for you and if he doesn't treat you the way you deserve to be treated, then don't go back. But I want you to know this about him..."

Sam turned toward me, her eyes locked on to me, hanging on my every word.

"When we were younger, we were stupid and we knocked this window of the Chinese takeout there on Union Avenue. We thought it was all fun and games until this woman came out and chased us for blocks."

"What?" She chuckled.

"Yea, we were amazed at how fast she could run. She had grey hairs, quite pudgy, and she was wearing this sweaty black apron and all but we couldn't get her off our tail." I chuckled, reminiscing at the youthful episode of mischief. "Ricky turned back and let him catch her, so I could get away."

"What happened?"

"Nothing." I bat my eyebrow once. "They called his mom down and she laughed in the woman's face for wasting her time but that wasn't the point." I rubbed my cheeks as I laughed for a moment re-living the passing memory. "Ricky is the kind of guy that if he loves someone, he'll take the fall for them every single time. He'll come around..." I placed my hand over the number 16 embroidered on the shoulder of her jersey. "I'll drop by and speak to him."

"Thanks." A smile returned to Samantha's face, refreshing to see as it could light up a room. "So, what happened when you left with Christina?"

I was a lot a loss for words. I couldn't find it in me to lie to her but at the same time knew that if the news got back to Melissa, I was falling on my sword.

"She's bad news, her..." A slight rage filled Samantha's eyes; her emotions had a way of consuming the environment around her as I could feel her anger in the air.

"I am going to trust you here and tell you a secret, okay?" I took a deep breath. "But it has to stay between us."

"Ok, what is it?" She remained frozen awaiting an answer, she let out a yawn. "Dear me, I'm shattered from cheerleading."

"Why don't I walk you home and we can talk about it?"

"Corey!" Foxy grilled me.

"I have a crush on Melissa, she's the girl I'm chasing after. I've always had a crush on this girl since..." I looked up at the moon rising above the horizon. "...since forever." I paused for a moment, carefully selecting what I said next. "When Ricky invited me to come meet the two of you that night at Greis Park, I was nervous beyond belief because I have daydreamed in Math class about this girl countless times."

"I wish Ricky would say half of those things about me..." Sam glowered and looked down at the ground. "But your secret is safe with me."

Trust, the act of falling back and *trusting* that you won't be let down or that the one you confide in will be there to catch you. Call it instinct but Sam didn't have to say or do anything, I knew I could trust her.

"I'll try to help you with Dukes but she loves to date these guys who treat her with no respect. Matt is controlling and manipulative, she hasn't been around in days because he has her at the end of her tether. First, they go on a break, then he takes her back and they are all lovey-dubby. It's a matter of time before he starts with his antics again."

"Well, she wouldn't have that problem with me."

"I know..." Sam's blue eyes locked into mine, they were piercing and when they were set upon you, nothing else seemed to exist. "I can tell." She sighed. "I'll see what I can do, I can be quite persuasive. Lord in Heaven knows; I wish that Ricky and I can be more than just sex." Samantha ran her hands through her hair.

"So why don't you change that?"

"I'm not that strong Corey." Foxy chuckled. "If I wanted to be with a guy who would be my best friend, I think you seem like the perfect candidate."

She looked at me as if she understood me while also feeling understand. It was as if she knew what was inside my heart and she wasn't rushing to pre-tension. My brother was right about her, she was a gentle soul who was vulnerable but had a quite nobility about her.

An engine screeched as a rusted-out car entered the car park, its headlights made a brief intersection with Sam's eyes, drowning out all of the night around it. "There's my ride." Sam waved. "Where are you heading?" She turned to look back at me.

"I was going to go to Ricky's actually."

"I'll ask my Nan, if we can drop you along the way." Samantha approached the car and opened the door, conversing with an elder woman who wore a teal sweater and large-framed glasses that drew attention to her judicious eyes. White frayed hairs escaped from below a red bonnet.

"Hop in."

"Thanks." I gripped the door handle and slipped into the backseat; the plush leather weathered from years of usage contoured to my back. The cabin was warm with the heat on blast.

"Hello." Sam's grandmother greeted me, carrying an Old South drawl like her granddaughter. "A friend of Sammie's?"

"I'm Corey." I spoke to the woman who looked at me sharply from the rear-view mirror, inspecting my every movement.

"Nice to meet you, son." She pushed up on the driveshaft and the car rolled out of the parking lot. "I take it, you are you coming back our way?"

"Actually, I was hoping I could get dropped at my friend's, if that's okay..."

"Nana, Corey is going to Ricky's." Her tone was gentle and submissive, full of respect and reverence for her elder. "They are friends from football..."

"Ricky, is that the brown-skilled fella that you are palling' around with..."

"Yes..." Sam spoke at length and nearly growled.

"That kid is trouble..." She gave Samantha a side-eye.

Foxy pouted and held her forehead.

"Sammie, dear, I only have your best interest at heart." Her grandmother's eyes shifted back to me with a lukewarm smile. "I tried warning your mom about your father, he was a smooth talker too."

The engine revved behind us as we passed a Dunkin Donuts. Two teenage girls stood in front of the glass vestibule sipping on Coolatas, indulging in the drink and warm summer night. I watched them to see if I could recognize them but they blurred past as we made our way down Sunrise Highway, heading in the direction of one of the two towering Rockville Centre water towers, a white hulking column reaching into the sky with a red light at its apex.

"So where do you live?"

"On Holmes Place..."

"You don't say?" A fuller smile broke from her face for the first time. "We live on Central, just over yonder. It's good to know that my granddaughter has a friend close by..."

"Your granddaughter is a very kind girl so..." I clapped my hands together nervously, when I looked up at the rear-view mirror, Foxy's grandma looked more relaxed. She was a woman of few words but her expression said it all.

"He's right there, Nana." Foxy interjected, pointing at the apartment above the hobby store. The store was black and shut for the evening but the lights above it where Ricky's family lived were fully lit. I always had a good time when I stayed there, Ricky's mom would make rice and beans with some jerk chicken and his sisters garrulous laughs would fill the flat as they played a medley of pop songs with the volume turned up. Ricky's home was far livelier than mine which was quiet and introspective.

The car pulled over the curb and I reached for the warm metal handle. "Thank you for the ride, it's nice to meet you." I put my hand on Sam's shoulder, briefly stroking some of her silky hair by mistake. "I'll let you know how it goes. Call me if you need anything."

"Thank you, Corey."

I shut the door and waved as the car drove off. When I glanced up at the window, Ricky's little sister Minnie was waving at me. Her brown eyes curious and full of excitement. "Corey is here!" Her words legible on her small lips. Before, I could press the doorbell, the large blue door flung open with Ricky standing in the doorway.

"What's up, brother?" He came out and slapped me five, pulling me in for a hug. "You look different man..." He grinned.

"How?"

"You got more pep in your step."

"What can I say, I had a good day yesterday." I bantered.

"Care to elaborate?"

"It's all good." I licked my lips. "Can you tell me what is going on with you and Foxy?"

Ricky rolled his eyes. "Did she tell you something?"

"She just seems really upset."

He nodded. "So, she did tell you something." Ricky placed his hand against the door frame. "That bitch needs to get a grip."

"She's not a bitch dude."

"Look, she's my girl and I got this shit." Ricky put his hands on my shoulders. "I know you trying to help me out and I appreciate that, but she's trippin." He rolled his eyes again. "I've been dating her for less than a month and she's way too attached. Every little fucking thing that I do is overanalyzed and scrutinized to the eighth degree."

"I'm just saying Rick not everybody is nonchalant like you when it comes to relationships."

"Yea and not every is so uptight and serious like you either." Ricky pat my shoulder. "Matter of fact, she reminds me of you, man..." He laughed.

"Thanks." I simpered.

"But you're my boy."

We smiled at each other.

"In fairness, she's a nice girl. Maybe, you just need to make her feel safe with you..."

"Which is why she is confiding in you, right?" Ricky laughed and put his arm around me. "Tell me, did you fuck Christina?" He asked in a low voice.

"What makes you say that?"

"Shut the fuck up, I can tell." His voice grew but his proximity didn't. "But I want to hear it from you..."

"Yes." I let out a deep breath. "Twice, actually..."

"That's what's up bro, congratulations."

"Thanks, but there is more to it than that."

"No, there aint anything else to it. Don't catch feelings!" His grip intensified around the back of my neck. "Don't get sentimental over a slut."

"Is that what you think Sam is?"

"No!" He sighed. "I was talking about Christina." Ricky shook his head. "But don't let Foxy get you caught in her web of melodrama. If it was such a big deal, she wouldn't put out."

"I think you got it wrong, man."

"Nah, brother..." He looked up at the apartment. "Cuidado, nina." Ricky spoke at length at his sister who was trying to open the window to get our attention. "You the one who got it twisted."

I was perplexed at the meaning of that statement. In that moment, I thought he was trying to drop some sagacious advice on affairs of the heart and the opposite sex, but in reality, he was talking about something grander and greater that was forming right beneath my nose.

"You want to come up for some Cena?" He patted my back. "We got those plantains on."

"Damn..." A smiled unraveled across my face. "You are tempting me..." The faint whiff of oil and spices tickled my nose, beckoning me upstairs.

"It'd probably do you well for practice tomorrow..." Ricky shrugged his shoulders. "Plus, Mom, Minnie, and Joanna were asking about you."

"You better not mention your older sister asking about me or Mike may get jealous."

We both broke out in laughter; Ricky clapped his hand once as he couldn't control himself. "Word, he's had it bad for Jo." He put a hand on his hip. "He's busting my chops about her every time I see him."

"Ricardo, esta listo!" Ricky's moms voice echoed down the vestibule from the top of the steps.

"You coming?" He pointed behind him with the tip of his thumb.

"I'd love to."

Ricky smiled and put his hand around my back, leading me up the stairs where I was greeted with hugs and kisses by the rest of Ricky's family. I never understand how he could be so cavalier with Samantha's feelings but so loving and affectionate toward his sisters. Surely, Ricky wouldn't want them to be treated with such disregard as he does Foxy? Growing up with doting sisters made him seek constant female attention but Ricky prided himself on being independent, never wanting to be smothered like his younger sisters. Nevertheless, any tension that built in our conversation over Samantha quickly dissipated as we passed salad around the table and traded jokes over a glass of fruit punch.

Chapter 7 – New Beginnings

Practice was a drag, and much of the team likely felt the same as we were labored and fatigued from the oppressive heat and humidity. Ricky was showcasing talent impeccably, cutting up field for big gains and taking the ball the full distance several times against our defense. I was where I expected to be, standing on the sideline playing with a roll of white tape which I used to wrap around my wrists. I looked behind me and watched the cheerleading squad conducting a practice of their own. Christina led the squad in cheers and Foxy was trying keep up. Both noticed me looking at them, Samantha made a silly face while Christina glared at me with disdain.

"What up Ma?" Ricky's voice spoke at length. I shifted my attention to him as he stood there with his green helmet on, chewing on his mouthpiece. The entire team was laughing but when I glanced back at Foxy, her eyes were full of scorn, wounded by the gaff.

"Ok, let me see Montgomery and Russell at Wide Receiver." Coach Kenny called out.

"Wait, what?" I looked over at Coach, the look of disbelief couldn't be hidden beneath my helmet.

"Flanker, right?" Coach tried to hold a steady authoritative tone but he nearly cracked.

Last season I rode the bench, it was my home away from home. I only played a total of five plays last year and that was on defense at safety when the games were blowouts and that was only if we were the team blowing the other team out.

"Yea..." I muttered, both excitement and nervousness flowing through me.

"Let's go!" Coach spoke at length and pointed to the field, a smirk breaking from his stoic demeanor as I tore off the tape and sprinted out to the huddle with Danny following. Marlon Green our star wide receiver ran off along with Damarcus Landry. While

Marlon didn't drop his hand to give me a low five to encourage, DaMarcus tapped me on the head as he passed. "Get it Gingy." He cheered as he passed.

"Come on brother." Ricky put his fist out to me. "Time to eat."

"Play Action 13 Curl." Our quarterback Brendan Adams went through the cadence until Ricky interrupted.

"Brendan, Corey he is sick on the post. If he gets an inside step, no one is catching him." Ricky gave me a wink. Brandon leered at Ricky, aghast that he was calling for an audible as the running back.

"It's on me, if it gets fouled up." Ricky rested his hands on his knee pads. "But it won't."

"Okay..." He shook his head. "Play Action 15 Post on two, Play Action 15 Post on two, ready?" Brendan clapped his hands and broke the huddle.

"Break!" We all screamed and went to our positions.

I lined up across from our starting cornerback William Jean-Baptiste. I glanced over at Christina and Foxy both watching on.

I listened to the cadence; my heart beat I am surprised didn't drown out the sound. On the second hut, I stutter-stepped and broke inside. Brendan faked the handoff to Ricky who then pulled off a great acting job as if he was running with the football. The linebackers flushed to Ricky and this opened up things for me over the middle. When I was fifteen yards down field I pivot-stepped at a forty-five-degree angle and broke for the middle of the end zone. Brendan pump faked and threw it deep, throwing a beautifully placed ball as I had time to get under it and complete my route. I had a good three steps on Willie when I caught the ball in stride and took it to the rest of the way. Ricky ran up field and met me in the end zone.

"Just like a pick-up game at the park!" Ricky picked me up and smacked my helmet.

I was joined by several teammates in the end zone both congratulated me and celebrated as if it were a real game. I jogged back to midfield and handed the ball to coach.

"That's it!" Coach gave me a quick hug. "That's what I was looking for!"

"Thank you, coach." I was wearing a smile ear-to-ear.

"No need to thank me, good route!" He patted me on the butt as I was met by the rest of my teammates on the sideline who congratulated me as well. All except for "Greenie" who ran back on to the field, as if it never happened at all. I looked back at Foxy and smiled at her. She pumped her fist at me modestly as Christina and Katie were addressing the squad. Practice ensued for another hour until coach finally ended the festivities for the day. I was fortunate enough to get several reps at receiver and I even made a few more receptions.

After practice, I found myself back in the same place I was many days previously, sitting on the bench near the locker room steps waiting for Ricky to emerge.

"You were something else today, kid." Sam plopped down on the bench beside and patted my lap. "They don't have an answer for you once you get into space." Sam picked up a bottle of Red Powerade and put it to her lips, her white bodysuit beneath her green cheerleading vest soaked in sweat.

"No Gatorade, huh?"

"Gators..." She wiped the brow of her lips. "Ewe..." Foxy placed the bottle between her thighs escaping from her green "lollypops", what cheerleaders colloquially called spandex short shorts. Admittedly, I caught myself staring at her thighs but tried to distract myself with a quick rub of my sweat-soaked t-shirt against my face covered in grime.

"Maybe you are right about Rick..." I chuckled and playfully tapped her thigh with the back of my hand. She wrinkled her eyebrows and glared at me, before breaking to a smile.

"Hello, kids." Melissa slid next to Samantha, her hair down over a red tank top tucked into black jeans, her eyes covered in sunglasses. Butterflies filled my stomach and I tensed up, she looked really good.

"Hi." I waved.

Samantha squinted at me, her eyes warning me to relax and when I focused on her, I eased up.

"Hear from Matt?" Samantha crossed her arms.

"Yea..." She moved her head forward and caught her hair in her hands. "We are back on a track." Melissa flipped her hair back and rested her head against the bench. The news filled Melissa with elation but to me it was a gut punch. But I feigned a smile, jealous that this guy could have her as he pleases when all I wanted was one chance with her.

"I am glad it worked out for you."

"Thanks." She half-smiled. "How was practice?"

"Corey, made an amazing catch today actually." Foxy answered on my behalf, flipping the half bottle of thirst quencher in the air before catching it. "In fact, I think he will get some reps at receiver."

"I don't know about that, you got Greenie and Lando."

Samantha raised her hand. "You did great, have a bit of confidence." She put her finger over her tongue and faked a gag. "Dukes, this kid has breakaway speed, they are going to have to bracket him."

"Bracket him?" Melissa smiled and crossed her arms.

"What you do is, you put a corner on him and press and then roll the safety over the top to keep him in a box..."

Melissa arched her eyebrows, clearly confused by Samantha's advanced football acumen.

"...it's to take away the post route or the seam, cause Gingy on the fly or a deep post likely can't be covered."

Melissa glanced at me, hoping I would elucidate.

"What she said..." I pointed at her with my thumb. "I'd trust her calling the plays more than anyone..."

"Cheers." Sam briefly chuckled and touched the side of her head against mine. Wrinkles formed in Melissa's forehead.

"Sam..." Melissa's tone was serious as she tapped Foxy's leg, her eyes were locked on what she focused on. Sam swung her head back, her hair nearly whipping me in the face by accident while doing so and her exuberance evaporated at the appearance of Ricky and Christina exchanging in pleasantries at the top of the steps.

"Well, I'll be!" Sam shot up from the bench and stormed over towards Ricky and Christina. I leapt off the bench as Melissa sped up flanking Foxy.

"Foxy, wait!" I attempted to step in front of Foxy.

"Let me go, please." She tried to step around me but Melissa passed both of us.

"Yo, it's not what it looks like." Ricky threw his hands up.

"Really bitch?!" Melissa took off her sunglasses and snapped them shut, placing them on the neckline of her tank top with a look of pure rage in her eyes.

"Dukes, I got this!" Foxy screamed, as she tried to get around me but I gently kept her at bay.

"It's not worth it, Sam." I rubbed her arms. "You are better than this."

The words disarmed Sam as Ricky stepped in front of Melissa. Despite the intervention, a clash seemed imminent between Melissa and Christina who was dressed in the green lollypops and a matching green sports bra, her toned core and arms covered in sweat. Seeing her like that, made me re-think what I had done as she looked sexier than ever.

"You really are just a homewrecking fucking slut!" Melissa was face-to-face with her.

"And you are just a tease." She smirked and looked at me briefly before she backhanded Melissa in the face. Her hair splashed behind her as she clutched her lip. Her cheeks reddened by the strike.

Melissa retaliated without thought and kicked her between the legs.

"Ahh!" Christina cried out and doubled over holding her stomach, gasping for air, her hair draped down as she clutched her groin tight, winded from the pain.

"Does that hurt, you stupid bitch?!" Melissa grabbed Christina's hair and pulled back to throw a punch. "You'll never fuck again!"

Before she was able to land another blow, I jumped in front of Christina just in the nick of time. Melissa's punch connected on my jaw instead, my adrenaline alone numbed me from the impact though it was hard.

"Really Corey, you're going to protect that bitch?!" Melissa lunged forward but Ricky stepped in front of her again as I hooked Christina around the waist to pull her away from Melissa. However, Melissa was deceptively strong and by rage along imposed her will and shoved Ricky out of the way. Ricky endured the onslaught and threw his arm around her stomach, pulling her backwards as she kicked out like a caged animal.

"Let go of me!" Christina threw an elbow at me which released my hands from around her waist. "All of a sudden, you are a knight in shining armor?" Her eyes flamed with a mix of confusion and betrayal.

"You're such an asshole!" Foxy screamed in Ricky's face and stormed off.

"Sam!" I let go of Christina and ran after Foxy as she paced toward the gate.

"Let her go, she's a drama queen!"

"Yo Rick, you're a fuckin dick bro," I turned around and scolded him. His confident smile soon turned into an empty gape.

"Don't lecture me, dawg, you fuck her." He pointed at Christina walking in the opposite direction. "When you have a crush on my girlfriend clearly..."

My eyes shot to Melissa, the object of my affection. Her hair was thrown all over the place, blood forming at the corner of her lip as her eyes bulged with fury. "You fucked that skank?" She screamed, betrayal and disgust poured from her eyes. This is the last thing I wanted to foil any hope with her and Ricky in his hubris, forgot that.

I shook my head at Ricky and moved my head once in the direction of Melissa, he soon disarmed, visibly ashamed he just blurted out what he did. But I didn't have time to follow-up, Foxy was gone and the state of how she could be haunted me. I sprinted out the gate and saw Foxy was long down the street, walking away with her head down.

"Foxy!"

I sprinted past teammates exiting the front of the school, weaving through the foot traffic until I caught up to her, 100 yards down.

"Are you alright?"

Tears were flowing from Samantha's eyes.

"I am sorry, I don't know what he was thinking." I pulled her in for a hug.

"It's alright." She sniffled. "I don't know why I do this to myself." Sam raised her hands and swiped a tear. "I just need a minute to take a walk and cool off."

"I can't leave you here on your own."

"I'll be swell." She looked over her shoulder. "I am going to go to Duke's. If I was you, I'd be more concerned about that at this point."

"Sam, I am worried about you..."

"Many thanks, but it's not necessary." She looked down, lost in her thoughts.

A car turned the corner with the bass blasting, as *Down and Out* by Cam'ron escaped the windows of the passing white Ford Thunderbird.

"Will you call me later then?" I stepped between Sam and the street, as the car went past. The driver shot a look at Sam and then glared at me, as the car carried on down the street. I watched as it kept going until the tires screeched as it took a sharp turn at the corner.

"I need to know you are okay..."

"I will do." Sam wiped her nose. "Thank you." She smiled at me before I pulled her in for another hug and we went our separate ways.

Despite all the chaos and calamity of that afternoon, things went back to normal as if they had never happened fairly quickly. Ricky apologized to me for me what he said and I said my sorry to him, and as was the case with friends who are brothers, the fight never happened. We just picked up where we left off and made stupid jokes and hung out as we did any other day. Ricky also came full circle with Samantha, from what she told me in our phone conversation later that evening, he apologized for speaking to Christina and told her he would never do so again. After a few sweet lines and words, Samantha was eating out of his hand again and seemingly the events of earlier that day were a distant memory. The only question that remained was where I stood with Melissa and in that moment, that seemed to most pressing of all.

Chapter 8 – The First Game

It was the eve of our first game of the season and as customary, we had a walk through on Friday's: Helmets only, jerseys with no pads, and pants. After warm-ups and calisthenics, three whistles blew as Coach Kenny called us to center. We circled Coach who was dressed down like we were, no team logo polo and khakis, no suit and tie. Coach was wearing a red Georgia Bulldog jersey with a block number 3 on the back, the name Shockley written above it draped over black And 1 basketball shorts with white Nike Air Force One's on his feet. Coach Kenny reminded me of Mike with his short hair buzzed and the beard edged up, he looked like a high school student more than a football coach. One may think that too until you heard him speak.

"Boys, let me tell you this. Last year you were 2-6 and our guests were 6-2." He raised his finger. "But I want to tell you that this is a new season and with everything that happened before, is gone. The past doesn't exist and the future doesn't either. We have now, what will you do with?" Coach's eyes moved across the team surrounding him, his look met each and every player and had an ability to ignite a fire in our souls. "As for now, we're going to go through some special teams and offensive sets quick and we'll get out of here, so we can be fresh and ready for tomorrow." He glanced down at his clipboard. "On Kick Return, I want to see Davis and Montgomery as the return men." I gulped as I slowly gazed at Coach, who noticed I was nervous at the unexpected announcement.

"Just follow your blocks, Corey." He smiled. "You got this."

Ricky came up behind me and patted me on the back, his touch re-assuring and encouraging.

"Kickoff, on the 35." Coach pointed and trotted off.

I ran out to the twenty-yard line, every step furtive as if I was stealing someone's place, waiting for the right person to come back and take it. I turned and looked over at Nathan Davis one of our running backs who was also assigned to kick return. He nodded at me, I turned to the sideline and looked for a familiar face to ground me in this moment. There stood Foxy amongst the other cheerleaders, she waved across at me. Although I couldn't hear her, I read her lips. She was yelling "Get em Gingy."

The kickoff came next, and as expected, the ball sailed straight toward me. I took a step forward as the pigskin cradled in my chest, I followed the blockers in front of me and saw a lane open on the left side. There I hit the jets and accelerated through the hole to the next level where I had followed two more blockers in front of me until I was forced out of bounds at around the midfield. My teammates cheered and jumped, patting my helmet with enthusiasm.

"That's a good return!" Coach gave me a tap on the butt. "First O, on the ball." Coach turned back to me and pointed. "Gingy, rotate in for Greenie on the next play."

I paused for a moment, what did he say? Play with the first team? I wasn't even on the second team last season. I threw my hands on my hips and tucked my chin against the puddle of sweat on my chest as I watched our first unit head onto the field. On the ensuing play, Marlon Green was in a one-on-one with our second cornerback, Brian Flaherty and gained a step on with a quick shimmy. The two hooked up on a bomb that Green caught in stride and took down the field for a touchdown. He made it look easy and trotted back along the sideline to the pats of teammates.

"That's what starters do, ya dig?" Green flipped the ball to me and I dropped it on my shoes, still tense from the dig. But I had to put it behind me or at least I tried, I got my reps in with the first team and made a few catches that impressed Coach Kenny but still Marlon's words lingered. *Did I belong? Was I ready for this?*

Animosity seemed to be the theme of the day, as it didn't only come from rival teammates. When I emerged from the locker room,

Christina shot me a nasty look amongst a group of cheerleaders circled near the top of the steps. I weaved through clusters of teammates all engaged in their own conversation until I saw Melissa ahead on her cell phone, pacing back and forth, her voice rising until she erupted into profanities, the sobs breaking through her anger. Her olive skin shined under the sunlight as she threw her hands to her sides, fists clenched. Melissa's dark blue New York Yankees t-shirt crinkled against her as she let out profanities. Seeing her distressed, I approached slowly, a crushing sensation radiating throughout my sternum from the fear and anxiety that came with it.

Mel shut the phone and squeezed it in her hand, placing her other fist against her forehead as she leaned into it.

"Hey...." The words skittishly came out in the form of a stutter. "Is everything alright?"

Melissa slid her cell phone back into her tight blue jeans, scowling at me as she did so. "You're the last person I want to talk to right now."

"You looked upset, so I just wanted to make sure you were okay..."

Her eyes moved side-to-side but she didn't respond, her brown hair gently tussling in the soft breeze. "And I also want to tell you that if you ever need anything, I am here..." I nodded once and bit my lip, turning away to head to gate and walk home.

"What the fuck?" Her voice pierced the air, sharp and accusing as she stormed up behind me. "You don't even really know me and you're going to put yourself out there like that?!"

"Well that's how it starts..." I stuttered. "I am sorry for upsetting you yesterday."

Melissa's attention turned to the right and I joined her, just beyond the fence at the end of the field.

"Good shit today, brother!" Ricky called out to me, wearing his green home jersey with a white number 45 outlined in gold, his arm around Foxy who was dressed in a grey tank-top showing a slight amount of midriff, her fair skin glowed under the sunlight. Her auburn hair was set in a long ponytail descending down cutting above the curvature of her butt which was hugged by her tight blue jeans. She waved at the both of us with a warm smile.

Melissa broke her frown at the sight of her friend, her white teeth escaping from her pouting lips. "I love you, bitch!"

Foxy blew a kiss to the both of us and gave us a thumbs up. Melissa's smile soon evaporated as she set her attention back on me.

"Why do you even care?" She crossed her arms.

"Because I do..." My passions bubbled up in me, my cleats dug into the ground, as I looked her firm in the eyes. "I like you, Melissa."

Her eyebrows rose slowly. I could feel my chest tighten, my pulse quickening. This wasn't how I imagined things would go—but maybe, just maybe, it was the right thing to do. I had to tell her... even if it scared me.

"I always have...."

Melissa's lip descended, stunned at my revelation but she wouldn't say anything back to me.

"I take it that was Matt?"

Her eyes shot once at me to confirm even if she didn't say anything. "You shouldn't let him treat you the way that he does, he should appreciate you."

Melissa peered away again, crossing her arms but despite her apparent disdain, she didn't go anywhere. "I am sorry, I don't mean to overstep." I raised my hand once to ease any tension. "And I am sorry again for yesterday I was only trying to stop you from getting into a fight with Tina."

"Why did you leave with her?" Melissa simpered. "Was Ricky talking shit or did you really sleep with that whore?"

I paused for a moment, unsure of how to answer it. I could tell her the truth and risk losing her forever or lie to her and save it, knowing fully well that this entire situation would be built upon falsehoods set in sand.

"I left with her because I couldn't leave with you." I put my hands behind my back. "I hope one day that will change." I nodded once at Melissa whose eyes had softened, she seemed unsure of what she was actually hearing and I took that as a cue to make my way to the gate. Mel didn't say anything as I walked on and I didn't look back but I could her feel her eyes burning into the back of my neck. I felt her presence follow me all of the way home though I left her standing by the practice field.

When I opened the front door and I stepped into our house, I was met by the aroma of chicken cutlets cooking on the stove. The thunderous footsteps of Mike echoed through the halls.

"There he is." Mike approached me and rubbed my head. "Are we going to beat Plainedge tomorrow or what?"

"We're going to try." I pulled out a seat to join the table, my thoughts distant from the game on the horizon.

"Yeah, that's probably the last thing you thinking about."

He chuckled as I pulled up

my seat kitchen to the table. His remark was ironic since it was true, it was the last thing I was thinking about but Mike didn't realize who these thoughts were focused on.

"Mikey, knock it off..." My mom stood cooking the cutlets over the stove, a sizzling sound from the skillet encompassed the kitchen. "How's Ricky doing?" She plucked a cutlet out of the pan and put it on a white china plate set next to the oven top.

"He's better..." I replied skittishly.

"I am sure he is." Mike winked as he put some salad on to his plate.

"On that heartwarming note..." Mike placed a cigarette between his lips and headed out for the porch. "I am going to step out for a smoke quick."

"Hey bro, can I talk to you about something?"

Mike looked down at me, all the teasing and ribbing left him as he could sense the urgency in me. He gestured me to follow him and I rose from my chair. We headed toward the porch, as we did so the cell phone rang in my pocket, it was Foxy.

"Hey what's up?"

"Hey Corey, how are you?"

"I'm good, just got home." I opened the door and stepped out onto the porch. "What's going on?"

"Can I come by?" Her words were filled with distress. "I need to talk..."

"Do you want me to come to you?" I held the phone to my ear and looked out toward Hendrickson Avenue, my eyes wandering amongst the parked cars in the various driveways.

"I need to get some air and walk it off..."

"Sure, I'll meet you, half-way then..."

"Don't be daft." She laughed. "It's only a short walk, I'll be over shortly."

"As you wish."

"Thank you, see you soon sugar." The phone went silent.

My brother leaned against the railing as he puffed on his cigarette, studying my every move. "How can I help you?"

"I got a situation." I threw my hands at my sides and sat on the steps.

"What kind of situation?" He moved his wrist to check the time on the face of his Casio watch.

"You know how I like Melissa?"

"Yeah." Mike sat beside me. "What about her?"

A DAY WE MET IN LYNBROOK

"I think I messed it up by fucking Christina."

"Word?"

"Word..." I nodded. "But I broke things off because I didn't want to mess it up with Mel."

Mike covered his eyes and jerked violently from the laughter.

"Well, what do I do?"
"You don't have to do anything, what have been telling you about keeping your options open?"
"But they hate each other..."
"And who's problem is that?" He continued to laugh as flares of cigarette smoke trailed around him. "You got to do what's good for you." Mike puffed on his cigarette and let a brief cloud of smoke flush around his face again. "And while we are digging, I wouldn't recommend you become immediately available whenever Melissa's dysfunctional relationship ends..."
"Well I told her I liked her..."
"And how that go?"
I shrugged my shoulders. "She didn't say much." I itched the top of my head; the feeling provided a distraction from what the anxiousness that was consuming me. "I don't know what to do."
"It sounds like you did it." Mike said. "Personally, I think you put too much emphasis on this whole romance gambit."
I looked down the street and saw Foxy, she smiled as she approached, her headphones hanging around her neck and her black hoodie blending into the dusk
"...it'll come brother don't worry. When you least expect it and you'll know what to do though when it does..."

She waved at me as she neared the house, I waved back. "You remember Samantha, right?"

Mike leaned back. "How could I not?" He chuckled. "All of a sudden, you a fucking pro with the women?"

"It's not like that, Mike."

"Right..." His eyes lit up from amusement. "It sure don't look like that."

Foxy walked up the steps, straightening her hair in her hands at it fell over her black Tennessee Volunteers sweatshirt, covering the orange T and E. Her eyes matched her jeans which hugged her hips and thighs, tucked into white adidas sneakers with orange bands.

"Hello." She drew her headphones down and tapped the white face of her silver iPod. "I'm Samantha, we met last week..." She stepped onto the porch and adjusted the American flag which was about to slip of its holder.

"How could I forget?" Mike smiled.

"You can call me Foxy if you prefer...."

"Because of your looks, right?" Mike winked at her though the remark was clearly innocent and benign. He batted his eyebrows at me, gauging how I'd react. Inevitably, the comments made me tense but Sam eased all tension with a chuckle. "It's nice to see you again, Mike."

"The pleasure is all mine." He smiled with a warmth, taking back a step from his one-liners and witty remarks genuinely refreshed by her presence.

"Thank you, darling."

"She's proper Southern." He smiled at Samantha.

"Well she is a Vol, you know..."

Mike smacked his head. "Geez, I would have never thought that as she is wearing their freaking Tennessee sweatshirt." He put his finger up and shook his head. "Straighten him out, will ya?" Mike flicked the cigarette toward the lawn and made his way toward the door. "He's whacked out."

"Come on man." I blushed from the embarrassment.

"We'll sort him." Samantha played along.

"I knew I could count on you, you aint a Dawg after all..."

Foxy smiled at the dig at the Georgia Bulldogs, a rival of Tennessee and funnily enough Coach Kenny's team. "Never that..."

"I am going to head back inside." He leaned toward Foxy. "Samantha, it's a pleasure as always." Mike stepped inside and winked at her again, as if she was a lost little sister that he was doting over.

"Sorry about that, he's a goof."

"Don't be silly, he's lovely..." Foxy flicked her hair. "Do you care to go for a walk?"

"Yeah sure, let's go." I hopped down from the steps and led the way.

"Volunteers." I pointed at her sweatshirt. "I should have figured."

"They are only my favorite team." Foxy stuck her tongue out. "Hopefully one day you will see what the craic is..."

"The what?"

"Irish saying..." She flicked her hands. "...a fun experience..."

"You learn something new every day...." I raised my eyebrows. "But being that Rick is a Gator fan, it's no wonder you and him don't get along..."

"Yeah well we don't agree on anything why would get on with football teams?" Foxy sulked

"Granted the Gators, do suck, don't they?" She giggled and showed lightheartedness in her remarks. "So, you told Melissa that you liked her, aye?" Samantha sighed. "The timing was a bit off in my opinion."

We walked onward as the sound of a whizzing car passed at the end of the road.

"It just came out..."

"After you were seen leaving with Christina. To be fair, that's the last thing she needs right now she in such a deep mess with this Matt kid. It's kind of like Ricky and I, but much worse." Foxy looked up at me with a glower in her eyes. "Unlike Ricky, Matt is trying to take a break so he can legitimately cheat on Melissa."

"History has a way of repeating itself." I said it under my breath not thinking.

"What?" Foxy stopped in her tracks.

"Girls seem to always go for guys who don't do the right thing. They struggle trying to fix him."

"Are you referring to me?" Foxy's tone became defensive.

"Did something happen with you and Ricky today? You guys looked you were good..." I shrugged my shoulders. "But you seemed a bit down on the phone."

"Yeah..." She sighed. "He's distant and he seems disinterested at times, I always catch his eyes wandering."

"You might not expect to hear this coming from me but I think you can do better."

Samantha's forehead wrinkled, a bit of confusion and shock from my comments. "...Corey that is your best mate..."

"He is but I've had it out with him over all the stuff he pulls." I peered up at the electrical lines above the railroad tracks behind the row of ranch houses that lined Hendrickson Avenue. "Normally, it's with some girl I don't know but it's different with you."

Sam smiled.

"I got to come clean about something though..."

She tilted her head. "Go on..."

"I didn't just leave with Christina, what Ricky said was actually true."

"What?" Foxy's eyes bulged for a moment until she crossed her arms. "Wow..." She arched her lips. "You and Christina Caputo..." Samantha carried on walking. "Best not tell Melissa that..."

"Well she's asked me about that today but I didn't say anything. I don't see what difference it makes at this point."

"A lot, actually..."

"I blew it with Christina too, I told her I couldn't do this anymore and she is tight with me also."

Foxy about-faced. "Can't say I have any sympathy for her." She raised her finger as she practically scolded me. "She pretty much body-snatched Dave Schmidt from Melissa..."

"Actually, he played her too. She told me she was really crazy about that guy."

"I'd go see a witch doctor about an ingrown toenail before I believed a thing she ever said."

Her response was cross, her eyes darkened with a rare show of anger.

"Guys assume she's easy so she plays the role because no one gives her a chance." I gazed up at a passing cloud. "And yet I became the very thing she thought I would never be..."

"Doesn't the devil wear a business suit?" Sam replied as we stopped at the corner of Webster Street and Whitehall Street in close proximity to the red blinking light near the entrance to Westwood train station. The light was a careful observer of many conversations had and many exchanges viscerally played out in the paved asphalt behind it.

"I am not going to lie to you, Sam." I gently gripped her sweatshirt. "I actually liked her; The Lord gives us second chances so I was trying to give her one. I only hoped your friend would give me one chance..."

She opened her arms. "Come here..." Samantha embraced me and I did the same. "I know you're a good fellow and you try to see the silver lining in every dark cloud." She stroked a strand of her hair. "I respect that about you but trust me, Christina is bad news..." Samantha put her hand to my wrist. "I'll have a word with Melissa and see what I can do. Just don't do anything rash again, will you?" Foxy nudged me as our shoes clattered against the slabs of concrete as we crossed the parking lot and walked over the train tracks to the Malverne side. We halted at the basketball court which hung beneath the branches of the sagging oak trees. It was dusk near twilight; the air was hot and thick with the sounds of cicadas flooding the night.

The streetlights had just turned on and I appreciated the brilliant green of the trees and the grass field that sloped down and back up towards the playground.

"So, what do I do in the mean time?"

Samantha's eyes wandered toward the lights at the train station which turned on. "Nothing, just stay clear of Tina..."

I felt spiteful and resentful, I wish things could be so easy. That is why I always I admired my brother's carefree approach. He just did what he pleased and dealt with the consequences later. He lived in the moment and he did what he had to do to get what he wanted. I wish I could be like that.

"I'll always be your friend and want what is best for you but I am glad you aren't going to be hanging around her, I can't trust Ricky anywhere near her."

"Then why are you with him?"

"Cause maybe I am gullible and trying to "fix him"." She pouted and made quotation marks with her fingers.

"Not at all, Sam. You are just a really fair person." I smiled at her. "I'll try to speak to him as well and see if we can work all this crap out for the both of us..."

Samantha's eyes wandered toward the train tracks as the gate went down. "That would be grand." Her eyes shut briefly as she turned back to me. "Thanks, Corey...."

"Don't mention it." I put my arm on her shoulder and stroked her once. "So, what are you doing now?"

"Nothing planned..." She rubbed her hands. "Albeit, it is a bit brisk..."

"I know you like college football, so we do have a tendency to play the video game..."

"Say no more." Foxy shoved me lightly. "I'll eat you for breakfast."

I raised my eyebrows at the audacity of her comment, as she led the way back to my house. As we ascended the steps, I noticed that the lights were off and the car was out of the driveway. I put the key into the door and turned the key, the bell chimed as the door opened and I let Foxy go pass. When we entered, it was pitch black, a green light blinked where the air conditioning unit stood in the wall, rattling as it blew cold around the room.

"Mom?" I called out but there was no reply, only the faint scent of chicken cutlets left from when Mom was cooking dinner earlier. "They must have gone out...." I flipped the switch on and the brass chandelier illuminated. "Please make yourself at home." I extended my hand toward the couch and Foxy sat down on it, crossing her leg as she flicked her hair behind her.

"Would you like something to drink?"

"A glass of water, please." She put her hands on her lap.

"Sure." I made my way into the kitchen and grabbed two glasses from the cupboard and placed them on the counter top which were shiny with a scent of lemon. I opened the refrigerator door and looked in. Two plates were covered in aluminum foil and on the side shelf, there was a fresh carton of orange juice, milk, half and half, and a two-liter bottled water which I shook loose and poured two glasses full.

"Do you want any cutlet?" I yelled out to Samantha.

"No, thank you." She replied cordially. I shut the door and came back into the room, handing her a glass.

"Cheers." She took a sip and placed it on the side table next to a picture of Mike and I as kids with our grandfather, an image of the two of us wearing plaid shirts tucked into khakis with our hands in our pants, our late Grandpa placing both his hands on our shoulders. I placed my glass on the floor and turned on the television. Fuze was the channel it was set to and when the image on the screen appeared, the video of *Don't Tell Me* by Avril Lavigne was midway through. Foxy hummed the song as Avril Lavigne broke her.

"I love her." Foxy giggled.

"Do you want me to leave it?" I kept my finger pressed to the up button on the cable box, the number 56 illuminated in red on the screen.

"There is no use in delaying it, it's time for you to get your lesson, fool." She teased and took another sip of water, her nose and lips descending into the flowered glass.

I chuckled and pressed the down button on the box until it reached 03.

"President Bush was hot on the campaign trail today as he met with teachers in a public hall meeting to discuss the No Child Left Behind Act..." The television speaker spoke in the background as I powered on the PlayStation 2, the screen soon went black before the music for the PS2 turning on filled the room. I unraveled the cords for the two controllers and passed one to Samantha as the intro for NCAA Football 2005 started.

"Are we doing Miami versus Tennessee?" My eyes were basking in the white glow of the television screen. "Or do you want to try something different?"

"It's up to you." Samantha shrugged her shoulders.

"Might be fun if we were teams that we normally wouldn't be."

"Fairy snuff." She rubbed her chin. "How about we click random three times for each of us and we choose from there?"

"Sounds like a plan." I sat on the lip of the couch and we took our turns. Samantha drew Penn State, Wyoming, and New Mexico State. I drew USC, Vanderbilt, and Marshall.

"How about a rivalry game?" Samantha raised her eyebrows. "Battle of I-10?"

"Sure..." I took a sip of water. "Who's the other team in that?"

"UTEP..." She pointed at the screen. I arched my lip impressed at her knowledge once again as I didn't even know such a feud existed.

"My personal favorite outside of my own stead is Floyd of Rosedale."

"Iowa and Minnesota?"

She nodded once. "All that malarkey over a pig at a fair..." Samantha studied the screen and sat up, focused and determined. Samantha went on to utterly embarrassed me in a wire-to-gate route that resulted in her winning 42-3. When the final score showed, I sat back and scratched my head.

"Well I didn't expect that..."

"I know you were trying to be a gentleman and I appreciate that."

"To be fair, I was trying after you were up 14 but I had no chance anyhow." I laughed. "You had an answer for everything I threw at you."

"Thanks for that." She put the controller down and stretched. "If you couldn't get your run game going, you were one-dimensional. I was loading the box, so when you tried to bounce it outside on a sweep, I would send the linebackers on a slant overload to blow it up." Foxy looked over me with a wry smile. "And I don't know why you kept blitzing when it would play into my screen game. Once you backed off, slants and draws. It's like putting a hen in the oven." Her drawl was especially evident after the delivery of the adage.

The front door opened and in came my mother with a stack of envelopes from the mailbox with Mike following her.

"Well, well, well..." Mike shut the door as my mom put the mail on the white side table.

"Hello..." My mom's eyes dilated at the sight of Foxy. "I didn't know my son was having a lady over." She raised her eyebrows at me. "I am Corey's mom."

Foxy put her hands behind her back and bowed her hand. "I am Samantha." She extended her hand. "It's a pleasure to meet you, ma'am."

"She is well mannered." Mom cracked a joke and took her hand. "I am Mary." She pressed her cheek against Sam's. "My son I see is no good at introductions, but you are quite the gentlewoman, aren't you?"

"I am sorry about that." I tried to interject but was cut off by my brother.

"Shut up." Mike pointed at me with a smirk on his face. "You are right, Ma..." He glanced at the screen and saw the score. "I thought you were chivalrous, Corey. You could have taken it easy on the girl..."

"Actually..." I waved my finger around. "Sam did that to me..."

Samantha looked down at the floor with a modest smile.

"So, you know your football too, good for you sweetheart."

Mike laughed. "Maybe she should be playing for you and you can bench Ricardito..."

"I wouldn't doubt her." I cupped my hand and directed towards Foxy. "She calls a great game too..."

Mike nodded with approval. "I like her, she's got moxie."

"I never seen Michael so complimentary." Mom picked up a pile of envelopes and put it against her chest. "It's truly a pleasure meet you, sweetheart." She gently rubbed Sam's shoulder.

"Much obliged, Mrs. Montgomery."

Mom chuckled. "Call me Mary." She gently tapped her cheek. "You'll make me feel old and these two characters always remind me..."

I scowled. "When do I?"

"Did Corey offer you some of our chicken cutlets and mash?" Mom glared at Mike. "We hard to dart out to the library because someone forgot to tell me they had a form due at midnight..." She smacked Mike gently with the back of an envelope.

"He did, many thanks."

"Come on then." Mom put her hand on Mike's shoulder. "We better get this application done for the apprenticeship rehabilitation program." Her shoes tattered across the floor as she made her way to the door to the kitchen. "Nice to meet you, Sam. I hope to see you around soon, we'll have you around for dinner."

"Thank you." She smiled politely. "It'd be wonderful to join."

"I'll leave you lovebirds to it." Mike patted my shoulder as he followed my mom to the kitchen.

I rolled my eyes and grunted with irritation while Samantha's cheeks were flushed.

"Don't mind him..."

Foxy wiped the back of her head, pretending it was sweat while making a whoosh sound, prompting a laugh from me.

"Want to go sit outside?" She nodded her head once and we stepped out onto the porch. Foxy and I spent the whole night outside on the porch talking about everything we could imagine. Conversation was natural and effortless, time seemed to go by in a blink. Before we could even determine how long we had been out there, it grew late into the night and I walked her home. I still look back at that quaint stroll through the neighborhood, the air was cool and still. There we no dogs barking or kids laughing, only the faint screams of fire engines rushing to a far-away call and the streets growing mute again, it was just the two of us in the warm summer eve. A calm before the storm.

With the next dawn came a new season but we endured the same old results. Walking off the field, my cleats felt heavier than usual, weighed down by the crushing reality of another loss. As we huddled, I couldn't help but glance at the scoreboard again: 31 to 7. We started off strong but Plainedge proceeded to make a mockery of our defense combining for 424 yards of total offense in the inevitable rout. Coach Kenny was supposed to be the change that we needed and yet the more things changed, the more they stood the same. The same could be true for Samantha with Ricky and me with Melissa. As I glanced at the scoreboard one last time, its harsh red glow reflected more than just the numbers—it mirrored the patterns in my own life. We'd fought hard, but in the end, some things felt unwinnable.

Chapter 9 – The Fair

It was a chilly autumn eve where you could curl up under the blanket and enjoy the simple pleasure of a warm bed to get away from the escapades of the day. My heart skipped as I was awoken by the ring of my phone in the bed beside me. The time read: 2:37, on the screen, it read Foxy. I pressed the green button and pressed the phone to my ear.

"Sam?" I answered still startled from the piercing ringing, I heard sniffling on the other side. "What's wrong?" I sat up and stretched, her misery injecting adrenaline into me.

"He left me..."

"What?" I swung my feet around to the foot of my bed. "What can I do to help?"

The phone went silent, briefly muffled by Samantha's sniffles.

"I don't know where to start." She sighed. "I don't think he cares anymore and it couldn't have come at a worse time because my mama and papa are supposed to come visit around Christmas time."

"Sam, that's like three months from now." I leaned over, staring into the darkness as I listened to her speak.

"But I don't see my parents often; Ireland is a bit of a long ways. I want them to think I am doing well." Foxy exhaled. "Sometimes I think they second guess sending me to live with my Nan."

"Well, do you want to live with them?"

"That's another conversation..." She sighed again, more demoralized than she was just seconds before.

"I think your parents are very proud of you." I smiled. "Look at all that you have done, already..."

"Thanks, Corey." Her sniffles had vanished.

"So, how did all that happen anyway?" I laid back down on the bed and looked up at the ceiling.

"Well my Nana and Grandpa are from Tennessee originally. When my Mama was younger, she, my uncle, and my grandparents moved up here. She didn't like it much and my Mama ever the eager traveler went to Ireland and there she met my Papa."

"So how come you didn't end up there?"

"When he found she was pregnant, he tried upping sticks here but it didn't pan out. They tried to settle in Tennessee with the rest of my folk but there was no work and not too long after I was born, they went back to Ireland and I lived with my Auntie until they had things sorted in Ireland."

"Have you been to Ireland?"

"Loads of times. It's really green." She laughed. "I'd spend the summers and holidays with my parents there and went to elementary school down south. I lived on the Emerald Isle for two years but when my grandpa died, I moved in with my Nana to keep her company and I've been here ever since."

"So that's where you get your screenname from...IrishSouthernBelle."

"526..." Sam finished my sentence. "my birthday is May 26th.

Her wit was a treat to indulge in.

"I have the old-fashioned Irish surname with the e at the end. So, its spelled...F, o, x, e. Thus, my nickname Foxy..." She yawned. "Any who, I should get on back to bed..." The phone went silent until her lazed intonation animated. "Oh, but before, I go...Mel is single."

"What?" I shot up from my bed and sat up. "How? When?"

"Matt left her, like no one could see that coming..."

My eyes lit up at Sam's coy remark.

"If you want your chance at her, this is probably it."

"I am sorry, I don't mean to be so excited especially when you are down..." I leaned back against the pillows.

"I get it, I wish Ricky had that same energy for me...." She yawned again. "I better get going..."

"Foxy..."

"Yea?"

"Ricky doesn't know what he is missing out on..." My thoughts diverted from Melissa, strictly to encouraging Samantha. She was a good friend and she didn't even realize it.

"Thank you, Corey..." I heard her smile break through the static on the phone.

"My pleasure." I twinkled briefly as we shared a comforting moment of silence together. "Good night Foxy, pleasant dreams."

"You too, sugar."

The remainder of the week trickled by as we got ever closer to the fabled town fair. Despite my numerous efforts, it was difficult to get a word in edge-wise with Ricky outside of practice. He had no problem keeping it casual but evaded me on the subject of Samantha. I didn't get the chance to talk with Melissa either, she skipped town for Pennsylvania faking sick from school to get away from the misery caused by her break-up leaving Foxy to fend for herself. We had each other though, Samantha and I were together nearly every day after school, her staying for dinner a couple of nights under Mom's invitation.

From last year's Feast to this year's was a blur. The months used to creep by but now the time passed in a matter of minutes. So much had happened in such a small span of time and seemingly the older I got, the quicker the time went.

It seemed like an hour ago that I was stood by the entrance to the annual fair at Our Lady of Lourdes Church, joined by my brothers Mike and Shawn and we were standing in the same place again a year later at the annual tradition. Mike and Shawn weren't alone though, they were out in force with many members of Dem Rep beside them. All wore green bandanas and all were representing to the fullest extent. Mike wore a camouflage t-shirt with a matching fitted worn backwards. Shawn stood beside him in a green Notre Dame

Fighting Irish jersey and green New York Yankees hat backwards worn over his head. Both men wore baggy jeans and black sneakers to complement their ensembles. Slick and Numeralz stood beside the two as they all smoked their cigarettes and sipped on alcohol concealed in water bottles. The entire crew surveyed the grounds for any prospects of trouble and upheaval.

The fair however was not a battleground by any means, it was a family affair that offered a cornucopia of rides and amusements ranging from a miniature Ferris wheel for toddlers to a zeppole stand that offered rare confections that adult patrons formed long lines for. There were classic fairground games, often accompanied the roars of a boy followed by his handing a stuffed elephant to his significant other. Sweet aromas filled the air, accented by signage with cotton candy, candy apples, and donuts written in large bubble lettering.

"So, where's your girlfriend?" Mike took a sip of his water bottle.

"What girlfriend?"

"Foxy." He teased.

I waved my hand with a smile.

"Terror, them two are attached at the hip." He pointed back at me as he chuckled. "She was pretty much living at our house all week."

"You know Melissa went to Pennsylvania, right?" I shot Mike a wry look.

"I thought Foxy was from Tennessee...." Mike leaned back and smirked at Shawn who gave each other a dep with their first as they continued to poke fun.

"She's an Irish lass, too isn't she?" Shawn feigned a brogue accent and fist-pumped Mike again who laughed some more.

"Him and Samantha were up watching romantic movies all night, last night." Mike added.

"Sounds like she is a keeper Corey." Shawn cleared his throat. "How's the football going?" He bit his lip for a moment and watched as some hooded figures entered the ground from the other side of the yard.

"Alright, I guess." I shrugged my shoulders.

"He's being modest." Mike put his arm around me, gloating on my behalf like a typical proud older brother. "Corey is a monster."

"Yea, well you always had that Devin Hester speed, Dawg." Shawn gleamed with pride as he turned back to survey the fairgrounds, I joined them until my eyes stopped on Samantha heading towards the entrance. She had down her hair in pigtails, her plaits descended onto black overalls which had only a lime green sports bra beneath them. As she came closer, I found myself engulfed by all kinds of energy and excitement that I hadn't felt previously.

"Foxy!" I called out to her. She halted in her steps and looked around for a moment. Once Samantha saw me, she waved and hurried over.

"Is that her, Corey?" Shawn lit up a blunt, the scent of marijuana emanated from the blackened end of the cigar. "She's cute..."

"Terror, I keep telling him. He doesn't want to listen to me about that one." Mike put his hand out for Shawn to pass him the blunt. "She's a dime piece."

"I'll see you guys later...." I waved to them as I left to greet her.

"Hi." I hugged Samantha.

"Howdy." She grabbed her pigtails as she giggled.

"You remind me of Polly Pocket..."

She made a funny face at me. "I can't say I was going for that."

"...but in a good way."

"What are you on about?" She smirked. "I didn't know you liked to play with dolls."

"Well, they look even better with a bow." I grabbed her pigtail carefully and held a flower that was in her hair to keep the braids tight. "You look amazing."

"Thank you." Samantha smiled. "So, what's going on with them?" Samantha moved her head toward my brothers. Both Shawn and Mike waved at her when they noticed she was glancing over. She waved back with a friendly smile.

"They are just here doing what they need to do."

"I've never been one for riddles." Foxy grabbed one of her auburn pigtails.

"I'll spare you the trouble of an explanation." I put my arm around her and escorted her away from them. We made our way across the fairgrounds, passing a Test Your Strength game, until we stopped at a cotton candy booth. I placed a dollar bill on the shelf and took hold of a cone of red fluffy cotton candy.

"Thank you!" I held the cone out for Samantha, who gently clawed into the confection and placed it in her mouth.

"How's Melissa?"

Mambo Number 5 started to play in the background as our attention was directed a dance floor formed beyond a series of benches cloaked in red checkerboard tops.

"Struggling..." She took another handful of cotton candy. "No matter how hard I try to lift her spirit, it seems she can't come out of this."

"I guess she needs time...." My eyes wandered to the basketball toss game. "Do you want a stuffed penguin?"

Foxy's eyes lit up.

"Let's get you one then." I put my arm around her waist as she held the cone in her hand, angling it toward me to take some for myself. As we circumnavigated all the families and couples perusing the fairgrounds, I saw the girl from the brawl. She was wearing the same get-up that she wore on that faithful night. I glanced over at her trying to determine if that was in fact her and she caught me doing so. She shot me a look and smiled to affirm my inquiries.

"Is she a friend of yours?" Samantha gazed across at her.

"A bit of a long story..."

"Oh...do tell."

"Remember that fight I told you about?"

Sam nodded once.

"She was there."

"Well that's a lovely place to strike up a conversation." Sam took another piece of cotton candy and bit into it.

We both shared a laugh, diverted from the moment. I was happy to see Samantha having a good time given the week she had.

"I should have known...."

We both about-faced to the sight of Christina standing alongside Ricky. Foxy's playful and giddy demeanor became solemn and lifeless.

"What are you doing, bro?" I placed my hand in front of Foxy.

"I could ask you the same, man."

"Will you at least speak to her?" I pointed back towards her. "She's been distraught this entire week."

"I am not interested in talking to her man..." Ricky kissed his teeth. "...she's your problem now." He flicked his hands and Samantha's eyes soon welled up with tears.

"You are such a jerk!" She screamed in Ricky's face. Christina stepped towards Samantha but I intervened coming between the two, stopping Christina from any form of an advance. I don't think Foxy was looking for a fight though, she was broken and shattered. The expression on her face brought me anguish, her sweet eyes were filled with tears, and her lips quivering. She looked like a lost little girl even if she was 17.

"Oh, so now you are going to protect her?" Christina went nose-to-nose with me. "Since you did the same thing with me, I suppose you'll fuck her and leave her too..."

The words cut through me, stinging as they were full of ire and I could understand why she felt that way. Christina thought I was different, but in the end, I treated her like every other guy before me did though that was never my intention.

"I was wrong for the way I treated you and I am sorry for that. But she has nothing to do with this Christina."

"You are right, this one is entirely on you." Christina snickered.

When I looked back to see where Samantha was, I saw she had stormed off toward the exit. Ricky didn't pursue her; he didn't even care to have a parting word with her.

"Dude, she deserves better than this."

"Don't offer me any insights, meng." Ricky sneered. "You don't know even know what you want…"

"Well I know one thing, Rick…" I looked over at Christina. "All you ever see is the body but never the heart."

"Apparently, I can say the same thing for you." He took hold of Christina's hand.

"Maybe, you are right." I turned my back to them both and chased after Foxy who had now left the churchyard.

I looked north and saw her pacing up the street alone in the direction of her home. Judging by the wobbly and shaky steps she was taking; she was clearly crying. I sprinted towards her as I grew close, her sobs and sniffles became more apparent with each stride.

"Samantha." I stepped in front of her and grabbed both her arms.

"Corey, please, I just need to be." Tears were pouring down her cheeks, her porcelain skin glistening where the tears streaked. I pulled her toward me and embraced her, I could feel her sob violently in my grasp.

"I am sorry, Samantha." I massaged the back of her head as her cries became louder. "I'm here for you." I held her close, others passed by occasionally rubber-necking at the scene of my comforting Samantha in the midst of her despair, curious to know what was going on or moved at the sight of compassion.

"I don't know what's wrong with him." I dried her tears and placed my hand under her jaw, lifting her face towards me. "He's an absolute fool." I smiled at her; she returned the pleasantry for a moment. I pulled her back in and hugged her once more, kissing her on the forehead while I did so.

"I wish you didn't leave so quick, I wanted to get you that penguin." I pulled her back in for a hug and felt her smile against my chest, followed by small jostles indicating she was laughing. When I moved back to look at her, she was in a full fit of laughter.

"You are a goofball..." She put her hands over her mouth to catch her breath.

"At least your laughing..." I wiped her nose with the back of my finger. "Come on." I put my arm around her back. "I'll buy us some Chinese food and we can drown our sorrows in some soap operas."

• • • •

I OPENED THE DOOR TO Samantha's bedroom with a brown paper bag full of Chinese Food in one hand; The aroma of Wonton Soup tickled our noses, as she walked past when I held the door for her and she turned on the light.

The wood floor shined as if it had been mopped recently, her bed was centered in the room and neatly made. A white blanket with three pillows with orange pillowcases placed on the center. Above her bed was a large Irish flag; on the bed a stuffed animal which was Smokey: the mascot from the Tennessee Volunteers. Three sliding oak closet doors were behind me and a matching bookshelf across from me. To my right was a dresser with a miniature Tennessee Volunteers helmet placed upon it. On her wall was a poster from the Volunteers' 1998 National Championship season and above a desk with CD player upon it, a large orange Tennessee Volunteers flag with the grand white Power T. She had also put up the State of

Tennessee flag which the Volunteers carried onto the field with them, as well.

"You really do love the Vols don't you?" I placed the bag on her desk and looked around all of the mementos.

"I reckon you already know the answer to that." She shook the orange mouse connected to the matching shell of the computer and clicked the mouse twice before *Taproot*'s song *Mine* played low in the background. We sifted through the bag removing various items, our faces not far from each other as we did so. Finally, the collection of trays and plastic cutlery was set out on the desk.

"We'll sit on the bed."

I grabbed a container of Beef Lo Mein and Sesame Chicken before I followed her.

"Shall I give thanks or you?"

I put the food down on the floor beside the bed. "Please..."

Samantha put her hands together and closed her eyes, I joined her. "Heavenly Father, thank you for blessing us with this food and please bless our time together. In Lord Jesus' name, amen."

"Amen."

The way she said Amen was different, it sounded like ah-main, it had a nostalgia to it.

I reached down to the floor and opened one of the cartons; steam met me as I glanced down at the red pieces of chicken and broccoli. "So, have you ever been to a Tennessee game?"

"Many times." Sam twirled Lo-Mein on her fork. "I was there last with my cousins two years ago when we beat Kentucky for the Barrell." She scooped the Lo-Mein into her mouth. "Neyland is something else, there is nothing like hearing one-hundred thousand strong signing Rocky Top at night. Gutted, I am not going to be there this year..."

"Why not?"

"Cheerleading." She sulked. "It's like a full-time job."

I laughed.

"It's a crying shame, cause I could really use a trip to the Heart of the Valley."

I glanced over at the screen of the computer and the visualizer was on bursting with lights of different colors with each power chord which provided an immersive temporary distraction. "That is really cool..."

"Thanks, it was Allie's. She didn't like the color of the iMac, so I had it off her for next to nothing..."

"I think the color sold it on its own..." I bit into a piece of chicken and winked at Foxy, she smiled back at me. "Sorry about that, you were talking about Neyland...."

"Yeah, before I joined cheer it was easier. I was there when we played Notre Dame, Georgia, Alabama, and the overtime win against Florida." She looked at my chicken. "May I try one?" I turned the carton around for her to poke her fork in. "Thanks." She wiped her mouth. "I've been to both Dublin and London with my Daddy to watch the rugby and nothing compares to Knoxville..." She took a piece of chicken and dropped it over her Lo Mein. "He said it himself..." She glanced up at the flag. "My Mama's side of the family is from Shiloh way..." She glanced over at the radio as *Be Quiet and Drive* came on by the Deftones. "It's less than an hour's drive to the checkerboards..."

For those that don't know, Tennessee's end zone is comprised of an orange and white checkerboard, Foxy just assumed I would get the reference, since to her the center of the universe apparently was in Knoxville, Tennessee.

I glanced over at her bookshelf and saw a shamrock miniature placed in front of a collection of books. Adam Smith's *Wealth of Nations* the most noticeable title from the spines due to its large font and gold lettering. "Have you read much of Smith?"

"Just finished it." Foxy wiped her mouth. "I found his thesis on the wages of labor, absolutely fascinating."

"How did you get into cheerleading?"

Foxy took another spoonful of Lo Mein and looked over at me, as she swallowed.

"You're not really the...."

"Cheerleading type..." She smiled as she finished my sentence. "I love football and cheerleading allows me to watch it up close and personal." Foxy dabbed her lips. "...plus, I can meet new people and not be this random girl from down south with a bit of an Irish brogue when she gets emotional..."

I looked over at her at a moment and glanced back at the books on her shelf: Wilde, Browning, Descartes, Fitzgerald, and Ginsberg were on noticeable amongst them. I was both impressed and envious, as she already made her way through some books that I hadn't had the chance to read yet. She was clearly very imaginative and certainly someone that thirsted for knowledge. I don't know why she hid that because as being such a way often interferes with daily life in more ways that can be counted.

"The one drawback from cheer is that it can obviously get in the way of Volunteer games but I can tape them and watch it once I am home, if need be."

"So, you never miss a game?"

"Heck no..." She shook her head with a determination.

"I don't think I know anyone who has as much dedication as you."

Foxy shrugged her shoulders unsure of how to respond to the compliment. "Perhaps, they should cheer on the Big Orange and see what the craic is about." A smile broke from her face. When the music turned over the opening notes to *Faint* by Linkin Park, she looked like a kid on Christmas. "Tune." Foxy hopped off the bed and turned up the volume. When the guitars came in, she started to bang her head, her hair flying, flipping, and flaring with each movement she made.

"Favorite band."

"Really?"

"Shoot yeah...." She opened her hands and scowled at me. Sam carried on whistling the tune, as her hips swayed with each step she took. The humming soon turned into lyrics flying from her lips, an impersonation of Chester's screams to his singing, as she bit into her egg roll. I sat back and watched it all unfold, admiring her uniqueness and how she shattered preconceived notions effortlessly. Samantha didn't fit the typical cheerleader stereotype but that was a great thing. Truth be told, she was unlike any woman I'd ever met previously. Truly, she was one of a kind.

"What do you think about watching some *One Tree Hill*?"

"You are joking..."

"No, it's my favorite."

"Really?" She replied with a smug and playful tone.

"I can say the same with you and Linkin Park."

"Fair dos..." She broke a smile. "It's just not something you expect from most boys." She glanced down and swam her fork through more Lo Mein.

"We did basically have a romantic movie marathon last night?" I gave her a side eye with a smirk.

"True, but I thought you were trying to indulge me." Foxy deadpanned. "It is a pleasant surprise though." She giggled. "I'll tell you what, close your eyes and I will surprise you."

"Alright." I placed my hands over my eyes.

"No peeking." I felt Samantha get up from her bed and heard her open the door to her closet. A few moments later, I felt her sit back down on the mattress.

"Alright, darling."

I opened my eyes and saw a guitar in her hands.

"I didn't know you played…"

Samantha twisted one of the tuners and strummed it through once to make sure it was in the right note. "Only you and Dukes know now."

"That guitar has been around too, hasn't it?"

"It's a hand-me-down from my Papa. He performed all over: Liverpool, Barcelona, Berlin, he even made it to Sydney, Australia." She adjusted another tuner. "I used to sing with him when I was a kid and he taught me how to play."

"That's really cool, why would you keep this a secret?"

"To be fair, I don't when its useful. I do give guitar lessons as I am saving up…"

"I get it. When it's not football season, I work like a madman in Long Beach." I reached out to touch the glossy pine neck of the guitar. "What are you saving for?"

"Besides getting my own car and paying for essentials? I am going to Paris." Her smile illuminated as she strummed the strings. "I always wanted to gig in one of their cafes and busk in front of the Eiffel Tower."

"That sounds amazing."

"You are more than welcome to join." She smiled widely. "If Europe is your sort of thing…"

"I've always wanted to go."

"Good." Samantha stroked a stand of her hair back and gave me a smile with a side-eye.

"Well…" I slapped my thigh. "Are you going to play something?"

"I don't know." She grew bashful.

"Come on, it'd be awesome." I smiled at her. "Besides it will get you ready for when you light up the Rue de Lafayette."

"Very well, let's see if you know this one…" Samantha looked up to the lighting fixture which hung from her ceiling. She began to strum and play a few chords; it was the chorus from *Faint*. She laughed and then the melody shifted. She introduced me to her powerful and angelic voice and I have never forgotten the moment since. She sang *Michelle Post* by Hootie and the Blowfish and when she hit the outro, I truly marveled in the beauty, the texture, and the power of her voice and how it filled the room. I was in awe; I was enchanted; I was amazed. When she finished, I burst into an applause.

"Cheers." Sam stroked her hair and placed the guitar down.

"You are amazing."

Sam's smile grew wider, her cheeks turning red. "You are flattering me, mister..." Her twang was rather sharp in her reply, as she put her guitar down against a small oaken nightstand.

"So, the Vols got them Gators tomorrow, right?"

"Indeed." She nodded and sighed. "...and Ricky won't be there..." Samantha rolled her eyes at the irony of the statement. "He'll be with that fiend instead..."

"I'll watch the game with you..."

"Really?" She looked up at me. "But I thought you were a Hurricanes fan?"

"I am not a die-hard. Besides, it'd be great to watch it together."

Samantha broke a smile. "I can be a bit loud though..."

"I am not worried..." I shoveled some fried rice in between my lips.

"To put this in perspective for you, when we have an early kick and I have to cheer, I use old VHS cassettes to record the games..." Sam walked over to the bag and plucked an egg roll. "I've always loved Lady and the Tramp but when we played your lot two years ago in Knoxville, I taped over it cause the Owls were away at Malverne with the same kickoff time."

My eyes peered to a cardboard box with Vols Games written on the face of it in black permanent marker.

"I was going to go sick but the team needed me, so I had to make a sacrifice." She bit into the egg roll and dunked it into some duck sauce. "All that to get our doors blown off." Samantha shook her head as she reminisced.

"I wish you would have won." I smiled at her. "I prefer you be in good spirits as opposed to The U winning another game..."

Samantha raised her eyebrows, her eyes dilating as she set her eyes upon me. She seemed both perplexed and pleasantly surprised at what I had said. My loyalty to her over a football team as trivial as it may sound, touched her.

"I can't say I am giving up Smokey for ya, sugar." She chuckled subtly as she nudged me.

"I wouldn't expect you to." I pressed my hands over hers and her smile soon disappeared, our eyes met for a moment, frozen and fixed upon one another.

"What do you say we put on that *One Tree Hill?*"

Her cheeks crimsoned as she smiled back with a slight nod.

"I'll get it." I crouched down at the TV stand, pressing the eject button on the silver DVD player. As I looked into the reflection of the television screen, I could see Sam follow my every move, taking in everything I did as if it were new to her. It seemed that she was always waiting on everyone else that she didn't know how to manage that being her for a change. A smile broke to my face for a moment, as I watched her eyes study my every move in the reflection.

My eyes glanced down at the DVD case for Season 2, focusing on the image of Nathan and Haley. Their story felt too perfect, the kind of thing that only worked in scripted TV shows. Real life was messier, harder to navigate. People didn't just fall into perfect romances—they stumbled, got hurt, and sometimes found their way back to each other in ways that didn't make sense to anyone else. Or sometimes they meet someone they never thought they would and are never the same again...

A DAY WE MET IN LYNBROOK

As I set the DVD into the player, I caught Samantha's reflection in the screen. She sat there with a soft and curious smile. It made me think about how rare it was to feel truly seen by someone—not for what you could do or who you pretended to be, but for who you were when no one else was looking. Maybe love wasn't about perfection at all. Maybe it was just about showing up for someone, over and over, no matter how messy it got.

Chapter 10 – Orange Checkerboards and Smoke

The next day, I found myself back with Foxy in her bedroom as we watched the Tennessee-Florida game. If I had written it the other way around and Foxy discovered it, she would have confiscated it. The lights were off in her room, only the glow of the television chased away the darkness. I sat on the floor while Foxy stood with her hair down over a black t-shirt that had the Tennessee state flag colored in smokey grey. She wore orange leggings and a white scarf around her neck with orange and white checkerboard embroidery, the words VOLS sewn into the design in white lettering outlined in orange. Coach Phil Fulmer's words filled the room as Tennessee chewed on a piece of beef jerky.

"Want a piece?" She bit off a piece and handed it to me.

"Thanks." I put into my mouth, one end wet and warm from her saliva. The camera panned to the formation of "The T" where Tennessee emerged from the tunnel and Foxy's cheers were louder than the television. She shook her scarf and sang the words of *Down the Field*, as they marched out.

"Cheer and fight with all of your might." She pumped her scarf crumpled in her hand. "For Tennessee!"

The game however was filled with drama and Florida for the most part controlled it, taking a 21-14 lead into the fourth quarter that grew to 28-21. Tennessee would score with minutes to go but miss the crucial point after attempt. But the Volunteers would get a chance to have the last word as they would get the ball back with 43 seconds, starting at their 35-yard line.

"I still can't believe he missed the extra point..." Foxy shook her head.

"You just need a field goal."

"We have to get in range..." Foxy's eyes scanned the television as Ainge dropped to pass and threw an incomplete pass. Foxy threw her hands on her knees and shook her head. "What on Earth was that?" She peered over at me. "That was a wagon of a play, wasn't it?" She looked down and shook her head. "They are playing off with three deep. You can run the sweep outside with Gerry and we can get the first down." Her finger pointed. "We can clock it with a fresh set of downs." Foxy clutched her hair. "Don't be a gowl, Phil..."

On the next play, Ainge dropped back again but escaped the pressure and scrambled to throw the ball and completed a pass to Chris Hannon taking the Volunteers to the Florida 40-yard. Foxy erupted and jumped. The band soon started to play as the drum roll echoed in the background.

"V!" Foxy screamed. "O!" The music blared. "L!" She threw her hand out. "S!". She screamed louder and faster "V, O, L, S! VOLS! VOLS! VOLS!"

I watched on in awe, admiring her dedication and passion. Her love for Tennessee football was more robust than anyone I knew who played the game on our team. What a woman, I thought, how could Ricky not enjoy being around her? I didn't want the game to end because being with her in that room watching the game was an experience unlike any other.

Tennessee spiked the ball with 20 seconds left and needed about 10 yards to be in striking range for a game-winning field goal attempt.

"We need to get closer." Foxy has a laser-like focus on the television. "Run 10-yard hitches on the outside with the inside receivers running crossing patterns. Put Meach and Hannon in the slots and run a Middle-In, one of them will be open!"

Foxy might as well called the play perfectly as Ainge connected for a seven-yard pass on a hitch route to the outside. She cheered and hugged me, keeping her arm around me. "Dang, we don't have any timeouts!" Foxy started snapping her fingers signaling for a spike. Tennessee did that and stopped the clock.

"This is it." Samantha clasped her hands to her mouth. "We're kicking it now."

James Wilhoit, the Tennessee kicker trotted out, Samantha took my hand. The roar of the crowd came through the television as he stepped back and got ready for the attempt. Foxy's pulse throbbed through her hands into mine as he connected with the ball and it flew toward the goalposts. Foxy rushed to her feet and as it went through, she jumped into my arms. I caught her and she pressed her lips against my cheek in excitement. Her head swiveled as she kept hold of my hand as she watched the box score. The final, Tennessee 30 – Florida 28.

Samantha started singing Rocky Top at the top of her lungs until she plucked her hand away with a twinge of rouge under her cheeks. "Sorry, love."

An awkward silence filled the room although there was bedlam on the television set filling the room.

"I've never been so fired up when Miami won, congratulations..." I smiled at her.

"Thank you." Sam stroked her long hair back. "It's a good thing Ricky wasn't here, aye?"

"Nah, he'd be walking off with his head down for sure." I chuckled.

She grinned. "Nothing like a good comeback, huh?"

I nodded. Comebacks. Redemption. The feeling of something being at stake. That was what made games like this unforgettable. And maybe that's why I loved books so much too—because anything could happen. A story could start in one place and end in another, full of twists you never saw coming.

Football wasn't the only thing that gave me refuge from the troubles of life. And given the fact that we started off the season

0-2, there wasn't much to be excited about. But books—books were different. Between the front cover and back page, I could be somewhere else entirely, in a different time, a different space... a better world. A world where moments like the one I lived through with Samantha didn't just fade but stayed, not just a passing memory. A moment captured for others to find it, to feel it, and be there too.

I long aspired to be a writer but never put pen to paper, I didn't know where to start and the very thought of crafting some grand narrative seemed like scaling a towering mountain, though the greats would tell you it is a journey of both peaks and valleys.

The next day, the immortal words of Fitzgerald's *The Great Gatsby* melted the time away. I had spent hours reading it, nearing toward the end of the novel where Gatsby finally got Daisy back. It could have ended there and it would have been poetic: the struggle and industry of Gatsby to become wealthy just so he could take care of her; all he wanted was a girl, the money meant nothing to him.

I put the book down when the front door flung open and Mike stepped out on to the porch, covered in all green apparel with a look of determination etched across his face. At first, he didn't say anything, he only lit his cigarette before he looked back at his first exhale.

"What are you reading?"

"Gatsby..."

"Great book." He flicked his cigarette. "You're not going to the fair?"

"Nah. I'm going to sit this one out." I gripped the sweaty glass of red Kool-Aid and took a sip.

"Last night of the Feast, three-day weekend, and you want to stay home reading books?" Mike teased.

"Wild one last night, that Tennessee-Florida game. Wow..."

"Tennessee-Florida? I wonder where you watched that..." Mike smirked, like he already knew the answer.

"Foxy's."

"Mmmm..." Mike nodded his head as he looked at the book in my hand. "You know what I always liked about Gatsby?" Mike leaned against the porch riser, tilting his head up toward the sky. "He wanted his life to go like this." He lifted his hands, fingers tracing some unseen trajectory toward the clouds.

He let that hang in the air for a second.

"Maybe you should do the same..."

He smiled —a rare, almost gentle expression— and I knew what the metaphor was alluding to. But before I could respond, the white Thunderbird pulled up to the curb, its engine rumbling like a low growl.

"You want to ride with us, old sport?" Mike flicked the cigarette, I glanced out and saw the front passenger swing open as Shawn stepped out.

"Come on Ghost...don't pull a Jessie." A voice echoed from the car.

"Ay, fuck you man." Mike postured and opened his arms with discontent. "I'm talking to my brother!"

I looked on and noticed the visible presence of irritation in Mike's expression as he turned back to me. I didn't want to leave the comfort of the porch or my book, but maybe I needed to stop dreaming about stories and start living them. Even if that meant climbing into a car full of smoke and loud music.

"You know what?" I put the book down on the wicked coffee table. "Let's go."

"Alright..." Mike as he placed his arm around my shoulder and pat my back once, leading me to the car. "Make room for my brother."

Numeralz and Slick slid over, both extending to her hands to slap me five as I shuffled into the back seat.

"Little brother." Shawn greeted me a rub of the head.

"Little ghost." Numeralz pat my shoulder.

"What's good kid?" Slick greeted me, as Mike sat up front adjusting the seat to give me some more leg room. The bass in the car was bumping as *Get Down* by Nas came on. The vehicle left the curb and sped off into the night under the cadence of muffled acceleration and raised sub-woofers.

"Go up to the Sev, man." Mike put the window and lit up another smoke, the car window hummed as it descended and the car moved swiftly down toward Franklin Avenue.

"Do you think we'll be seeing them tonight?" Numeralz's eyes fully set on Mike with a rolled up blunt pressed behind his ear.

"Either way, we'll handle it." Mike put his hand on the window as the cigarette smoke wafted into the air as we stopped at the Five Corners where the towns of Lynbrook, Malverne, and Lakeview met and the streets of Hempstead Avenue, Franklin Avenue, and Lakeview Avenue converged. It was a confluence of urban tributaries walled by a gas station, shopping center, car mechanic, and drive-thru teller and bank: a center of commerce amidst a suburban backdrop. Shawn lit up a smoke and turned left, heading over the train tracks along the edge of Malverne before we stopped at the traffic signal on Cornwall Avenue. To the left, down the road was the path back to Westwood, to the right an area I had not been too much in my life: North Valley Stream. The road was a medley of Victorian-style and Colonial-style houses pitched back on green lawns freshly cut and raked in a tapestry of brown-leave covered verges extending to a point where one saw the road vanish into a bend. The car carried on forward as the music gyrated through the vehicle until we arrived at the 7-Eleven.

Mike hopped out and threw his cigarette down. "Coffee and a Hostess, right?" He stepped on it and pointed at me.

"That'd be great, man."

Mike shut the door and put his head through the open window. "Anyone else?"

"Cop some of those PBR's for me?" Slick spoke, the alcohol on his breath combined with the aroma of marijuana in his clothes filled the air around me. He wiped his nose with the collar of his white shirt.

"Can you get me an Oatmeal Crème Pie and a bag of chips?" Numeralz spoke up. "I am hungry as a motherfucker."

"You always hungry, motherfucker." Shawn snorted as he took a puff of a cigarette. "And you only weigh just over hundred points soaking wet."

"Chill, dawg." Numeralz pulled the blunt from behind his ear and gave it a whiff. "Spark this..." He handed it to Shawn who removed a cheap purple lighter from his pocket.

"You want any of this piff, Corey?"

"I am good, Jerome." I raised my hand. "Thank you though..."

"You sure, man?"

The scent of marijuana soon filled the car as Shawn frayed the edges black as he puffed on the blunt.

"And call me, Numeralz, my dude."

"My bad, man..."

"You good." Numeralz took a hit of the blunt and blew some smoke onto his phone as he opened it and pressed a button on his side. "Where you at?" Two beeps followed.

The small parish grounds were as we left it the night before, a medley of attractions and amusements. I circled several times before I caught a glimpse of Melissa for the first time. Her hair was down, wearing a black tank top that cut off mid-belly button with matching black yoga pants. As soon as we made eye contact, Melissa sped off in the opposite direction.

I threw my hands on my hips and sulked. When I turned my head in the opposite direction, I saw another familiar face: the girl from the brawl. She was here again and was joined by a few of her friends, lost in the merriment of their own exchanges. The girl looked sizzling, wearing blue ripped jeans and a red tank top that cut off at her midriff and flaunted her abs. Her chestnut hair descended with long gold earrings shining against it, complementing her olive skin. All I could do is lust and gawk, but she caught me and shot me an inviting smile. I put my hand up and waved once, she raised her eyebrow and gave me a military salute with two fingers. I had to go for it.

"Hi." I felt the heat in my cheeks as I broke the ice.

"Hello." She smiled.

"I'm, Corey." I extended my hand to shake hers.

"Sarah." She extended it back to me.

"It's nice to meet you."

"To you the same..." She tee-heed.

"I have seen you around before." I circled my finger through the vacant air. "Never got the chance to say hello..."

"That's awfully kind of you..." She raised her eyebrows with a playful smirk.

"Look, I am not really smooth." I let out a deep breath. "You have to understand how nervous I am to even come up here. I mean look at you, you're gorgeous."

"Well that was a hell of a pick-up line."

"It's not like that."

"I take it you live around here, Corey?" Sarah giggled.

"Yeah, just up there in North Lynbrook". I pointed in the wrong direction. "Sorry, I mean that way." I chuckled and reoriented myself.

She laughed. "That's cool, I am from RVC."

"Oh really? My brother and I used to live there."

Her eyes narrowed at the mention of it, she glanced around the park for a moment before her glowing eyes centered on me. "Who's your brother?"

"You probably don't know him."

"Probably not." She shrugged her shoulders. "I have an older brother too; Jay is always out somewhere doing who knows what."

"Same with Mike..." I put my hands on my hips.

"Mike is a great name." She laughed nervously. "But I don't know if my brother would feel the same." Sarah blushed. "Sorry, bad joke with some truth in it."

I chuckled. "So, are you staying for a bit?"

"No."

"Well if that's the case, can I take you for a coffee at some point? That is if you could spare me the time."

"Well you are straight to the point." Sarah leaned back, impressed at my forwardness.

"I try to be, my brother said it's the only way to be." I placed my hands in my pockets.

"Your brother sounds like a wise dude." She broke a playful smile.

"Plus, if you are going, I don't know when I am going to see you again. So, it's do or die for me..."

"I didn't plan on going home though..." Her smile grew wider. "I was just going to go get a slice of pizza."

"If it's no trouble, may I join you?"

"Sure..." She adjusted her tank top, it was there that I noticed the belly button ring for the first time, piercing and glimmering against her navel. "You seem like an interesting guy..." Sarah led the way and I followed her to the gate. As we stepped out, Melissa emerged from the crowd with a nasty scowl on her face.

"Having fun?" She smugly remarked.

"Mel...I...." I extended my hand towards her and she swatted it away. She glared back at Sarah and sped away into the bustle of the fair.

"What was that all about?" Sarah leered back at Melissa.

"She's going through a rough time."

Sarah raised her eyebrows at me, subtly accusing me if I were the cause of her discontent.

"Her boyfriend left her and she hasn't taken it well..."

"What do you have to do with it?"

"I liked her." I glanced back to find Melissa in the madness but there was no sign of her. "But she didn't like me back."

"So, I am a backup plan?"

"No." My thumb drew to my teeth as I nipped the nail. "I've seen you around a few times, but I've been afraid to go up to you...."

"Well I am glad you did..." Sarah's tone was matter-of-fact and straight to the point. "If you didn't pick up my cue, then I would have to do it myself." She shot me a wry smile.

"I've never been good at that stuff."

"I don't know that any boy that does." Sarah motioned her head in the direction of town towards the pizzeria.

The walk from the fairgrounds to the pizza parlor was about five minutes at maximum, but it felt far longer. We took a short stroll through Lynbrook town in route until we made our way into the pizza parlor and grabbed two padded corner seats.

I carried over two pieces of pizza each on white throwaway plates, the crust sticking to the waxy sheet between the paper and the pizza to collect any smears of grease, loose cheese, or bubbling sauce.

"Here we are..." I placed both slices down on the table and grabbed some grated cheese, pepper, and garlic from the trash receptacle across from us.

"Thank you."

"Let me go get the drinks." I stuttered and went back to the counter to grab two paper cups filled with Diet Coke, I was careful not to trip or stumble as I made my way back to the booth as Sarah's eyes locked on me.

"Have you been here before?" I placed her drink beside her.

"Never." She took a napkin from the dispenser and placed one across from me before she did the same for herself.

"Thank you..." I pulled the warm slice from the plate and folded it in half like a paper airplane. "Any good pizza spots in RVC?"

"Can't say there is." She followed suit and took a bite into her pizza, wiping her mouth with a napkin as she chewed. "That sauce is on point..."

"How about Our Lady?" I took a sip of soda.

"I prefer it to St. Anthony's..."

"Why is that?"

"My brother fucked it up." She shook her head. "He got into some scuffle over there and I am not in all that gangster shit." Sarah took another bite of her pizza.

"I know what you mean. My brother just came home from jail because of some dumb beef he had with people from your neck of the woods."

"I probably do know him then...." Sarah squinted her eyes and took a sip of soda. "Mike..." She nodded. "Yeah, my brother used to know a guy called Mike..."

"If that were the case, it likely wouldn't be for anything good." I chuckled.

"You are probably right, knowing Jay." Sarah took another sip of soda. "It got messy as there was this whole ordeal over some girl." Sarah waved her hands. "Speaking of which, you're single?"

"Yup..." I said softly, my nerves started to catch up to me.

"And you clearly you are looking for a girlfriend?" She sat back in her chair and eyed me up, I grew tense once it registered with me that this girl actually had interest.

"Yeah..." I wiped my mouth. "I mean if it doesn't work out, we could always be friends but you are a bombshell..."

"Thank you." She blushed. "So, tell me how does a boy and a girl simply become friends?"

"Do you remember that girl that was all weird when we left?"

"How could I forget?" Sarah raised her foam cup an inch and placed it back down. "She was Grade A Salt."

"Her best friend has more or less become my best friend."

"And she is a girl?" Sarah leaned forward and my eyes wandered to her cleavage, despite my efforts to maintain eye contact. "She is." I diverted my sight toward my half-empty cup of soda. "You'd like her. Sam is really down to Earth and very warm."

"And you never wanted to get with her?" She flicked out her hair and stroked back a strand behind her ear. "I saw her yesterday when she was with you." Sarah placed her hands on the lip of the table. "The one with the pigtails...."

"So, you were looking at me?" I flirted.

"Obviously..." Sarah giggled.

"Her nickname is Foxy. But the way she got the moniker is really interesting actually." I remarked with a smile. "Her last name is Old English because her dad is from Ireland and her last name Foxe is spelt with an e at the end."

Sarah raised her eyebrows and crossed her arms. "And this girl is just your friend?"

"Yea..."

"Are you sure?" She grabbed her slice of pizza and looked down at the glisten of the cheese. "Doesn't seem like it to me."

"Do you want to ask me a third time?"

"I am just saying, it seems like you are quite fond of her." Sarah bit into the slice and ripped away a piece of crust. "And I kind of picked that up off her too when I saw you together..."

"You would get along great with her. I think she'd become a sister to you." I picked up my half-eaten slice of pizza off the paper plate and re-folded it before taking another bite.

"I am sure she's great." Sarah wiped her lips. "But I don't play any games though Corey, I must warn you."

"I get it and neither do I." I put the piece of pizza down. "I don't even know how I can even sit in the same room with a woman like you, but I asked you here because I am genuinely interested."

Sarah's tense glare eased into a friendly smile. "And I am here with you now because I am interested too..."

The conversation eased after that: we kept it casual and fun. We talked about our favorite movies, foods, music and all the usual subjects you would expect to discuss as you first got to know someone. After we returned to the fair, I parted ways from Sarah but not before getting her phone number and securing a potential second date. I was ecstatic and couldn't wait to tell Samantha and my brother about what happened. However, neither were present when I returned so I carried on home.

As I made my way past the North exit, I caught a glimpse of Melissa leaning against the wall smoking a cigarette by herself. Her make-up ran down her eyes and eye shadow puddled beneath her lashes. When she looked up and saw me, she threw her cigarette, and attempted to evade me again. This time I pursued her and wasn't going to stop until I spoke to her.

"Melissa! Wait...."

"Leave me alone Corey." She brushed me off.

"No...wait!" I grabbed her waist and she turned around. Her eyes were emboldened with agitation.

"What do you want, Corey?"

"What's wrong?"

"Plenty." She about-faced.

"What does that have to do with me?"

"You tell me how much you like me and I hear it from Foxy. But you went off that slut and you've moved on to someone else!" She sped away.

"Hold on!

"Leave me alone!"

"Melissa, I want to be with you."

"Are you sure?!" She swung her hair back. "Maybe it will be Foxy next week!"

"That's what I wanted the entire time!"

She turned around and we locked eyes.

"I always wanted you. I mean I don't even know what to say half the time." I looked away nervously. "I know you've been hurt and I know you've heard it a million times before probably but only an idiot would take such a beautiful woman for granted."

I took a step closer. "The first time I met you, I was under a spell." My eyes went left and right to the various houses with their lights on and curtain drawn, unknowing of what was unfolding in the very street they lived on. "Ricky and my brother always poked fun at the crush I had on you."

I itched the side of my face. "Ricky brought me with him in the summer when we first me, because that's all I ever wanted." I threw my hand out. "You can ask Foxy, she'll tell you. It's always been you Melissa!"

"She did tell me that too actually." She replied sternly.

"You were with Matt and I felt like I never had a chance." I looked deep into her green eyes. "But if you gave me one chance, I wouldn't know what to do with myself because it would be like living in a movie. I wouldn't blow it..."

Her eyes softened, flattered and humbled by my revelation. "I am not that special..."

"To me you are...."

Melissa looked at me, her green eyes searching mine like she was trying to find something she didn't even know she'd lost. For a moment, I thought she was going to walk away again. Instead, she bit her lip and let out a soft, trembling laugh. 'You really mean that?' she asked, her voice barely above a whisper."

We stared at each other, as if it were a stand-off and we were prompting the other to make the next move. Minutes ago, I was seething over the successful pizza date with Sarah but it had all gone blank, this was my moment. I was going to capture it or go down in a blaze of glory. Everything else seemed like an afterthought, it's amazing how infatuation can consume you in a heap of passion. The only sounds that could be heard were the hums of the power station in the distance.

"I do..."

"But I need to know the truth." Melissa curled a fist in her hand. "did you sleep with that whore?"

"Yes."

"Why?" She clenched her fists harder.

"It was a mistake but as soon as I realized it would cost me you..." I grazed her knuckles with my hand. "...I put an end to it."

"Why was Foxy covering for you then?"

"She was only trying to help us and didn't want to get caught in the middle of it." My fingers managed to enclose her fist. "She cares for both of us and wanted us to be happy together." Melissa's fist soon released, her finger subtly plucking at the tips of mine.

A bass soon filled the air set to a beat of Classical Music. Melissa's tracked to the direction of the music though the source couldn't be found.

"Francesca..."

Her eyes turned to me, the name inciting her to stare a hole in me.

"It's a song by Myth the Poet about a guy who likes a girl and she doesn't even know he exists."

"Is that how I made you feel?" Her hands took mine, finally we were locked in each other's clutch.

"No..." I plucked at my collar and gave it a slight tug. "I made myself feel that way because I never thought in a million years that a girl like you would give me the time of day." Her grip intensified as I confessed my feelings. "But if you did..." I swallowed harsh. "If you did, I would hope I could freeze that time so it never ended..."

"I think we can make that work" She closed her eyes and charged forward as she pressed her lips against mine. My eyes bulged when I felt her lips make contact until I shut them and savored the kiss. We continued to swim our tongues through each other's mouths as our lips danced together. Not once did I hear the many sirens and yells in the distance, I only learned of the brawl that had broken out just a few blocks away at the fair through the thread of text messages churned out by the rumor mill.

It turns out that our star receiver Marlon Green was involved in the altercation in the parking lot in the row of stores next to the churchyard. Ironically, Greenie had picked a fight with some of Mike's cohorts and he was thrown through a restaurant storefront window. As he crashed through the glass, he landed in a plate of sushi that a family were sharing, the table collapsed with yellowtail and salmon thrown everywhere. Greenie was arrested and undoubtedly once Coach caught wind of it, he would likely be suspended indefinitely. This couldn't come at a worser time as our football team looked to be short-handed now more than ever when we needed our best player most; and yet I didn't care because I felt like I was on top of the world. Melissa was finally mine!

Chapter 11 – Victory Formation

I woke up the next morning with a euphoric feeling of triumph. It was 11:17 when I stared at the clock, suddenly I was struck on the side of the head with a pillow.

"Get the fuck up, let's go have a smoke!"

"What the fuck?!" I slowly rose and stretched, letting out a yawn. "Yo, what happened last night?" I sat up.

"I could ask you the same." Mike smirked. "The word on the street is that you..." Mike pointed at me. "...finally got with your lady friend..."

"Yep." I blushed; the smile could not be contained. Needless to say, I was still in shock of what happened. "But I was asking you about Greenie..."

Mike squinted and looked up at the ceiling. "Wait, the kid we put through the glass of Narita?" He started to laugh. "We turned that motherfucker into a dragon roll..." His laughter became more hysterical. "You should have seen it."

"Why did you do it?"

"I didn't." He glowered at me. "Slime was down there and apparently that kid tried to juke us for a dime bag and when we tried to address the dispute constructively, he got fucking stupid." Mike's face was bereft of any emotion. "We had to let him know his place..." He rubbed his hands together.

"But now, we've lost our best wide receiver, Mike!" I sat up and dug my nails into my scalp.

"Oh fuck, that's right..." He threw his hand to his side. "I should have remembered that he plays for the football team..." Mike shook his head and shut his eyes for a moment, acknowledging the trouble it caused. "Didn't he pick on you though?" Mike leered at me, as if that somehow justified what happened in the grand scheme of things.

"That's not the point." I could feel my forehead crease.

"Well I'll never lose sleep over fucking up a dude who was messing with my little brother..." He shrugged his shoulders. "You can be their guy now..." He threw his hands out again. "...and if some left-field way we can play a role in that somehow, I'm glad..."

"I don't want to become a starter because the other guy...."

"Didn't do what he was supposed to." Mike interrupted. "He could have been at home reading his playbook and staying out of trouble like you. He made a decision not to do that..." Mike's lip stiffened. "Thus, you earned the opportunity..."

I sat back and let out a sigh. "When you are going to get away from this stuff?" I put my hands down on the top of the mattress. "Don't you ever want more out of life than being trapped in Lynbrook throwing guys through the windows of a sushi restaurant with the risk of going back to prison?"

"I appreciate the words of wisdom brother but they are not necessary." He reached into his jean pocket and removed a partially crushed pack of Marlboros. "...It was I that was hoping to speak with you..." He threw the cigarette onto the bed and made his way to the bedroom door.

"About what?" I spoke at length.

"Come outside..." His voice trailing as he made his way outside. I hadn't even gotten out of my pajamas yet and had a cup of coffee, Mike however was already dressed ready for the day.

I lurched from bed and dragged myself out to the porch, Mike had positioned himself on the banister comfortably in his usual spot with a hot mug of coffee carefully resting next to him. He put his cigarette in his lips and I followed, it was soon met by the flame of Mike's Zippo. He took his first drag and started up with his shenanigans.

"You've been on a roll lately. And normally, I would be happy for you that landed another piece of ass." Mike exhaled smoke.

"She's not a piece of ass." I contested with an undertone of irritation in my voice.

"But I don't think you are seeing the bigger picture here..."

"About what?"

"I don't think she is the girl you actually want." Mike flicked his cigarette.

The words were sobering and lifted the early morning haze. "The other girl?" I took a heavy drag of the cigarette and nearly coughed doing so.

Mike shook his head with a boyish smile and took another drag as he leaned against the railing.

"Who?"

"Foxy..."

Our eyes met for a moment until I shot up from my seat, cigarette still in hand. "But she's all tangled up with Ricky..." I took another drag and put the cigarette out against my shoe as it was too coarse on my lungs.

"That don't mean shit." Mike took another drag and put his hand against his arm, the cigarette smoke cascading around him. "Besides, she's always hanging out with you."

"Well we are friends...."

"Do you see the way she looks at you?" Mike leaned forward. ""Or the way that you look at her for that matter?" His eyes enlarged to clue me into some revelation that I clearly did not see. It was odd though because Sarah had alluded to the same thing yesterday.

"And don't tell me about Ricardito, that fuckin' kid tries too hard." His eyes darkened with anger. "He wants to be like Usher with the girls..."

I broke out in laughter at the comment.

"He's acting like an idiot." Mike leaned back. "That girl is sweet as candy and she's really fucking hot." He raised his hands. "If you don't mind me saying..."

I raised my hand to assure him offense was given.

"More than Melissa, man..." His eyes narrowed. "She is a nice girl; classy and respectful." He pointed as his cigarette me with each adjective.

"If you like her so much..." I opened my hand to him.

"She's not for me, she's for you." His eyes shifted for a moment, etched with focus and determination. "...not to mention, I have my own agenda." He tossed his cigarette onto the walk. I looked up at Mike, lost in my interpretation of the riddle.

"So, I'm just supposed to go for her?" I threw my hands out. "After, I just got with her best friend?"

"Shut up with the excuses." He cringed. "Do you like her, Corey?" Mike raised his eyebrows.

His words hung in the air, too sharp to ignore. I wanted to brush him off, to argue that it wasn't that simple. But it was, wasn't it? The way Foxy smiled, the way she laughed at my stupid jokes—none of it felt like just friendship.

There was a serenity and beauty that followed Samantha everywhere she went. Being amongst her was calming and tranquil, but I thought that was the way it was supposed to be around people you cared about. But perhaps, I had it all wrong.

She was breath-taking and became more idyllic the more time I spent with her. The subtle things that she did which showed her innocence and kindness, her cute sayings, and I admit that when she wore those spanks that cheerleaders wear on hot summer days, I did check out her backside several times and was filled with all sorts of primal emotions. But I had Melissa, that was the goal from the get-go and I got what I finally wanted.

"There is no point ruining a good friendship. If Melissa and I got married, Sam can be the maid of honor at our wedding."

"That would be a shame because I think it should be the other way around..." Mike shook his head once. "When I see you two together, you are yourselves. You have a connection."

"You would with a friend, right?" I broke a smile at the passion Mike was exuding in his dissertation.

"It's more than that." He glanced down at the hedge in front of the house before he looked back at me. "Tell me what do you really know about Melissa?"

"What?"

"Name five things you really like about her, other than she has tits, an ass, a flat stomach, green eyes, and she's got that olive Italian skin." Mike rubbed his chin. "Last time I checked, Samantha has blue eyes and is certainly a bit fairer, but she's got a better ass, equally nice rack, insane body...." He threw out fingers to count up.

I raised my eyebrows, stunned by his logic and thought process. He had an uncanny way of veiling what should be prioritized in mature discourse while integrating silly and childish points which undermined his point.

"Don't get bent out of shape, I led with that on purpose, little brother..." He rubbed his chin further. "...your reaction when I started talking about her looks says it all." He shook his head and laughed. "I'm not telling you what to do, Corey," Mike said, leaning forward, his eyes sharp. "But when you're with her, does it feel like you're putting on a show, or does it feel like you can just...be?"

There was something about the way Samantha saw the world—like she was always noticing the little things that everyone else missed. Being around her felt...easy. Comfortable. Mike was right but maybe that's just what friendship was supposed to be and Mike was mixing up his words. Or was it me that was confused?

"You don't even realize what you standing right in front of you, waiting for you take it." He put his hand on my shoulder. "Forget Melissa, she doesn't even know what she wants." Mike waved his hand across in front of me. "But Sam, she's special." He spat. "She reminds me of someone I used to know..."

"Jessie?"

Mike glared at me out of the side of his eye, he put his hands on his hips but he wouldn't reply. His expression would suggest that my words had some merit to them. "Think about what I am saying." He rubbed his nose as he made his way for the front door.

I leaned back against the porch railing, Mike's words rattled in my head, louder than I wanted to admit. Was he right?

I took out my phone to text Melissa a good morning but saw that I had received a message from Coach Kenny that read: Good morning, Corey. I don't know if you know yet but Marlon is gone for the foreseeable after he was arrested last night for various forms of misconduct. I've seen you develop and we've been getting you reps at Flanker. Now, I need you to step up. We've been working towards this moment together and it's your time. I know you will do great. See you at practice tomorrow.

I re-read Coach Kenny's message, the words "step up" hitting harder than they should. Stepping up on the field felt easier than stepping up in life. Because if Mike was right—then I had a whole other decision to make. And I wasn't sure I was ready for it.

Chapter 12 – Holy Ghost

I left practice feeling like I had a second wind, the chemistry I had developed with the first team was clear. Still, I was shocked that I was finally getting my shot let alone it working out. But then again, I have always doubted myself, second guessing every minor detail and pondering the what if's? I was pre-empting the worst-case scenario before the first point on that road map was crossed. Trust in the process and don't be outcome-oriented, it's all in The Lord's hands and even if…it's about process, it's about faith, it's about not letting the past dictate the present, and not letting the present dictate your future. One has all the time in the world until the only thing they want in the world is time.

As I approached home, I trotted along with energy in my steps. I was tired, sweaty, and smelled awful but I felt invigorated until I saw Mike sitting on the steps who appeared despondent; his eyes fixed straight ahead as he was locked onto whatever he was imagining.

"Yo…"

"How was practice?" Mike replied but didn't move his head or eyes to acknowledge me.

"Got in some reps with the first team actually…"

Mike nodded once as I placed my hand on his shoulder, walking around the steps around him.

"Can I ask you a question?" His voice rung out behind me.

"Sure, about what?"

"The Lord." His response was monotone and dry, his posture remained the same as I first saw him.

"I can do my best…" I walked towards him and then around him as I descended the steps. "…but He will provide the best answers."

"That's just it! You make it look so effortless." His voice finally had a glint of emotion in it.

"I don't know about that, I haven't been representing Him well with some of the things I have been doing, as of late." I threw my hands, standing on the spongy green lawn as his reply formed at his lips.

"How do you have faith in a being that won't manifest himself in front of you when all you ask for simple proof He is there?"

"How do you know He already hasn't shown himself?"

"Come on..." Mike replied sarcastically as he jostled his head upward and wrinkled his eyebrows.

"He works in mysterious ways man. Many who come to know and love The Lord look back on their life and they see His work is done inch-by-inch. It is only until you see the bigger picture that you realize."

"And you've seen him do stuff?"

"Yeah..." I swayed for a moment. "...He's answered prayers and I am pretty sure He can do a lot more than that when He wants to."

"Okay..." A smile broke from Mike's face. "And what have you prayed for lately?"

"I haven't." I looked down. "Life has had a funny way of distracting me." My eyes shot up to meet Mike's. "But I should start with you."

Mike's eyes softened, the remark had touched his heart but he didn't want to break his tough and composed exterior. "And you just so easily accept that you are in some relationship with this guy?" Mike snickered as he pulled out a pack of cigarettes from his pocket, raising his eyebrows as he did so.

"You know Mike, contrary to what a lot of people believe, it is not the easier road to have faith in The Lord."

"How is that?" He chuckled as he lit his cigarette. "With God, you don't have to face your mortality with anxiety or fear because you believe in this Heaven place. You have a meaning to life and an explanation for why we exist and every unknown thing has an explanation...." He made a funny face. "...it was God..."

"He is so kind and gracious that He'll probably let that slide because He loves you and wants you to know the truth..."

"What truth?!" He flicked his cigarette.

"I mean according to you none of this shit matters, right? We might as well maximize our happiness while we still can because we don't know what happens in the end..."

Mike listened on, intrigued at my forthcoming dissertation.

"...let's just live life and fuck it all. If there is no God, then your actions mean nothing..."

"Who says you need a meaning?" Mike held back a laugh. "You think most of the bullshit that goes on this world has a meaning?" The smoke billowed out from his cigarette and surrounded his black t-shirt in a cloud of white, his eyes piercing as he set his gaze upon me.

"We live in an age of science, where we don't use it as a tool to educate and understand but rather exalt ourselves and dismiss belief in the very being who gave us all of this." My eyes set on a bumble bee crawling into a hydrangea blooming on one of the end bushes. "Look around you, man, does it all look meaningless?" I waved my hand around in the direction of the lawn. "Like one big accident?" I moved my hands toward the sun. "It sure don't look like it."

Mike arched his eyebrows steeply, for once looking to me for answers instead of his normal role in providing them.

"There are many troubled folks who enter in to a relationship with The Lord and it is then they realize that they have become found, they are not lost anymore." I placed my hand on his shoulder. "He wants to help you but He does not wave a magic wand and make all your troubles disappear."

"That's fair..." He dragged on his cigarette.

"It's a common misconception, but He does give you a chance...

Mike raised his chin at me and glanced over at me, he looked lost but desperate for knowledge.

"Even if you could break down the chain of events, isn't the timing impeccable? He operates beyond science and reason. Miracles, aren't luck, brother..."

"You're not going to sell me on miracles." Mike chuckled as he exhaled the smoke, the grey cloud passing by in front of me. "I haven't had any miracles happen to me."

"Well this girl Jessie, she seems like she was a life-changing event, right?"

Mike stared at me, reluctant to speak. I didn't know much about this woman but given his reactions, her presence was very much everywhere in Mike's life though she was physically absent. There was something he was afraid to talk about when it came to her but just as I thought he would reveal the story behind her, I was met with defiance. "Who says that God had anything to do with that?" He tapped some ash from his cigarette. "What if The Lord sent Foxy to you and you are sitting here being stubborn about it?" He shook his head with a smirk. "I think you are blowing it with the Volunteer..."

"Funnily enough she would be honored if you called her that." A smile broke from my face.

"Maybe one day you'll realize..." His eyes locked onto whatever it was he was staring at across the street when I arrived. "...like I should with Jessica." He shifted his feet. "Have you ever seen Him?"

"Yea..." I shut my eyes for a moment and felt a peace wash over me, the spirit filling my body with a joy that wasn't there seconds ago. "He's with us, now."

He squinted at me, a look of confusion and bewilderment spelled across his sun-bleached face. "Where?"

I looked up to the sky for a moment and smiled at the light coming through the trees. "God is love, man..."

Mike took another drag of his cigarette, the paper burned quickly as a long column of grey ash formed at the tip.

"And love isn't an easy thing but it's the only thing matters, it's what guides us and leads us to a place to be more like Him."

He set his gaze upon me and once again remained quiet, he was clearly taking everything I said and thinking about it. "Love is eternal man, just like The Lord. But with Him all things are possible, I'm living proof of that." He grinded the tip of my sneaker against the gravel stone in our footpath. "...it's more than being an ape made of molecules man, that's not what you or me or Jessie or Foxy or Mom simply are. That love is bound in the spirit man, a spirit given to us in love by His grace."

Mike nodded as he put his cigarette out against the sole of his boot. "What about atoms, you can't see them either, right? But you can see them on a microscope."

"Have you ever seen one though?"

"Touché." He smiled with his lips shut.

"It takes as much faith to not believe in Him as it does to do so." I clasped my hands together. "But I know why you avoid the subject because if God is Love, that's giving someone power to destroy you. I mean you are completely helpless no matter what they do. It's having the ability to run free all the while you are bound to that other person, trapped in some invisible cage. No matter how far you go, you always go back to them; no matter where you go, they are always there with you. But there was never any need to run."

"So why do you run from Samantha?"

His response cut through me and left me speechless, it seemed topical but poignant. There was a reason why this was coming up again here and now but I didn't have to time to reply. My cell phone rang out to the default Nokia ringtone. The screen lit up with the word Mel <3 spelled across it.

"Let me guess..." He stood up and brushed off his blue jeans. "Melissa..." He made his way up the steps to the door. I flipped open the phone and hit the green button to answer the call.

"Hey!" I greeted her enthusiastically. "I was actually just talking to my brother..."

"I won't keep it long." Her tone of voice was sullen.

"Mel, what's wrong?" I initiated.

"I don't where to start..."

My eyes hovered to the blades of grass, all blades leaning up to the sun and rocking gently in the subtle breeze.

"I like you Corey, I do, but..."

"But?"

"But I don't know if I am ready for this..."

The words hit me like a punch to the stomach.

"I just don't think it's right."

"I don't understand..." My voice nearly broke, filled with angst and ache. Funnily enough, I thought I was being mocked and soured, here I was talking about The Lord and moments later I was met by an unbearable break in my heart. How many instances though were we stuck looking at a tree when The Lord sees the whole forest? I'd look back at that moment one day and realize it was all a part of the plan, but I couldn't see it then.

"I am not saying that I don't want to be with you. I just need some space."

"But we can take it slow..." My following words cut off by her firm reply.

"No, Corey. I just need to make sure."

"Of what?"

"That this isn't some rebound. I have been through a lot lately with Matt and it's easy to dive into something new and exciting." My eyes set downward as tears filled them, finding a momentary diversion in a black ant crawling along the gravel between the two verges of grass.

"Remember, I am not saying I don't want to be with you..."

"That's what it sounds like to me." I sniffled as I dabbed my eye, glancing down the road in the direction of Westwood.

"I am sorry, I'll see you at school..."

A lump formed in my throat, I didn't know what to do or say, I was at a loss for words. Before I could form any response that would convince her to re-think what she was doing, I heard her hang up the phone. She was gone, the silence replacing the sound of her voice which only minutes before I had hoped would never cease.

I retired to the steps and threw my hands on my legs; I should have mourned the loss of the relationship. I should have allowed myself to feel but I couldn't bare the pain. Instead, I took out my phone and scrolled down to the name Sarah. The phone rang twice before she picked up.

"Hey, you!" Sarah's voice was filled with eagerness. "I was just thinking about you..."

Heat filled my cheeks, a smile returned to my face. "Say, I was wondering. Are you doing anything tonight?"

"No..." Sarah sighed. "...other than avoiding my brother as he misfit friends who have some sick obsession with Lynbrook actually.
"

"Someone has to..."

"...He was curious when I told him that I met a guy from there. You said you had a brother named Mike, right?"

"Yeah..." I looked over my shoulder to see if Mike was anywhere to be found.

"I think he used to be friends with him but now they have beef..."

I was perplexed at the claim but my mind started to put the puzzle together. Her brother was called Jay. What was Jay short for? John, Jake, or *James*.

"Is Jay short for James?"

"Yea..." She chuckled. "...how did you know that?"

"Does he have a nickname?"

"I never liked it much, but his friends call him Truck..."

My stomach sunk but it made perfect sense, it explained why she was there the night of the brawl. I didn't know what to do next: hang up the phone and add to the rivalry by making a scene or give it no power and play it off? I liked Sarah and I didn't want a bunch of pettiness to get in the way of something that could be potentially great otherwise.

"Hello?"

"Yeah..." I stood up. "...look I don't want to make things weird but I think my brother and him don't really get along to well..."

"That's what he said..." Sarah replied.

"But you said there was a problem over a girl?" I scratched the side of my head. "I only heard about the whole issue between their crews and what not."

"Honestly, I never gave it much thought because I am my own person and so are you. I've had enough of my brother's immature feuds with God knows whoever..."

I looked back at the front door for a moment, remembering all the times Mike was outside plotting to get revenge or assert himself against his enemy. "I can relate to that..."

"I was worried that it might be a problem, but I told my brother I'll date whoever I want."

She had done more in a sentence than Mel ever did and I didn't have to jump through hoops to earn her affection. This girl was independent, she thought for herself, and she was fair.

"I agree, I don't think our siblings should have a say in how this goes." I swung myself around to face the street, giddy from the flow of the conversation. "It should just be you and me..." A smirk formed at my face. "I like the idea of it being a date too..."

"Do you?" She flirted back.

"Yea and you are a lot better looking than your brother."

Sarah's laugh filled the phone.

"How about we meet at seven by the VFW Hall and we can go grab some food?"

"Sounds good to me."

"And if I do really well, maybe you will consider coming to the game tomorrow, we are playing South Side after all..."

"You have this all figured out don't you babe?" She flirted again.

"I try..."

"I think we can make that happen. See at you seven." She kissed into the phone.

I hung up the phone, Sarah's laughter still echoing in my ears. For the first time all day, a genuine smile broke across my face. Maybe things could be simpler. Maybe Sarah was right—our brothers didn't have to dictate how this would go.

I stepped back onto the porch, glancing at the spot where Mike had sat earlier, the faint smell of cigarette smoke still lingering in the air. His words stayed with me, a quiet tug in the back of my mind. But as I looked up at the fading sky, streaks of gold and orange cutting through the clouds, something shifted. Melissa's words, Mike's questions, even Sarah's easy confidence—they all swirled together, leaving me restless. For now, I had a date with Sarah: a new start. And maybe, that was enough.

• • • •

THAT NIGHT, I HAD FORGOTTEN about the sting of losing Melissa when Sarah and I shared a hamburger and made out on the swing set in a school playground, just the two of us. We were there all night and no one knew we were there. But still even then, I was numb to it all. It was like I was living someone's life. Reality came crashing back when I came home that night, discovering Mike lying on the couch on the porch with an empty bottle of Budweiser tucked under his black hooded sweatshirt. He looked like a throw-over quilt clad in black lying on a patio couch, curled in a ball. As I made my way up the steps, Mike's eyes opened, his dilated irises glistening in the moonlight.

"Are you alright, dude?"

Mike rubbed the bridge of his nose.

"How long you been out here?" I drew close to him and helped him to sit up, sweeping away the bottle that clanged against the wooden floor.

"I don't know, an hour or two..." His voice was hoarse. "The boys left me off here as they usually do..."

"Here..." I handed Mike a bottle of water in my hand and unscrewed the cap. Mike took hearty gulps, the plastic crackling and crunching inward from the force at which he drank. He belched and ran his hand over the dome of his hand.

"Man..." He sipped slow. "That was stupid."

"You were doing good with the drinking, what happened?" I sat beside him.

"I should have kept it going but it was all too much I suppose." He placed his elbows on his knees and hunched forward. "I'll be okay though. You are going through a lot with your girl there..."

"No, tell me..." I cut him off.

"I tried to warn you about Melissa..." He sighed. "I am sorry, man." He put his hand on my back and rocked me gently. "That's why I was trying to steer towards you Samantha, that girl wouldn't do that to you." He peered upward toward a beam of moonlight which caught both of us on the porch.

"So, this is about Foxy, again?"

"No..." He feigned a smile. "But I don't want you to make the mistake that I did." Mike reached down and clutched the empty bottle. "Letting a great thing slip away." He put the bottle gently down on the table. "I saw her tonight...."

I arched my eyebrows prompting him to continue.

"Jessie..."

I sat up and drew closer to Mike. "Where?"

"At Nathans..." A smile less forced returned to his face. "I used to play Dance Dance Revolution in the arcade with her."

"Foxy and I have done the same thing..."

"See, I told you she's perfect..." He chuckled before growing somber again.

"You never told me the whole story about her."

"Eh..." He flicked his hand. "It doesn't matter..." He looked down at the ground, his eyes watering up as he fought back tears. "She wants nothing do with me..."

"Just tell me, big brother." I put my arm around his back.

He nodded and shook for a moment, sniffling as he took out a cigarette, offering me in which I declined.

"Before I got locked up and went upstate with Dad, James or Truck as you know him, or Jimmy as I called him started up the Rep..." Mike lit a cigarette. "It got serious pretty quick, next thing I know we were selling put and playing dice behind the movie theatre like it was a pick-up game of stickball." He exhaled a large column of smoke. "Jimmy always talked about this girlfriend he had, that used to nag him." He took another drag, the cherry glowing bright red. "And he'd brag about how he would be cheating on her with all these other girls and you know me..." Mike put his hand across. "I was never one for mistreating someone for the sake of it..." Mike shook his head. "He seemed proud that she was unaware of what was going on. I was never with that though." He returned his elbows to his knees, clutching his hands together with the cigarette escaping from between his knuckles. "One day, I was waiting for Jimmy by the

Lotto store on Maple, you know the one down the block from our old house."

I nodded.

"I met this girl and she was drop dead gorgeous." Mike smiled ear to ear. "Beautiful blue eyes, long brown hair. Perfect body, I mean I was in love..."

"So, I see where the whole Foxy obsession comes from now." I teased and Mike shot me a soft smile.

"Her name was Jessica...Jessie, as she was called." Her eyes twinkled with the joy at the mention of her name. "So, her and I struck up a conversation and we were talking for like twenty minutes or so before Jimmy runs up the corner and says *Yo bitch*" to this girl. At first, I looked around unsure of who he was talking about until Jimmy put his arm around her..." Mike paused and I thought back to the conversation with Sarah. Now, it fully made sense.

"This is all over her, isn't it?"

"You already know the answer to that." He smiled. "You are a smart kid, Corey. When we were at Westwood that one day and you said to me it seemed kind of personal just to be over snitching. I smiled because I knew I couldn't put it past you."

I gleamed at Mike, a look of reverence perhaps escaping me as my brother opened up to me.

"She became my best friend. She understood me and she didn't idolize me for being a thug and I needed that." His eyes filled with both pain and joy. "You know Corey, out of all the shit I may teach you in life, the one thing that I can surely tell you if you can find someone that is like your best friend, whom you could always smile at seeing everyday who becomes more and more beautiful every time you see them." He interlocked his fingers together. "That is what matters." Mike took another drag of his cigarette. "I can chase money and love sex, but I'd walk away from all this shit tomorrow if she came back." He tapped the top of his cigarette. "That's where the whole thing with Samantha comes from. I see it now and when you see it, I hope, you'll remember when this conversation...."

I reflected on what he said for a moment, not realizing then the importance of these words. I just thought Mike saw a similarity and was projecting his past onto my future. Usually, we have an uncanny ability to assume such things when the ones who are warning us are truly doing it to protect us, even when it feels like it's unnecessary.

"So, what happened?"

"Basically, every time Jimmy came around with her, Jessie and I would sit and have these long conversations, we'd laugh and we'd share intimate details about each other. We exchanged numbers and some nights she would come home from Jimmy's house, crying and telling me all the horrible things he said to her or did to her." Mike rose to his feet. "This is why I really hate this motherfucker more than anything else. She cared so much for him and he tortures her emotionally. You think I care about snitching?" He took another drag and a deep breath to collect himself. "I knew going in that he couldn't hack it." Mike circled his tongue against his cheek. "Anyways, the three of us were at some party on Jefferson Avenue and she lived down south in Oceanside on Woods Avenue. James was too drunk to get her home and passed out, so I walked her home." He smiled again. "I knew he was going to leave her, he told me." Mike put his hands against his chest. "So, I confessed that from the moment I saw her, I was head over heels for her..." Mike put the cigarette out against the railing. "She said she felt the same, so I told her to leave him and I'd be there for her. And once she did, I was leaving the Rep." He broke a boyish smile again. "That's why you never saw me, I always wanted to be with her. And it was real, we loved each other."

"So how did this all end?"

"We thought things would run their course but he never pulled the trigger. The crew noticed I was going scarce as I was spending more and more time with her. Finally, we decided we were going to tell him." Mike leaned over the banister, his posture all the more philosophical. "Problem was as soon as he saw us when we met him at the Green, he started calling her names, and was threatening to hit her, so I had to plant him." Mike curled his fist and looked at it. "From that day forward, the Rep splintered and the Sovereigns was formed. The bozos that left with him were the one who believed his story that the leader fucks his brother's girlfriend behind their back." Mike crossed his arms. "That's why it's a running a gag with the boys, they say if I didn't pull a Jessie, that none of this shit would have ever happened." He sat back down on the couch. "The dangers of following your heart." He turned to look at me. "Still I say fucking do it."

I looked out toward the street and recollected the jeers of Mike's friends in regards to not "pulling a Jessie."

"One day the Rep and the Sovereigns met one day on Park Avenue and we mopped the floor with them. From there, the only way Truck and his cronies thought they could stop me was to resort to other measures. For example, this idiot got bagged peddling chiba in the parking lot of the high school because he was doing it in front of a detective in a taxi cab." Mike started laughing at the thought of it. "...in exchange for his cooperation, they let him off with an ACOD if he said where he got it from. He pointed the finger at me..." Mike's eyes lightened again. "They were watching us for some time and you would think that is enough to do it, but it wasn't. The Grease started targeting our guys and eventually they had enough to scoop Houston Dan, because he was selling quarter ounces to several Sovereigns who actually had flipped. Basically, they were using the police to wipe us out while they had other motherfuckers moving in to where our boys were working." Mike shook his head. "Naturally, I wanted to stick around and ride this out with my brothers before moving on but Jessie made me promise to walk away at that point and I did. That's why I went upstate." He itched his chin. "But when I was gone, it only got worse. It had escalated into a full-blown turf war."

"All over one girl..." I sat back against the couch. "So how did that to get to the night?"

Mike leered at me out of the corner of his eyes, the day everything changed. He looked forward again before he spoke. "When I came back, I proposed to Jessie and she said yes." He removed a small ring box from his sweatpants and held up a diamond ring to the moonlight. "I carry this as a reminder. In knowing the difference between quitting and walking away." Mike walked over and placed the ring in the palm of my hand. "I wish I had known that then. Instead, we met up with those guys in the Green and I did a number on Truck once and for all." He dropped his head. "That's when I got arrested."

My eyes never left the sight of the twinkling ring in my hand until I looked up at Mike who put his knuckles in front of me, showing a scar. "That's from the night, I lost her. I punched the mirror in my jail cell and sadly it's not the only scar I have from it..." Mike stumbled forward to the door, nearly collapsing. "Hopefully, it won't take all that to realize Foxy is your Jessie." He held the door for a moment. "I am going to bed."

The door slammed shut behind him and a chilled wind blew across the porch as I clutched the ring, its cold metal biting into my palm. The weight of it felt heavier than it should, like it carried all of Mike's regrets. It wasn't just his words—it was the way his voice cracked, the way his hands shook as he held that ring. It was the pain he carried, and the warning he was giving me about not letting a good thing go to waste and knowing the difference between quitting and walking away. I didn't appreciate its true meaning then but soon enough I would learn what it meant intimately.

Chapter 13 – Home Away from Home

I grabbed my CD player and threw on my headphones. It was a warm day, the kind that begged you to be outside, and for once, I didn't mind the walk. My relationship with Sarah was growing stronger, and for now, our brothers seemed blissfully unaware of it. Most days, I forgot about the tangled web of family ties. When we were together, it was just us.

But today was different. It was the first time I was going back to Rockville Centre since the night everything fell apart—the night that sent Mike to jail. Nervous energy coursed through me, part excitement to see Sarah again, part dread at venturing into a place I'd avoided for years. Rockville Centre wasn't just another town. It was a graveyard of memories, a place I'd promised myself I'd never revisit until I had a reason bigger than my fears.

"Here goes nothing..." I texted Sam as I walked down Hendrickson Avenue, heading toward the Five Corners to catch the bus. Hoobastank's Crawling in the Dark blared in my ears, its beat syncing with the steady rhythm of my steps.

Though it was only one town over, stepping off the bus at Morris Avenue and Merrick Road felt like entering another world—one I used to know like the back of my hand. The familiar and unfamiliar collided as I looked around. The China Buffet still stood tall on the corner, its neon sign buzzing faintly in the sunlight. The faint scent of fried food drifted across the street, mingling with the distant hum of traffic. It was strange how the town felt frozen in time, yet completely different from how I remembered it. I couldn't shake the feeling that I was seeing it through a new lens, one shaped by years of distance and everything that had happened since.

I crossed Sunrise Highway and passed by the gas station and Hickey Field which was offset to the back, the same as I left it. I had many fond memories of Hickey Field when I was a kid; I remember little league and pick-up games with some of the neighborhood children. I passed the Electric Company and took in the sound of the motor turbines humming as it blew warm air from its vents.

I hung a right on Maple Avenue, across the way was the firehouse, the fleet of trucks sitting on the ramp shining in the afternoon sun, ready for the next call. Beyond it, stood the infamous Village Green: the place where so many lives were changed. Every step closer brought back fragments of memories I'd tried to bury. The shouting, the blood, the flashing lights of the cop cars—they were phantoms of a night I'd long tried to forget. But today wasn't about the past. It was about Sarah.

The Green was just as it was on the events of that night where Mike and Truck squared off, the life-altering event a small footnote in the annals of its history dating back to Victorian times. Though it was nestled in the center of a suburban town, if you threw yourself down in the grass in the middle of the field, you'd think you were miles away from everything. All you could see is blue sky and lush green oaks which canopied the park on its perimeters. There were some nights when I was a child I would lay in the field and stare up at the sky until dusk and just think. When I finally sat up the blood would rush to my head and I'd be itchy beyond belief. You'd look across to Lee Avenue and see the streetlights begin to illuminate and hear the sounds of sprinklers cascading through the twilight.

"Corey!" I heard Sarah's voice yell across to me. She was sitting on the rail of the gazebo in the Village Green, looking hotter than ever. Her long black hair was straightened and her red lipstick shimmered. She was wearing black legging pants and a white-beater, her brown leather coat draped over her arm- the same brown leather coat I saw her at the brawl in Lynbrook.

We approached and I placed my arms on her stomach and kissed her. She playfully nipped my lip and giggled.

"What's up?"

"Nothing just taking a trip down Memory Lane." I gazed up at the top of the hulking water tower. "I used to live around the corner on North Forest..."

"Really?"

"Can we go a take a look?" I smiled at her.

She pecked my lips. "Okay..."

"But first things first." I grabbed the back of her head as I engaged in an intense lip-lock with her. We made out intensely for twenty minutes, grabbing, groping each other until we were forced to come up for air.

Minutes later we stood at the intersection was North Forest Avenue. The words Lotto written in big white letters in the awning of corner store caused a dizzying nostalgic trance.

"It's still the same."

"Why wouldn't it be?" Sarah teased.

"My brother he used to hang out here a lot." I forgot the context of the situation briefly.

"Mine too." Sarah feigned a smile. "You want to go in? I got you on an Iced Tea if you're thirsty."

"That would be great."

Sarah led the way across the street and I couldn't help but have my eyes glued to her butt, Mike was right again. I kept remembering what he told me about hips on a woman at the Brookvale diner. I couldn't help but find humor. I opened the door for Sarah to let her in and followed her. Inside there were two kids wearing black t-shirts and bandanas with denim shorts. My knee-jerk reaction was that they were some of Truck's associates.

"Yo Richie...Keith!" She yelled out to the two kids who were completing a purchase at the counter.

"Hey Sarah, what's up?" The smaller of the two kissed Sarah on the cheek in a platonic manner. Sarah reciprocated.

"Nothing chilling what about you?"

"Rich and I just came to get a pack of smokes." The kid answered.

"Keith, Rich. This is my..." Sarah stiffened up upon completing the introduction.

I smirked. "I'm Sarah's boyfriend, Corey. It's nice to meet you" I extended my hand to Keith.

"Nice to meet you too Corey." Keith gripped my hand firm, a blatant show of respect. "This is my brother Rich."

I extended my hand to Rich, but he was more solemn and reserved.

"What's up Corey." He shook my hand strongly.

"I'm sorry to ask, but can I buy a smoke off you for my boyfriend and me?"

"No worries, Sarah. I got you both." He flipped open the box of cigarettes, the center flipped the other way.

"A Lucky..." I pointed toward it.

"You know what they say about them..." He plucked two cigarettes and handed them to Sarah. "Come on outside."

We followed them out. "Are you from around here?" Keith sparked his blue disposable lighter and kept his hand in front of the flame, lighting Sarah's cig and then mine.

"I used to live right down there actually." I pointed to a large green house across with a sprawling wrap-around porch across from another fire station.

"No shit." Keith turned around and looked back. "I live on Cedar Avenue, and Rich lives on Raymond...."

Rich smoked quietly in the rear enjoying his cigarette.

"Small world, Sarah and her brother are pretty much my neighbors." He rubbed the side of his cheek. "How do you two know each other?"

"We met at a fair in Lynbrook. The rest is history."

"The OLL feast?" Keith smirked. "No surprise, I hear there are a lot of attractive women there..." He pointed over at Sarah. "Like homegirl here. She looks after herself with all the lacrosse, volleyball, and swim team over here."

Sarah blushed. I wondered if there was more to their relationship than simply passing acquaintances, their rapport was obvious.

"Yea, I can tell she is quite athletic." I smacked Sarah's butt.

"Stop!" She giggled

"Anyways, I'd love to stay and talk some more but we got a train to catch to Brooklyn." Keith extended his hand. "It's great to meet you dude."

"The pleasure is all mine..."

The two turned their backs and exited, Sarah watched them walk down Maple Avenue in the direction we came, casually smoking on her cigarette.

"You good?"

I put my arm around her and slapped her butt again.

"Can't keep your hands to yourself, can you?" Sarah tossed aside her cigarette. "Where to now?"

I pointed towards my old home.

Sarah took my hand and we headed there until we finally stood in front. It looked exactly the same, the same mother-daughter Victorian house with the old worn in porch. The wood was original from the house, two white doors stood in front of the steps. The left door was the entrance to the lower floor apartment, the right door lead upstairs. I glanced down at the porch again and reminisced about days I would sit on the steps or the rails along the porch and look out at the firehouse and Fireman's Memorial Park across the street. I recalled spring days when the dogwood trees bloomed filling the streets with a pungent fragrance.

"I used to live downstairs, first floor." I threw my hands on my hips as I sized up the house. "Things were a lot different then, a lot simpler."

Sarah smiled; her eyes filled with intrigue as she listened.

"Call me crazy, but a part of me misses it."

"What do you miss?"

"Before everything changed, my brother and I were just some kids…"

"It's funny, all I ever heard was bad things about him, but through knowing you and hearing

How you speak about him. I realize you never really know someone until you know them."

"I know what you mean…" I watched as a plane passed by over us, its engines whining as it descended from the sky, likely landing at Kennedy Airport which was only 15 miles away. "So, what's the deal with your brother?"

"He's not a bad guy…" She shrugged her shoulders. "…just insecure. My mother and my father they can have high expectations. My dad he worked hard to get us in the house we live and he still works hard day in and day out. My mom met my dad when they were younger. They both grew up in Brooklyn and when my dad was eighteen, he joined the military. When he came home, he took out a VA loan and started a business. He owns the deli on Brower Avenue and not to mention he is a volunteer firefighter across the street over there. He also teaches EMS out at the academy when he gained his paramedic license. He pushes us but I'm a straight-A student plus I work with him at the deli and play three sports a year. James, he never wanted anything to do with that. He was a shy and quiet kid often got picked on and he used to skip class because of that. Dad was always hard on him." Sarah paused. "I suppose where this all comes from."

"I just don't get how a girl as sweet as you can be related to someone like him."

Sarah grilled me upon that statement. "You know I can say the same about you."

"Yeah but my brother, he is a family guy. He is loyal, he wears his heart on his sleeve..."

"That whole thing with Jessie though..." Sarah gave me a side-eye.

"My brother adored her; your brother treated her like shit."

"You don't know the whole story." Sarah's voice raised with disdain tinged in the tone.

"You're right..." I threw my hands at my sides. "Let's drop it..."

"Fine by me." Sarah snickered.

"Want to go check out the backyard?"

Her frown soon turned to a smile, as she nodded yes. I led her by the hand quietly into the backyard of my old house, seeking refuge in the old shed that was always vacant. I found it just as I remembered it. There Sarah and I had sex for an hour and no one even knew we were back there. Sarah and I made the most of it and once we were done, we made a stealth exit, the only lingering presence was the scent of raw and passionate sex that surrounded us. Sarah's hair was mangled and we were both sweaty.

"Well I am going to be sore later." Sarah chuckled.

"You might have a horse throat too." I teased.

"Shut up." She playfully tapped me. I poked her behind again and she grabbed me by my shirt, exerting her strength on me with another kiss.

"You hungry?" I ran my hands along the smooth flesh of her love handles. "Should we get some pizza again?"

"Sure..." Her hands gripped the back of my neck, as she pulled me in for another kiss.

Despite the turbulent trajectory which brought us together I found myself in a pensive state. I had wondered if the acrimony between Sarah's brother and mine had never materialized could her and I have met on more amiable terms? It was a gamble for both of us to engage in such a risk. But nevertheless, Sarah in many ways reminded me of Foxy. She had a personality that was easy to get along with her and talk to her. She was goofy, she was funny and she was independent. All of the qualities I admired in a woman.

We were near to town, back on Merrick Road, and our conversation on the way went off tangents that led to more tangents, we never once spoke or thought about brothers, it was just us. Ahead of me, a large sign for 7-Eleven.

"Want to stop for a coffee?"

She nodded again, clutching my hand as she brushed up against me. "I'll get us some Butterfingers."

"Oh, you shouldn't have..." I feigned the accent of an older man as I reached for the door to open it for her.

As we stepped in, a cold blast of air met us from the air conditioning. The brown tiles shined from being recently mopped, sporting a luster from the fluorescent lighting above. We made our way past the racks of pastries and assorted groceries to the island where the coffee pots brewed fresh which you could smell upon entry.

I stopped at the French Vanilla and took the pot by the handle and poured some in to a large green foam cup. "Get whatever you like gorgeous." I glanced over at the selection of creamers, milks and syrups. I grabbed a red stirrer and stirred the coffee aimlessly while I gazed over at Sarah who prepared her own concoction. She passed by and smiled at me as she headed for the checkout lane. I placed a lid on my cup and turned to join her, it was then that the door swung open demanding our undivided attention.

"Oh fuck!" Sarah's eyes bulged.

"Well what the fuck is this?!" Truck charged forward like a bull, wearing black from head to toe. Flanking him were his enforcers All Day and RJ. All Day had the more menacing look of the two as his beady brown eyes were filled with malice. In a similar ensemble to his confidant and leader, PJ's freckled face did not bear any pleasantries. His cropped brown hair faintly visible from beneath his fitted Los Angeles Dodgers baseball cap.

"James, hold on." Sarah stepped in front of me but PJ and RJ walked around her. PJ slapped the coffee out of my hand, the brown liquid scolded my hands and dripped onto the floor.

"What the fuck you doing here?" RJ grabbed me by my shirt and pinned me against the Slurpee machine. I threw my hands up in defense as my collar crumpled in RJ's grasp.

"Hey...Hey...Hey!" The cashier ran from the back to break up the scuffle. Truck grabbed Sarah and moved her out of his way to confront him.

"What the fuck you going to do, Wally?!" Truck puffed his chest out.

"Truck, come on man..." The scrawny, clean-shaven post-adolescent whined. His red uniform shirt was clearly oversized and his name tag read Bobby identified a clear misnomer in itself.

"If you want me to settle that debt for you, you'll let me handle my shit with my guest here, okay?"

Wally stiffened up and looked back helplessly. Sarah meanwhile came over and tried to pull RJ's arm. "Let go of him!"

"Chill, Sarah!" RJ shrugged her off and kept his grip on me unabated.

"Let go of him!" She tried to release me from their grips with her own strength and almost did so until Truck pulled her back and placed his hands around my throat.

"What the fuck are you doing with my sister?!" He was nose-to-nose with me, you could smell the tequila emanating from his breath. The smell was nauseating, but it was the rage in his eyes that froze me. I wanted to fight back, but every muscle in my body felt locked. Sarah's voice cut through the chaos, but even then, I wasn't sure if we were getting out of this unscathed.

"Answer him motherfucker!" All-Day bounced me in to the machine again, one of the plastic cups tumbled on the floor next to me.

"Let him speak!" Sarah shoved her brother and he lost his temper and threw her in to me. I forced my arms free to catch her and brace her from the impact. Her hair splashed in my face as her backside smashed into me.

"Go ahead, go ride his dick some more Sarah." Truck mocked her.

"Whose dick I ride is none of your business, you fucking sicko." She cocked back her hand to slap him but I took hold of her wrist. She looked back at me with disbelief. All three member of the Street Sovereigns were also caught off guard by the act.

"It's alright gorgeous. This isn't the time for it." I put my hand around her stomach and rubbed her to calm her.

Truck kept his steady gaze upon me. "For once, Little Ghost is right..."

"Fuck you." Sarah lunged forward with her fist curled up. "I'll kick the shit out of all three of you!"

Truck stood tall and looked down at his sister with disgust, neither did anything after that but the stare down provided all the dialogue. The fluorescent lights buzzed overhead, casting harsh shadows across Truck's face as he leaned in. Behind me, the hum of the Slurpee machine mixed with the faint click of Sarah's shoes on the tiles. It all felt too loud and too quiet at the same time, like the air had been sucked out of the room.

"This is what you really want, Sadie?" He looked down at her from the bridge of her nose.

"Yeah, I do!"

"And what about you?!" All Day drew close, his fist smacking the machine inches away from my face.

"What about me?"

"She's what you are here for?" He raised his eyebrows.

"Why else would I be here?"

"Answer the fucking question!" RJ surged toward me but Sarah met him with a curled fist and nasty look.

"Shit." He laughed as he took a step back. "You are lucky Sarah was here to protect you, little bitch..."

Truck grabbed both of his running mates' shoulders and pulled them back. "Fine, I'll tell you what sis..." He waved his hands and both RJ and PJ took two steps back. "If you want to be with him, that's fine."

"I didn't know I needed your permission." Sarah crossed her arms.

"Hell, I'll do you one better." He pointed at me. "I'll keep this between us." Truck shook his head as she smirked, rubbing the bottom of his pointy chin. "I won't say shit to Mike and as long as you do right by my sister, you won't even see my face in Softbrook..."

RJ and PJ both glanced at Truck, two brolic mopes confused at what their ringleader was saying.

"None of us..." He looked sternly at both his cohorts. "If you are the only one here coming in here..." He raised his finger and shook it. "For my lovely sister..." Truck smiled briefly at her. "...We're cool..."

Sarah backed up into me, shielding me. I gently grazed the smooth bare skin between the lip of her leggings and her white top which bore midriff.

"Sarah, if he makes you happy, I can let this go." Truck's tone was sincere, baffling me that he become so gentle despite being imposing and intimidating, seconds ago. In that moment, Truck seemed approachable and perhaps even kind until he set his gaze upon me. "Be careful though, you know who his brother is..." Truck taunted and puckered his lips at me.

"Motherfucker!" I clenched my fists, my body trembling with adrenaline, as I lunged off the machine but Sarah took hold me of forced back against it, her gaze locked on her brother. The three Sovereigns broke out in laughter.

"Just, let me handle this." Sarah spoke in a whisper before she flicked her hair and stared down the three of them. "You don't scare me, James," she said, her voice unwavering. "If you're done, leave."

"Going." Truck raised his hands in retreat. "But Corey, remember this." His finger erected again, pointing directly at me. "If you my break my sister's heart, I swear, I'll break your fucking face..." He flinched, simulating as if he was going to step to me and attack. I tensed by response; the three goons shared another laugh. "You good?"

I nodded once.

"Alright..." He spoke out of the corner of his mouth to his two deputies. "Let's get the fuck out of here and leave my sister with her new pet..." Truck turned toward the door. "You two have a nice day..." Both PJ and RJ followed Truck to the door, RJ kicked the coffee cup across the floor, smearing all the coffee across the glistening surface.

"Nice mopping job." He laughed wickedly as the three exited.

Truck slapped some money on the counter. "That's for the spill and whatever else they want to get, ight?"

Wally approached the point of sale and counted whatever was placed down.

"That's cool, Truck." He pocketed the cash in his blue work pants and headed towards the back.

The door swung shut behind them, leaving an eerie silence in their wake. I exhaled a breath I hadn't realized I'd been holding, my shoulders slumping as the adrenaline drained from my body.

"Are you alright?" Sarah's voice was soft now, her hand brushing my arm. "I'm sorry about that..."

"I'm fine." My hands trembled as I straightened my shirt. "We should have gone for a bagel with a shmear, instead..." My pocket buzzed, and I pulled out my phone to see a message from Foxy.

How is it going?

I typed back: Fine. *We ran into Truck, and he threatened to kill me if I broke Sarah's heart. Thankfully, she calmed everything down.*

"Who are you texting?" Sarah's gaze hardened, her voice cutting through the fluorescent hum of the store's lights.

"My friend," I said, shaking my head with a forced smile. "Foxy."

"What did she want?" Her tone was cool, her eyebrows raised as she leaned back slightly.

"She was just checking in," I said lightly.

"Didn't know you were close like that with her." Sarah tilted her head, her laugh short and dry. "Let's get out of here." She turned and headed for the door. I followed, stopping briefly to check my phone again.

My goodness! What are you going to do? Foxy's reply buzzed on the screen, the concern practically leaping from the words.

Nothing, I typed, watching Sarah's hips sway as her hair flowed behind her. *I'll just let it go. It's no big deal.*

I hit send, and for a moment, it felt like the danger was behind us. But deep down, I knew better. This wasn't the end—it was only the beginning.

When I arrived at home, I had finally forgotten about Truck's threats that malingered in my mind until I stepped through the door and turned the lights on. Mike was sitting on the couch deep in thought, dwelling on something heavy. *Did he find out already? Had Truck said something?*

"What are you doing man?"

Mike's eyes were red, wet still from perhaps a brief episode of tears. "Your buddy was looking for you...." He said, bereft of any emotion. Was he angered? He must have found out!

"Who?" My words trembled as they left my lips.

A brief smile filled his face. "Who do you think?"

Truck came to mind, his name forming on my throat until Mike interrupted me. "...Foxy, you dweeb..."

"Oh..." I smiled as I let out a sigh of relief.

"She came by but I told her you were out somewhere." His smile grew wider. "She seemed to be quite worried about you but she wouldn't tell me why..."

My stomach dropped; I knew what was worrying her but I didn't want to say anything to reveal the truth. Not now, not yet...

"She's waiting for you, watching something to do with a Black Diamond Trophy."

"West Virginia versus Virginia Tech."

"That's it." He pointed at me. "That gal is worse than you when it comes to football..." He chuckled.

"I'll head over there now..." I threw my hands at my hips and turned to the door.

"She's not there..." His words speaking softly to me over my shoulder. "She's waiting for you."

When I turned around to look at Mike, his smile was even larger than it had been since I stepped in. "She's upstairs, watching the game in my room."

I looked up into the black gape of the stairs, Foxy up there tucked away behind the closed door waiting for me to come through it to greet me.

"I hope you don't mind..." Mike laughed. "...I thought the poor girl would be bored out of her mind waiting around..."

"That's really kind of you."

"You should talk to her man."

"Actually, I was going to invite her to the breakfast next week..."

"Good." Mike smiled. "That's a good start..." He nodded. "But before you go, there is something I wanted to tell you..."

I took a half-step towards my brother, leaning in to know he had my full attention. This couldn't be about Truck, right? Surely not...

"I been doing some thinking..." He reclined back against the couch. "About what you said..." His hands clasped together. "About a lot of things..." Mike leaned forward. "I was wrong about The Lord..."

I grew stiff hanging on his next words, I had never listened more intently to Mike than I did then.

"...He was there all along." Mike's head dropped, as if he were praying then and there, a moment of submission in our living room in the quiet and dark. "...He sent me an angel to lead me out..."

"Jessie?"

Mike nodded. "I've been too proud and arrogant to accept it. But I suppose that's normal, I always wanted out of this but didn't know the way because this is all I've ever known. It's only when you look back that you realize He was sewing everything together to put things right. I blew every chance he gave me..." He rested his hands in his chin. "But not this one, I'm taking his hand..."

A joy filled my soul, I was glad that I didn't tell him about what happened with Truck in Rockville Centre. I was happy that I had reached out to Sarah, maybe this can all play a part in driving him further into this new life that The Lord had given him.

"I never gave Him a chance because I never gave myself a chance. But I've asked Him to forgive me. I asked The Lord to come into my life and make me his dwelling place, I wish to repent, I wish to leave these burdens at The Cross. I just pray I'll be good enough for Him..." Mike's head collapsed into his hands.

I stepped forward and put my hand on Mike's shoulder. "Mike, God doesn't ask you to be perfect, He loves for who you are."

Mike lifted his head and smiled at me from the corner of his eyes. "I just hope He will use me."

"He will."

"He's changed your life as He has mine." Mike turned and gazed forward, his laser-sharp focus now fixed to a new target, one not set in his own designs but something greater. "Perhaps, He will take me to change someone else's life."

"I am certain He will." I gently jostled Mike to encourage him.

"I just don't know where to start." Mike gazed at me again from the corner of his eyes

"You already have, brother." I opened my arms to him and Mike rose to his feet to embrace me. We held each other tight for a moment.

"I'm really happy you Mike." I pressed my hands against his shoulders.

"Thanks." He pointed toward the steps. "Now, don't keep her waiting any, longer will you?" He teased. "It's rude to ignore my future sister-in-law."

"Right, I am going..." I made my way up the steps and stopped at the first door at the top of the steps. I heard the roar of the television through the door as the commentators gave a play-by-play of the football game. I opened the door and there sat Samantha on the edge of Mike's bed, her eyes bulging at the sight of me coming through the door, her silhouette glowing in the light of the television.

"Thank, God." She rushed forward and hugged me. "I needed to make sure."

"I am glad you are here." I smiled at Samantha. "I have a surprise for you."

Her eyebrows arched.

"...I just got to get a few things out of my room and we'll take a short walk."

"Okay..." Foxy peered back at the television, an impact play in the game gauging her attention for a fleeting moment.

When we exited the house, Mike had already disappeared somewhere in the evening. It was twilight and the crickets soon began to symphonize with the environment as Sam and I passed the blinking red light just before Westwood. The air was warm yet humid, still comfortable as a gentle breeze would sweep through in a cool whisper.

We crossed over the train tracks and approached the basketball court. The streetlights had just powered on and yet the only noises you could hear were the sounds of those crickets buzzing in the night.

"So, you brought me here to play basketball?" Foxy joked as she twirled her hair.

"No." I placed the portable radio down, keeping my backpack draped over a shoulder. "Not quite." I smirked. "Close your eyes." I plucked a package from my backpack. Foxy covered her eyes and I saw her move a finger to try to peek.

"No cheating." I laughed and she soon covered her eyes again. I ripped off the plastic and removed a grey Lynbrook football sweatshirt with the number 17 embroidered in the middle. Every member of the team purchased one and I did so with the sole purposes of gifting mine to her.

"Open them..."

"You can add this to your hoodie collection, you are a part of the team..."

Samantha smiled, clutching the sweatshirt. "Should I fetch you a cheerleader vest then? It might like pretty good on you..." She snorted as she let out a laugh.

"As you know, our team breakfast is next week. I wanted to know if you would be my guest? You are a very important person to me and I want to share this with you, I was hoping you'd say yes."

Her blue eyes became glassy and her lips shriveled. "I'd be honored."

"Thank you..." I approached her and she hugged me with a tight grip. I held her and brushed the back of her hair. "I got a couple of other things for you too..."

"What?" She pressed her hands to her chest, overwhelmed by the events unfolding. I reached in to my pockets and placed two tickets in her hand. "I know it's not Paris but it's a start. And since Les Misérables is one of your favorite books, right after Thanksgiving we'll head into the City and watch it, we can make a day out of it."

"Oh, my Lord." Samantha held back a tear. "You didn't do have to do all this."

"I wanted to." I rubbed her back. "You've been through a lot lately and I wanted to do something nice for you. You deserve it."

"Thank you." Samantha smiled and pressed her lips against my cheek. "It's a date." Foxy looked away. "Sarah is a lucky girl..." Her southern twang really came through. "Melissa is a bloody fool..." The Irish accent blended in behind her smile.

"Sam don't let Ricky ever make you feel like you were never second to anyone. You never were and you never will be. It's the worst mistake he ever made in his life, in my book..." I put my hands behind my back. "You'd make someone really happy one day."

Her eyes locked onto mine, something unspoken passing between us. The words I'd meant to offer as comfort felt like they had shifted into something deeper, something more, piercing the both of us. Maybe, we were supposed to make each other happy? I couldn't figure out the mysterious reasons why it hurt so much for it to not be the case. Foxy was the one person who had to be there, I couldn't imagine it any different. In a matter of months, Samantha became closer to me more than anyone.

"One more thing..." I made me way over to the stereo and powered it on. Jimmy Eat World's *Work* began to play.

"Another one of my favorite bands." She smiled, her eyes shining in the glow of the streetlights. In that moment, it felt like the whole world had narrowed to just the two of us.

I walked over and extended my hand. "Can I have this dance?" I said in a formal tone to be playful.

"Well, sir, you must." She curtsied with a smile. I placed my hands around her waist and as she placed her hands around my back. We slow danced on the basketball court as the music played. I fixed my sight on the blue of her eyes and the kindness that radiated from them. We swayed to the music, the faint glow of the streetlights framing us as the world around us faded. Her head rested on my chest, and for a moment, everything felt right.

"Thank you, Corey." Foxy spoke softly.

"No, Samantha..." I whispered, brushing her hair gently. "Thank you."

Chapter 14 – The Spawning of Progressions

Days flew by and I still didn't tell Mike about what happened in Rockville Centre with Truck. I didn't want to. I had been praying for The Lord to continue to guide him and grow him, and I didn't want to play a role in somehow throwing him off course, even if that was actually bigger than myself. Given the fact Sarah and I were sneaking around within Truck's good graces, I didn't see any use in saying anything. Melissa remained a phantom. She was an entity that was the most prominent in every thought I held yet she was vacant to the naked eye. The opposite was the case with Sarah. Sarah was fun, she was sexy, and she actually had an interest in me.

We finished our Friday practice, excited and clapping in chorus together. Coach made his way in to the center of the circle we formed. Although we were 1-3 coming off a crushing defeat, we maintained an air of confidence and were extraordinarily exuberant. Coach raised his hand. The team quieted.

"Okay guys, tomorrow is a big game. Tomorrow we host Wantagh. As you know, they haven't lost a game yet. They're going to be coming in here tomorrow flying high." Coached flicked his clipboard and waved his finger high. "But let remind you men that every game starts with both sides tied at zero." He smacked his hand. "And anytime you ever feel you don't have a shot heading into something, remember that. Whatever it may be..."

All eyes were glued to coach, his words sent ripples through our hearts. "That right there shows you that we all have a chance to make something out of nothing if we are willing and able, it comes down to us. I don't care what records say or what the final tally says either."

The team clapped and roared until coach raised his clipboard, any rapture soon brought to a silent hush.

"On to some formal orders of business, tomorrow is our team breakfast, bring your mother, your father, sister, brother, pet dog, whatever you want."

Rumbles of laughter swept through the huddle.

"...warm-ups will be at the usual 12:00 PM time. Game at 2:00 PM." Coached twirled his hands. "...finally, as you boys remember, I told you that after four games we would elect two additional captains. Without any further ado, your first captain, Willie Jean-Baptiste." Coach paused so the team can applaud. Willie entered the center, receiving high-fives and pats on the back. He smiled, shaking Coach's hand.

"Congratulations, Stick Em. Your effort and enthusiasm have been influential." Coach glanced at his clipboard before continuing. "And your second captain... Corey Montgomery."

I froze, my body stiffening. My name. My heart skipped.

The fact it was real was confirmed when my teammates began clapping, followed by a series of slaps on the pads and helmet rubs. It was surreal. I slowly made my way to the center, unsure if I was walking into a prank.

"Congratulations, Gingy." Coach looked me dead in the eye as he shook my hand firmly. "You earned this."

"Thanks..." I murmured, overwhelmed

Even after receiving practice ended and I sat on a picnic bench waiting for Sam to get out of cheerleading practice, my mind was swirling. From benchwarmer to captain in the blink of an eye. It didn't feel real; it was something only God could do in such a way. I'd always wondered why nice guys finish last, but I realized something: champions are the last ones standing. They endure the heartache, the struggle, the pain—and they come out on top.

My head was clasped in my heads until I heard her voice.

"You asleep, sugar? Foxy smirked, wearing her cheerleading uniform with no green sleeves beneath her white, gold, and green vest top or any white leggings below her forest green skirt.

I looked up at Foxy with a beaming smile, excited to tell her the news but more she was there.

"Can I have your bookbag?"

Foxy smiled and handed it to me. "Such a gentleman..."

"But still full of surprises..."

We exchanged a half-smile as I swung the pink Jansport around my shoulder and we started our walk which always began with simple exchanges of how each other's practice went. But I sat on the news for a while, it was only when we made our way through the quiet residential streets of North Lynbrook that the opportunity to share the news had presented itself perfectly.

"So, what was that ruckus all about at the end of your practice today?" Foxy glanced up at the dangling branches of an oak tree that hung over the street.

"You may not believe me, if I told you..."

"Try me."

"Somehow, I got voted captain."

"Praise The Lord, that's amazing." She embraced me as her eyes sparkled in the sun which hung low. "Congratulations, Corey. I knew you had it in you, when I saw that catch you made on the first day that I met you, I said man that boy can play."

"You were actually paying attention?"

"Why wouldn't I?"

"Well, you know..." I smirked and she knew I was making a reference to her and Ricky.

"Oh, whatever...." She shook her head with a grin. "That's yesterday's news."

"Well we wouldn't be here had it not been for all that..."

"Too right." Foxy flicked her hair. "So what time is the breakfast tomorrow?"

"9:30, so I guess we best be on our way at nine."

"Sure thing."

"Yea, just watch out for my brother." I rolled my eyes. "He's a troublemaker."

"Oh, Mikey?" Foxy waved her hand. "I'm not worried about him. I think he likes me."

"He does." I gently grabbed her wrist. "He tells me all the time that you are a lovely girl."

Foxy smiled. "That's awfully kind of him." She threw her hair back. "Speaking of which, did you ever tell him about..." She arched her eyebrows meaningfully.

"I'll just let that blow over, this whole thing with Sarah may run its course and there is no need to cause any drama."

Samantha's eyes moved side-to-side, deep in thought. "What if it doesn't?"

Her question hung in the air longer than I liked. What if it doesn't? I didn't have an answer—not one I wanted to admit, anyway. The thought tugged at something deep in me, but I wasn't ready to face it—not yet. I forced a smile, hoping it would be enough to mask the doubt.

"Sam, it'll be fine." I insisted, maybe more to convince myself than her. "Besides, he's turned a corner recently, there is no reason for him to look back..."

"And Melissa?"

"If she ever comes around, I'll cross the bridge if I get to it." I shrugged my shoulders. "The thing with Sarah may be over by then..."

She tilted her head, studying me.

"Mike always told me to take things in stride and not get ahead of myself. That's what I am trying to do here..."

"Very well..." She nodded. "You know I never understood the trouble, people had with him. I think they should to get know him better..."

Her words, so simple yet so insightful, caught me off guard. They were philosophical in a way only Samantha could deliver—softly, without pretension, yet undeniably wise.

"That's what I love about you Sammie, you give everyone a chance."

"Perhaps, a couple with you?" She stuck her tongue out playfully.

"Especially me." I made a funny face back at her.

"But that's what happens when you root for teams like Miami." Foxy pushed me jokingly.

"I think I like Tennessee more at this point..." I smirked at Foxy, and we shared a moment smiling at each other. "Plus, we all can't have a cool and clever nickname with this really awesome backstory behind it." I teased, nudging her.

"That much is true." She paused and pressed her finger to her lip, as she looked up. "Mike is Ghost, and what are you?" Samantha squinted. "Pumpkinhead?" She tee-heed and I picked her up, she squealed as I started running around with her. In the midst of frolicking, we soon arrived in front of her home.

"I'm really glad you're coming with me tomorrow..." I set the bookbag on the bench propped against the side of her house.

"I am honored at the invitation, Pumpkinhead." She winked. "I mean Gingy..." She placed her hand over her mouth with a grin.

"Try not to stay up late and watch too much football." I slipped my arms around her and gave her a hug goodbye.

"Well there is a good one on tonight: Utah and BYU. You know they both hate each other since it's the Holy War." Foxy beamed with enthusiasm. "Hard nose defense versus an efficient spread offense. The problem is slip screens are like Novocain, give it time and they always work."

"You would know better than anyone." I chuckled. "I swear I learn more about football when we watch a game together than I have anyone else..."

"Well if you are up for it, we can watch the game maybe and I can fix you some supper..." She shrugged her shoulders. "Nana is out of town, so looks like it's the tried and true pasta and sauce..." She saluted playfully.

"I would love that." I grabbed her backpack off the bench and held the first door for her as she jingled the keys and placed it into the lock, following her into the house.

As the evening continued on, Foxy made some sweet tea, her mother's recipe and I helped her in making said sauce. We sat in the living room and watched the Utah vs. BYU game, though our conversations dominated our time and we didn't really watch the game. Whenever our eyes wandered to the television, Foxy was literally calling plays from the base of her couch. Samantha's eyes lit up as she studied each snap of the football. Her enthusiasm was contagious, and it made the hours fly by in a blur.

"Sadly, it's time for me to go." I rose to my feet. "Thank you for having me."

"My pleasure." Samantha smiled as she followed me to the door to let me out.

"Before I leave you, there is something I wanted to give you." I reached into the backpack and removed the white A&P bag which carried my away jersey, white with 17, and Lynbrook spelt in Hunter Green. Gold accented and outlined the darker toned 17. When I removed the bag and showed Samantha the jersey, her eyes widened with surprise.

"It's customary for your guest of honor to wear your jersey at the Team Breakfast." I placed the jersey in her hands. She traced the 17 with her nail, visibly amazed by the gesture I bestowed upon her.

"Thank you, Corey..." She hugged me. "But I can't take this."

"You must..." I smiled at her. "I only need it back when we have an away game, if you don't mind..."

She hesitated by slipped the jersey over her white tank-top and grey sweatpants, comfortably draping over her. "How is it fit?"

"Perfect." I stepped out into the night air and saw my breath escape toward the moonlight. Sam followed me outside as I held the door for her.

"You best sign it for me then..." She grazed the bridge of my nose with the tip of her finger and our eyes met for a moment. I didn't know if it was the jersey or something else, but there was an electricity in the air. I felt it in the way she smiled, in the way her fingers brushed against mine. But I didn't say anything; I just smiled back.

There was a weird tension in the air, one that I cannot put my finger on as to what it was or where it was coming from but it was there and we drew closer. My eyes focused on Samantha's lips as my hand reached toward hers and she clutched mine.

"I'll see you tomorrow." I said softly.

She nodded, and I could feel her hand slip from mine as she returned inside. The door closed behind her, and as I walked back into the cool night, my fingers trembled, my heart racing. Tomorrow couldn't come fast enough. I wanted to be around Samantha again—her presence calmed me like nothing else.

Chapter 15 – Work and Pain

"Corey! Let's go we don't want to be late to pick up your girlfriend." Mike yelled up the stairs to me.

"Coming dude." I sprinted down the hall to Mike who stood by the doorway twirling the keys to our Saturn in his hands. He briefly paused to look at my jersey and smiled.

"Nice number." Mike looked down at the ground, clearly humbled by what he saw.

"I wouldn't wear anything else..."

He looked back up at me. "Thanks a lot, little brother that means a lot to me."

Mike adjusted his blue tie at his collar, the white shirt was neatly pressed and tucked into khakis. He had put a lot of effort into how he looked for the occasion: no fitted today, just sporting his crew cut and chin strap that he always did.

"You're my big brother, I love you and I look up to you."

He smiled and extended his hand to me, our hands clapped as he met as he pulled me in for a hug.

"I am honored..." Mike released the hug. "Now let's go pick up ya girl." He smiled.

"She's not my girl..." I sighed.

"Not yet, she isn't." He spoke to back me and jingled the keys, making his way to the door. "Soon enough though..."

I rolled my eyes as I followed him to the Saturn, both of us hopped in.

"It's only a matter of time..." Mike rolled down the window and lit up a Marlboro and tossed me one as well. He pulled off from the curb and put *Dirt Off Your Shoulder* and in a handful of minutes we were at Samantha's house. She was already outside sitting on the bench upon the landing of the stoop. Samantha wore her hair down but she seemed to have ignored the fact I gave her my jersey; it was stuffed into her black cloth bag that she wore over her right shoulder. Instead, she wore a blue halter dress with pink polka-dots that hugged her figure marvelously. It was a classy and vintage and contoured perfectly to her curvy physique. It complemented her alabaster skin and auburn hair which dangled down over her ample cleavage. She had done her eyelashes and accented her piercing blue eyes with mascara. She placed a thin layer of red lipstick over her plump lips. She reminded me of a starlet from the Golden Age. She looked absolutely breathtaking.

I pressed my white shirt and the black tie beneath my football jersey, I was glad I could at least match her in formality.

"You really ought to get on that as soon as possible, dawg." Mike threw his cigarette in the street and wafted the smoke. "She looks stunning…"

I hopped out and opened the door for Foxy, my jaw was descended to the floor as she approached. My heart skipping a beat which each step she took.

"I am sorry if I didn't wear your jersey, I just wanted to look a bit more dolled up since I am your guest and you are being nominated captain." She hunched her shoulders. "I can put the jersey on if you'd like."

"Please don't…" I smiled and held open the door for her to enter. "You look amazing." She blushed, as she smiled gently, revealing some of the faint freckles beneath her eyes.

"Corey, go sit in the back with her." Mike looked back at me as she slipped into the backseat. I followed his imperative but he didn't need to advise me. There was a magnetism and a radiance about her that was overpowering.

"What's up Foxy?" Mike looked at her from the rear-view mirror.

"Hey Mike, you all right?" Foxy fastened her seat belt. "Thank you for picking me up."

"My pleasure." Mike put his foot the gas and pulled away from the curb. "Hopefully Corey will remind you but in case he doesn't..." He smirked at me from the rear-view mirror. "...you look great."

She subtly nodded and smiled. After we parked, Mike ran ahead to find our Mom who was volunteering across the street at the community center, leaving Foxy and I to walk on our own.

"You are going to steal the show today." I locked my arm with hers.

"Stop, Gingy. It's your day." She blushed.

"At least, you stopped calling me Pumpkinhead."

"For now." She rolled her eyes at me as we made our way toward the building. When we stepped into the gymnasium, we were met by a crowd of teammates escorted by parents, brothers, and girlfriends alike. I noticed Ricky and Christina over at one end talking to Willie. I also saw Coach Kenny with his wife speaking with some of the parents and players in another alcove.

"Come on." Mike put his arm on my shoulder and led us towards Ricky. An awkward encounter borne out of Mike's ignorance of the situation. Ricky was another brother to Mike, as Shawn was, all the stuff that was going on between us was irrelevant to him.

"Ricardito, what's up MVP?"

"What's up Mickey, how you been bro?" Ricky bantered.

"What going on with you and my brother? Mike drew us both in under his arms. "Are we going to start playing some NCAA again or what?"

Ricky stared me down with an ice-cold disposition. Christina and Foxy also glared at each other. The tension drowned out the muffled sounds from the numerous guests engaged in small talk and brief chit-chat.

"Anytime he wants to get his precious Gators beat, he knows where he can find me." I put my hand out to Rick.

"Fuck you, motherfucker." Ricky pulled me in for a hug. "I'm happy for you man." He patted me on the shoulder.

"We wouldn't be where we are with you." I returned the pleasantry.

"You see, this is what I like. The spirit of resolution." Mike joked but there was an obvious hint of sincerity in it.

"You came with Foxy?" Ricky's eyes shot over at Samantha; it was as if he was seeing her in a new light.

I nodded. "I don't mean any trouble by that..."

"Fuck it man..." He waved his hands. "She never looked that good for me when we were together..." Ricky raised his eyebrows. As I turned to respond, I saw Coach making his way past some of the other guests and greeting all.

"Coach." I raised his attention as he had a spare second.

"Corey, what's up my friend?" Coach extended his hand and I shook it.

"Coach, there are some people I'd like you to meet."

He smiled at Mike and Foxy, adjusting his black suit jacket before holding his green tie against his starch white shirt.

"Coach, this is my brother Mike."

"Wonderful to meet you, Mike." Coach extended his hand to my brother.

"The pleasure is all mine, Coach." He took it firmly. "It looks like you are turning things around..."

"We're trying..." He glanced back at a woman who sat at the table, wearing a floral-print dress with long blonde hair descending downward against her shiny toned skin. The woman held a child on her lap, a boy shaped like a ball with pudgy cheeks, curious blue eyes, and short faint hairs of blonde.

"Is that your wife, Coach?"

He smiled and nodded. "And my son..." He turned back to me. "I'll introduce you to them." He glanced at Samantha.

"This is Samantha..." I put my hand around her back and extended an arm forward.

"Lovely to meet you, Samantha. You are Corey's girlfriend?" Coach looked back at me with a smirk. The question inadvertently put me at unease because I didn't know how to answer it, given how Foxy was blushing, I felt there was no right way to answer it.

"Corey and I are very good friends..." Samantha extended her hand with a chuckle, giving me a side-eye.

"I see..." He peered at Mike, who responded to Coach's query with an eye-roll.

"If my name was Melissa however, it might be a different story." She shot a wry smile at me, faltering for a moment, before it returned. "She'll be at the game today, by the way..."

"Really?" My voice pepped up at the mention of it.

"Yea, I had a word with her..." She glowered. "...you best show out..." Foxy smirked.

"It's good to know Corey has such wonderful people beside him. It's nice to meet you both." He bowed slightly. "If you'll excuse me..."

"Coach..." Mike extended his hand forward to stop him. "I just want to thank you for giving my brother a chance. He really goes hard with the football and I am really happy that he is finally doing his thing out there."

"There is no need to thank me." Coach said firm. "Your brother is a pleasure to have and he works really hard. It's no wonder he was voted captain."

"You're captain?" Mike opened his arms.

"Yeah." I said softly.

"When did you plan to tell me?"

"I don't know." I murmured. "...it's not that big a deal..."

"Why didn't' you tell your brother, Pumpkinhead?" Samantha arched her lip. "He's hopeless, isn't he?" Foxy teased, her eyes sparkling in the direction of Mike.

Mike laughed at her antics as he placed his hand on my shoulder. "That's the style, little brother."

I put my hand around his back, as he ruffled my shoulder. He didn't need to say anything else; his joy could not be contained as he looked near choked up at the course of events.

• • • •

THE BREAKFAST COMMENCED and we helped ourselves to a buffet of breakfast foods, ranging from French Toast and eggs to biscuits and hash browns. We ate heartily and laughed merrily enjoying our meal. My mother joined us and mentioned how beautiful Samantha was; both of us were bashful as a result. Foxy sat between my mother and I; Mike sat next to me. My mother sat next to Ricky who was joined by Christina.

Coach walked across a stage set up in the middle of the gym and rested his both hands on an oaken podium: the Lynbrook Union emblem fixed to the center in gold. "I want to thank you all for joining us today and would like to take a moment to pay homage to the players. Our job as coaches is to train, teach, and mentor but..." He smiled. "...I learn so much from them and I want to thank all of our guys for what they do on the field and off." Coach paused so those in attendance can applaud. "We are going to name each member of our team and give you all a chance to give them the recognition they deserve. Every member of our team is important, everyone on this squad contributes." He gripped the podium firm. "When one thinks about a captain, many assume that the best players take on that role because being a superstar is not a prerequisite..." He paused again. "That's not how we do things here...On this football team, to be voted a captain, you must be elected by your teammates and coaches, it's a family decision." Coach looked around the crowd. "All four were selected by their peers. Two at the beginning of the season and two mid-way through, that way those who really step up can lead us when it matters most." He gathered his words. "We would like to take a moment to recognize them. First, Brendan Adams. Brendan was our starting quarterback until the second game of the season when he suffered a season-ending injury. We appreciate Brendan and his dedication to this team despite the tragic setback he has encountered." Coach paused to allow Brendan who stood with a casted leg to receive recognition.

"Second, our running back Ricardo "Ricky" Moreno. I can't begin to tell you the talent this kid possesses. He is an explosive player and he has put together a very impressive resume in his three years as a varsity half-back. But Ricky has never been about himself, he is the definition of team player." Coach led another chorus of cheer and clapping.

"Our last two captains as mentioned were elected at the midway point of the season. They were both announced yesterday after our practice. The first is William Jean-Baptiste, one of our starting defensive backs. Throughout the season he worked with upcoming receivers after practice to help them adjust to coverages they might face in game situations. Willie's enthusiasm and energy is contagious and his raw emotion inspires many." Coach paused again so all in attendance could recognize Willie Jean-Baptiste.

"Finally, there is so much I can say about our final elected captain Corey Montgomery." I suddenly felt an arm get placed around me. My brother smiled at me proud and my mother was misty-eyed. Samantha placed her hand under the table and held my hand, glancing over at me with a smile of pride and excitement.

"For those of you who don't know Corey, he's been playing football with us for four years. This is my first year as head coach of the Lynbrook Owls but from what I've understood Corey for most of his career did not see much playing time. This was never indicative of the talent that Corey possesses. He is elusive and he could be the fastest player on our team. Thus, we call him *Gingy* which is short for the Gingerbread Man because you can run as fast as you can, but you can't catch Corey cause...you all know the rest." The audience laughed and Mike slapped the table in full cackle.

"Gingy" Sam gaffed, as she leaned back in her seat.

"His compassion and kindness are what is most demonstrable. He is loved by his teammates for his dedication and spirit. He too is the definition of team player." Coach smiled at me and stepped away from the podium, the gymnasium roared with cheer. I did not know how to react or what to say. I just smiled and nodded my head in appreciation of the words that I wish were true.

This was especially true when we finally took the field. Maybe it was the food coma, or maybe the moment was just too big for us, but nothing went as planned. Within minutes, we were down 14-0, and it only got worse from there. Our offense stalled, our defense crumbled, and Wantagh looked every bit like the undefeated powerhouse they were.

Melissa showed up, just as Foxy said she would, but her attention was glued to her phone. I'd been excited to see her, hoping maybe this was my chance to prove something, but her disinterest cut deeper than I wanted to admit. Not that I could blame her. We looked lost, listless, like we didn't belong on the same field.

By halftime, the score was the least of our worries. The real question wasn't whether we could beat Wantagh—it was whether we could even get out of our own way. The locker room was heavy with silence as we trudged inside, heads down and hearts sinking. No one dared to speak.

Then Coach walked in, his eyes scanned the room. We needed something, anything, to pull us out of this. And judging by the fire in his eyes, he was about to give us exactly that.

"When I was twenty-two, I met this woman. She was gorgeous—drop-dead stunning. The kind of woman who could make a man forget his name just by walking into a room. I was at the firehouse, exhausted from training all morning, looking and feeling like hell. I knew I wasn't in any shape to win her over."

Thinking about the entire saga with Melissa, the analogy seemed to speak to me in more ways than one.

"Turns out, she was part of the medical company, and I didn't think I'd ever see her again. Worse, a friend told me she had a boyfriend. I was crushed. Most people would have called it quits right there. 'Plenty of fish in the sea,' they'd say. But something in me couldn't let it go. I didn't know much about her, but my heart knew what it wanted."

Coach paused, glancing around the room. "Here's the thing. Sometimes, we get so wrapped up in what looks impossible, we forget to fight for what matters. I could've walked away, but I decided to find out the truth for myself. And you know what? My friend was wrong. She didn't have a boyfriend. That moment taught me something: never make assumptions about what you can or can't have until you've put in the effort."

Coach's voice grew louder, more impassioned. "That's the thing, I knew there was something special about her, and I wasn't going to quit just because it got hard."

I was supposed to be focused on the football game, but I was thinking about Melissa sitting on a cold iron bleacher with her hood up over her head. That was what I wanted.

"Great things never come easy, gentlemen. Whether it's love, football, or life, you're going to face obstacles. You're going to suffer, doubt yourself, and question whether it's worth it. That's where hope comes in. Hope isn't some magical solution—it's a decision. It's choosing to believe there's light ahead, even when all you can see is darkness. It's clawing and scratching your way toward the things that matter most, no matter how many times you get knocked down."

He slammed his hand on the bench, the sound echoing through the locker room. "So, tell me men—are you ready to show them what hope looks like?"

"Yes, Coach!" The team's voices rang out.

As the team cheered, I raised my hand. "Coach, what happened to the girl?"

The guys chuckled at the timing, but Coach didn't miss a beat. "She's my wife," he said simply, his grin wide. "She was at the breakfast today...."

The room fell silent, the weight of his words sinking in.

"And that's my point, gentlemen—stick around long enough, fight hard enough, and you'll give yourself the chance to win."

We stormed onto the field like a different team. Every tackle, every block, every yard felt like a battle won. When I caught a pass and sprinted into the end zone for the game-tying touchdown, the roar of the crowd sent chills through me. For the first time all season, I felt unstoppable.

We rallied back and handed Wantagh its first loss of the season. It was more than a victory—it was a statement. And as the celebration unfolded around me, Coach's story lingered in my mind. If he could fight through rejection and doubt to win over his wife, why couldn't I? Maybe Melissa wasn't pushing me away because she didn't care—maybe she was running because she didn't know how to deal with the idea of us. I needed to let go of Sarah, I needed to be like Coach and be brave enough to run after Melissa.

Chapter 16 – Wash Out

It was a rain-filled Wednesday. Practice had been canceled and my plan was to head to Rockville Centre and surprise Sarah. I kept thinking about Coach's speech and thought maybe it was only for a football game, after all. As I passed the White Castle, approaching the train station steps, my phone rang. I looked down and saw it was Melissa. It couldn't be...

"Hello?" I answered with a bit of hesitation and disbelief.

"Hi Corey." Melissa replied.

It felt surreal hearing her voice again. After all this time, all the wondering, all the doubt—it was her.

"How are you feeling?" I put my hand to my ear, attempting to drown out the sound of rain drops splashing against the asphalt.

"Better, thank you for asking...you were something else on Saturday..." I could hear her smile break through the phone and my chest tightened. She sounded happy, was this it? Was this the moment everything turned around?

"Thanks..." I stepped away from the steps and headed towards the trestle.

"I am glad that Foxy invited me to come because I was thinking..."

My heart pounded, each word from her lips feeling like it was pulling me toward something I'd been waiting for. Like Coach's words had somehow come to life, whispered into existence just for this moment.

"Is there any way you can come by and we can speak?"

I pumped my fist and paced forward, taking a breath to regain my composure. I couldn't stop smiling, but a small voice in the back of my mind whispered: what if this wasn't what I thought it was? I pushed it aside and focused on the road ahead.

"Fox is supposed to come by when she is done and she has the car, maybe you can go back with her."

"Sounds great..." I stepped under the trestle, finding refuge in the hulking grey columns that were dry and out of the reach of the rain. The smell of urine and alcohol ripe in the air despite the steady rain. "...I am on my way..."

"Great, I'll see you soon."

"I'll see you soon..." I muttered the words nervously as I sped onward to Melissa's house. The rain felt relentless, slapping against my face and soaking through my jacket. The wind cut through me like a knife, but I kept going. Each step felt heavier than the last, but the thought of Melissa—of what this might mean—pushed me forward.

After minutes of trekking through the rain, I finally stood outside her home, a small Cape Cod-style house, white with brown paneling positioned next to bustling evergreen tree. There was no fence that lined the perimeter of the lawn and backyard that formed an L, since it was a corner property. The light was on in the front left window with a white curtain drawn glowing in the window. The front door was a white swinging screen door with a black horse-drawn horse ornament melded into the panel. A black mailbox hung on the linoleum sealed shut and protecting the letters and memoranda from the torrent. I made my way over the granite walkway and saw a broken-down Oldsmobile rusticated and abandoned sitting in the driveway, as if it had been sitting there for years. Behind it, a large patch of overgrown grass before a brown picket fence stood erect behind it.

The door opened as I made my way up the steps and there stood Melissa. Her hair was up today and under a scrunchie, wearing a grey sweatshirt with the words Penn State written on the front in navy blue with white piping.

"Hey..." She opened the door and I followed her in. "Come in, take your shoes off..." She shut the door behind me as I plucked at the soaked wet black laces of my sneakers, immersing myself in the distraction of undoing my shoelaces to escape where I actually was. I was in a place, I never thought I'd be, nervous beyond comprehension.

"I'll get us some green tea...." Mel scampered off into a shadowy dining room which led to a brighter kitchen behind it. I took off my coat and put it on an open brass hook that lined the wall next to the door, I threw myself down on the plush grey couch as Melissa came in with two mugs of tea, her navy sweatpants swaying with each step as she handed me a plaid-colored mug, warm to the touch.

"Thank you!"

"You are welcome." She did before she folded up on the couch beside me. "So, listen, I owe you an apology..."

I sipped on my tea and studied the green of her eyes as she initiated.

"I made a mistake and I am sorry; I didn't know how to react to someone like you." She sipped. "It's a weak excuse but my ex-boyfriend said the same stuff you did, and all he was trying to do was get in my pants."

"I understand..." I sipped. "That's always the issue, when someone is actually sincere, they get tarred and feathered because some guy before him pulled the same antics for all the wrong reasons..."

"But I think you are really nice guy and we deserve to give this a chance...."

I elated though I tried to keep my emotion to myself, I was nonetheless star-struck and a nervous energy had overtaken me.

"Really?" That's all I could say given how star-struck I was.

She nodded.

"You are not messing with me, are you?" A smile broke to my face. "Because if you aren't, I am all yours."

"I am serious..." Melissa put her mug down on the mahogany table beside her on a white lace coaster. "Foxy had a lot to do with this, you know..." She laughed. "...she wouldn't leave me alone until I came to my senses and if you'll have me...."

"Have you?" I interrupted her and took her hand. "Melissa, I'd never want to let you go."

She beckoned me to lean toward her, I followed and placed my mug down on the coffee table in front of me and reached across the couch to kiss her. The kiss turned into a heavy make-out session that lasted nearly an hour, when it was interrupted by a knock at the door.

Melissa grunted and looked up at the ceiling for a moment, as she skipped off the couch and made her way to the door. When she opened it, Foxy stood outside, her black hooded coat far drier, her hair escaping downward from below an orange beanie with a white fluffy ball at the dome.

She waved at me and I waved back vigorously. The nervousness that I feel dissipated when she walked through the door, the house felt more like a home.

"Well, I am glad you two have straightened things out finally." Foxy took off her coat and put it over mine, joining me on the sofa. "Dukes, I take it you've made up then?" She reclined backward and stretched her legs out on the coffee table, her dark blue skirt dry and free of wrinkles.

"We were about to until you arrived." Melissa jabbed playfully, as she went back to the kitchen.

"Sorry for that..." Foxy smiled at me, but there was a sadness in her eyes that could not be hidden. It was as if she was putting on a brave face to lend support while something else was brewing beneath. As elated as I once felt, I was empty again, my heart was with Samantha and the desire to know what she was hiding.

"Is everything alright, Sam?"

"Yes, Gingy, I am as happy as a pig in mud..."

"What a weirdo..." I chortled.

"Bless your heart." She stuck her tongue at me and I laughed some more. Melissa joined us once again and handed Foxy a mug of tea, before sat beside me.

"Do you want to go make up?" She pulled me in to her bust and kissed the top of my head. I looked at her with excitement upon her recommendation.

"Sure." I kissed her chest.

"Mmm..." She moaned. "...that feels nice." Melissa sat up and handed Samantha the remote control. "The television yours, my bestest of friends." She took my hand and led me to the steps. "My man and I are going to go have a quick nap."

"Play nice, you two." Samantha started to flip channels, sat up, with her mug in hand. Melissa and I went to her room and made love for over an hour. We tired ourselves out and passed out in the bed together. When we awoke, Foxy was lying in the bed with us, cuddling with Melissa: the two looking like siblings huddled together for warmth and protection.

Samantha soon sat up and yawned, Melissa squinted her eyes as she pressed her palms to the bed and lifted her head. "I am worn slap out..."

"What on Earth, does that mean?" Melissa sat up slightly, the intrigue in the use of the term filling her with a second wind.

"I am knackered..." Foxy rubbed the side of her face.

Melissa playfully tapped Samantha's leg.

"I am tired...."

"Why don't you just say it like that?" Melissa teased.

"Shut up, Dukes..." She poked Melissa in the chest.

"Ow!" She smacked Foxy back in the arm, not hard.

"Hey!" Samantha whined. "I am going to go." She leaned down and embraced Melissa tightly, the two sharing a tender moment together. "Do you need a lift?" She asked me, I glanced over at Melissa and she signaled me to go ahead.

"I'll call you later?"

Melissa smiled, I planted a kiss on her once more and followed Foxy down the steps, grabbing our coats as we went out to the car. I hopped in to the front seat and placed on my seat belt, the cloth was frigid and cold, the glass had fogged up. She turned over the car and put on the heat to clear the windshield and warm it up.

"So, I've been wanting to know how it feels?" Foxy flicked on the windshield wipers to clear the glass, the vents roared as the fog started to dissipate.

"How does what feel?"

"To have Melissa, finally..." Foxy switched on her turn signal and pulled away from the curb, the car revving as it made it accelerated.

"Amazing..." I sat back.

"Do try to be more enthusiastic..." She bantered, and I remained numbed nearly, still in shock that what happened earlier actually transpired.

"I reckoned you would be considering you gave me that whole shpeal about what your coach said." She slowed down and came to an intersection, her long auburn hair swung left and right with each movement even though she had it in three pony tails. Her piercing sapphire blue eyes thoroughly studying the road. "Whatever happened to Sarah?"

I didn't answer at first, but as we reached the red light, the answer formed.

"I don't know to answer that, obviously our brothers hate each other and...."

Foxy raised her eyebrows before she turned on the radio which was hooked up to her iPod. *A Decade Under the Influence* by Taking Back Sunday surrounded us softly in the background.

"Good tune from a local band..." She looked up at the light, and hummed the chorus, turning down the defogger as we waited for the light to turn. "The lyrics are spot on..."

I have a bad feeling

"... you can't expect to be with Dukes and then have Sarah nibbling on the other end of the string..."

"But what about what Truck said?" I watched stared into the red light.

"Maybe you will learn something from this..."

I squinted at Foxy, who looked irritated, her eyes had enlarged with an anger hiding behind her darkened eyes. "...concerning impulse control..."

"What is that supposed to mean?" The intonation of my voice grew a little defensive.

"I love you to bits Corey but think about it for a moment. Christina, Dukes, Sarah, Dukes, you are like a bloody ping-pong ball." She shook her head modestly. "Bouncing all over the dang place."

I sighed but couldn't help but crack a smile at her remarks. "You are right."

Foxy smiled back at me.

"I'll make appearances less frequently, maybe she'll just break it off and move on, at least it won't provoke him..."

"And how long will that take?" The light turned green and Sam pressed the gas. "Dude, if I am truthful with you, I wouldn't go for that. I wouldn't want there to be someone else, if we were together..."

Samantha and I shared a brief gaze at each other, the car went silent. Foxy appeared haunted and pre-occupied, her eyes started to water.

"What's on your mind?"

Foxy shook her head. "I just want you guys to be happy..."

"Are you happy?" I put my hand over hers, patting it with an almost brotherly-like affection.

Foxy paused as she came to a stop at the light on Sunrise Highway. Samantha nodded but didn't say anything, sorrow filled the car from behind her glassy eyes, my heart broke at the sight of it.

"Samantha?"

"Don't mind me..." She broke a smile.

"Please..." I placed my hand over hers, but she raised it gently in response.

"It's fine..." She swung her head, her hair following her in a streak of dark auburn. "Just be careful with this situation, it sounds dangerous..."

"He's probably bluffing." I said, trying to convince myself as I reclined. But the memory of his threats lingered, a shadow I couldn't quite shake. "I shouldn't be afraid of this fucking idiot, he's the one that got my brother sent away over nothing." My teeth nipped into my lips. "I am just trying to keep the peace but it's no good for either of us, if we are going through the motions."

"Whoever you want to be with, commit to them and stick with it." Samantha made a left onto Route 27 (Sunrise Highway) and carried on down the middle lane. "Don't second guess it."

"With Melissa, it was always been her. She just never stuck around long enough for me to be able to settle in."

"You ever think maybe that none of them are right for you?" Foxy muttered.

I gave Samantha a side-eye. "Including, Mel?"

"Maybe..." Samantha sighed...

The car came to a halt as she stopped at the intersection over Horton Avenue, I looked beyond the elevated train and imagined Greis Park behind it, where Samantha and I first met. What if she was right? It was strange because though I enjoyed their company and found all of them attractive, I didn't feel like I could be candid and open with them like I was Samantha. I thought of that as a sign but I know I overthink things. Maybe, it's because Sam and I were such good friends and went through things together while these other girls were idealized in an overture of romantic cadences that left all that heard it, desperate for more. Was that how it was supposed to be?

"I wish they were more like you..." "The words slipped out before I could stop them, and for a moment, the air between us felt heavier.

Samantha and I gazed at each other again, our faces grew closer toward each other before "Thanks..." She looked down and laughed it off, her cheeks flushed, and I wondered if I'd said too much—or not enough.

Much wasn't said for the rest of the ride, but Samantha's words lingered in my mind. As the streetlights blurred past, I resolved to end things with Sarah. It wasn't fair to her, and it wasn't fair to me. Still, a part of me wondered if I was underestimating Truck. He was volatile, sure, but would he really start a gang war over something so trivial? Sarah might not even tell him or better yet, she may be in agreement with me and be amiable.

I glanced at Samantha; her profile illuminated by the glow of the dashboard. Her face betrayed no emotion, but her earlier words echoed: *"Be careful with this situation, it sounds dangerous."*

I had Melissa, I had Foxy, and I had football. I had to cut my ties with Rockville Centre like Mike did and move on. As the car slowed in front of my house, I made a silent promise to myself: whatever path lay ahead, I wouldn't drag Melissa—or Mike - or Samantha—into the crossfire.

"Empty Apartment" by Yellowcard came on the radio, Samantha turned the volume up and started to sing the lyrics. As the music filled the car, I leaned up against the door panel stealing looks of

Samantha. Tears were now trickling down her cheeks but she wouldn't look over at me. Melissa was the dream I'd built up in my head for years—the girl who was always just out of reach. But now that I had her, why did it feel like something was still missing?

I glanced out the window as the homes and streets passed by, the lyrics from the song piercing my soul as the crescendo of the song started to play. My eyes watered, my lips started to shake. Someday...some point in the future. Foxy and I would be sitting in a room somewhere perhaps a long way from here listening to this very song, singing that it's okay. Indeed, it's finally okay and we could look back at this moment and remember what it was like when we were younger and it was still all in front of us. I elated at the notion of it but agonized at the idea of it not happening, just some girl I was close with from two decades ago, lost in the past somewhere. The tears escaped my tears at the thought of it, I twitched my head gently to see her once more to know she was there with me now, relieved that she was gripping the steering wheel tight with wet cheeks and glassy eyes. What if Sam was right?

What if what I always wanted was sitting next to me and I was too afraid to face it? I knew what she was to me and I knew what I should have done, but as is the case with anything magnificent in life, it never comes easy.

Only days later was I sitting back in that car with Samantha, recollecting that conversation. The street ahead was slicked with a wet shine from a passing shower, the skies were blue with few clouds visible. The leaves were starting to change color and the smell of Autumn was in the air.

"Let's get this over with." I reached for the car door handle; Sam glanced over at me with her grey mittens still wrapped around the steering wheel.

"Do you want me to come with you?"

"No, thank you." I smiled at Foxy as she flicked your hair around. "I appreciate it, but it's best you stay here."

"Very well, I will keep an eye out for you." Samantha nodded and turned off the ignition. "Come on back, when you done."

"Thanks, Foxy, you are the best." I opened the door and took a faint whiff of the Vanilla scent thick in the upholstery before I closed the door, adjusting my coat as I looked back at the old Chevy Corsica, Sam sat in as she waited. The blue body had faded elements on the rear of the car near to the bumper and black markings across the door, but it ran well for Samantha's grandma, so it stayed in operation.

As I turned toward the moss-gate entrance to Fireman's Field next to the high school, Sarah rose off the guardrail, happy to see me. She wore an ensemble similar to that of which she wore that Sunday afternoon when I came to Rockville Centre to visit her. However, this time she was wearing white leggings with white leather boots, complemented by a blue tank top which exposed some of her midriff. She tossed a cigarette she finished into the sewer caps and met me half way. Sarah had her hair down and dark sunglasses, which framed her face and inexplicably made her pink lips pop.

"If I was you, I wouldn't be wearing that around here." She looked at the green Lynbrook football jersey tucked under my baggy black duffle coat which was partly zipped.

"They beat us, I don't know why it is an issue."

"I guess I will have to protect you like I normally do." Sarah zipped up the coat fully. I tensed up, feeling a bit of nerves from the forthcoming conversation, I felt both nervous about the outcome and a guilt for how it may affect Sarah, but it had to be done and the sooner I did it, the better I'd feel.

"Sarah, I am really sorry but I need to come clean about some stuff..."

"Okay..." She went in for a kiss and I backed away.

"I am not sure you are going to want to do that after this..." I looked down and placed my hands in my pocket, Sarah's eyes already darkened as the anger was building before, I could say one word. Her volatility filled the air and I knew this was a journey into perilous waters but I reminded myself this could be far worse, if it continued on.

I prayed silently as Sarah took me by the hand and led me away from the vicinity around the high school. I didn't pray for my mistakes to be undone or for the consequences not to be severe, but rather find peace in knowing I was doing what was truthful, honest, and right, honoring Him.

We rounded the corner of Muirfield Road towards the dead end out of the line of sight of any on-lookers or security guards, where it was just the two of us. I glanced ahead to see that Foxy remained parked in front of one the houses that lined the street. Foxy kept her gaze upon me but tried to remain subtle as to give off any kind of notion that this was an ambush. Sarah and I were in a more remote location adjacent to the curb in between two Cape Cod style homes which at the moment appeared vacant.

"So, what is it?" Sarah flipped the top of her pack of Newports.

"May I have a smoke please?"

She nodded once and I took one out, then she opened her silver Zippo to light it for me.

"Thank you."

She drew the light to the tip of her cigarette, not even acknowledging my gesture of gratitude.

"Listen there is no easy way to say this, so I'll going to do the best I can."

"I already know where this going." She crossed her arms. "But go ahead...."

"Sarah, I like you; And the past few weeks have been awesome. I mean you are one of the hottest, most beautiful I have ever laid eyes on." I stuttered. "You are fun and your strength is impressive." She smiled, visibly appreciative of the remarks.

"But my heart has been conflicted for some time. Out of respect for you, I'm not going to lie to you and make up some story, I want to be honest."

"You're breaking up with me, aren't you?!" She raised her voice.

"Wait..." I grazed Sarah's wrist and she pulled away violently.

"I never said that..."

"What else could you mean?" Sarah interrogated.

"My heart belongs to someone else..." I took another drag and exhaled violently.

"So, you are breaking up with me!"

I looked up at her and didn't answer.

"Who is it?" She smacked my shoulder and I glanced down the street for a moment at Sam who was sat in the car reading a book.

"It doesn't matter..." My eyes glanced away toward the green lawn in front of a house beside us, the tips of the blades were sparkling in crystalline from the passing shower.

"No, actually it does." She smacked my shoulder again; her voice went louder. "You can't fuck me and not tell me who the fuck this person you are in love with is!" The volume of her voice was a dissonance that filled all of the street, I saw Foxy look up from the car and place her book down, alarmed to keep watch.

"Is that your best friend you were telling me about?" Sarah leaned into me. "Foxy, is her name, right?"

"No."

"That's who is it?" She stepped closer to me getting near to my face, her fist curled up. "And what am I, your fuck-toy to hold you over for the time being?"

"Sarah if I didn't like you so much, I wouldn't have even risked it going to Rockville Centre knowing what may happen..."

"Oh..." She condescended with a smugness. "So now, you're some fucking hero because you got on a bus and came to see me?" She laughed. "Afraid that my brother was going to jump you with his pussy ass friends?"

"I don't know what his problem is..." I wrinkled my eyebrows. "You or I have nothing to do with this..."

"I think you know the problem..." Sarah crossed her arms again. "Ask your brother or maybe now you can ask this mystery girl who I don't even know about. What is she like a superhero or something, she has to keep her identity revealed?"

"I am trying to make this right by you but I don't know how...." I tried to step aside and move away from her. However, Sarah wouldn't let me leave.

"So does Foxy jump building and fuck you better you also?" Her nose was near to mine, I could feel her breath blowing against my lips. "Cause maybe I should find out where she is at and go kick her ass myself!"

"You need to back off on that." It was the first time that I was stern with her but the threat made my blood boil. "She has nothing to do with this..."

"Oh, so it is her?" Sarah turned away and when she looked down the road, her eyes stopped at the car. "And you brought her?" The woman shook violently and curled her fist again. "That's ballsy...."

She took one step in the direction of Foxy and the car which was still a considerable distance away, I however wouldn't let her go any further.

"Will you stop, please?" I grabbed her arm to pull her back, what followed was a brief breeze and a smack against my face.

"So, you were fucking me this whole time so your loser ass brother can get back at Jimmy?"

I held my tongue, I could have responded in kind but I had to de-escalate, I had to be rational and reconciliatory. Forgive her, she doesn't know what she is saying and don't seek to one-up her. The Lord always directed such conduct and at that moment, I had a chance to apply His teachings here, to grow from this experience.

"If that's what you honestly think, then I was wrong about you." I tossed my cigarette toward the sewer. "I wish you all the best...."

"I guess bitch shit like this runs in the family." Sarah mocked me as I walked on but she seemed more infuriated that I wouldn't give her a response. I thought she wasn't like her brother, but then again, I didn't really know her. I thought she had more grace and class, but in that moment, she carried herself in the same antagonistic and provocative that her brother did, and it was abundantly clear that she wasn't much different than him, after all. The best way to react was to not give her any attention, as any attention would be better than none.

"I should waste that slut you came with, just like my brother will waste that soft mark of a brother of yours."

I had done well until she disrespected Sam and Mike in the same sentence; I admit, I snapped.

"Will you shut up already?"

"Why don't you make me?!" Sarah taunted.

I waved my hand and kept walking.

"Keep walking because you know I'll whoop your ass."

I continued to work onward toward the car as it turned over. Foxy put the window down and waved me in to the car. "Come on, let's go sweetheart."

"Did you forget what he said?"

Foxy looked ahead with concern on her face, that prompted me to turn back to look at Sarah who was charging forward. "Break my heart and he will break your face." Her steps became more paced and intense as she came closer. "That is after I get that bitch out the car."

"What did she say?" Foxy's eyes filled with shock.

"Take one step closer and I'll be sending you back to your brother in a package!" I pointed my finger at her and it caught Sarah off guard. I looked at Sam and said I am sorry on my lips quietly. "Don't fuck with me, there is a reason why my brother ran shit and not yours..." I stood in front of the car, glaring across at Sarah who seemed ready to fight but equally shocked that I would speak to her in such a way.

"I'll tell him you said that and I will also tell him this was all some plot to get at him. You just wait and see; he's going to wipe out you and your brother and the rest of those green wearing faggots!" She started to laugh maniacally - it was cliché villain style but maybe that was all an act. I honestly thought she was above that but the old saying goes the apple doesn't fall from the tree. In many ways, she was worse than her brother and it took away any remorse or regret in my decision. It was obvious that this woman was bad news.

"Fuck your brother!" I gave her the middle finger and made a brief sprint to the car. Sarah gave chase and I dove into the car and slammed the door shut. "Lock it!"

Sam pressed down on the lock button on the panel and reversed down the street as Sarah sprinted forward. "Is she for real?" Foxy looked back for oncoming cars and turned into a driveway. "Mini-Truck" came charging, forward her white leggings shimmering under the blight fall sunlight. As the car swung out and

Foxy completed the turn to head in the opposite direction, Sarah threw a punch at the car as it was my side that was protruding outward, fortunately her fist only hit air as the car had already moved from where it was.

"Does she want get run over?!" Foxy watched her pursue the car, screaming obscenities from the rear-view mirror.

"She's nuts." I looked back as she sprinted down the road, Foxy stopped at a four-way stop sign and rolled through continuing down the road at a speed that Sarah wouldn't be able to meet. When the car got some distance, I looked back and could see Sarah standing there with her hands on her hips, out of breath, shaking with anger as her fists were curled.

"I think you dodged a bullet there, kid." Foxy snorted as she held back a laugh.

"It's all a bunch of horsepoo." I waved my hand and knelt up against the side panel of the door.

"You've come a long way, Gingy." She turned on the signal and looked left before she turned right onto Long Beach Road to get along ways from where were. "You used to be unable to form sentences and now you have gals chasing after you, literally..."

The tension soon dissipated as I was utterly amused at Foxy's wit, we both shared a hearty laugh from that well-timed remark and soon after we arrived back in Lynbrook; the rest of the ride was rather anti-climactic, it was actually quite peaceful and I soon regressed back to a state of tranquility.

After Foxy dropped me off at home, I plopped down on the sofa in the living room, face first and drifted off to sleep for twenty minutes when I was awoken by a vibration in my pocket. I lifted my head and let out a yawn to get my bearings before I reached into my pocket and removed the silver clam-shell Nokia cell phone, it was a text message from Sarah.

"Hey babe, I'm sorry for what happened earlier. I should have never slapped you and bugged out the way I did. I'm sorry for what I said about you and your brother, I was trippin' I lost it. Please call me back, I just want to speak to you and tell you once more how sorry I am. You have to understand, I was really upset because I really like you Corey. Call me back and I'll make it up to you ;-)."

It must be a trap, I thought. However, I was in the wrong too. I said some things I shouldn't have and I felt that I owed her an apology too. Perhaps, she had some time to cool down and reflect on what happened; maybe, we could end this peacefully. That would be great, that way no one else had to be brought into this.

I trusted that her motives were sincere even if the text seemed a bit contrived, since Sarah didn't call me a hundred times and berate me with constant threats, as I have seen in previous occasions of relationships gone sour. It was worth it to take a shot and see if we could talk things out and maybe we could be friends. Perhaps such a friendship would ultimately this feud between Mike and her brother, maybe they could learn from our example. I felt inclined and hopeful at the notion, so I went ahead and called her.

"Hi, Corey" Sarah greeted after the third ring.

"Hi, Sarah."

An awkward silence filled the phone, the living room started to buzz.

"I wanted to apologize for what happened today. I was a bit riled up but I do like you Sarah..."

"Shit happens..." She replied with a more vacant tone in her voice.

"I never wanted to do anything to hurt you. I hope we could stay friends, as I think you are really cool."

There was a bit of muffling on the air, it seemed that Sarah was outside somewhere. I heard Sarah talking to someone else, even laughing faintly but I could not confirm.

"Sarah?"

"Hold on a sec...." She giggled as I heard another voice faintly ask, *is that him?*

"Yo, motherfucker!" A foreign voice creaked through the speaks but as soon as I heard it, I recognized it. It was the same voice which made adamant threats at me in the 7-Eleven in Rockville Centre: it was Truck. Right then and there, the pit of stomach fell through the floor.

"Can you put Sarah back on the phone please?"

"I gave you a fair warning and I didn't smear your stupid ass all over the walls like a five-year-old with shit on his hands. My sister for some reason really dug you and when she came home this afternoon and told me what you said to her and what you did to her, I parted with any idea that I would show you any mercy." He chuckled. "It's a shame, if you stuck with my sis for a while, I may even have come to like you, but you are Ghost's brother, so it might have been a longshot..." His tone remained sardonic. "But you made this easy, so you listen to me you stupid fuck. I don't know where you live but if you find yourself walking through Pussbrook tonight, I'd do what they taught in you football. Head on a swivel kid, because you will see black and grays at some point. Whether it's you, your brother, Terror, or even that girl you were with. If they are walking, our guys will seem them. Cars are everywhere and you don't know which ones are them...." He laughed. "But they know you..."

I had to warn Foxy, she was at practice at the high school and I had to get to her somehow before she left. I couldn't let anything happen to her in case she was walking home, but more importantly I needed to see her and make sure she was okay. I had to warn Mike!

"One thing my brother didn't tell you, not only are we going to destroy you, we are also going to destroy your fucking cunt girlfriend, your brother, and his bitch ass crew too. It's just a matter of time, motherfucker." Sarah's voice was piercing through the speaker. "To think, all this could have been avoided if you just didn't sneak around and keep your dick in your pants you bird!"

"Corey!"

I shot up from my seat, shut the phone, and withdrew it from my ear; my chest tightening as Mike walked into the living room, his brow arched in curiosity. "What's gotten into you?"

I hesitated. I could tell him everything right now, but what good would that do? Mike was relaxed for once, untouched by chaos. This was the situation I dreaded the most and didn't want it to somehow get worse than I already imagined. But I had to get to Foxy, first.

"Can we take the car? I need to get to the high school."

Mike leaned back, eyeing me with suspicion. "Yeah, we can..." He placed his hand under his chin. "...is there something I need to know?"

I faltered. "No, I just...I need to help Sam with her English Lit report."

Mike shook his head. "Why don't we pick her up and bring her back here?"

"She's got cheerleading practice," I said quickly, avoiding his gaze.

"So, bring her after, we'll feed her dinner like we have a million times before." Mike wrinkled his nose even more.

"I need to get there now."

"Are you sure there is nothing else?"

I wanted to tell him, I wanted to come clean but he looked so relaxed and at peace, for one he wasn't bothered about any small antagonism but just taking the day in stride. I couldn't disrupt that and I couldn't reveal what I had been doing, it would crush him, or so I thought. Perhaps, these were idle threats and Sarah just trying to scare me to have the last word. I'd be assured once I got down to the high school and saw Samantha.

I shook my head. "I want to drive because I need to practice for my driving test..."

I justified my actions then by saying there was some truth in it, but that was a lie. I wanted to take the quickest route to the school, I couldn't waste another second.

"That much is true." Mike cracked a joke and dangled the keys in his hand, plucking them from the white table behind him. "Let's go then..."

As we stepped outside, my phone buzzed again. *I will find you, little Ghost – yours affectionately, Truck.* My stomach dropped, and then another text came in from Sarah: *Your slut girlfriend is dead.*

I texted Samantha immediately: *Please stay in the school. I'll meet you by the gym.*

"Are we going?" Mike stood by the passenger door of the car leaning over the roof. "For a man who doesn't have time, you sure move slow..."

"I was just letting her know I was on the way." I held up the phone, my voice taut, and slipped into the driver's seat. The keys felt cold in my palm, trembling slightly as I jammed them into the ignition.

The tires screeched as we tore onto Whitehall Street, the car lurching forward. Mike leaned against the passenger door; one arm braced on the dashboard.

"What the fuck?" he admonished me, his tone light but his gaze sharp. "You are not going to pass driving like that."

I didn't answer, my focus glued to the road ahead. Every red light was a lifetime. My phone buzzed in my lap—a phantom vibration, nothing more. No response.

The telephone poles blurred against the rain-slick asphalt as I pushed the speedometer higher. What if something had already happened? What if I was too late? I gripped the wheel tighter, swallowing the lump in my throat. Another red light. I checked my phone again. Still nothing.

I slammed the gas as it turned green, the car skidding slightly as we rounded a corner. "Corey, slow the hell down!" Mike snapped, but I was past listening. I had to get there—before everything fell apart.

• • • •

WE PARKED IN THE REAR of the high school, behind the gymnasium where many cars were parked in rows and all eyes were on the lot.

"Do you want to tell me what the heck is going on?" Mike put his hand against the headrest. I skittishly glanced at him; the truth buried beneath but erupting to the surface. Foxy! I didn't have time, the sooner I knew she was safe, the sooner I could breathe again.

"I mean you seem rather drastic for an English assignment..."

"She has an immediate deadline..." I flung the door open. "...we don't have much time..."

"I am sure this is all because she forgot to finish her report..." Mike chuckled as he got out of the door and swapped with me. "If you see cousin Daisy, tell her I said hello." He rolled his eyes, as he got back into the car. "Luke Duke over here..."

When I opened the screen to my phone, there were more threats from the terrible siblings, but I had also seen a new message from Ricky saying: CALL ME ASAP. I pressed the green button and placed the phone to my ear.

"What's up?" I initiated.

"Yo!" The tremolo in Ricky's voice showed he was in a state of panic. "What the fuck is going on?"

"With what?"

"There are all these guys wearing black and grey in the center of town." I drowned out Ricky's voice now, realizing that these were no longer threats or idle words. "They look identical to the dudes that your brother and Shawn whooped, the night we were with them..."

"Hold on..." I put the phone against my chest and looked back, Mike had already left. The bumper of the gold Saturn now blurring away in the distance as it turned back toward Broadway. Broadway led to town. But Mike hated driving through town in the daytime with all the traffic, so I prayed that would be the case today. I had no way to warn him, he left his cell phone where they keys were before we left. This was all my fault and I pray for Mike's sake that The Lord show him mercy for my failure.

"Have you seen, Samantha?" I sprinted across the road and trotted along the side of the school until I reached the front colonnade. I froze to see if there were any Street Sovereigns in the area.

"Nah, man..."

"Let me call you back in a few..." I snapped the phone shut, as I scanned between the green columns and the students forming small circles, engaged in conversation under the façade. Lynbrook Union High School fixed to the brick in stone.

> I opened the phone and rang her; it went straight to voicemail.
> Where could she be?

A small and gentle hand touched my shoulder, there was no malice or menace in its touch, it was warm and inviting. Nevertheless, I flinched.

"Woah!" I recognized that Southern drawl anytime:

"A bit jumpy, aye?" She smiled and kissed me on the cheek.

I threw my arms around her and never held her tighter. A stray strand of hair danced into my face as I held her. Weirdly enough, Samantha didn't seem to be in a rush to go anywhere, her embrace was warm and comforting.

"Thank God." I sighed with a breath of relief, in that moment everything gone around us didn't matter, I was at peace.

"It's nice to see you too..." She held my arms, confused and perplexed. "What's going on?"

"I tried texting you and ringing you, and I didn't hear back from you..." I looked in to her blue eyes which were shaded with concern and preoccupation. Her lips were stiff. Samantha's auburn hair was down and she wore her cheerleading vest and undershirt with grey sweatpants, a line of midriff escaping from beneath the undershirt and sweatpants, her toned core rarely exposed. In the anxiety of it all, I found solace in how beautiful she looked and the joy of being in her soothing presence. As much as I wanted to protect her, I was strangely aroused at being there with her in that moment.

"That's because was my phone was off..." She wrinkled her eyebrow. "You are acting weird; can you tell me what's the issue?"

"We need to get you out of here..." I took her hand and she followed, as I led her a few steps toward the nearest entrance to the school. "I'll call Ricky back and see if Christina will come down..."

Foxy halted us in our tracks. "Hold it right there..." Her eyes were filled with betrayal, as she let go of my hands. "Ricky and Christina?" She crossed her arms. "Why would I get in the car with them?" Her expression darkened, a mixture of worry and something sharper—betrayal, maybe.

"You remember what happened with Sarah?"

Sam's expression shifted immediately at the mention of the name. Foxy looked away for a moment for her eyes rejoined mine. "...Dear Lord...."

I nodded once and shut my eyes. "Her brother and his goons are all over Lynbrook and Ricky was warning me."

Two soccer players passed close to us, laughing loudly as they joked blissfully unaware. One clutched a Gatorade bottle as he eyed up Samantha, passing into the open door into the eastern corridor of the high school. I stood in between her and the two, my back to the street as she was closer to the gold concrete wall. If anyone was going to get to her, they were going through me first.

"They are looking for me..." I stroked her arm. "...and they mentioned you." Instinctively, I curled my fist but Sam gently tapped my knuckles with her fingertips to relax it. "But I am not worried about me, I came here because I wanted to make sure you were safe."

Samantha's eyes softened, clearly moved by the gesture until she regained her focus, her resting pout returning to her as she deliberated the next move. "Katie was kind of enough to offer me a lift. Come along."

I took her hand and she led us into the corridor, the floors were glazed over in electrolytic cleaner shining brightly from the white fluorescent tubes above, descending from the ceiling in silver bracketing. The walls glowed in their luminescent white paint, directing all to a colorful mural which presented an annotated history of Lynbrook back to when it was first called Pearsall's Corners. Today was a blink in the chronology of this town but the day in itself seemed like one that would last forever as my stomach did cartwheels at the thought of what may come next.

As we walked through the bright, sterile hallway, I couldn't shake the feeling that we were being watched. My eyes darted to every corner, every doorway, but there was nothing—just the echo of our footsteps on the polished floor. The only constant that gave me comfort was the feeling of Sam's hand in mine as we walked, until a junior varsity cheerleader dressed similarly to Foxy passed by and gave us a funny look.

"We are in this together." Foxy leaned back. "...but I don't know if we should be doing that..."

"Doing what?"

"Holding hands..."

She let go, her fingers slipping from mine like water, and I caught the flicker of something in her eyes—regret, or maybe just caution. I stared at the glossy floor, avoiding the question in her gaze.

"Let's go git your ride..." Samantha's voice was steady, but her eyes carried a hint of unease as she walked ahead. I followed her through the school, and we emerged into the rear parking lot where Mike had dropped me off earlier. As I ran forward to open the door for her, I stopped short as my gaze locked onto two men in black t-shirts at the far end of the lot. They were deep in conversation, but one of them glanced briefly in our direction before returning to his companion.

"Wait..." I stepped in front of Foxy's path, shielding her instinctively.

"What's a matter?" She asked, her hand on my shoulder, warm but firm. Her touch steadied me, but my focus didn't waver from the two figures. They didn't seem to notice us—or care—but the knot in my stomach tightened.

"Nothing, I thought I saw something..."

A teal Geo metro hatchback rumbled up to feet in front of us, until the car stopped. Katie glanced up at the two of us, her black sunglasses shining in the sunlight as she remained unaware of all that was unfolding.

"Kate, is there any chance we can give Corey a ride on back?"

She didn't respond, her fair skin glowed despite her lack of expression.

"He can get out with me at mine, but he is at a loose end..."

Katie nodded once. "...get in..."

I hurried forward and opened the door for Foxy.

"Thank you, sugar..." She got in and I shut the door, as I slid int the backseat behind her.

The car hummed off as Katie drove it down to the left bank of Carpenter Avenue. I looked down the block and scanned the area. To my horror, I saw a trio of Street Sovereigns propped against the wall of the school. They were clothed in black and grey, their customary colors with black bandanas draped out of their back right pocket, a tradition of their set.

The car slipped past undetected, as they were indulging in a smoke, lost in their own jeers and frolics. As we approached Sunrise Highway, Katie slalomed through some of the residual school rush hour traffic which created a gridlock at the intersection. As she continued to weave her way into the left turning lane, I cautiously surveyed the landscape of Gothic style buildings which housed a wide range of storefronts.

Ryan Cabrera played lowly over the radio, as Foxy and Katie cracked jokes, noticing three more junior varsity cheerleaders walking home together in matching uniforms to that of Samantha.

The forward arrow turned green and we carried onto Atlantic Avenue, trailing a white Chrysler Concorde from the late 90's with three passengers whose silhouettes were pointing out the window, the car's brake lights flashed intermittently. They were looking for someone, I was convinced that it might have been some more Sovereigns looking for me, but anxiety has a way of making fictions a reality.

We soon rolled past Angelica's Pizzeria, the red lettering on the sign reminding of their homemade sauce they would spread across freshly baked dough. There on the sidewalk, adjacent to the pizzeria amidst the line of parked cars and minivans, some of the major figureheads of the Street Sovereigns RJ and PJ were walking toward the front entrance with two other unknown companions that eerily grilled every car that passed by.

"Friends of your brother, Corey?"

I angled my back against the window, to avoid any eye contact and detection. "Good one, Kate..." I feigned a laugh to hide my worries and downplay any potential commotion. Foxy remained silent and soon it awkwardly filled the car.

"Fox, did you finish your essay for Current Events?" Katie laughed. "I can't believe you wrote a paper on college football." She scoffed.

"It was an analysis of the current BCS system and how to fix it." Foxy countered. "...using relevant data of course..."

"I can't believe you actually went through with that." I chimed in.

"The system is broken and we need to fix it." Samantha replied coyly. "I am just telling us how to do it..."

"I need to read that..."

In that moment I had forgotten what I just saw seconds ago. The problem was merely what I made of it, it seemed minute, compact, and beatable. That was until, I felt my pocket vibrate. I had received another text message.

"We are going to cut off your pretty girlfriend's tits and shove it down her throat. We are going to gut your brother like the pig that he is!!!!! <3 LOVE SARAH and TRUCK.

My fists clenched as the words burned into my mind, fueling a fire I could barely control. I looked out the window, searching for a target, ready to explode. My hand slowly crept toward the door handle. But I had to keep it cool, I had to keep both Samantha and Katie safe. I didn't have much time to make any other movements as Kate hit the gas and crossed Merrick Road and then Peninsula Blvd until we were now in North Lynbrook.

I looked down at the message and my spirit re-ignited, I had to set this straight. I was done with the bullying and hostility. We were far enough away where I could still walk back into town and square off with them, and yet Foxy was a minute away from her house driving wise.

"Kate, can you stop the car please?"

Her eyes snared to me in the back. "I thought you were going to Foxy's?"

"Just stop the car..." I blurted it out.

Samantha turned; her face etched with worry. "Corey, what are you doing?"

"I need to handle this," I said, my hand already on the door handle. Katie turned onto one of the side streets before Central Avenue where Foxy lived. "Fine, get out..."

"Thanks for the ride." I ripped open the door.

"Gingy!" Foxy yelled to halt me, but I shut the door and paced out on to the sidewalk. I dialed up Sarah as I started walking back towards the town. This was it, if I was going down, I was going down swinging but I wouldn't run.

"Hello Bitch!" Truck answered the call.

"Corey!" Sam's voice cracked with urgency.

I looked behind me and saw Samantha had followed me out. My plan was foiled before it got started, I wasn't going to bring her into this. Over my dead body. I ran back towards Samantha and put my arm around her back, guiding her back to the side street.

"Let me explain something to you, motherfucker!" I roared into the speaker. "Don't you ever threaten my brother or my friend ever again because if you do, I will fucking find you and so help me Lord, I will fucking kill you. Do you got me?"

Truck went silent for a moment, while Foxy was throwing her hands at her side.

The silence was soon interrupted with a chuckle. "You got balls, but you are stupid. This isn't going to be some fist fight." He simpered. "It's just you getting massacred with your brother and that bitch you are sweet on." Truck taunted. "Foxy is she called?"

My eyes locked into Samantha's.

"...my sister will make quick work of her."

"Unless you and your sister want to die. Stay the fuck away from her and don't say another word..." I didn't yell, I was calm in my reply and I meant what I said. "Otherwise I will make sauce out of your blood, you spaghetti-eating fuck."

"When I see you, I see you." He hung up the phone and I was ready to throw it in a fit of fury. "Fuck him!" I turned and punched the Stop sign.

"Corey! Slow down, pal." Foxy grabbed the back of my shirt.

"Samantha, you can't be out here." I shut my eyes to compose myself. "It's not safe..."

Samantha embraced me rubbed the back of my head. I held her tightly, hanging onto her for dear life. I was nervous, I was afraid, I was frustrated, I was pissed off. The emotions swirled like a whirlpool in my stomach. However, in her embrace I felt relief. She released me and looked into my eyes with a soft gaze.

"It's going to be alright."

I took a deep breath and stared down the street clueing every car that passed at any of the intersections that ran parallel to Hempstead and perpendicular to Davison Avenue (the street we were standing on). I looked back at Foxy, whose hair was slowly tossing in the wind. Truck's comments about her seem to get the worst reaction out of me. I understood Mike and his rivalry, the gangs, and even my involvement as I wasn't a civilian when I backed up Mike. But Sam, she had nothing to do with it all and her being in danger is what I most feared. grew worried about her safety. I knew that her house was just around the corner and wanted her to get home safe.

"If you get all hysterical like this, you're going to fall in to an early grave." She grabbed my wrist.

"The only one who is going is that scum..."

Samantha halted me in my rant and stroked my hands. Before I could respond, a black Trans-Am turned the corner, its slow, deliberate crawl sending a chill through me. The tinted windows and throaty rumble of the engine screamed trouble. The carburetor let out a plume of black smoke as it rumbled towards us.

"Sam, get behind me, please..." I said, my voice low and firm.

"That don't scare me none." She clutched my hand hard, her fingers intertwining with mine. "I am not leaving your side."

"Sam, they don't care if you are girl."

"Good for them, then..." She stood firm as the car approached.

"Samantha, I'd rather get buried in shit before a hair falls off your head." I tried to take her hand and lead her away, but we didn't have much of a chance. The Trans Am slowed to a creeping halt and the window slowly dropped, my heart pounding through my chest as I saw my nervous complexion descend with the window glass.

"What's good?" A voice called out from the blackness of the window, until a skinnier male about five years older than I, popped his head out. His jet-black hair was matted against his head, his diamond earing twinkled against his caramel skin. "Don't mean to roll up on you like that but I am a bit lost."

My pulse was throbbing, my body shaking though I put on a brave face. I stood in between her and the vehicle, completely shielding Samantha and ready to defend her at all costs.

"I am trying to find Lester Avenue..." A smile broke from his face. "...could you point me in the direction?"

I glanced at the street sign for Pearsall Avenue, exhaling as I steadied my voice. "Head down to the end of the block, make a left, and it'll be on your right."

"Good looking, homie." His eyes were unreadable as his earing caught the sunlight. "Ma'am." The window slid up and I was met by my reflection of Samantha and I shoulder-to-shoulder, hand-in-hand. Our hands soon released again, as the car rolled away. I watched until it disappeared, my body trembling with the adrenaline still coursing through me.

I looked at her, her blue eyes steady and unyielding. "I'll walk you home."

We walked in silence, the wind rustling through the trees, the weight of the day pressing down on us. When we reached her house, I paused at the steps, my hand lingering on hers, as I remained on the outside of the street with her to my inside.

The silence was awkward and eerie, louder than the gusts of wind that rustled the branches, leaves, and trees. The imminent sentiment of peril was evermore ubiquitous, I was most on edge when we approached the front steps of Foxy's house, which were only yards away but they seemed like miles. I kept envisioning what my tactics would be if a car full of Sovereigns pulled up right now. Every blink I took, I conceptualized a new strategy. I prayed that all my petitions would be answered and we could safely get Samantha home.

As Samantha stepped onto her porch, the black Trans-Am reappeared, crawling down the street with the same deliberate menace. Its carburetor growled like a predator stalking its prey, the sound reverberating in the stillness of the late afternoon.

"Come inside for a minute," Samantha said, her voice steady but urgent. She grabbed my hand and pulled me through the door, her movements quick but controlled. The lock clicked into place behind us, the sound unnervingly loud in the silence of her home.

She turned to face me, her blue eyes searching mine. "I'll show you that report."

I nodded, though my mind was miles away, replaying every second of the Trans-Am's slow crawl. Was it a coincidence, or were they watching? My hand twitched, my fists tightening as I scanned the room, every shadow feeling like an encroaching threat.

Samantha disappeared into another room, her voice floating back over her shoulder. "I'll be right there."

I paced the small entryway, my pulse pounding in my ears. Through the window, I saw the Trans-Am's taillights glow as it passed by.

Samantha reappeared, holding a thick folder of notes and papers. She set it on the table and opened it, her fingers trembling slightly. "An eight-team playoff" She pointed to the charts and tables, her voice soft, "we can use each of the major bowls as a playoff game with each BCS conference champion and the highest-ranked non-BCS conference champion qualifying."

I tried to focus, nodding absently as I leaned over the paper. But my ears strained to hear any semblance of the engine outside.

"...the ratings should be a mean of the computer rankings over the course of the season with strength of schedule rated into the formula..."

I glanced over my shoulder, squinting through the linen curtains to see if the car had returned, the road was empty, like an abandoned house that was left still in the wake of a haunting poltergeist.

"Corey," she said gently, placing a hand over mine. "Look at me."

I did, her calm gaze anchoring me for a moment. "We'll be okay," she said.

Her words settled in my chest, heavy but grounding. I took a deep breath, the fire in me dimming slightly. She was right—we couldn't let them dictate our lives, couldn't let fear take over. Samantha drew close to me and leaned in. "the two remaining highest ranked teams would be wildcards..."

Our faces drew close, our eyes studying each other's next move until our faces got closer to where our lips were exhaling into each other's.

"To think, I used to be some kid that rode the bench that no girls looked at...." I gulped. "...and now I am here with you."

"I don't know why that was ever the case..." She spoke softly, her voice smoother with a faint tremolo in it. "But things can change...."

Our respirations grew more intense, our lips closed in even more on each other as my eyes shut and I can feel my lips inches away from hers until I finally pulled back for a moment.

"I should go..." I crept back a step or two. "...I need to tell Mike about all of this..." I took a deep breath, hoping to gather myself.

"You should do..." Samantha sighed and nodded; her cheeks reddened as she led me back to the door. "Besides, Nana is going to be home any minute. You know what she is like..." Her hand gripped the brass doorknob. "When you get home, call me please."

"I will." I opened the door and was met with a rush of cool air, carrying with it the weight of uncertainty that seemed to press against my chest. I hesitated, scanning the street, my pulse quickening as my eyes darted between shadows and corners. The street was clear—but for how long?

"Promise me..." Samantha's voice was firm, pulling me back to her. She held up the pink Motorola RAZR, its faint shine catching the porch light.

"I promise," I said, my voice steady, though my heart was anything but.

As I stepped onto the porch, the wind carried a faint, distant hum. I froze, listening. It could have been the far-off sound of traffic—or the growl of the Trans-Am's engine. My fists tightened instinctively; my body braced for whatever might come next.

Behind me, Samantha stood in the doorway, her silhouette framed by the soft glow of the light from inside.

I turned back to her, forcing a small smile. "Thank you, Sam."

"It's what I'm here for," Her hand lingered on the doorknob, her lips curving into a faint, reassuring smile.

As the door closed behind me, I felt the absence of her presence like a cold wind. The street was still, the silence both a comfort and a threat. I scanned the street one last time before stepping off the porch, my steps resolute but cautious.

The hum grew louder—or maybe it was my imagination. Either way, I walked forward, ready to face whatever came next.

Chapter 17 – Somewhere in Franklin Square

I waited for the lock to catch before going any further, gazing up to the sun which beamed through the trees, desperate for a moment of solace. It'll be fine, I reassured myself with every swift step I took. A relatively short walk seeming like the longest I have endured. The closer I got to home the more I hyperventilated until my house came in to view, I was relieved at the sight of Mike sitting on the steps with The Bible in his hand. I was worried about an unlucky encounter and yet Mike who was a bigger target than I, seemed blissfully unaware. He wasn't dressed as he normally was, he had shaved and looked more formal in a collared shirt and khakis with polished boots.

"What's the occasion?"

"I was thinking about maybe going out to church later." He closed his Bible.

"What?!" My eyes bulged. "But I thought that there was no chance that you would ever...."

"There aint nothing but trouble out there, man..." He smiled as he clutched The Bible and glanced out into the street. "Tell me have you ever read the book of Jeremiah?"

I sat down on the steps next to Mike. "Many times, actually..." I couldn't help but draw comparison in that moment to when he was caught in the cistern.

"It's quite amazing, you know Jeremiah experienced some terrible things but he always stayed true to God." Mike gripped The Bible firm with both hands. "The Lord said, I have plans for you to succeed and prosper." He shook his head. "I blamed our Heavenly Father for everything that went wrong when I should have embraced him." He stroked his cheek. "If only I had realized this sooner..."

"It's never too late, brother." I placed my hand on his shoulder. My actions betrayed what I should have done, but instead I shut my eyes for a moment and prayed The Lord would sustain my brother and that this whole incident with Sarah and Truck will pass through a change of heart.

"There is one thing I wish to iron out..."

Truck? Perhaps the prayers were answered faster than I could ever imagine. Was he going to put this all to bed? If that were the case, should I even tell him about what happened or would it be better for me to forget about it too?

"...I want to show these guys that, God has a plan for them too and there is no need for any of this." Mike glanced at me. "I just don't know where to go from here. This is all I've ever known."

"Well you have to take the first step before you see the staircase."

Mike smiled. "Wise words..." He lit up a cigarette. "So, what's going on with you?"

I was overjoyed that he thought about dropping all of the gang lifestyle and embracing his new life. I had waited years to hear it and now a guilt washed over me. I couldn't say anything, perhaps there was a way I could die on this hill alone, a long way from Mike and Samantha. I had to support him, I had to encourage him, I had to make sure he didn't get pulled back in.

"Don't worry about it."

Mike looked over at me as he took another drag of his cigarette.

"I cannot wait to see what The Lord has in store for you, bro."

"Neither can I, little brother." He smiled and got up to head inside.

I remained sitting on the steps in a contemplative state, pondering all the possibilities that can come as a result of the situation with Sarah. Maybe this was all just a scare tactic and charade. Maybe Sarah would come to her senses and things would settle down in a few days. I didn't want to be the reason why Mike stumbled, I didn't want to be the brier of thorns that ensnared him but the wind that kept him on the straight and narrow path. But what if I didn't tell him and it all came to the surface? He would feel betrayed perhaps more than he ever had been previously, even though that was never my intention.

My phone beeped and when I took it out, I saw it was a message from Foxy: *Are you home safe, Pumpkinhead?*

I didn't even start to type my message on the small keypad, hitting the button on the left shoulder with Call written above it on the screen in block letters.

"Hey there, partner." Foxy greeted me. "Did you stop somewhere in your travels?"

"Sorry, Sam." I held the phone close to my ear. "I was talking to Mike." I looked over my shoulder to see if anyone was listening. "He's going to church later."

"Really?" Her surprise was evident in her response.

"I can't say anything and screw this up." I pressed my fingers to my head and squeezed my skull that throbbed from the stress. "If it's The Lord's wills that I fall on my sword for this, so be it, but I can't make this any worse."

"The fear of man is a snare, but whoever trusts in The Lord is safe." Samantha replied. "Proverbs 29:25".

Her words were encouraging and comforting, as if the Spirit had filled her and me to bring solace to the situation.

"You are right, but I think we should stay in tonight. The three of us can watch a movie or something and give it a bit of time." I turned around and moved onto the porch, finding some form of security under the portico. "I'll ask my mother for a ride and see if she can grab you along the way. I don't want you walking across town."

"Have a bit more faith, Corey. There are many things we do not have control of."

Her words were sagacious and apt, and they would come true in more ways than one by her account.

"You are right..." I leaned back against the door. "But I won't let you walk anywhere on your own given the situation presently. I wouldn't be able to live with myself, if the slightest...."

"I am not even going to have it out with you..." She interrupted. "Let me know when you are on the way." Samantha sighed, indicating her appeasement.

"I will give Melissa a ring now and get everything figured out."

"Sounds like a plan, sugar. Speak soon...."

"Bye, Sam." I pressed the red button on the phone and closed the shell, sliding it into my pocket and heading inside. I sent Melissa a text proposing the plans and she was happy with it. On the way to Melissa's, my mother and I stopped to pick up Foxy. I stormed out of the car to stand vigil when Samantha exited her house. Mom and her had a laugh about the overzealous demonstration of chivalry but nevertheless Mom was encouraged by it and Foxy appreciated it though she knew that there were other variables in play that only she was privy to.

The evening was growing late as the three of us sat on the couch, watching *A Bronx Tale*. The room was dark only with the glow of the television filling the room with any form of light. I heard Foxy's respirations beside me as she leaned her head against my left side. Melissa's head was lying on Foxy's lap, her body across mine with her legs extending the length of the couch. Foxy ran her hand through Melissa's head, massaging her scalp to where she was drifting off to sleep while Samantha and I watched the movie. When the conclusion reached and Sonny died, I couldn't help but think of Mike. I was worried one day such a fate would await him. My head collapsed into my hands as I clasped them over the bridge of my note.

He could be out tonight somewhere and his past could inconspicuously catch up with him like it did Sonny. And I could have stopped it, if only I said something! Heavenly Father, please protect and watch over your son, because He loves you, you shall rescue Him. I recited the verses of Psalm 91 under my breath as the credits rolled.

Melissa got off my lap and exited the couch, the lights soon flicked on with the sound of a snap. "Are you alright?" Melissa placed her hand on my hand.

"Yea, I'm fine. Thank you."

"Did the movie get to you, hun?" Foxy sipped her soda.

"Hey Fox, you wanna stop hitting on my boyfriend?" Melissa snickered with a smirk.

Foxy and I looked at each other with arched eyebrows.

"Dukes he was yours since the moment you met him, you got nothing to worry about with little old me."

"Good to know." Melissa jumped onto my lap and kissed Foxy on the cheek. "Too bad, he has to compete with us, first, hmm?"

"Naturally..." Foxy flicked her head and put her hand around Melissa's shoulder, their heads touched in a brief show of mutual affection. My pocket vibrated twice, I reached around Melissa's waist and plucked the phone from my pocket and saw it was Shawn.

"Cuz, what's up?"

"What's up little brother, where is Mikey at?" Shawn had a sense of urgency in his voice. It permeated through the speaker.

"I don't know, did you trying calling the house?"

"Yea, no one answered."

"Well I guess he's still at church."

Melissa and Samantha stopped conversing and looked at each other for a moment, Church spelled out on Melissa's lips in the form of a question as Foxy nodded once to confirm.

"Repeat that again..."

"He's a changed man bro."

"Well if you see him can you tell him to call me ASAP!"

"Yeah sure." My forehead wrinkled, anxiety filling at me the possibilities of what this may be related to. "Is there anything I can help you with?"

Silence was on the other end of the line.

"Little brother whatever you do, make sure you stay off the street tonight. A lot of Sovereigns driving around town in record numbers."

A shiver shot down my spine as my heartbeat accelerated, what I had dreaded had come true.

"What do you mean?"

"I don't want to scare you man, but the walls talk and apparently they are looking for you."

I watched as Samantha got up from the couch to grab her coat. Terror filled me and I leaped from the couch. "Hold on a minute..." I marched toward Sam and gently took her wrist. She halted in her steps as I put my hand against the door to make sure it is shut. Shawn had never stopped talking but I wasn't paying attention until I knew Samantha wasn't going anywhere.

"...This is probably some bullshit that they are trying to pull to get at Mike for whatever reason they can make up, but play it safe, ight?"

"Ight..."

I looked at Samantha and though there was no verbal communication, we both understood the bigger issue at hand and what the call was in relation to. She made a face at me to signal the need for me to speak with Melissa.

"Can someone tell me what's going on?" Melissa looked at us both perplexed.

I pulled ten dollars from my pocket and placed it in her hand. "I am getting Foxy a ride home." I took out my phone and called for a taxi.

"All-County..."

"Hello, I need a taxi for one from Scranton Avenue to Central Avenue."

"Well send one over." The dispatcher said with no emotion or tone in her voice.

"Thanks." The call disconnected and I slid my phone back into my pocket.

"Whatever secret you two are keeping, do you mind sharing it with me?" Melissa's voice was tinted with envy.

"My cousin just called me and told me some stuff is going down and I don't want to take any chances. We got to make sure Foxy gets home safe."

Sam placed the money back in my hand.

"Samantha, please..." I let the money touch my palm but I don't take hold of it. "For Melissa and I." I placed my other hand over hers and pressed it to the ten-dollar bill

She sighed. "Fine, Corey. I'll pay you back when I can."

"There is no need to..." I waved my hand.

A silence filled the room but a tension rattled in between the faint whispers of the heat.

Melissa sat up, peering at both of us as I stood against the door and waited for a horn to honk. Once I did, I looked out the peephole and saw the white taxi parked by the curb. "Alright he's here." I opened the door. "I'll walk you to the car."

I placed my arm around Samantha and held open the door for her.

"It's brick out here, tonight..." I cupped my hands and blew into it briefly, as she sauntered out. As we made our way down the footpath toward the taxi, I kept my arm tight around her waist as I looked left and right for anything that looked out of place while listening for anything other than the faint rumbling of the old Crown Vic parked ahead of us. The only thing I could see is the shadow of the telephone poles under the orange streetlamps; the only thing I could hear is the faint rustling of leaves.

"I understand why you are nervous but you don't think this is a bit much?" Breath escaped from Samantha's mouth as she spoke.

"You never know with these people." I opened the door for her. "Let me know when you get in please?"

"I will do but make sure you fill Dukes in about everything." She nodded and got in; we both shot a look back at Melissa who watched from behind the outside glass door. "She looks as lost as a priest at a hen party and completely cut out..."

"I'll speak with her." I shut the door and went around to the front of the taxi. The driver lowered the window, you could feel the heat escaping from the car. The driver wore a black winter hat and a black hoodie. He had darker skin that glistened from the moonlight; he had a distinguishable bushy black beard and a warm smile behind it.

"Good evening, sir."

"What's going on, young buck?"

"My name is Corey." I extended my hand toward his.

"Calvin." He shook it.

"Calvin, may I ask a favor?"

He nodded.

"Before you drive off, can you make sure she gets in the house safely?" I handed him another five-dollar bill.

He looked over his shoulder and a smile broke from his face. "It's like that, huh?" He handed me back the five-dollar bill. "It's no problem, I got you..."

"Thank you."

He nodded and raised the window. I watched as the car drove off before I went back into the house and shut the doors behind me; locking both before settling in.

"Do you want to tell me what that was all about?" Melissa sat back on the couch. "Either you and Foxy are planning to elope together or you are really paranoid. Which one is it?"

"My brother is in trouble." I looked down at the ground as I clasped my hands over my nose. "And it's all my fault."

"How?"

I looked at her and joined her on the couch.

"Talk to me...." She sat up beside me and started to rub my back. "I want to help anyway, I can."

I turned to hug her and embraced her snugly. We didn't say much, I just wanted to feel safe and forget about everything going on in the world outside. Melissa turned over the channels on the television behind us and *Maps* by the Yea Yea Yea's started to play behind us. Soon after, Melissa and I both received a message from Foxy that she arrived home safely.

"Come on..." Melissa yanked me off the couch. "Let's go take your mind off whatever is bothering you..."

She led us up to her room and when she stepped in, she about-faced and pressed her lips against me until we fell on the bed. Melissa shot up from the top of the blanket and locked the door before she pulled off her tank-top; we made love for over an hour.

Melissa lie sprawled out and I held her, finding refuge in the stillness of the night and the cool brisk air that filled her room. I tried to put my mind at ease and fall asleep beside her but all I could do is obsess over figuring out a way to present this entire situation to Mike without provoking him to turn back to his old ways. I prayed for Providence that he averted any trouble that lurked through the streets of Lynbrook. I prayed for everyone involved, that they would all have a shift in attitude and go peacefully, their own separate ways if they couldn't reconcile. I prayed for forgiveness and forbearance for the bad decisions I continued to make and the sins I committed.

Finally, I fell asleep but didn't realize it until I jolted awake at 3:13 in the morning. Melissa remained motionless perched on my chest still comfortably asleep. I looked around the room which was silhouetted in darkness. The only light came from the streetlight shining through the window from the street below. I looked over at my cell phone and saw a message from Foxy that said "Thank you again, good night :-)". I also saw two missed calls from Home around 12:30 AM. A voicemail was left as well. I assumed I was in trouble because I did not make it home and I would deal with that inevitability when it came, but I wanted to enjoy whatever tranquility I could feel in that moment, finding sanctuary from all the turmoil that circulated through the neighborhood. I started to press the alphanumeric keys on the phone, making sure there were no misspellings as I wrote out "As long as your safe, I'm happy." before I sent it off in response to Foxy. Even if there was no threat to Samantha, I would have felt better if I was sleeping on the bench next to the front door of her house. That way, I was there, prepared and ready for any event I imagined, as unlikely as it may be. Nevertheless, she was safe and I thanked The Lord for that – that's all I truly needed.

"You awake?" Melissa whispered.

I could feel her look and when I glanced down at her, Melissa's concern was spelt across her face.

"I'm just having a tough time sleeping."

"Does this have anything to do with what you were telling me before?" Melissa sat up and curled her knees into her chest. "I have been trying to pry it out of you, but it seems you only want to tell Fox..."

"It's not like that, Melissa..." I let out a deep breath. "I just didn't want to make anything worse..."

"You won't." She ran her lips against my neck and brushed her face against mine. "Just talk to me..." Melissa softly grazed my arms.

"I know you may have trouble trusting me cause of what has happened between us, but I promise you, you don't need to keep anything from me..." She rubbed my arm with more intent as I sat up.

"Do you remember how he used to be in some bad shit? Like the gang and all that?"

"Yeah."

"Well, they are going around the neighborhood."

"Who is?"

"The guys that he has beef with." I lied back down. "I was worried that Sam wouldn't make it home alright. But I don't want to think about that anymore, I want to be happy to be here with you."

I felt Melissa's finger press against my lips. "Everything is going to be okay."

"I don't know about this time; I have a bad feeling." I glanced at her. "I sure hope you were worth all of this."

"What do you mean by that?"

"I shouldn't have said that..."

"No, tell me what you meant." Her tone grew stern.

"When you decided that you needed space after that night that we first kissed, I thought you were going back to Matt again. So, I met this other girl a while ago and we hooked up."

"Wait, so you just moved on just like that?!"

"Let me finish..." I grabbed her gingerly. "I didn't know if you were coming back, so my brother told me to keep my options open and don't sit there feeling sorry for myself. I always wanted you, Melissa..."

Melissa's eyes became glossy as she heard me confess my feelings.

"And I just didn't want to hurt anymore, and I saw this girl at the fair and we talked and she really liked me so I hung out with her. Thing is I really liked her you know? But she wasn't you..."

Melissa blushed. "So, what happened?"

"This happened..."

Melissa gripped my face with both her hands.

"And the thing is this girl happened to be the sister of my brother's arch enemy. These are the people they have beef it. I didn't know this going in, I found out after the fact and I didn't realize how serious it was until we were hanging out in Rockville Centre and he threatened me."

Melissa looked at me with great concern but also one of shared remorse. "Oh, no..."

"I haven't told Mike because I don't want to mess up all the changes he is making and I don't want him to feel betrayed. I was afraid to leave Sarah because of what might happen but I wanted to be with you."

She interrupted me with a powerful kiss, throwing her body across me as she pushed herself against me and stroked the side of my head. I threw my arms around her back and held her close.

"When I listened to coach describe what happened with him and his wife when they first started seeing each other. Everything was going well, then everything got screwed up. Coach hung in there and he stuck with her when everyone else told him to forget it. But guess what? he's married to her now."

"Well I suppose we owe Coach a thanks, if we get married." She laughed.

"I didn't think it would come to this because Sarah told her brother off for threatening me but when I left her, she thought it was some ploy to get back at her brother and that I was cheating on her with Samantha..."

Melissa looked away for a moment. "Funny how she felt threatened by Fox, as well."

"She is crazy and she was saying all sorts of awful things about what she wants to do to Sam..."

"She's not going to do anything to Foxy or you, it's all talk..." Melissa replied sternly as she took my hand and held it. "I'll fight them with you if I have to."

"I don't want you to fight anyone." I kissed Melissa on her forehead. "...I brought this on myself..."

"No, this is my fault..." She laid on my chest again peering out the window. "I should have been with you from the beginning..." Melissa ran her hand up me. "But you should tell your brother, it's what it needs to be done and it can make this a heck of a lot worse."

"I know..." I caressed her. "...it won't stop..." The words slurred as I fell back asleep unknowingly until I awoke to the buzzing of the alarm clock. The silence of sleep was aerated by the chirps of birds and the buzzing of insects. The bright glare of the sun's mighty beams cascaded off the trees and windows which caused me to squint my eyes as soon as I opened them. Melissa remained asleep in my arms. I very cautiously woke her.

"Mel?"

I tickled her a bit and she giggled as a response. I reached over and grabbed my phone and noticed I had two more missed calls from home with a voicemail. I completely forgot to listen to the initial voicemail in the midst of it all. Immediately, I picked up the phone and hit the talk button for home. As I wedged the phone between my chin and shoulder, I hit the snooze on the alarm. The phone was answered with haste.

"Mike!"

"Yo! Where the fuck are you?"

I gathered my composure, thinking whether this was the right time to come clean. I balked, yawning as I elicited my excuse.

"I am sorry, I fell asleep at Melissa's..."

"Listen, you're lucky I'm in a good mood man. I had to endure an interrogation by Mom when I covered for you, I told her you were with Shawn."

"Thanks bro, I owe you one."

"Yeah, you better play the game of your life today."

I felt Melissa's eyes on me. "Have you spoken to Shawn?"

"No, why?"

Another chance to tackle the difficult subject that I was keeping deep inside, but again I failed to deliver. "I was just wondering if he was on board with all of this..." I looked at Melissa again and could tell by her expression that she was urging me to reveal what happened to my older brother. "After the game, could I talk you about something?"

"Sure, do you want to tell me now?"

"I have to get to the game or I'll be late..."

I was unsure if he already knew and was testing if I would be forthcoming or if it was his typical mellow and indifferent manner of response he leveraged on many occasions.

"Alright, then..."

"I'll see you later."

"Yep..."

I hung up the phone and peered over at Melissa. "I'll deal with it after the game."

We shot out of bed and each grabbed a Pop Tart along with some coffee, watching College Gameday on the television as we waited for Foxy to come pick us up. I remained focused on the game; I was fixated on playing my best as I thought this might be my last chance, I ever get to make Mike proud before I told him the bad news.

When I was out on the field against Sewanhaka, I had the best performance of my entire high school career: everything went right. We established our running game with Ricky and the Sewanhaka cornerbacks could not cover me. There was a point in the game where they were rolling the safety over to double-team me. At the end of the day I finished with nine receptions and 147 reception yards plus two touchdowns. We now won two in a row and our record stood at 3-3, it was a brand-new season and we made that clear to ourselves and all competitors with the 24-0 rout.

As we took off our shoulder pads and helmets when we filed off the field toward the bus, it became eerily silent. A gentle breeze kissed my face as I looked back at the field once more time accented by the shadows of dusk. The large hulking brick edifice of the school itself was pitched back and the clock tower in the center of the structure was illuminated in gold.

We arrived at Lynbrook around twilight, cars lined Union Avenue many running with their headlights on. When I stepped off the bus, I saw Mike with Shawn, Melissa, and Foxy all waiting against the fence for me. They all smiled at me as I led the team back to the locker room behind Coach Kenny. When we all sat in the locker room, Coach Kenny addressed us quickly and told us how proud he was that we played up to our true potential that day against Sewanhaka. He named it our hallmark victory because we played a complete game on both sides of the ball. He awarded me with the game ball for my play in the game. I was humbled but felt undeserving of the acknowledgment, I wasn't a truthful man but perhaps when I exited the locker room, I could finally warrant some of the acclaim. As I emerged from the steps, the four of them were awaiting me.

"What's that you got in your hand?" Mike called out to me.

"The game ball."

"You deserve it!" My brother hugged me. "You were incredible out there."

"I was watching you tear them motherfuckers up, they couldn't stop you." Shawn rubbed my head. "Good shit, Corey."

Melissa came next and kissed me. "You were amazing babe." Foxy ripped the ball from my hand as I held it loosely.

"But no amazing enough. Turnover!" Foxy ran with the ball. "Come on now Corey, you need to cover that up, all-star." She kissed me on the cheek and placed the ball against my chest.

"Jeez, Fox." I smirked.

"You were awesome." She put her hands on her hips. "It was merely a matter of time."

"We're going for ices tonight." Mel took my hand and shot a look at Samantha.

"As soon, as you do what you need to do." Foxy leered at me; both girls moved their head in the direction of Shawn and Mike.

"Won't it spoil the mood?"

"Corey...." Melissa scowled, Foxy joined her in a matching expression. "...we discussed this."

"You'll feel better once you've gotten it over with." Samantha put her arm around Melissa's waist. "Think of it like getting a flu shot."

I glanced over at Mike and Shawn leaning against the fence in deep conversation with another fellow who was parked up in a yellow Plymouth Hemi Cuda. *Hey Ma* by Cam Ron was playing out from the speakers of the car, the bass vibrating against the steel frame of the vehicle's muscular body. "And we are going to get it on tonight." Samantha and Melissa sang the lyrics to each other and started to dance together, their arms clutching each other with a sisterly love. I laughed for an instance and enjoyed their moment of youth and jubilance.

I peered over at Samantha who batted her eyebrows toward Shawn and Mike, her long auburn hair bobbing up and down against her white undershirt.

"It'll be fine, babe." Melissa ran her hands down Samantha's back and started massaging her shoulders.

"Your hands work magic, Dukes..."

"It's cause, I want to cop a feel..." Melissa teased as she grabbed Foxy's backside. "That squishy butt of yours..."

Foxy squealed. "You have the best bum out of the two of us..." She pinched Melissa's butt in playful retaliation.

"Please, I wish I had your ass, Fox..."

The two giggled as they bantered, a charming diversion from what was to follow. Nevertheless, the light-heartedness gave me a chance to ground myself. Maybe I overreacted, maybe I was thinking about it too much, maybe I was wrong. Maybe this whole thing was going to blow over after all.

Foxy wrung out some sweat from her hair and folded up the top of her undershirt to expose some of her abdomen. It caught my attention for a moment as I gazed at her belly button. Melissa snapped her finger at me and gestured toward Mike and Shawn who were far ahead. "

I'll go take care of this while you two do whatever it is you need to do..." I looked at them wryly, as I ran off to catch Mike and Shawn.

"Yo bro!"

Mike turned around "What's up?"

"Do you have a minute?"

"Yea sure." Mike stepped aside. "Give me a sec, Shawn."

"Sure thing." Shawn walked ahead.

"I needed to talk to you."

"I know." He smiled. "What's it about?"

"Melissa."

"What about her?" Mike put his hand on my shoulder.

"Well remember when I told you, I was seeing that girl Sarah?"

"Yeah I remember..." Mike grinned. "What happened? You dump her and she's a little upset?" He teased.

The anxiety started to build within me as I swallowed to gather my composure. "There is a bit more to it than that..."

"Is there a big brother involved too?" He smirked.

"Yeah that's it, but her brother." I stuttered. "Her brother is Truck." Mike's visage suddenly narrowed to a scowl of fury.

"What do you mean, her brother is Truck?"

Mike was clearly confused and he turned to Shawn. "Yo! Terror!" He summoned Shawn. It seemed that at the drop of a hat, Mike had reverted back to the man I thought he left behind. The steely look of fury had filled him again. "You were seeing a girl named Sarah and she was from Rockville Centre; I should have known..." He threw his hand at his waist "That fool had a hot sister named Sarah, motherfucker!"

Shawn quickly paced over to Mike's side when he heard him shouting. Unlike Mike, Shawn had shown no intent of leaving Dem Rep behind by any means, he was sporting a green bandana tied below a green Notre Dame Fighting Irish fitted. He also wore a white t-shirt with black and green trimmed shorts. He was reppin' Dem Rep to the fullest.

"What's up Ghost?"

"You were telling me earlier that those bitches we were running around town in record numbers, right?"

"Yea like a bunch of ants swarming bread crumbs..." He pointed at me. "...Supposedly looking for him." He looked out of the sides of his eyes at Mike. "...that's a bunch of bullshit though, right?"

"Unfortunately, not..." Mike's took a deep breath, seemingly the spirit of hostility left him. "So, I'm going to give you one chance to tell me the truth. How long has this been going on and when did you find out this was Truck's sister?"

"Wait, what?" Shawn scowled.

"I knew for a couple weeks." I looked down ashamed.

"A couple weeks?!". Mike opened his arms, as he voice rose. "What you mean a couple weeks?!"

"And I thought that was them inventing some story to come in and start something!" Shawn cornered me. "What the fuck did you start?!"

"Chill!" Mike put his hand in front of Shawn. "He is still our little brother."

"Sarah said she was from Rockville Centre, so I took the bus over one day to visit her because she was always coming down here to see me. "

"Ok and?" Mike scolded me.

"Just hear me out, please." I put my hands up and appealed to his temperance. "I had been seeing her for a couple weeks, as you remember. I told you I saw her at the fair and shit wasn't going well with Melissa and I followed your advice and kept my options open."

"Yeah, that's great, but not with that motherfucker's sister!"

Suddenly, Foxy and Melissa who were chit-chatting aimlessly focused their attention on the three of us and began to make their way over to us.

"It was only when I went over to Rockville Centre to visit her and we went for pizza."

Shawn yoked me up and forced me against the fence. "Fuck the pizza and fuck you too!" Mike grabbed Shawn and put him against the fence.

"Enough that's your little brother! What is wrong with you?"

Shawn adjusted his shirt which was then wrinkled up by the force of Mike grabbing him. Foxy and Melissa ran up at the sight of the commotion.

"Ladies it's fine, we're just talking." Mike turned toward the girls. Shawn brushed his shirt off and gave them a thumbs up. "You good?"

Shawn nodded.

"Go ahead." Mike set his stare upon me.

"We were walking through parking lot to cut across to 7-Eleven and we ran into Truck and his boys. She didn't even know he was there either. But despite the fact that the threatened me, he said long as I was with Sarah and kept her happy, he said he'd live you alone."

Mike turned to the right and glanced over at Shawn.

"You got to believe me Mike!" I pleaded and looked at Shawn. "I'd never put you guys in harm's way. Ever!"

"What were you going to do? Stay with this girl forever and keep shit from me?" Mike sighed, a look of disappointment replaced his anger and irritation. "Eventually I would have found out."

"No, I just was going to do whatever I had to do for the time being to make sure you didn't get dragged back in." I was close to weeping, the words strained as they left my dry throat. "But then she came around..." I pointed at Melissa.

"So, now it's her fault?" Shawn spat.

"No, but what I was supposed to do?"

Mike and Shawn threw their hands on their hips and ran their sneakers through the grass, looking at each other for answers.

"You found The Lord, man. The last thing I wanted to do was tell you when you were finally deciding to leave this all behind?"

Mike looked down at the ground and ran his boot over the tip of his other.

"You were planning on dropping the flag?!" Shawn glared at Mike. "He's telling lies, now, you believe this?"

"He's right."

Shawn's face dropped. "What?!"

"I am going to leave..."

A look of betrayal coursed through Shawn's eyes.

"...but not before taking all of you with me."

"Ghost?" Shawn ran his finger across the top of his lip to catch some snot dripping down from his nostril.

"No Shawn, enough of that. I am done with all the fighting, the drugs, and the bad decisions. Cause God knows, I made plenty of them." He bit his lip and shook his head. "Little brother is right; I am a man of The Lord now." He placed his hand on his hip. "And I need to handle this in a way that reflects Him and brings glory to Him."

Shawn appeared bewildered and gazed over at me looking for answers. I threw my hands to my side.

"With my new life in Him, I have been afforded the opportunity to help people like us. I can show them there is another way to get through all the heartache and all the pain that life dishes at us. There is another way to show the world how tough we all are, and it ain't no set and it ain't no guns and it ain't no flags. Cause they all mean nothing!"

Samantha and Melissa's shadows stood behind me as they listened onto Mike's monologue.

"...I lost the greatest thing that ever happened to me because I couldn't walk away from this bullshit when it counted. So now, here I am, walking, but walking a higher path. A path I never thought I deserved to walk, a path I thought I would never walk."

Melissa's eyes grew glossy as she was clearly moved by Mike's words. Shawn meanwhile was at a loss for words. Foxy appeared moved like Melissa but was still catching her breath from running up to the skirmish. Her abs flexed and relaxed as her lungs rose and fell while she adjusted her black bike shorts on her waist.

"Guys, I shouldn't have led Corey on, you can blame me..." Melissa muttered. "I told him, I got him with this..."

"It's not your fault." Mike smiled and took another drag. "But thanks for having my brother's back though."

"Mike, hun." Foxy stepped forward and he turned towards her, oddly as if his little sister was speaking to him and she had his undivided attention. "This has been a very trying period for us, this Sarah gal had gone full-blown Mrs. Hyde and Corey here was sincerely up a tree about this whole mess and how to approach you..."

Mike smiled and even chuckled, as her interjected. "Thank you for all of that Samantha, my brother is very blessed to have someone like you who cares so much about him and others."

"What do we do now, Ghost?" Shawn looked to Mike for answers, a loyal confidant and soldier awaiting the next movement from the leader he adored. His devotion to Mike was beyond one of colors, it was family. His motives were beyond what was good for the Rep, it was about what was best for Mike. His support remained unwavering.

"Nothing." Mike peered across at a service door opening to the school as a custodian wheeled out a barrel of trash. "We can't have Truck do anything to little brother but I know what he wants." He glanced over at Shawn. "...this has to end, it's no good for any of us..." He turned towards me. "I'll take care of this Corey, don't worry about it." Mike drew close and put his arm around me. "I am sorry if I raised my voice at you..."

I looked up at him and nodded.

Shawn came over and put his hand around the back of my neck. "My bad for the way I treated you little brother, I lost my cool."

I peered at Shawn from the corner of my eye and nodded again. "It's fine, I apologize for keeping this from you both."

Mike and Shawn's eyes oscillated across the playing field and back to each other, as they strategized their next moves, squinting as they glanced at the setting sun across the field.

"How much you want to bet that this guy would stoop down to the level of getting his sister to sucker him into being with her, so he can have the moral high ground on this one?"

"Perhaps you are right..." Mike broke out a pack of cigarettes and packed them against his wrist. "...but I won't give that to him." He unwrapped the pack and removed a cigarette, placing it to his lips. "Core, you go have a nice evening with the two of them." Mike lit up the cigarette. "...you earned it..." He exhaled the smoke. "Just please do me a favor, don't ever keep this stuff from me again..."

"I won't." I nodded. "Thanks, Mike..."

"You good..." He replied coolly.

I took Melissa by the hand and Foxy took Melissa's other arm as we made our way to the gate.

"Corey!"

I turned around to look at Mike.

"You played a heck of a game today." Mike smiled at me as he took another drag of his smoke. "I'm proud of you, bro."

I threw the game ball to him. He made a one-handed catch look easy.

"What's this for?"

"You give the game ball to the most valuable player."

He smiled back at me.

"I love you Mike."

"I love you too, little brother," Mike said, his smile warm but weary.

He pointed his cigarette at Samantha, the faint cherry glow like a beacon in the night. "Foxy, my brother is a lucky man and doesn't even know it."

Samantha shook her head and laughed softly, her auburn hair catching the glow of the streetlights as she walked beside Melissa. As we made our way to the gate, I glanced back at Mike. He leaned against the fence, a faint trail of smoke curling into the twilight. For a moment, he looked invincible—a man reborn, ready to face the world. Little did I know, those words and that image of him would linger in my mind forever.

Chapter 18 – The Ice Shack

In Valley Stream, the Ice Shack was a small hut that served over 100 flavors of Italian Ices. On summer nights, Rockaway Avenue was filled with the chatter of children and food traffic snaking back toward the pavement. On that chilly October eve, the streetlights were already lit and the brisk autumn air tickled our cheeks. The shop was illuminated in fluorescent colors from the outside, inviting the stray passer-by to enter and have a scoop. As we opened the door, the heat from the vents caressed our faces still raw from the frost-hinted air.

"Little Ghost!" Numeralz put his finger up to the air and put his hand out to me, I slapped him five and gave him a hug as I carried onto the register with Sam and Mel following. Numeralz was there with some other guys associated with Dem Rep as they gave us all a cordial and respectful acknowledgment as we passed toward the register.

"What are you having, Corey?" Melissa looked over her shoulder as she was closest the case. My eyes perused the options until they settled on Strawberry Cheesecake. "I'll try that one." I pointed at it, Melissa eyed up the option and smiled back. "Good choice."

"Thank you, babe."

Melissa smiled again and glanced at Samantha. "Fox?"

"Orange and Vanilla, please." She put her hands in the pockets of her blue jeans. "I am a traditional gal."

"You think I didn't pick that up?" I raised my eyebrows at her.

"What?" Samantha flicked her hair.

"The colors of Tennessee..."

"It's a coincidence." She chuckled and nudged me with her elbow.

"I am sure." I put my hand around her back, our heads slightly tapped to each other. When Melissa looked over her shoulder, I saw a brooding glare in her eyes until she forced a smile back to her face. "I am really glad, that things worked out with Mike." She interjected.

"Me too..." I took hold of our cups of ices. "Thank you..." I smiled at the worker behind the counter in a blue polo shirt which matched the tops of all the others wearing the same uniform. "I feel like everything is going to be alright now...."

"Good, that's why you don't keep things to yourself." She winked at me and put her arm around Foxy's waist as I led them to the door and opened it for them.

We sat together the three of us, enjoying the still evening talking about movies and music, for once it was good not to talk about football or anything serious, and have light conversation. As we chatted and giggled at our silly remarks, I noticed that some of the ice had dabbed the top of Samantha's nose, glowing orange even more vividly under the streetlights that glowed in matching hue. It's such unique details that often accompany a memory, no matter how pleasant or harrowing it may be.

"Sam, you have some ice on your nose."

Melissa looked up and slapped her thigh, laughing. "What a mess..." She handed a napkin to Foxy, who took it reluctantly.

"Are y'all pulling my chain?"

"No..." Melissa took another lick of the swirl of red and purple cotton candy ice. "She's hopeless..." She chuckled and shook her head. "She can't see it, give her a hand, please..."

I laughed as I gently dabbed the napkin against the tip of her nose and smiled at her. Sam's eyes twinkled back at me, dilating slightly as a gentle smile filled her face. We got lose in the gaze, one that was encapsulating and drowned out the world around us.

"So that's the bitch you dropped me, Corey?" A voice shouted interrupting the peaceful moment. Across from us stood Sarah with her arms crossed, sporting a leather coat and black leggings which matched her eyes filled with rage and malice. Her waves of hair descended around her face, crowning her scorn.

"Sarah?"

"Is that her?" Melissa rushed to her feet.

Samantha nodded.

"Bitch you need to back up." Melissa huffed but I placed my arm firmly around her gripping one of the loops of her blue jeans as I pressed my hand against her black tank top. "It's cool, beautiful. I got this."

"No, you don't." Sarah snickered back at me.

Foxy raised her hands. "Whatever the trouble is, can we talk about this like civilized folk?"

"I remember her..." Sarah laughed and pointed at Foxy. "So, is she the sidepiece or was it me?" Her finger moved in the direction of Melissa. "And you are his girl, apparently..."

"That's right and what are you going to do about it?" Melissa jeered as I kept my hand tight around her stomach, her abdominals flexing as her adrenaline continued to build in her.

Some Dem Rep members and Numeralz began to take notice, keeping a close eye on me as they chatted amongst themselves.

"That's enough, Sarah."

"Yea, why don't you watch what you say about my man and my friend!" Melissa sneered.

"So, it is her?" Sarah stepped towards me and Melissa. "I really thought it was red-head over there."

Melissa emerged from around me and got face-to-face with Sarah. "Are you going to do something?" She looked at Sarah from the bridge of her nose. "You little plastic trick."

"Come on..." I stepped in front of Melissa and Samantha ran over to pull her away. However, Melissa cunningly stepped around me and evaded Samantha to push Sarah into the wall. A loud thud crackled through the air as her back met brick. Sarah cringed and pushed off the wall to lunge at Melissa.

Once again, I attempted to get between the two and voices started to yell from all directions. Numeralz and Slick jumped into break up the fight and Foxy tried to reason with her friend away from the mass of bodies that were now engaging in taunts and threats. In the midst of the pandemonium, I heard a gun cock. It was a noise distinct and clearly discernible, very quickly it brought everything to a hush.

"I'd step the fuck away from her now. If I were you!" A voice commanded, emerging from the group of patrons was Truck, himself.

"Tell ya bitch to back the fuck off!" He waved the gun around in the air and alarm filled me. When he pointed the firearm in the direction of Melissa and Foxy, I had already stepped in front of both of them to shield them.

"Sarah, come here..." Truck summoned her with his hands. She slowly strolled over to Truck who was backed by some of his cohorts. "It's okay, sis..." He put his arm around her and kissed her on the side of the head.

"Now before I lay you out..." Truck fixed his pistol on me and though I was scared, I was happy it wasn't Samantha or Melissa that was the target. "...let me remind you of the ground rules."

"Fuck you." I glared at him and his eyes raised with surprise. "You are the one that brought the piece out."

"The safety is on." He laughed as he clicked it off. "Do you want to fucking test me, motherfucker?"

"Go ahead."

"Corey..." Foxy's hand latched to my wrist.

"Sam, step off to the side please." I kept myself in front of her to ensure she wasn't in harm ways. "I am sick of his shit." I stared Truck in the brown of his eyes. "...this is between you and me."

Truck laughed with his gun still locked on me. "You are right..." He gave me a nod of respect. "I will give you one thing: you have a lot more balls than your brother." Truck nodded once more. "I honestly mean that." His gaze fixed on me with a peek of respect shimmering in his dark eyes. "But nevertheless, if they deal with you..." He pointed his free hand at Foxy and Melissa. "...they are involved too."

"You leave them the out of this, motherfucker!"

"You know what?!" He looked at his reflection in the steel chamber of the pistol. "I wanted it to work out with my sister because she really liked you. So, I did that for her." He started to advance on me. "But what did you do? You broke her heart and now as promised, I'm going to break your face!" Truck clutched his pistol in hand but his path was impeded as various members of Dem Rep and the Street Sovereigns started to converge on each other.

"Step away from my brother!" Another voice took over the crowd.

Truck paused in his tracks, as well as both gangs who were feet away from scrapping it out; it was Mike. My brother always came through in the most inexplicable of ways.

Truck looked down, unsure of what to do next, the situation had taken an unexpected turn and clearly not gone according to plan. He circled in his tracks and scratched his head. "It was only a matter of time, Ghost."

Mike stepped in front of me and pushed me of the direction of the firearm. Samantha drew close to my right and Melissa drew to my left. I could feel my jersey rising on Samantha as she took each breath in anticipation. I looked at her out of the corner of her eyes and held her hips tighter; Melissa was more composed leaning into me as she watched Sarah with an icy glare.

My brother was not dressed in any colors or gang paraphernalia. It was clear he was neutral; he wore a white t-shirt and black jeans.

Shawn flanked Mike forming a barrier between Melissa, Foxy, and I, he nodded back at us.

"You are wrong. Truly, this has always been about you and I, James..." Mike looked over his shoulder at the other members of Dem Rep. "Take a step back, boys."

Shawn looked over at his compatriots and nodded at them to take a step back. The Street Sovereigns present, stood vigil unsure of what was happening; they were expecting a fight but instead witnessed discourse.

"I am sorry."

"You're sorry?" James rose his eyebrows, stunned at what he was hearing.

"I am sorry that it had to come to this." The streetlight seemed to glow against Mike's T-shirt in that moment as if he were chosen to speak and bring reason to the crowd that surrounded him.

"Are you serious, Ghost?"

"My name is not Ghost anymore Jimmy, its Mike." He clutched the bandana is his hand, ready to let it go. "I am sorry for my brother; I know he broke your sister's heart but..." Mike looked back at me. "He's still unsure of what he wants..." A faint smile was directed at Sam and then back toward me. "...conflict causes confusion."

"What has happened to you, Mike?"

Clearly, Truck expected a melee or a chaotic brawl to spill out onto Rockaway Avenue. He was visibly shaken and scared as the situation was once again out of his control.

"I think it's time we put this to bed James."

"So, are we supposed to just be cool now?" Truck shook his head. "Pretend that we don't have years of hatred between us!" He huffed.

"That's up to you, that can end today..." Mike attempted to reason with him further.

"We can't just let this go to bed! This shit is live more than ever especially now that you sent your brother to hurt my sister!"

"That's not what happened and you know that!" Mike raised his hand. "You and me have always handled things personally."

"I'll give you that." Truck crossed his arms.

"He didn't even know that Sarah and you were related. I can also make the argument that your sister attempted to seduce my brother as a ploy, but I am not accusing her or you..."

Truck lifted the gun and pointed it downward at Mike. "You shut the fuck up! How dare you, ever insult my sister as to say she is some whore that I would sick on your little brother to get at you." He appeared flustered; Truck was saving face in the worst possible way. He wanted a way out but didn't want to look weak. You can see the confusion in his eyes.

"I am not saying that, Jimmy. But put the gun down..."

Truck lowered the pistol. "And then what?"

"You tell me, Jimmy." Mike put his hands in his pockets. "Is another brawl between The Rep and your boys going to solve anything. Does someone have to die before we finally get this shit right?"

"No Mike, the only people that die are you and your pathetic excuse of a crew over there." He waved the gun. "You guys die! Just like you always should have!"

"Is that what you really want?"

Truck held his tongue. He wanted to say no but he couldn't, so he said nothing and gripped the gun tighter.

"This is about Jessie, isn't it?"

The question took all the wind out of Truck's sails; you could see Mike hit a nerve, even if he didn't mean to.

"I think you know, Mike."

"Jimmy, you treated her like a doormat but I wanted her for a wife."

All eyes were glued upon Mike. From me it was a look of pride; to his gang-brothers it was disbelief; to Samantha it was captivation in the romance of it all; to Melissa it was shock.

"And out of respect for you, I waited until you and her were through but I couldn't deny what was there." Mike looked over at Foxy and myself. "I didn't want to have any regrets...."

"Nah, you don't fuckin understand Mike, I loved her." Truck shook with the pistol held tightly in his hand.

For the first time, Mike seemed to show some empathy towards Truck. "Well if you loved her Jimmy, why did you treat her the way you did?" He kept a calm tone.

"Because, I was afraid..." He swiped his forehead. "That you all would make fun of me."

"It should have never mattered what we thought, Jim."

"You are right." He lowered the gun. "When I was a kid, my dad used to tell me all the time why can't you be more like Sarah? Why can't you get good grades? Always calling me a loser!" Truck shook as he pointed the gun at Mike yet again. "You know what it was like..." His hands shook. "...that's why we were boys."

Mike nodded.

"I didn't want people thinking I was soft when I was with you guys because everywhere else someone had something bad to say about me! But then what do you do? You steal my girlfriend!" Truck started to scream ferociously. "It wasn't enough for you to jump me and then your little brother starts fucking with my little sister!"

"Did you forget that you snitched me out, Jim?"

Truck went silent, frustrated by Mike's tact. He looked around at his compatriots to see if there was any frailty after Mike's remark, a secret he hoped to keep tucked away in his past.

"It's done now, Jim." Mike extended forward. "Let's put this behind us and go have a cup of coffee. Maybe, we can finally have some peace."

RJ nodded a show of respect at Mike, Shawn reciprocated the goodwill by giving RJ a nod of respect in return.

"We can leave everyone else to enjoy the rest of their evening..."

"No, fuck you." Truck pointed the gun carelessly. "You aint talking this down!"

"Point the gun at me, Jim!"

"Tell me Mike, how does it feel to have something you love threatened to be taken away from you?!" He took a step to find a gap to angle the pistol in my direction, but he couldn't. Shawn and Mike were a fortress and we were safe behind the walls.

"Don't you dare point that gun at my brother again..." Mike replied firm but he was losing his composure. "I will tell you one more time, leave him out of it, or else...."

"There is the Ghost, I know..." Truck began to breathe heavy. "But you are right, maybe I should just shoot you instead." The gun shook in his hand, Truck was rattled and you could see it. Though he wore a tough exterior he didn't know what to do next. He was scared, he was scared for his life and he wasn't thinking.

I left from Foxy and Melissa and stepped in front of Mike, putting a hand on his chest. "Mike, let's get out of here..."

"Corey, get back!" Mike pushed me behind him. "Jim, let's take this down a notch."

"Now you want to de-escalate?" He shouted. "Make up your mind, Mike!"

Both sides started to yell at each other and exchange hostile words until eventually they rushed each other. I turned my back for a moment to move Melissa and Samantha toward the street to safety, using myself as a buffer to protect them. Before any fists were thrown, a gun went off and echoed through the night. Both parties froze in their tracks, all focused on a body lying on the ground.

Truck stood with the gun still smoking in his hand as he stared at the body with horror. The body lying on the ground was Mike. Blood poured through his white shirt from his stomach, spreading across his shirt and soaking him in a pool of red. You could see it on Truck's face, he knew he made a grave mistake - he squeezed the trigger by reflex not intent.

Mike was on the ground shivering as I rushed to him, patrons, allies, and enemies scattering in every direction away from the scene. The gun fell out of Truck's hand as his complexion grew pale with sheer lament.

"Mike!" I put my hand around his head and held him up. "Someone call for help!"

In the background Shawn was on his cell phone calling an ambulance, others sprinted and shouted for assistance but Truck stood there frozen.

"I didn't want anything...." Mike shook violently. "...to happen to you..."

Mike took my hand and I held it with my other. "Stay with me, big brother!"

Foxy and Melissa were on the phone calling for help as well with tears trickling down both their faces.

As I looked over at Sarah, she was trying to break Truck from his trance, pleading with him to flee but he couldn't move, he stood there with tears running from his eyes as he looked down at Mike lying on the floor.

"I am glad I won't be going to hell..." Mike chuckled as he expended every ounce of effort to talk. "Do me a favor..." Blood flooded into his mouth, staining his teeth.

"Mike, please...."

He grabbed my shirt, his fingers going limp as he held onto me. "Give the bandana to Jessie..." His head started to move back. "...it's the one I started The Rep with..." Mike began to breathe less frequently. "I am finally out...."

"Mike..." I started to shake. Shawn came over and joined me. When I looked up, I noticed Truck and Sarah were gone.

"Help is coming, Ghost." Shawn knelt down beside me. Both of us looked around for any sign of an ambulance or police car as the girls sprinted back towards us.

"Tell her I love her." Mike wept. "I should have walked away."

"I love you..." I became hysterical. "You saved me..." I felt his blood-soaked hand reach up and touch my face.

"That's what big brothers are for." Mike stopped breathing and went limp.

"No!!!!!" I cried hysterically on top of him. I didn't hear the sirens or anyone else come, just the words of my prayers until I felt someone pull me off of Mike. It was one of the EMT's clad in a grey work shirt and matching pants, his face indiscernible behind my tears.

"Please help him." I grabbed the clean-shaven black-haired technician.

Shawn placed his arm on my shoulder. I focused my attention back to the EMT's that placed Mike on a stretcher. I leapt from my feet, growling as I rushed forward to lift a bench.

"Corey!"

I turned back to the sound of Foxy's voice, tears had soaked various spots of her cheeks. She opened her arms and invited me into them to seek refuge. She placed my head against her breast and rubbed my head with tenderness. I closed my eyes and pretended that it wasn't actually happening and that this would all be over soon; it must be a nightmare. Only an hour ago, I was walking past the sign welcoming us to Valley Stream, but that's how it always goes, you never see it coming.

As the sirens painted the street in flashing red and blue, I closed my eyes, desperate to wake up. Maybe this wasn't real. Maybe in five

A DAY WE MET IN LYNBROOK 255

minutes, I'd be back on the porch with Mike, joking like we always did. But the blood on my hands told me otherwise.

Foxy's embrace tightened around me, her tears warm against my neck. Melissa's hand found mine, anchoring me as my world crumbled. My brother was gone, and the world felt emptier, colder. In that moment, I didn't feel the autumn air or hear the chaos around me. All I felt was a hollow ache, and all I could think was: *I wasn't ready to say goodbye* but Mike was dead.

Chapter 19 – Flowers for a Funeral

I didn't sleep much that night, if it all. Melissa stayed with me but all I did was lay in bed and stare at the ceiling. I was numb and I didn't know what to feel as it still didn't seem real. Why didn't Truck shoot me instead of Mike? But did he really want to shoot anyone? It didn't matter anyhow.

I slithered out of bed and threw the comforter over Melissa as I went out to the porch. My mother was in her bedroom and the door was shut but I could hear faint sniffles muffling behind it. I wanted to check on her but I didn't want to wake her in case, I was wrong. She was reluctant to leave the bedroom as it was and if she had finally managed to escape this grief and sorrow that was everywhere in our house, I would be relieved to know she found some respite.

I sat on the couch and stared out into sunlight as I removed Mike's pack of Marlboros and his lighter which were recovered off his body. I lit up a smoke, placing a false hope that the cigarette would bring him back somehow and I'd see him leaning against the railing philosophizing as he always did.

I checked my cell phone and saw missed calls from Ricky and Coach Kenny. There was a message from Foxy which said *I am with you tonight even if you feel there is no one*. I wish she was here now, she understood, and she was there.

I didn't know who else to call or what to say to anyone else: so, I called no one. After thirty minutes of sitting on the porch in silence and dense introspection, I got up and started to walk with no destination in mind, I just wandered. Somehow, I found myself on Central Avenue. I lit up another smoke and took in the landscape of colonial-style houses and oak trees. There was nothing in particular I was focusing my attention on until I found myself approaching Foxy's house. I looked up to her window and thought what she might be doing. The curtains were drawn so maybe she was still resting. As I got down to the intersection of the next street (Woodlawn Avenue), I heard her call out to me, just like she did last night in the aftermath of the shooting.

"Corey!"

I turned around and smiled for a brief moment at the sight of her. Her hair was still messy, fresh out of bed, but she had a radiance about her that followed her everywhere she went. She was wearing an orange Tennessee Volunteers tank-top with a picture of Smokey their mascot on it and white UFO pants with long black flares.

There was a relief that came with her presence, her simply being there made me feel at ease and even joyful. I didn't know what to say to Foxy but I didn't need to.

"What are you doing here?" Foxy grabbed me and pulled me in for a tight embrace and I threw the cigarette away from her before I gripped her tightly.

"I needed to see you..." The words muffled as they lift my trembling lips. She rubbed the back of my head. I didn't say anything more, I just enjoyed the comfort that it brought while I gazed over her shoulder focused on the concrete before the grief finally sunk in.

"I went for a walk and ended up here." I looked towards the grass wafting in the gentle autumn breeze. "I can't sleep."

"Would like to come inside?" Some strands of her hair flicked a passing breeze.

I reflected back to everything Mike ever said about Foxy in that moment. She had to know.

"Mike thought you were special."

She broke a smile and held her hands together. "Thank you for sharing that with me. That's awfully kind."

"He couldn't say enough nice things about you." I recollected with a chuckle. "About how you are sweet, funny, and smart. I can keep going but I wouldn't want to inflate your ego."

Foxy smiled, delighted that I was in good spirit in that instance. "It means the world to me." I flicked her hair. "Sorry if my hair gets all over you, it's a mess."

"You look beautiful, Foxy."

"Thank you." Foxy blushed and nodded, her cheeks raising to reflect her modest reaction to the compliment.

"I should have listened to him." I looked up to the sky for a moment.

"About what?"

"You."

A shame filled her, perhaps that she couldn't do any more to acknowledge what I told her or full of remorse that such a conversation was being had while her best friend was back at my house asleep in the bed.

"You are grieving and I understand that when you lose someone, these things can replay in our heads. Corey, you are with my best friend..." She drew close. "You are unlike any guy I've ever met. You're really good to Melissa and you are a great friend to Ricky. Your teammates love you, your brother loved you, and I love you." Foxy hesitated for a second, as her tongue rolled over the last part of her response. "You have a good heart." She let her hair out of her scrunchie and I gently guided it out to help her.

Her words lifted my spirit, they made me want to pray that they would be true and that I would do everything to fulfill them. In that time spent having that brief dialogue with Foxy, I had completely forgotten about everything. Everything seemed safe, peaceful and back to normal, as if I expected to see Mike at home to rip on me after I went down to see Samantha. I looked into Samantha's blue eyes and saw Mike smiling back at me from me.

Foxy moved her head toward her house. "So, have you had a word with her yet?"

"Who?"

"Your girlfriend?" Foxy raised her eyebrows. "She's called Melissa, does that ring a bell?"

"I don't know, maybe it's a sign." I threw my hands on my hips. "A sign that her and I were never meant to be. Look what happened as a result."

"Whoever you are meant to be with, you will be. Trust me." Foxy sat under the small apple tree on the front lawn. "But you are with her, now..."

I sat beside her. "Forget about her..." my pulse thumped in me as the words forced themselves from my mouth. "You deserve to be with someone that should be blessed in your presence."

"I say the same for you Corey, but you should give Mel a chance..." Foxy turned her head and set her gaze upon me, her blue eyes had a way of drawing me in where there was nothing else perceptible around them. "It's what you wanted, right?"

"I don't know..."

"This is all raw right now, it's to be expected that you'll push away people that are close to you." She leaned her head against mine and looked out toward the street.

"I would never push you away..."

Foxy turned her head and her eyes seemed to brighten, as if they were looking deeper to resolve a mystery hidden within me.

"I don't know what to think anymore, Sam." I grabbed my nose. "Maybe he is right..." I sniffled. "Maybe you are my Jessie."

"Jessie?" Foxy glanced over at me with a look of intrigue.

"A woman that he loved." I rubbed the bridge of my nose. "She made him want to be the best of version of himself."

"I see..." She put her head back against mine as we both reclined against the tree.

"She made him believe that life can be really great. He said she was his greatest blessing that The Lord could provide in this life and he was grateful to him for it."

"Strong words from a man who was keen to shag Katie in a bush."

I laughed heartily for a moment. Samantha's wit and dark sense of humor were second to none.

"That's why Mike liked you so much." I tapped her thigh. "He said you were genuine...."

Samantha's cheeks parted as a wide smile filled her face until she grew serious again.

"And kind...."

The words caught in my throat; the blowing of the wind reminded me again that was he gone but Samantha was still there. A hollowness filled me, what happened to everything? What happened to me? The tears filled my eyes as my voice broke. "He's dead." I broke out in tears and Samantha threw her arms around me. Such episodes and outbursts came in the days to follow until when I finally saw Mike's body lying in a casket for all to pay their final respects; it was surreal. Mike was always a man that was lively and energetic, to see him motionless with no life, with no expression on his face was foreign to me.

The turnout for his funeral was enormous, among all those in attendance, members of Dem Rep all dressed in suits and ties with green bandanas tied around their right wrists with the name Ghost written across it to pay homage to Mike. Coach Kenny stood in the rear with most of the team beside and behind him, including Marlon Green. Christina Caputo and various cheerleaders were also there, vividly portraying Mike's remarkable ability to bring people together.

Foxy held my hand and Ricky sat beside me on my other side. I looked back into the second row at my dad sitting in disbelief, his starch white shirt tucked into black dungarees as he twitched his moustache; some involuntary spasm to help process what he was seeing.

He came with my step-mother Catherine, a woman with long flowing blonde hair over a black wool top and trousers, she was a bit more full-figured and perhaps five or ten years younger than my father. This was the woman that he left Mom for and it was the first time I was properly introduced to her aghast that such tragic circumstances brought such an encounter together.

I remained in a world of my own, I couldn't form words. I saw in the front row reiterating the same prayers and wishes that I would wake up from this, that this would all over be soon. The service went by in a blur as the pastor finished his benediction and invited all who wish to say their final farewells up to the front and kneel before the casket. As the procession filed, each member of Dem Rep placed their bandana in the casket with Mike. They each said a prayer and kissed their hand before placing it upon Mike's forehead. He had left it all behind but it didn't matter to them, as blood was thicker than water. My teammates followed and paid their respects to my fallen brother and extended their support and love to my family and me, each in their own way. I collapsed my heads into my hands until I felt a hand touch my shoulder. When I looked up it was Marlon Green standing over me.

"I'm sorry for the loss of your brother and I'm also sorry for the way I treated you." He extended his hand to mine and I took it.

"Life is too short for grudges." I replied.

"If you need anything, I'll be here if you want to talk."

"Thank you, Greenie."

"And if you ever want to go over plays when you are ready. I'm back with the team as an assistant.

"I really appreciate all of that." I pulled him in for a hug and he met me with a pat of the shoulder.

"Anytime Gingy." He patted my shoulder once more before exiting.

Coach Kenny approached me after he spent some time to console my mother who was crying in my aunt Pattie's arms. When

Coach approached me, he didn't say anything, he pulled me in for a hug.

"My condolences, Corey."

"Thank you, Coach."

"There is nothing that I can say or do that's going to change the way you feel right now. I will do everything I can to support you and help you get through this. If you need someone to talk to, it can be any time of any day, I am only a phone call away. If you need help with anything, we will be here for you." He released the hug and put his arm around me as he glanced back at the casket. "If you need to take a break from football right now, we'll be waiting for you when you are ready..." Coach looked into my eyes. "Take your time with this...."

Despite the beautiful prose, I couldn't shake the heavy woe I was feeling. After arriving home from the service, I spent the night with Foxy and Melissa and barely ate. Samantha was relentless in her attempts to lift my spirits. She called up a favor from her friend Alison and acquired a 24-pack of beer for the three of us to drink. I dove in head first and after a few hours of sitting on my porch with the two girls, I became rambunctiously drunk.

"That was really sweet of Foxy..." I stepped on the porch. "I couldn't thank her enough." I placed the can of beer on the table and collapsed on the couch. "It's a shame we went..."

"We can go back, if you really want too..." There was a tinge of displeasure in Melissa's voice as she sat beside me and sipped on her Budweiser. I had sprawled out, sloppy, disheveled and all over the place as I drunk double the amount she did and thus I was severely intoxicated. Looking back, I am amazed that I can even recall the events with any form of fluidity.

"It's all good..." I fought through the spins and sat up, a momentary throb before my head felt less heavy. "And now for the burial on Friday." My fingers shook as I put a cigarette between my lips. "I still can't believe it." I took the first drag after I lit the cigarette and stared into the solace of the night.

There was a silence that followed which was all the more awkward, a dissonance of two minds in two different locations though physically present in the same space.

"What time is it?" I looked at my watch. "Good Lord, its 2:30 in the morning. Don't you need to get home?" I sipped on my beer and glanced over at Melissa.

"I am staying with you." She rubbed my hand. "Did you forget?" She feigned a smile.

"I don't know Mel, maybe it's best if I am alone." I placed my head back and the porch began to spin when I closed my eyes.

"You just said you wanted to see Foxy a minute ago, if you don't want me to be here..."

I interrupted her with a raised hand.

"Stay please, I am no position to walk you home..." I slurred my words as the alcohol continued to set in. The cigarette fell out of my hand and on the porch. I heard Melissa jump to her feet and stamp the cigarette out. Every step was loud and pronounced against the solid work panels.

"Samantha is going to come down right?" I abruptly opened my eyes again to see tears in Melissa's.

"She's coming, right?"

I rose to my feet and nearly toppled over doing so until Melissa extended her hand to grab me.

"Let's go get her."

"Corey, I don't understand..." She sniffled. "I am trying to be here for you and you have your girlfriend who you apparently always wanted to be with, and all you think about is her best friend."

"She's also my best friend, you know..."

"Corey, if I were going through the same thing, I wouldn't ask Ricky to sit next to me in the service, I'd ask you..."

"Don't tell me what you would do, it's not like you are the one going through it, right?" I snickered.

"That's not what I am trying to say."

"What are you trying to say?" I snapped again at her.

"I just want to know if there is something wrong."

"Well there's nothing wrong other than fact my brother is dead!" I got off the bench and stumbled as I made way to the door. I halted and looked back at her, signaling her to come in with me as I held the door for her. "Don't you want to come in?"

"Do you want me to come in?" Melissa cried.

"Of course, I do..." I held open the door once more and she walked through the threshold before we made our way up to the room. When I laid down in bed beside her, I fell asleep right away and was woken up a few hours later by Melissa who was fidgeting.

"Is something wrong?" I muttered.

"No, it's fine"

"What is it?" I honed every ounce of strength to communicate to her whilst my face was immersed in the pillow.

"This is the wrong time..."

"No, it's not." I dragged my head out from the pillow and looked over at her.

"You said a name when you were asleep."

"Let me guess..." I chuckled. "Foxy?"

Her face dropped at the mention of it.

"There could be a million reasons why, I am bit fucked up as you know..."

"Well wouldn't you be a bit concerned if you heard me say another man's name while I was asleep?"

I sat up abruptly and caught a case of vertigo that pounded my head. "Do you hear yourself?" I rubbed my forehead to alleviate the throbbing. "Seriously?"

"Corey, I just want to know."

"Know what?" I threw my hands up.

"If you want to be with me or Foxy?"

"What kind of question is that?" I clenched my fist. "Shouldn't I ask the same question?" A visceral rage filled me and I could no longer hold my tongue. "Are you sure you want to be with me this time Melissa? We all know you played me like a yo-yo for two whole months while you obsessed over some scumbag who was cheating on you!"

"I said I am sorry!" She yelled back at me. "What more can I do to show you I want to be with you?"

"Well for starters stop being jealous of your best friend!"

"You think I am jealous of Foxy?" Melissa quipped. "For real?"

She denied as much as she wanted and tried to put on a brave face, but it was clear. She had acted off in the funeral when she had to sit behind my mother with Shawn while Foxy was next to me, at my request. It had nothing to do with Melissa, Samantha was someone I felt safe to be vulnerable with and she was my companion through all of the twists and turns. Is it not possible that a man and a woman could share such affection for each other without a witch hunt?

"It seems pretty obvious." I retorted.

"Well I am not."

"Alright then, so leave me alone about this shit." I put my head back down. "I got bigger things to worry about, this aint The O.C."

"You know what? It's nearly six. Maybe I should just get home and get some sleep, I tried."

"WELL THEN GO RIGHT AHEAD!" I shot up from my bed. "Leave like you always do Melissa and don't let the door hit your ass on the way out. Next time please make sure no one's brother dies as a result of your back and forth bullshit!"

Melissa was expressionless. She looked as if a nuclear bomb had dropped and as if she were gazing at the blast. As soon as I said it,

I felt horrible. I put my head down, overcome by remorse and grief that I would say such a terrible thing.

"I'm sorry." I softened my tone. "I shouldn't have said that."

"Is that what you really think?"

I shook my head, "No..."

"I am going to go for a bit and forget you said that..." She made her way to the door. "Call me in a few hours when you've sobered up...."

"That's what you always do..." I spoke under my voice.

"What?" Melissa turned back and glowered at me; her eyes glowed with anger. She looked like she was ready to cry but equally ready to fight.

"All this talk about Foxy" I shot to my feet. "Well guess what? She wouldn't fucking leave me, she never fucked with my head, and she never played games with my heart!" I stepped forward and got in Melissa's face. "So, maybe you should be jealous, not because of how I feel about her mind you..."

Rage bubbled in the capillaries of her eyes as tears flowed downward. I can tell that she wanted to slap me but instead she about-faced, opened the door, and slammed it behind her. I heard her boots clatter as she walked down the steps toward the main door. As I looked out at the window, I saw her brown hair trail her as she walked away.

To this day, I remember her gaze, it was one of disappointment that matched her anger and hurt. She expected more from me and I let her down, and even now since it has long been put to rest, I still feel horrible for the way I treated her. Melissa never deserved that, no one does.

But in that moment, I felt good; I felt relief from all the pain I was feeling and in control. She could never make up her mind about me and had she, there never would have been a Sarah. But that wasn't fair to put on her and the pursuit of Melissa led to one that was even greater. I didn't know that then and found myself soon overwhelmed by another surge of sorrow. I broke down on the windowsill and cried hysterically, alone.

Chapter 20 – Samantha Jayne Foxe

I thought that once the funeral and burial had passed that I could move on finally, that there was closure and I could quell the agony that I was feeling. I was wrong and I tried sorting things out on my own by skipping school and dodging practice. I didn't care anymore and I tried to further numb the sting of Mike's death with alcohol and cigarettes. People kept telling me that time would heal the wound, but the more that time passed the more it hurt.

His departure was even more evident; the absence of the smell of Newports burning in the wee hours of the morning was a gut-wrenching reminder that he was gone and was never coming back. My brother had been searching for redemption; he was searching for a chance to atone for the mistakes that he had made. Some would say that anger should be directed at God, for letting this tragedy happen. However, that would not be fit. The Lord was not going to be the convenient scapegoat that many have used in haste. The object of my scorn was Truck, the man who took Mike from me. The same man who pointed a gun at me and caused Mike to act as he did.

Truck became to me what Mike was to him. However, the cause of resentment could never be more different. Truck was envious of Mike because he was the embodiment of what he could never be. James "Truck" Marion's grudge was based on a feud he truly had with himself. He was angry that he let Jessie slip away and Mike was there to pick up the pieces. He was jealous that he didn't have the drive or courage that Mike had to go for what he wanted. The villain felt he could only rectify his internal dilemmas by destroying the epitome of those successes he wished he could have attained.

All statues crumbled and to me, Truck was a monument of acrimony. A reminder of all that is wrong in this world: a target I wished to destroy. In my rage, I was committed to devising the wickedest schemes to bring forth his end. I sat at Westwood Train Station with a 40-ounce bottle of St. Ide's in my hand and smoked a cigarette lit by Mike's lucky Zippo lighter. I gazed down at Mike's bandana and clutched a knife in my hand. In a cyclical pattern, I continued to review my strategy and what I planned to do when I found Truck. The son of a bitch was out on bail, so I assumed he was probably at home. Like the coward I imagined him to be, I was sure he would be hiding. Nevertheless, my rage reassured me that there was no place in this world safe enough for him. My plan was simple: I was going to take the bus over to Rockville Centre and wait until he left his house. I didn't care how long it would take, as long as I got the chance to kill him in the most intimate and personal of fashions. I wanted to look him in the eye and make it slow. This was my obsession that consumed me, I had not spoken to Samantha, Ricky, or Melissa for days. All I could imagine is the surge of relief I would feel once the dagger pricked his skin. Once the look of terror filled him, when he knew this is where it ended, and it was ending because of what he did.

I shut my eyes and felt the chilled breeze draped around me, cloaking the darkness of Westwood with a stillness after it settled. *Enjoy this serenity while you can*, I thought. The bus stop is only a five-minute walk and once I was on, there was no turning back. I took another drag of my cigarette as the gates fell, the chimes humming all those close to stand back from the passing train which soon rushed by. Once, it was quiet again, I took it all once more.

"Heavenly Father, forgive me for what I am about to do." I flicked my cigarette. "I love you, big brother." I smashed the bottle of lager against the ground in a fit of rage.

"Corey!"

I looked behind me and there stood Samantha. She had her hair in a bun and wore my Lynbrook Football sweatshirt along with plaid pajama pants.

"Sam?" My rage quickly disarmed at the sight of her.

"I have been trying to call you."

"I am sorry, I left my phone in my room before I came here. How did you know I was here?"

Her eyes glanced down, as I should have known the answer to that question. "What's that in your hand?" She reached into my hand slowly as she noticed the bandana wrapped around the knife.

I pulled back swiftly, covering the blade to ensure she didn't touch it or it touched her. "It's nothing."

She grabbed my open hand with a soft yet firm grip, her eyes alarmed at the sight of the knife. "What's gotten into you?"

"I'm need to take care of something, please let me go!"

"What are you going to do?" Tears began to trickle down Samantha's cheeks. "Kill him?"

"Samantha, he has to pay for what he has done!" My muscles began to spasm from the fury I felt radiating within me. "All he wanted was another chance. A chance to do things right and leave the negativity behind. Because of Truck, Mike will never have the chance to be the person he was meant to be!"

"I am sorry for what you are going through and I'd give anything to change that." She attempted to reason with me. "But this isn't right. The way you treated Melissa, the truancy, and now this?!"

"I am getting on the bus and I am going there to finish this." I gently took her hand off my wrist and about-faced towards Whitehall Street. Rage and anger had consumed me and I refused to wait any longer to settle this account. But Foxy told hold of my wrist and squeezed it, reminding me of what my mother would do to me when I misbehaved as a child.

"Put it down." She pressed my hand downward.

"Okay..." I knelt down and placed the blade on the ground away from her.

"You are wrong, Mike became the person he truly was meant to be because he always was that person." Sam cupped my hands in hers. "When he was with Jessie, he was the best version of himself. When Mike was with you, Mike was the best version of himself also. In fact, Mike did the greatest thing any person can do, he gave his life for someone he loved." Samantha grazed my thumb with hers, her hands far smoother to mine. "The shooting was an accident and even so, Mike made sure you were safe. Mike didn't come to provoke a fight but he came to bring peace to both sides. Even in his final moments, he was loving to all." Tears fell down her face. "How could you even think of this after everything?!"

"Sometimes you have to do what you have to do." I pulled my hand away.

Samantha reached for my arm. "Have you learned nothing?"

"I learned everything from him!" I jerked my arm free a second time. "And I am not letting this go!"

"Do you reckon he would want you to throw away football?"

I bit my lip.

"What about Ricky? or your mom?" Her eyes narrowed. "What about me?!"

The thought her of absence filled me with a pain that was just as profound as the grief I was feeling.

"Stay here with me." It was hard to detect whether her soothing touch was one that came from a sister or a lover, or perhaps both in this occasion but I had to get vengeance, he couldn't get away with what he did. Psalm 59 needed to be acted out in order for me to be satisfied.

"Sam, I love you, and I care for you..."

Foxy tensed at the words.

"...I am truly sorry for the way I acted towards Melissa and the way I have been in general lately." I placed my hand over my chest. "I've been horrible and wish I could snap out of it..." I bit my lip and held back a tear. "But it never ends..." The words formed in my mouth before they could escape my lips. "...You are the last person I'd ever want to hurt and normally I don't want to hurt anyone ever..."

And even then, somehow in the midst of my remorse and regret, I still wanted satisfaction. In my sordid thinking, I thought it would make things right if I took Truck and put his sister what he put me through. As energizing as revenge could be, it truly only causes more suffering because all you do is put more of it in the world while it doesn't take away what you had endured. It doesn't fix anything, only forgiveness can do that. That's what The Lord Jesus taught and I didn't understand it then but part of recovery is appreciating the notion.

"I am sorry, Sam..." I started to walk away again but Sam yanked me back toward her and kissed me on the lips. The feeling of her kiss was euphoric and in abrupt fashion, the malice that festered in my heart dissipated. In a matter of moments, I lost my breath and sensations of warmth and bliss flooded my body. We paused and gazed into each other's eyes. For a moment, I felt feelings of faith and hope. Thereafter, the sharp pain of Mike's death encompassed me.

I cried in her arms and she held me tight, rubbing the back of my head as I clutched her. In the midst of it, Sam started to shiver from the cold, I took off my coat and placed it around her.

"I don't want you to get sick." I smiled at her and rubbed her shoulders. Sam leaned into me and placed her head under my chin, wrapping herself in my arms as she embraced me tightly. I had everything I needed right then and there, there was no suffering; there was no desires for reprisals; there was Samantha and I was overjoyed at that.

"What do we do now, Sam?" I sighed and placed my chin gently over the top of her head.

"Come again?" She looked up and wrinkled her eyes, confused at the nature of the question.

"Where does all this leave us?"

"Where do you want it leave us?" She looked out onto the park. "I've been thinking a lot lately..."

"About us being together?" I smiled, perplexed that this was even a possibility given the circumstances. That truly seemed too good to be true, because it wouldn't be like any of these other adolescent dalliances that are driven by lust, hormones, teenage television drama, or infatuation. This was another level, this was real, this had the makings of an epic bond that could last a lifetime – one rooted in loyalty, partnership, and genuine love for another. I always thought about what it would be like and candidates that such a fantasy could unfold with, little did I know this is how it happened: completely out of nowhere. Just over a few months ago, I didn't even know her but now I couldn't imagine life without her. She was the one person I had always hoped would be there, could we really only be friends? Whether I liked it or not, she wasn't going to be an adopted sister.

"Yeah..." Her eyes revealed the sincerity and the seriousness of her remark.

"Is that what you really want?"

"Dukes and I spoke about this before Mike passed away..." Her cheeks crimsoned.

I looked up at the sky for a moment, baffled by what I was hearing. "She must hate me though and I don't blame her..."

"She doesn't...." She smiled back at me. "We should have been together all along but after this all unfolded, I was going to sit on this for a while." Samantha sighed. "But then I realized from this event, that we could wasting time that we'll never have. If only, we realized it sooner..."

"Are you sure, you want to be with me?" I raised my eyebrows. "I can't bear anymore heartbreak, not now..."

"More than anything..." She smiled gently and nodded, assured in what she was saying. As much as I was grateful and eager, I was terrified.

"How about you?" Foxy kissed my cheek and tilted her head slightly with a youthful half-smile.

All I had to do was say, yes. I wanted to tell her that she was the most beautiful human being on the planet and I am a better person by simply knowing her. Instead, I looked across the train tracks to Whitehall Street, at a passing bus: The N33; The plot soon consumed again and all possible contingencies. I could walk down the road to get the N15 in Lakeview and it would take me into Rockville Centre, that scoundrel could meet his fate in under an hour if I caught him on the street.

"I have to go and settle this once and for all." I rubbed her shoulder and started to walk towards the sump which led to a dead-end street which terminated at the edge of the park.

"Corey you can't!"

I took a cigarette out and placed it between my lips.

"Please for me." She yelled as her feet chatted against the sidewalk, giving chase to stop me. "If you go there and do what he did, you are worse than him!"

I threw the cigarette into the field and turned around abruptly, raising my hand in surrender.

"I wore your jersey for Homecoming even though you weren't there because I believe in you." Samantha stood firm with an impassioned gaze that overpowered everywhere she looked. "You are better than this."

"I have to square this away." I looked onward at the dead-end cul-de-sac that invited me to continue walking toward the bus stop with a glowing orange streetlight fixed to a lamppost. "May I walk you home?"

A DAY WE MET IN LYNBROOK 275

"No..." She crossed her arms. "...if you go through with this, you've made your decision..."

"Forgive me, then..." I pressed my lips to her cheek, she leaned toward me welcoming my return to her. "When this is all over, I'll come find you." I picked up the knife and marched off into the night.

Looking back that was the hardest thing to do. In retrospect, I still do not know how I could ever turn my back on Samantha. She didn't say anything back, perhaps she didn't imagine I would walk off from her and continue on with what I intended. Though I didn't have eyes in the back of my head, I could feel her looking on from behind me with great disappointment.

In that moment however, I was incensed. I continued on my trek down towards Whitehall Street, fixing my sight on the blade and its shimmering luster under the moonlight. I wrapped the bandana around the knife and reassured myself I made the right decision, plucking another cigarette from my pocket and igniting it in a glorious first puff. My mind began to recite many different verses of The Bible and though they were mere phrases flowing through my head, they were as loud as any preacher shouting them from the pulpit. In the midst of my rage, Mike's voice spoke to my heart.

"I lost my life, keep yours." The sheer thought caused me to freeze. He was right, should I continue onward I may lose it and I'd repeat the error Mike was attempting to erase. Love was staring back at me and I chose to pursue hate, what a folly. What would it prove? That I was careless and ungrateful?

Then I thought about Sam and what she had just experienced with me. I didn't want to put her through the agony of seeing my mugshot in the Herald. I remembered everything Mike said about her and I wanted her to be the Jessie that stayed, not the one that slipped away and could have been.

I stopped in my tracks to gather myself, take another drag of the cigarette and look up at the streetlight before I glanced back into the shadows of the park.

"Sam?" I called out to her but there was no answer.

I was helpless and didn't have answers but I realized I was blessed and grateful to have Samantha, someone so kind to come out into this blustery weather and attempt to prevent me from self-destruction. The Lord sent her, because He didn't want this; Mike didn't want this; I didn't want this, I tossed the knife down the drain and never turned back.

"Samantha!" I cried out as I sprinted back toward Westwood to find her but when I went back to where we were, she had already disappeared in the night. All that remained was a somber wind that dusted leaves across the dimly lit basketball court. I threw the cigarette and continued to sprint across the train tracks until I was on the Lynbrook side, nearly passing out from losing my breath. The air burned as I inhaled but I didn't care, perhaps I could catch her before it was too late!

When I got down to my street, my hands were resting over my knees. I trotted home and I tried calling Samantha but she wouldn't answer. Her phone was off, maybe I should go to her house and see if the light was on in her room, but it was late...

What was I thinking? She was there in front of me, she was mine, and I let her go. The emptiness left behind felt sharper than my anger ever had. That night, when I finally fell asleep, I had a dream. I saw the image of Samantha and me getting married. Her long auburn hair smoothly straightened and descending over a white satin halter corseted dress with a long flowing veil behind her. She didn't wear much make-up, but she never needed it, she was breathtaking as she was.

What was most poignant was the sheer joy my brother exuded when he saw Samantha and I hand-in-hand at the altar, as he also happened to be the minister leading the ceremony. *Remember what I said*, his words most resounding in the midst of the scene. When I awoke the next morning, I knew what I had to do.

Chapter 21 - The Only One

I was especially groggy that morning but the dream had been lucid and clear, like clean mountain air filling my lungs somewhere in the Catskills. The house was oppressive, all the curtains drawn with slivers of sunshine breaking through. The dishes were piled up in the sink, the overspill of used plates and silverware that were packed into the dishwasher. Empty bottles of soft drinks and coffee creamer were left across the counter top. I reached behind the debris and saw there was still a fresh pot left on the percolator.

I took hold of a beige mug that seemed half-clean rinsed it out with some warm water and finished off the pot. I opened the fridge and saw take-away trays and tin-foiled bowls cast across the shelves, on the door itself was a maroon carton of Half and Half, I shook it out and there was barely any in there. Beside it, a bottle of Caramel Cream Coffee Mate, I took some and dumped it into my coffee and made my way into the living room.

I coughed once and cleared my throat, as I shook the mouse on the desk, the flat screen of the computer finally awaking like I was, a red light turning green as the screen lit up. My finger turned the dial of the speaker as I double-clicked the icon for LimeWire and double clicked a MP3 scattered amidst the long list of icons, *Silhouettes* by Smile Empty Soul started to play. I remember when Foxy burned me a copy of their CD, sitting in her room with her and listening to the music as she reclined against her bed, closing her eyes as she took in the lyrics.

I stared at the triangular icon on the desktop, clicking on the triangular icon to open AOL Instant Messenger, after signing on, I was greeted with a welcome. I scrolled down the Buddy List and stopped when the menu turned blue over a name: IrishSouthernBelle526.

I peered out the window, before I clicked it and opened the chat box. A yellow post it-note icon was next to her name. Cheerleading <3. At a slow deliberate pace, I started to type: *Samantha, I am sorry...please forgive me...I Lo....*I reclined in the chair and shut my eyes for a moment, listening to the music playing until the song finished and *My Immortal* by Evanescence came on to follow, it made me think of Sam and how her complexion and face resembled that of Amy Lee. The yellow away icon dissipated next to her screenname and then became bold: she was available.

I sat back and shut my eyes again, listening to the piano play but the compulsion to send the message ripped my eyelids open. I deleted the text and started to type again. *Samantha, I am sorry. I can't stop thinking about you, I need you to forgive me, I can't forgive myself if I were to lose you...I Lo...*I paused again and looked down at the floor, when I gazed back up at the chat box, she was away again. Her status reading: *I am down but not out <3 :-**

"Fuck!" I dropped my head in my hands. Why procrastinate? She could have read it and you could have gone to see her but instead the room got bigger and colder than it already was. As I looked at the time in the corner of the computer screen, I saw it was 8:14 AM. I shot up from my seat and made my way to the door.

• • • •

AFTER AN HOUR OF WALKING in circles around the high school, the door to the Coaches Office stood in front of me. It was slightly ajar, meaning coach was in and that any that wish to see him could do so. I am surprised he didn't see me standing there for minutes with hunched shoulders as I gave myself a million reasons to go back home, but I didn't leave. I spurred myself forward knocking gently against the gold lettering which was peeling off the wood paneling.

Coach looked up, holding back a smile that instinctively filled him at the sight of me. He was wearing a green sport polo with the Falcon insignia over the right breast. His shirt was tucked in a pair of cream-colored khakis with complementing beige Timberlands. Coach had his facial hair edged up nice and neat as always.

"I had a feeling you'd come around." He got up from his chair. "Please, come have a seat, Corey..."

He shut the door behind me as I entered and pulled up one of the blue plastic chairs you commonly saw in the classrooms. "It's a shame you had to miss Homecoming last weekend; you only get one." Coach circled his desk to sit back down and look across at me.

"I didn't know if I was needed at this point"

"Of course, you were, you are a crucial part of this team. This week we're wrapping up the season against Lawrence. It's a big road game and obviously we have a chance at making the playoffs if we win." He took a sip of coffee. "We'd love to have you back but that's not what we need to talk about." He slid his coffee cup down. "I can't tell you how sorry I am for what you are dealing with and you will always have my deepest sympathies and support."

"Thank you, Coach."

"But what I won't accept is you ditching class and getting drunk." He sat up briefly and rolled his chair beneath him.

"What does it matter?"

"That's not who you are." Coach put his hands on the desk. "You owe it to yourself, your mother, your brother, and most of all to God to dig deep and fight through this and not let it derail you from everything you have done and can do."

"Well what if I told you that last night, all I wanted to do was to kill that motherfucker for what he did to my brother?"

Coach picked up his pen and tapped it against his desk for a moment. "Why didn't you do it?"

I leaned back and shrugged my shoulders. "A dear friend stopped me."

"Ricky?"

I stared at the grey file cabinet. "Samantha, actually..."

He smiled and nodded. "I had a feeling." His hands rubbed against his jaw. "How could I forget her?" He chuckled. "It is those with the wide eyes, rosy cheeks, and the cherry red hearts that always get caught up and sent in the wrong direction."

"That sounds like Sam."

"I wasn't talking about her but it's nice to know that you are thinking of her first and foremost despite everything that's going on." Coach raised his chin and glanced down at me, prompting me to consider that very point.

"The Lord knows your heart, so when he sees you are heading down the wrong road, He will send you an angel; a guide to point you back to the right path..."

The image of Samantha standing in Westwood watching me walk away flashed across me.

"Is that what you are saying Samantha is?"

"That's not for me to answer." Coach took a sip of coffee to cover his grin. "...now I know you are dwelling in a dismal place now, but whoever or whatever it is that will get you of there, run to it and never let go because that's the way out..." He took another sip of coffee. "Trust me..." Coach leaned back in the chair and watched me absorb his words. It wasn't some pantomime or presentation to sell me a used car, it was real, it was from a place of lived experience.

"Practice starts in twenty minutes. Do you want to give this one more shot?"

I looked up at Coach and nodded with a smile. I left the office and was welcomed back with joy by my teammates. However, over the span of the practice, I couldn't stop thinking about Foxy and the distraction caused me to drop a lot of passes when we ran routes. The message that I never sent to her; a fumble more catastrophic than the pigskin slipping through my fingers. It didn't help that I was getting winded easily from the cigarette smoking and felt like I didn't have my usual speed. I grew extraordinarily frustrated and irritated with myself.

I thought it would get better when we moved along to team offense to run plays. Nevertheless, the trouble seemed to trickle over. There, I stood on the sideline, anxiously waiting a chance to redeem myself. What happened to me? Did I deteriorate so quickly?

"Gingy!"

"Yes, Coach!" I buckled my chinstrap.

"Get back in there, we got to get those cobwebs shaken out."

"Yes, sir." I sprinted into join the huddle. As Danny called the play, I looked over at Foxy as I had numerous times over the span of the scrimmage. Although she was practicing with the cheerleaders, she would normally glance over at me. However, it seemed that she was intentionally ignoring me. I couldn't blame her, she opened her heart to me and I walked off, she probably felt embarrassed and belittled. I wish I could take that back.

I ran out from the huddle after the play called and lined up wide. I ran and sprinted down field with no one covering me. Danny threw the ball up and once again, I dropped it. I shook my head and ran back to the huddle.

A few plays later, it happened yet again. Once more after I glanced over at Samantha. Her long auburn hair was down her back and she was wearing black leggings which contoured to her thick legs and round muscular backside. Beneath a black sports bra which formed a y in between her shoulder blades, her arms, and lower back glistened as she was sweating profusely. She looked really hot, I could put my arms around her and smell her sweat to indulge in her, I was in submission to that fact. Everything about her was ethereal. All that I wanted was to see her look over and smile at me. I wanted to be right with her, I was at a point where I was ready to run to the sideline and pull her aside then and there, if it would allow us to reconcile. I stared back at her as I re-joined the huddle.

"Gingy, I am going back to you." Danny called across to me.

"You got this man." Ricky tapped the back of my helmet but his touch irritated me. "Don't sweat it..."

"Is that what you said when you were around Partridge last night?" DaMarcus laughed.

The unit all followed suit, except for me. I was still hoping Foxy would turn to at least acknowledge me. It must be all in my head, she wouldn't deliberately stonewall me but my guilt accused me of being the cause of such an event.

"Gingy, who you looking at?" DaMarcus's voice interrupted me as I continued to zero in on at the cheerleaders performing at the side of the school.

"He's got good taste." Ricky chuckled. "We got some dimes for cheerleaders, don't blame him..."

The guys all laughed in the huddle.

"You don't get it, do you?" I glared at Ricky.

"Get what, brother?" He looked up at me.

Both of us sized each other up, clad in our football equipment and dusty red practice jerseys, as if we were knights preparing to joust.

"Let me guess, you are just fucking another one on the side, aren't you?" I stepped away from the huddle.

"What are you talking about, homie?"

"No, don't give me that shit."

"What shit?" He extended his hand toward me and I slapped it away.

"How the fuck did you have the balls to treat Samantha the way that you did?" I gestured towards Samantha who was ignorant of the confrontation, in the midst of doing cartwheels and backflips.

"Foxy..." He laughed. "Again...." He waved his hand at me. "If you like her so much Corey, go for it." Ricky made a crucifix with his hands. "You have my blessing."

"I wasn't asking for it!" I shouted. "She is a wonderful girl, you know..."

"So, tell her!"

"She never deserved any of that man, fuck you!"

"No, fuck you." He pointed back at me. "And fuck your painfully obvious crush over Foxy that you are afraid to admit!"

"That woman deserves someone that will adore her and see how special she is. You think she is your fuckin' play toy!"

"Says the guy who was obsessed with Melissa, right? Now it's Foxy, Foxy, Foxy."

I took one more look over at her until I re-directed my attention toward Ricky. "You love her so much but go skedaddle when it's there. You don't think I know what happened with her, last night?"

My clenched fist opened, as if all the might had been zapped from me.

"She told me." His eyes grew larger. "But who really knows what the deal is as no one has seen you in a damn week!"

"You look at Samantha and all you see is her ass and a pair of legs, and nothing else." I stepped close to him and got in his face. "There is so much more to her..." Our exhalations crossed each other's faces. "...she's extraordinary, you should have considered yourself honored..."

"You want my advice?" Ricky took a deep breath and tried to reign this in. "You should have went for her from the get-go, man."

"You were with her!"

"Who cares?" He smacked his hand. "I never loved Sam but you clearly do..."

I froze for a moment, as if the words had pierced my soul.

"She's right there, now." He pointed at the cheerleaders who were stretching their legs under the press box still unaware of this argument unfolding. "Get off this field and go tell her..." There was no malice in his voice, only sincerity. He meant it. But when I turned to look, my stomach dropped and my heart broke. One of the soccer players stood beside Samantha, it looked like he was chatting her up. She was smiling—laughing, even—as if I didn't exist. I remembered him from the day Sam and I were in the colonnade and he was eyeing her up. His beady black eyes, flip haircut, and pimpled face made my skin crawl, but it didn't matter. She seemed to like him.

My chest tightened. What if I do love her? What if I'm too late? He was finally making a move, something I should have done when I had the chance. Of all the things that could go wrong, this one hurt more than any other.

"...but don't be jealous of me because you don't have the nuts to act on it!" Ricky's voice cut through my thoughts like a knife.

That was it. I lost it. I grabbed Ricky by his face mask, escalating into a full grappling match where the entire team had to pull us apart and separate us. The roars of the team and the bedlam that followed halted our practice, as well as the cheerleading squad. It was then that Samantha gazed over at me from the first time. No smile, no laughter, just shame. She looked at me like I was a stranger—like I was exactly the kind of guy she'd never want to be with. I couldn't hold her gaze. I looked down, my cheeks burning as regret twisted in my gut.

I couldn't live with myself and soon stormed off the field practice with my head down and found myself pacing down Horton Avenue, passing by where it all began, Greis Park. I glanced at the scoreboard and threw the football in a fit of rage, it crashed and caromed off the chain-link fence that bordered the park. "Piece of fucking shit!" I kicked the ball as it bounced across the sidewalk.

I continued onward until I paused when I reached the firehouse where Coach Kenny was a Lieutenant. In that solace, staring up at the brick veneer of the firehouse I began to remember what Coach Kenny told me about God providing us guides to help us navigate the shadows we encounter. My emotions intensified and further grew erratic. I began to ruminate on Mike's death and became remorseful for my actions with Ricky. In that moment, I was met by urgency and I sprinted home. I had to call Ricky; I couldn't lose him too.

Like a chicken without a head, I ran aimlessly believing the acceleration of my movement would diminish the overwhelming anxiety I experienced. Minutes later, I arrived at my home and Ricky was already on the steps waiting for me.

"Rick." I could barely catch my breath. I'm sorry man, I need to talk to you..."

"It's okay." He twirled a football in his hand. "Do you want to tell me what's going on?"

"I don't know what to do anymore..." I gazed down at the cobblestone slates. "This whole thing with Mike...."

"You are grieving brother, I get it." He tossed the football up in the air again. "But that's not the only thing I was talking about..." He smiled wryly.

"I shouldn't have lost it at practice." I pressed my palms against the railing. "...And you know me man, I'm not one to curse or to flip out. But I've been doing a lot of that lately; I haven't been myself."

"You don't need to tell me, man." He threw the football on the grass.

"I am really sorry; I appreciate you being here in spite of it..."

"I know we have had our differences lately but come on, he was like my brother too man." He patted my shoulder. "And I am not going to leave my other brother to mourn on his own."

I smiled at Ricky and thought about all the funny stuff that Ricky and Mike used to say when they taunted each other playfully. "You know what he told me, once about you?"

"What?"

"That you try to be like Usher with the girls." I laughed.

"Yeah, yeah. He thinks he can say that and get away with it with this stuff." Ricky looked up toward the sky. "Don't think I forgot about all your shenanigans, Michael!"

We both laughed heartily.

"He loved you though, that's why he broke your balls all the time."

"I loved him too." Ricky wiped his brow. "So, what is this whole thing about Foxy?" His eyebrows furrowed.

"I was just taking out my frustration on you."

"Yeah bullshit..." He picked up the football "I may have said some stuff I regret in our spat earlier but the one thing that is true, is that you love her, man..."

I didn't respond, unsure of how to reply. "

"You can't even show up to practice but you are ready to throw down for her on a moment's notice." Ricky smirked as we both watched a car drove down the street, the song *Surrender* by Ashlee Simpson blasting out the windows as two girls giggled in the car, as it passed.

"You are in love with her but you are scared, so that's why you left last night..."

"Did she tell you that?"

"Don't worry about it."

"I looked away, feeling the heat build in my cheeks. "What about the kiss?"

"I know about that too..."

I turned back to Ricky and squinted my eyes, confused as to what exactly was occurring.

"Do you think just because we haven't been talking that I wasn't trying to help you?" He put his hand back on my shoulder. "That we, weren't trying to help you." A grin filled Ricky's face. "You and I are better friends than that and Foxy and I can meet halfway when it comes to the matter concerning you..."

"What else did she say?"

"I am not saying anything else." He spat into the grass. "With everything that has happened, you're afraid you are going to lose her and things are going to be worse than they already are. Here is the thing you are missing: that's not going to happen and you are already worser off without her, anyhow." He rolled his eyes.

"Thanks." I retorted sarcastically. "What about that kid she was talking to?" I threw my hands out.

"Patrick McDonough?" He cringed. "...fuck that!" Ricky gripped the football and squeezed out his hands. "Foxy needs someone like you, someone that would stand by her and protect her."

"Isn't that what I am supposed to do?"

"You love her and you know it..." He threw the ball up in the air once and caught it. "Don't run from this."

He was right and I was afraid to admit it to myself, because for the longest time it seemed like a fantasy as well, even when I knew that this was actually real.

"...that's why you invited her to the team breakfast, and that's why you were ready to fight me twice now, fair included." He smirked. "We've been friends for how long and never even exchanged one foul word at each other and this woman comes around and we are ready to go to blows." Ricky smiled in gest, taking in the irony. "You were a sick maniac today..." He broke out laughing for a brief moment, before he looked at me with intent. "Funnily enough, you never got like that over Melissa. You gave Foxy your jersey and you sought her out when you had the so-called woman of your dreams lying in your bed waiting." Ricky brushed off his jersey. "You are the luckiest man on the planet and don't even realize it." He placed his hand on my shoulder firmly. "All you got to do is reach for her and she's yours. Trust me..."

I was taken back to Coach's office and what he said to me earlier this day. "Trust me." Trust. Trust in what The Lord has provided and the blessing He bestowed, it was beyond anything I could ever fathom or comprehend.

"Unless there is something, I don't know..." He raised an eyebrow. "Did you fuck her or something and you are not telling me?"

"What?" I raised my hands. "No..."

"But you want to..." He smirked.

"Do you hear yourself?!" My voice raised.

"Your reaction says it all..." Ricky chuckled. "...I was just proving it to you, yet again...you are in love with her."

"Mike did the same thing." I looked up at the sky and sighed. "I'd want a lot more than that with her..." The confession emerged, there was nothing more to say because my ability to speak left with the burden I was trying to conceal.

"And you can have it..." He spat once more. "Or would you rather Samantha in that polka-dot dress with a flower in her long reddish-brown hair down hair flowing over that fair skin with them sapphire blue eyes, with McDonough's arm around her instead?

I froze and started to breathe heavy, the thought felt like broken glass splintering further in my chest until it started to carve into my very soul.

"Judging by the looks of it..." He smiled widely. "...you are clearly not okay with that..."

"You are right." I threw my hands together. "I am in love with her." The words flew from my lips, as if they were forcing themselves from the bottle that they have been kept in. "I've never been more certain of anything..." I leaned back against the rail again. "Shit!"

"I am glad you admit it, finally." Ricky shrugged his shoulders. "What's the problem?"

"What if Foxy doesn't love me?"

"Do you honestly believe that? She pretty much said it!" Ricky shook his head. "And she never did anything like that with me either..."

I looked at him with bewilderment.

"...she might be clingy, but she's timid..."

I opened my hands to him, prompting him to continue his thesis.

"And despite the bravery of her pouring her heart out to you, the poor girl thinks you turned her away." He batted his eyebrows. "I have experienced being the giver of the bad news with her and she doesn't take it well. But you can still fix this..." Ricky leaned back. "Sam is forgiving and she wants you!"

"She doesn't even want to speak with me." A tear filled my eye. "I've let her down and I don't want to do that anymore."

"Shut up." Ricky spoke over me. "Go to her house, knock on her door." He itched the side of his scruff. "And tell her you love her."

I smiled for the first time in a long time, I couldn't help it.

"Give yourself a chance, at least..."

I grew nervous when he said that.

"What if we got this all wrong?"

"She deserves to be loved for her, right?"

I nodded.

"For that reason alone, you should tell her. And if nothing else, at least you went for it and did the first smart thing you did in a while..." He cracked another joke and placed his hand on your shoulder "...deadass, it's miles better than drinking and fighting, but personally, I think you'll be fine..."

Suddenly everything that Ricky, Coach, and Mike had told me all made perfect sense.

"I'm a fucking idiot!" I placed my hands over my head and circled. "Mike was right all along."

"Mike was right?" Ricky simpered. "That's it?"

"When she kissed me last night, it was like the greatest feeling I ever felt in my life. It was euphoric."

"If you're in love with someone it tends to feel that way."

"But I was more fixated on hopping on the bus and finding this motherfucker..."

"Is any of that going to bring Mike back?" Ricky leaned against the bannister to the steps. "You think that's going to square root this?" He snorted trying to hold back a laugh. "Besides, I don't think murder is really your kind of gig."

"Samantha said the same thing." I chuckled and removed the pack of smokes from my pocket. "When I was walking toward the bus, Mike told me not to do it..." I pulled out a cigarette, "It's like he was speaking to me from the Kingdom but I did go back for her..." I placed the cigarette between my lips. "But then she was gone..."

"So, you were going to tell her last night."

"This morning too but I backed off... "I looked over at Ricky as I lit the cigarette. "I had a dream when I finally got to sleep, her and I got married." I took a drag and my cigarette smoke blew in the wind. "She's the most beautiful woman I have ever seen." I waved my hand. "When I met her, there was something there but I told myself that you were with her and I wanted Melissa..."

"Word..." He plucked the cigarette from my lips and took a drag. "...and despite your corny prefaces, you should tell her what you just told me, as well." He put his hand against my shoulder and shook it with affection. "Go get her, Cap."

Chapter 22 – xo Irish Southern Belle xo

I realized that when love came knocking on Mike's door, he didn't win a million dollars. However, what Mike found was something much greater than money can ever provide. For years, Mike could never get his act together. He was obsessed with leading a life that only served to get out all the frustration, anger, angst, and resentment built up inside of him. When he described his relationship with Jessica, Mike defined all those negative moments as a pathway to her.

I was a fool, but like my brother, I wasn't stubborn enough to succumb to my own petulance. I walked to Samantha's house, determined to tell her how I felt. The walk seemed like an eternity although it was just a short stroll of a few blocks. Though my heart pounded through my chest, it assured me that it was her and only her - she was the one I needed to be with. The Lord blessed with me Sam, an angel to guide me through the darkest hours of my life and I couldn't hide from the brilliant light that radiated from her, it exposed every corner of my soul. For the first time since Mike's death, I had clarity and it provided me with an infallible tautology that mathematics could not quantify: I was in love with Samantha Jayne Foxe. I was never more certain of anything.

It was just near dusk; the skies were reminiscent of a pastel painting as the sun began to set. A cold wind gusted through the streets and swept up the crinkled leaves that had fallen. "*Hoodie Weather*" is what we like to call it as it is always best to take a sweatshirt with you when you venture out. Despite the frigid ambiance, the setting couldn't be any more romantic as a warm and gentle stillness filled me. I could finally take this in for what it was worth, perhaps everything that led me to it, needed to happen for me to be present in that brief passing moment.

I removed my cell phone from my pocket and pressed the buttons with shaking fingers until I was ready to call her. My heart was pumping and my breaths became shallow and rapid. Before, I could press the button to ring her phone, the front door opened.

Samantha walked the down the steps from her house as her long auburn hair tossed in the breeze. Her grey sweatpants sagged as she walked, framing her thighs as she wore them over a black tank top which was tighter to her body. Her hair was up, and she wore no makeup, but she didn't need it; she was stunning even in her simplest form. And in one look from her, I couldn't breathe, at all.

"What are you doing here?" Her lips stiffened.

"I have to talk to you..." I could barely finish the sentence without stuttering.

"You're not in jail, so I assume you never went over to Rockville Centre". Foxy inquired with a hint of sarcasm. "So, what changed everything then?"

"You."

Her eyebrows rose, she was visibly surprised by the comment.

"I was lying in bed all night thinking about everything you said."

"You could have fooled me!" Samantha snickered. "Judging by the course of events that unfolded at practice today."

"That's not what I meant." I looked away for a moment. "You know when we were at Westwood, last night?"

She arched her eyebrow again and nodded once. Any strength in her regressed back to a state of timidity.

"I ran back to find you..." I took a step toward her and reached for her hand. "I needed to tell you something..."

"Say what you need to say, Corey..."

My stomach began to turn from all the butterflies, I closed my eyes "I love..." I bit my tongue and her eyes bulged for a moment. Instead, I took a deep breath and looked at her with desperate eyes. "I don't know how to put this..."

I took her by the hand and yanked her toward me, she flew off the steps into my arms but I caught her and pressed my lips against hers. Once again, I felt that same euphoria from the previous night when she kissed me, it was as if I were floating on a cloud. I felt Samantha place her hand on my cheek and engage even further. When I pulled away and opened my eyes, hers were still closed. Foxy looked so innocent and as if she were child and she had just lost her breath for the first time.

"I love you, Samantha."

Samantha's eyes flew open.
"You love me?" Bewilderment filled the blue of her eyes.
"Yes, I am in love with you. You are the reason why I am still here; you and only you." I scratched my head nervously. "That's why I went back to look for you last night. I wanted to kiss you again and tell you that." Her eyes softened when she heard the words before a smile unraveled. It was if it were Christmas and she had just opened a gift that she had been asking for all of her life.

"And I'm sorry I left, if I could have done it all over again, I would stayed with you and woke up to know the joy of being yours." I let out a deep breath, as if a gorilla had just stepped off my chest. "I've been pissed off about everything lately and I've been screwing up. But you, you have been there through all of it. You mean more to me than anyone else ever has." I looked directly into her eyes yet again "That's why I nearly fought Ricky today, I was defending you..."

"Well, you are fortunate your coach was swell enough to let all that go..." She smiled.

"And then when I saw that kid talking to you..." I ran my hands down the bridge of my nose and let out a deep breath. "...I am sorry if I suck at this."

"I'd give you top marks." Her cheeks were rosy red. "Keep going..."

I smirked at her banter. "Everything feels uncertain right now, except one thing—I love you, Samantha." My disposition shifted from skittish and nervous to determined and passionate. "...When I am with you, nothing else matters. I want us to be together years from now and remember a day we met in Lynbrook..."

Samantha's eyes filled with tears.

"...And if you'd have me, I swear I'd never let you go...."

She covered her mouth and pulled me in for a tight embrace. "What about Melissa?"

"Sam, it's you." I rubbed her arms. "The Lord sent you to me and the sound of your voice could calm the most tempestuous of seas within me."

"That's very poetic..." She moved her head back and raised her eyebrows at the analogy. "Where did you get that from?" She released my hands and turned her back for a moment, a slight smirk appeared and evaporated on her face.

"I was worried you wouldn't feel the same..." I threw my hands at my sides. "I am sorry, I..."

"Hush up, Gingy..." Foxy about faced and pressed her lips against mine with her hands clutching my cheeks. "I love you too."

Right then and there, I looked up to God and thanked him. To this day I have yet to feel a rush of excitement and ecstasy that could rival that moment. She embraced me again and we kissed furiously. We lost track of time, our lips waltzing together as if it was the last day that we would ever see each other. She was my sunlight and with her came the blossoming of fresh flowers, full of color, life and splendor to my barren world.

We spent the whole night making love and it was nothing like I had experienced previously. Her touch made the hairs stand on my back, her lips tasted of a nectar, her warmth filled with me with ecstasy, and our bodies molded together like two hunks of clay destined to be one when we were one. It went on for hours and it was just us in the darkness. It was just Samantha and I and the chorus and raptures of our love and the passions that filled every inch of us.

Chapter 23 – It's All A Long Hello

I awoke to the greatest feeling I have ever felt. Samantha's hand in mine as she laid against my chest in my arms under the blanket. Our clothes were scattered across the floor, our flesh was each other's blanket. Her chest expanded and compressed against mine; her breasts pushed against my pectorals. Her hair was scattered across my face, my arms tight around her back as she nuzzled into my chest. I stroked her hair and kissed the top of her head as she slept peacefully.

"Good morning my love."

"Is this a dream?" She yawned.

"Thank God, no." I kissed her and engaged deeper with more passion before we stopped and locked eyes. The blue in her eyes were especially crisp, matching the autumn skies.

She smiled and brushed my face; we kissed again and the vigor ensued, as I slipped my hand under the blanket and massaged her breast.

"Mmmm." She moaned and ran her hand down me. "So, is this all you wanted to do all day?" She tapped my nose.

"I could." I rubbed her soft skin and held her face. "I need to apologize to Melissa."

"You do..." She nodded gently, keeping her cheeks tucked between my palms. "We'll pop by hers at some point today..." Foxy smiled as she pressed her lips against mine, I shut my eyes and enjoyed the taste of them. When I opened my eyes, I peered over and saw Mike's bandana resting on the nightstand. "And there is something else I would like to do also..." I stroked her cheek. "Would you come with me?"

"Of course." She smiled and we kissed again.

"But first." I rolled Samantha over and she squealed, as my lips continued to make their way down her neck, through her breasts, and over her stomach. We made love again for an hour and I was glad that my mother had gone away for a few days to stay with my aunt, otherwise who knows what consequences would await. Be that as it may, I would be surprised if the whole neighborhood wasn't interrupted from the sound of it. We fell back asleep and awoke again a few hours later.

I had the car and took Sam to the Brookvale for breakfast before we headed to Melissa's house. When we arrived, she was already sitting on the steps, the hood of her gray sweatshirt pulled over her head as she puffed on a cigarette. Her eyes lifted when she saw us, and despite her best efforts, a brief smile broke through.

I turned off the car, but before I could open her door, Sam jumped out and sprinted to the steps. Melissa stood, and the two embraced, Melissa's gray cotton sleeves wrapping around Sam's purple wool coat. Their voices were muffled, but I caught Melissa's words from a distance: "I'm happy for you."

"Thank you..." Sam said to her and she turned, her smile radiant. "...I'll get us those hot cocoas ready for the boardwalk while you two talk." She stepped inside, the door clicking shut behind her.

"Where are you taking her?" Melissa asked, smirking.

"Long Beach," I replied, shoving my hands into my coat pockets. "But I needed to stop here first."

Melissa rose to her feet, brushing a strand of hair behind her ear. "She looks happy," she said, her voice soft. "I've never seen her like this before. Gleeful—is that the word?"

"I hope so." I swayed slightly, my nerves bubbling to the surface. "I owe you an apology, Melissa. I was horrible to you." My gaze dropped to the ground. "I blamed you for my brother's death, but the truth is, I blame myself."

"For what?" Melissa's brows knit together.

"I kept thinking that if I never went for you, it wouldn't have happened. But that's not fair. If I never met you, I wouldn't have met Sam." I looked up, my voice steadying. "I'm sorry for everything."

Melissa crossed her arms, her sweatshirt's blue lettering obscured. "You were going through a lot. And I didn't make it easy for you." She glanced to the side, her voice wavering. "I never knew what I wanted, and when I finally did... there was no point in fighting what was already there."

I followed her gaze to the window, where Samantha's silhouette blurred behind the glass. Melissa smiled faintly. "I'm glad you two figured it out. Take care of her, Corey. She deserves it."

"I will," I said, stepping closer. "And I promise I'll never act that way toward you again."

Melissa nodded in appreciation.

"Is there any way we can be friends?" I extended my hand forward.

"Sure..." Melissa smiles. "We can be friends, as long as you don't fall for me." She opened the door with a chuckle as Sam emerged with two green travel mugs. "I don't want Fox trading places with me anytime soon..."

"What's this?" Foxy bantered, as I rushed towards her to take hold of the mugs.

"Just making sure I don't steal back the man you stole from me, you goon..." Melissa patted Foxy's butt playfully. "I don't think that will be happening though."

"Neither do I..." I said, meeting Sam's gaze. Her eyes sparkled with newfound hope, her smile lighting up the moment.

"She told me what you said..." Melissa took two steps toward the stoop and held the railing. "Many years from now, you want to look back on a day you met in Lynbrook..." She reached for the door. "Quite poetic, I hope it stays true..." Melissa shot a smile at Samantha. "Did he get that from a book?"

"He swears he didn't." Samantha bantered as Melissa embraced her tight, the two sharing a long hug of affection before Melissa released her and waved good-bye to the two of us. Shortly thereafter we were on our way to Long Beach, the tension lifted off of me. But there was still one more stop that I had to make.

We emerged onto Atlantic Avenue crossing over the train tracks into East Rockaway, passing both a Pathmark and a CVS, followed by the houses that lined the street until I saw a large glass greenhouse across the road from me when I stopped at a red light.

Samantha looked up at the sign for *Bea's Nursery*. "Are you sure you want to do this?" Her hands grazed against my arm.

"It's what Mike would have wanted, honey." I gently cupped her chin and carried on as the light turned green. I pulled into the parking lot and put the car off in park. A silence filled the air.

"Thank you, Sam."

"For what?"

"For being you." I smiled at her. "And for being here now." I kissed her and hugged her once again.

We entered the nursery to the fragrance of the various flowers emanating through the air. Behind the register, there stood Mike's former lover Jessie as he had described her. She hadn't changed at all but her identity was equally confirmed by the name tag worn on her green work shirt.

"Hello." She greeted me.

"Hello..." I nodded. "I'm Corey, this is my girlfriend Samantha." I turned to Foxy and smiled at her, just to steal another glance of her amazing face that beamed back at me.

"Nice to meet you both, I'm Jessie..."

Samantha acknowledged her with a quick nod and smile.

"I know who you are..."

Jessie moved her head back, startled at my comment.

"I am sorry to roll up here like this but do you remember Michael Montgomery?" I looked down reminiscing about my fallen brother.

She appeared perplexed.

"...I'm his brother..."

"Did Mike tell you I worked here?" She stepped from behind the counter, a hint of irritation and melodrama radiated from her glare.

"He didn't send me here..." I raised my hand. "...well he did, but not as you imagine it..."

"I don't really want to hear what Mike has to say, Corey, no disrespect to you..."

"It's not what you think." My eyes became watery. "It'll only take five minutes..."

"I'm going to take a smoke break." She looked up at the glass panels of the greenhouse. "Do you mind coming out with me?"

I followed her out the front entrance, Samantha's hand in mine. Moments later, we stood in the front of the store and watched traffic pass by on Atlantic Avenue. I pulled out the bandana and immediately she recognized it. Dried up blood stains faded the once green bandana to an opaque white-pink shade.

"I need to give you this." I placed the bandana in her hand. "Mike said you would know what it meant."

I looked at Sam for a moment who offered a supportive gaze back to me. Her gentleness and kindness radiated from her eyes. "A while ago, my brother told me that long ago, you and him were in love. He told me that every day he regretted the choices that he made because as a result they cost him you."

She took another drag of her cigarette as a tear escaped her eye.

"He would have given his life for you and Dem Rep was his life. But you have always been more important to him. He wanted me to let you know that he was out."

A smile broke from her face. "He's always been a good man, deep down." She put her hand on her hip. "...Mike..." She scrunched her face and smiled. "I don't get your brother sometimes. Why didn't he come and tell me? We could have worked this out..."

The irony of the statement was distressing, she was ready to forgive him and give Mike another chance. If only Mike could have lived to see it, I prayed that he somehow knew now so it would give him peace. As I looked up at her, my expression likely gave it all away, it was hard for me to conceal.

"He was going to..." I sighed. "...but Mike passed away." I broke down and Jessie soon followed.

"What?!" She covered her eyes and shook violently. Foxy rushed to her side, as did I.

"The life that he was leaving behind caught up with him. There was an accident and he was shot."

"But I just saw him in September..." She sobbed and we drew close to her.

"He told me and that was what made him want to change after he saw you at the fair. He told me about the times you guys shared and the first time that he met you."

Tears cascaded from her eyes.

"He told me that no one ever meant to you what he did and he would have stayed with you forever, if he could." I looked over at Foxy and took her hand. "I learned the value of this and didn't want to make the same mistake of letting her..." I gazed at Foxy "...slip away..."

"I've always feared this..." She sniffled.

"The night he was killed, he was trying to end a feud between the Sovereigns and Dem Rep. Mike was stepping down and attempting to help his fellows turn their lives around for the better too. In fact, the reason why he was shot was because he was there to protect me when the confrontation got out of control."

"Truck..." She swiped her eyes. "...they never knew when enough was enough...."

I embraced her as she trembled with the bandana gripped firmly in her wet palms. Foxy joined and embraced us both, until the hug broke and both our hands clutched the bandana together.

Jessie put her hands on my wrists. "He always used to tell me about you. He told me he was very proud of you and that when you got a little older, he didn't want you to get involved with gangs or selling drugs." A smile broke as she swiped another tear. "He hoped that you would pursue your dreams and meet a nice girl..." She paused to acknowledge Foxy. "...I have never met you until now but I feel like I know so much about you..." She placed Mike's bandana in my hand. "I think you should have this."

"Mike wouldn't have it any other way." I placed the bandana back in her grasp and closed her fingers around it. "You set him free from all of this. Thank you for that." I bowed and Sam curtsied in her own way. "If there is anything you ever need, do come by. We are family..." We turned toward the parking lot and took two steps before Jessie called out to us.

"Corey, can I give you something as well?"

I turned around and nodded, following her to the cashier register which was littered with business cards and a variety of notes written on an arrangement of loose-leaf, post-its, and aged napkins. The medley of stationery was kept underneath a plastic transparent cover which was placed on top of the station itself.

Jessie came from behind the register and approached me with heavy footsteps. Her high-heels careened off the polished wood floors.

"Call it a premonition but I feel that you should have this..." She handed me a note that was crinkled, crumpled, and seemed to have traveled great distances in many different pockets. "Mike told me you enjoyed reading and loved to write."

I took hold of the note and placed it into my pocket. "Thank you, Jessie."

She smiled back at me and nodded, then we parted ways. It didn't take much longer than me getting back to the car where I felt inclined to read it. I plucked it from my pocket and unfolded it.

"Do you know what that is, sugar?" Sam looked over my shoulder.

I skimmed down to the end. "It's a letter Mike wrote to Jessie, when he was upstate with Pops."

"I guess you weren't the only one with a passion for prose after all." Foxy rubbed my shoulder.

"I guess not, this is just before Mike came home and went to jail. It's dated to May 14th, 2003." I pointed at the date in the right-hand corner. "...I guess she has kept this with her every day since."

"Will you read it to me, love?"

I rubbed her cheek and kissed her once before I put my around her and started to read it aloud:

"My wonderful Jessica, I write to you this lukewarm May morning longing and aching for you. As you know my father Will and his wife live on the grounds of an old Grist Mill here in the Hudson Valley. This morning at the crack of dawn, I jumped in my father's pick-up and we headed to Pleasant Valley to pick up some lumber for a shed he was hoping to finish by the summer. As we made our way down Route 6A, we stopped off at a gas station to top up and as my father went into find the attendant, I took a step out of the car to catch a breath of fresh air. Across from this gas station was a creek that trickled aimlessly through the woods and grassy fields somewhere between Cold Spring and Fishkill. It was there that I saw a young man and young girl hand in hand merrily strolling through the tall grass. I simply watched and didn't interrupt, lighting up a cigarette to take it in.

These two were no more than twenty-one years old, but they were madly in love with each other: you could tell by their mannerisms, their fondness, and their affection towards each other. The girl reminded me a lot of you, wearing a white blouse and faded jeans, while the boy he was wearing a white beater and baggier jeans with work boots. He was clean shaven with a shaved head; probably in some sort of manual labor profession and she probably worked in some sort of trade as well. It was then that I knew what I truly wanted out of life.

I didn't know it until now but you have always been there guiding me. I haven't seen you in months but I know that should I see you again, no matter what comes my way, my life is perfect if you are in it." I had to stop for a second and regain my composure before proceeding. Foxy was silent as tears fell from her eyes. She took a moment to wipe mine, as I wiped hers.

"I know I cannot promise you wealth or even furnish you with lavish luxuries though I would love to, but I also know that none of that is as important to you as the truest gifts in life. I promise you that I can provide you infinite love that will never fail nor falter, and will always find a way to hold you sacred and most high in the face of any danger. I promise you that I will support you steadfast in any dream you wish to pursue, as it is not your dream, but ours. Finally, I hope to provide you with a family not just of brothers or mothers or cousins. I hope to create a family with you, our family. It is without question that when I return, I will place my bags down at the door, kiss my mother, hug my brother, and run to Lincoln Avenue to take hold of you and I hope I will never have to let you go.

I want you to be the mother of my children and the only woman I ever love. I would do it now if I could, but I am going to propose to you to be my wife and I will pray that you accept my hand in marriage. I love you more than life itself and would die tomorrow for you if it would ensure your happiness and health. I cannot wait to see your beautiful eyes and kiss your perfect lips.

I lose my breath gazing at you simply smiling in my direction. I only have one life to live, I was born in 1984 in Oceanside, New York and through all circumstance of human history, you and I simply crossed paths in front of a delicatessen. It could have been five minutes prior to and I could have bought a quarter water only to return home to my porch never knowing of your existence. Or I could have left 10 minutes after and walked down to the corner to get sidetracked by some other act of fate beyond my control. I could have been born in 1895 or 1995 and still never have known nor met you. However, in the one life I was given that can vanish at a fleeting moment, I just so happened to take a walk I will always remember and since then I've been ruined. I'll never be the same now that I've come to know you. Never more joyous was the occasion I first locked eyes with you. Until I see you again, Love, Michael." –

I finished the letter and that dream I made even more sense. Jessie to Mike is what Foxy is to me, but I was fortunate enough to realize this and act upon it when I had the chance. I placed my hand on Foxy's face yet again and pulled her in for a long and passionate kiss.

"I love you." I held her tight; In the silence of peering out the window from the parking lot, I was again learning from my big brother: how delicate and fragile such a tender moment like this could be and all that happened for it to occur, I would never take it for granted.

"I love you too." She closed her eyes and pressed her lips against mine, pressing her forehead to mine. Foxy ran her hand up and down my chest until she too peered out the window. "So, what comes next?"

"I am going to write about all this...."

"And then what?"

"We're going to the playoffs, my love." I looked ahead, determined as ever.

"Darling, I've always admired how far you plan ahead." Sam fluttered her eyelashes for a moment. "But I was talking about this afternoon, Pumpkinhead." Foxy giggled until it broke out until full laughter. I chuckled and pressed my lips to hers, as we descended into the seat kissing each other with slight nibbles hanging on the middle of our lips. I nuzzled up close to her and she threw her arms around me, squeezing me tight. "I could stay like this forever...." She shut her eyes.

I kissed her forehead. "...I was thinking the same thing." I held Samantha ever closer, ever more appreciative of the love that sprouted between her and I.

When people grow old and they face their mortality, almost always they reflect on the way their life panned out. Some smile and peacefully accept their fate and embrace their walk to their last breath. They are brave and content with hope and faith ever so strong in our good Lord. Others live in fear, dwelling on what they could have done or should have said or what they could have done differently.

. Death is absolute and once it comes there is no turning back. While you have the opportunity, the physical capability, and the time at your disposal to do whatever is what you want to do...do it. As long as you are alive, you always have time.

I believe if my brother could impart his wisdom upon us, he would encourage us to hopelessly fall in love. Leaving nothing behind and everything that is you on the line. For me it was simple, I was going to make the most of it; I was never going to quit; and I was just going to write. And thus, I dedicated this entire novel to you Samantha, because you inspired it.

Chapter 24 – The Day to Remember

Mike lived every day like it was his last, until one cool autumn night, it finally was. He didn't leave this world with many regrets, but the burden of losing the woman he loved weighed on him until the end. For a long time, I didn't fully understand that kind of love. Then Samantha Foxe came into my life, and everything changed.

Though Mike is gone, he still teaches me every day. He reminds me to never take love for granted, to appreciate every moment, no matter how small. I cherish the simplest things—lying beside Samantha, her head on my shoulder, or curling up on the couch, watching football together. Those were the moments that made life beautiful; a blessing that science nor philosophy could ever truly discern.

Coach once said I was a man on a mission. That mission became clear when we faced Lawrence with our season on the line. We were 4-3, clinging to a postseason dream, and trailed by 21 points at halftime. But we rallied, refusing to give up. I finished with 12 catches, 224 yards, and two touchdowns. Tennessee also beat Alabama that day, and Samantha couldn't stop singing Rocky Top. Her voice was like music itself, blending the melody of her heritage with the joy of the moment. Her southern drawl seemed to harmonize with the Irish elements of her accent in a cadence that was harmonic and smooth, I was amazed someone like her even existed in a place like Lynbrook.

From that victory, we went on a run. We defeated South Side in the first round of the playoffs, and at the celebratory party, I finally made peace with Melissa. We agreed we weren't meant for each other, but she was genuinely happy that Samantha and I had found each other. She only asked one thing of me: to take care of her best friend. That's a promise I've kept every day since and committed to even before we discussed it.

In the semifinals, we beat Bethpage 17-3, and then we punched our ticket to the Long Island Championship with a 21-13 victory over Coach Kenny's old team, Floral Park – Verbena Avenue. For the first time in our school's history, we were headed to "The Turf" at Hofstra University. There, we faced Nesconset High School, undefeated for two years. By halftime, we were down 27-0. Everything that could go wrong had. But Coach reminded us: With God, all things are possible. Don't let the scoreboard define who you are. Finish what you started.

We clawed our way back, cutting the lead to six. On the final play, with seconds left, we pulled off a miracle. A double reverse pass, and I caught the ball in stride, racing to the end zone as time expired. The commentators' voices still echo in my mind:

"*The Falcons will have one last hurl to the end zone and though it seems improbable, one has to admire the grit and determination of this team, as they simply wouldn't quick. Lynbrook will come out with four wide: Jean-Baptiste and Montgomery lined up on one side with Landry and Moreno on the other, Russell in the gun. Jean-Baptiste goes in a motion and they will hand it off to him on the end around, Moreno comes back on the double reverse and the defense is cheating up but wait a minute, he's going to throw. Ball's up and there is Montgomery extending his hands and he's pulled it in with no there to cover him and he's turned it up a field. He's in the clear and it's a footrace: 30, 25, 20, 15, 10. No one is going to catch him! No one is going to catch him! Touchdown Falcons! Touchdown Falcons! Lynbrook Union is Long Island Champions in one of the greatest comebacks you will ever see.*"

I ran straight to Samantha, handed her the ball, and she jumped into my arms. In that moment, I knew: she was the true MVP. She had led me here, through my darkest days, just as she had that night when I almost lost myself. Confetti rained down as my teammates mobbed me, but the real victory was knowing Samantha was by my side. That was my last game in green and gold and for many more of us, it was the last time we ever set foot on a football field.

• • • •

"IT'S WARM TODAY, ISN'T it?" Foxy fanned her hands, sweat formed on her chest, and arms. Her orange tank top cut off just above her hip bones exposing a bit of midriff before her black leggings hugged all the curves of her thighs and calves. She had her hair up and in a pony tail.

"Nothing like a Winter Heat Wave..." I took her hand.

"It is utterly repugnant...." She paused in her steps

"Good choice of words...."

"Cheers..." She broke a smile and kissed my lips. "May we sit, please?"

A cool breeze traversed the park, cooling both of us as we sat upon the metal bench set beneath a massive oak tree providing a canopy of shade. The rolling grass of Westwood was painted in a gradient of green where the sun broke through the trees that towered over the park.

"Sure..." I sat against the cool metal and put my arm around her. Foxy plucked her iPod from her bag and leaned against me. "Barely ever see the sun, when we go to Ireland in a few months, will we?"

"You are probably right..." I rubbed her shoulder as she put one of her headphones into my right ear, as she put the other in her left. "I warn you ahead of time, you might forget it's 2005 on occasion..."

"What's this?"

She hit play and *Away from Me* by Puddle of Mudd, broke through the silence. Foxy started to belt out the lyrics before she stopped herself. "Sorry, that's not what I mean to play...."

I laughed as I watched her hit swell, the orange shell with Tennessee's signature Power T on the face glistening under the daylight. "They are not bad for Gator fans..." She bantered.

"That's a lot coming from you..." I chuckled.

She shot me a look as the skipping sounds crackled through our headphones.

"I don't know babe, maybe you have turned over a new leaf..."

"Right..." Samantha replied smugly.

"I am just saying you are wearing orange...." I teased her and she glared at me with discontent. "And you know who that is for, thank you very much!" She smacked my shoulder.

I poked her stomach and she grunted from being startled. "You sneaky worm!" She threw her weight against me and pinned me against the bench, tickling me as I couldn't stop laughing. In the midst of all the fooling around, I held her so she didn't fall off the bench. Our eyes met and when they did, it was like everything else around us had stopped. We never took our gaze off each other until Sam reclined against the bench under my arm. She hit the play button and shut her eyes. *I Don't Want to Know* by New Found Glory started to play.

"Good choice, honey...."

She nodded in agreement as I put my left on her hand on her lap and took her free hand, my other arm kept around her as I shut my eyes and listened to the music, the sun breaking through the trees and landing on various spots of my face as the branches danced in the wind. The minutes of the song melted by and soon Foxy was sleeping on my chest, my eyes shut peacefully as the wind once again blew across. I felt as if Mike was there with us in that moment, his joy at us being together radiating in the warmth sprinkling through the trees.

My eyes opened to gaze up at the sky, wandering down at three teenagers across the park on Cornwell Avenue. Each had slushies in hand as they carried on walking toward Merrick Road, occasional laughs fading as they moved further away from the train station. I shut my eyes again with a smile on my face, as I leaned against Foxy's head, drifting off until I was awoken by a loud scream.

"Oh fuck!" A kid's voice echoed as he sprinted across the parking lot, his two friends sprinting behind him as a black Mercedes sped into the lot behind them, its tires screeching from the tight turn. It was the same kids from minutes before.

Foxy's eyes opened as she watched on with confusion. The windshield wiper flicked off the remaining purple and red slush which had formed a large puddle on the front of the car. The driver door opened and out shot a middle-aged man with a face full of stubble, his salt and pepper hair balding at the dome of his head. He drew his arms to the roof of the car and pointed his fingers at the retreating miscreants, forming a gun with his fingertips. His blue Phil Simms jersey flexing with his posture, the white number showing some cracks in it from wear, as the New York Giants top may have been as old as the last time the G-Men had won the Super Bowl in 1991. His baggy jeans draped over his white Nike's with a blue and red swoosh symbol.

"Boom!" He recoiled them. "Boom!"

Foxy watched on with shock.

"Boom!" He shouted a third time. "Where are you runnin?" He jeered, with a mischievous laugh. I placed my arm in front of Foxy's stomach, sitting up in a protective position even if there was no imminent threat to the two of us.

"What on the glad green Earth?" Her voice billowed from behind me as we watched the man put his hands back in his pocket.

The man removed a cell phone and put it to his ear. "Sorry, honey. I am on my way home now." He looked down at the phone and put it back in his pocket, then he glanced over at us and broke a smile at the sight of us.

It was like looking at Mike, only twenty years older. He had the same sly smile and deep gaze in his eyes. He gave us a nod of approval followed by a wink, as if he had known us. He took one more look at us, his smile growing wider at the sight of us sitting together on the bench, before he got back into the car and calmly drove off from the parking lot in the opposite direction from where the culprits had run. My heart clenched at the sight of that grin, so much like Mike's. For an instant, it felt like my brother had come back just to see me with Sam, letting us know he was happy for us. And in a blink, the car had long sped off into our memory, disappearing into the afternoon like a ghost from the past.

"Is it just me..." Sam turned her head towards mine, shocked with amazement. "...or does that gent look like Mike?"

"I was thinking the same thing." I looked up at the sky for a moment, the sun breaking through the trees until Foxy made a gun with her fingers. "Boom, boom, boom..." She imitated the stranger, a playful smile returning to her.

"Don't run anywhere." I smirked.

"I promise, I won't."

We shared a laugh as our lips came together. The memory of that stranger lingered only a moment before Sam's soft laughter and our interlocked gaze drew me back to her. The kissing intensified as I ran my hands up her back, and our eyes met again.

"Maybe, we should go take a nap instead? No one is home, you know..." I bat my eyebrows at her.

"Oh?" Samantha smirked and I moved in to kiss her again. "I like the sound of that." She met my lips and we engaged for a moment, as I cupped her cheek and she threw her hands around my back.

"Ready when you are..." I patted her thigh and helped her to her feet. "We'll enjoy our nap..." I gave her butt a playful smack and Foxy smirked at me, bridging her eyebrows.

"That's if we get to it..." Foxy giggled and I kissed her once more.

"I love you, Samantha…" I took her hand.

"I love you too, Pumpkinhead." She pulled our joined fingers up towards her and pressed her lips against the top of our knuckles. We stared at each other for a moment, setting a glowing gaze affection upon one another until I swung her hand once and we walked onward through the park, passing by the places and things that we had always known as our home, soon enough that was all going to change but Samantha and I had each other.

Samantha and I spent a year in Ireland before we went to college at the University of West Virginia. Samantha and I traveled around Europe, exploring Paris and Barcelona. We also made it to Knoxville for many Vols games. Each day, I fell more hopelessly in love with her. When we returned to New York, we became teachers, building a life together. Soon after, Samantha was pregnant, and we had a baby girl who had Sam's eyes. We named her Michelle Louise in honor of Samantha's father and my brother. Many may remember him for his mistakes, but we remember him as a loyal friend, brother, and son, befitting of such a tribute.

Ricky earned a full scholarship to Stony Brook, where he became a star. In his senior year, he led the Big South in total yards and graduated with honors. But ask him about his greatest accomplishment, and he'll still say it was winning that championship with us. He was the best man at Sam and my wedding.

Coach Kenny stayed in Lynbrook, despite offers from bigger schools and colleges. He believed in shaping young men in our community, and he did so as a coach, a Captain of his fire company, and a college professor. He's now in the Lynbrook Athletic Hall of Fame, alongside a few of my old teammates who've joined him as assistant coaches.

Shawn disbanded Dem Rep after Mike's death and helped organize a truce with Street Sovereigns to raise money for his burial. He and Melissa found comfort in each other and have been together ever since. Shawn now serves as a paramedic for the FDNY, and Melissa became a nurse. The four of us bought a two-family house in Floral Park and make it a priority to share Sunday dinners together, as we are family.

On October 24th, 2007, Samantha and I were married, marking the three-year anniversary of the night that we shared our first kiss. She was dressed as I imagined and our first dance was to *Your Guardian Angel* by the Red Jump Suit Apparatus.

And just as we were on that late Winter day years before, we were together at Westwood again, revisiting that very bench and that moment where it was just the two of us. Our daughter has grown into a beautiful, intelligent, and energetic little girl that takes after her mother in more ways than one. Even now, we take her to Westwood and reminisce about when we were younger, when it all started and it was all in front of us, rejoicing in the fact that it is now the three of us and the time we have shared with each other.

There was a point in my life where everything seemed to be shadowed by fear and anxiety. Doubt, was the only compass directing me on a path I would never be able to return home from. But then Samantha came and didn't realize she was always there guiding me. I wrote this story as my testament to her love and with a hope this will serve as a living monument that tells the whole world of her existence and withstands the test of time, like my love for her.

To anyone who reads this ten, twenty, fifty, one-hundred, or two-hundred years from now, know this: God's love is unyielding, and through His grace, I found my angel. Samantha Foxe, my sunlight, my love, my forever.

The End.

A Selection of Poems by K. Scott Fuchs

Note to A Loved One (2009)
A Truth be told -
I'm still burnt from being scold.
I put up these facades;
These fake faces, to disguise my true intentions.
I'm not the fighting type; I'm pent up with
Past aggression.
My heart is cherry red and it's never been more alive -
But I felt dead until you arrived.
Like a copper beam of life and joy that shot through me
My stomach and lungs full of tar and gook, now rinsed crystalline.
Soon I'll be grazing in the glorious of afternoons.
You are my sun, blanketing me with your warmth.

Master Shake Syndrome (2007)
I will not be a piece on your chessboard,
Cracking thunder -
At your leisure.
Your scruples molten shut,
At the sight of your lusts.
Your necessities prepared before you -
Feed your greed,
To be the king in your castle.
I'm not your pawn!
Knight me with your knife;
Your unholy hammer -
Will never nail me!

• • • •

CLARITY (2006)
I bring out the book of Psalms
I worship His crown
I kiss His feet
And surely, I know now that I will never cease -
But sometimes, I get addicted;
Other times, I get afflicted;
And even then, I get conflicted,
But in the end, on Him I depend.
Blood stains,
Brothers betray.
Bandanas strain,
I get disgraced -
I get disrespected,
Received wrongly and neglected;
Perceived incorrectly and rejected.
But sagaciously, I digress -
Cause in the end, on Him I depend.
It's a blurry road;
It's a curvy route;
It's bumpy and turbulent.
But out of the darkness comes the light.
Persistent and truculent
What is dreary is clear,
What is eerie disappears,
Full of clarity
Because in the end, on Him I depend.
Streetlight (2006)
I'm just another boy-
Daydreaming, staring at the streetlight.
It's just another hour,
I shiver with fright.

Anxiously awaiting
Alone, will I seize what I've always wanted?
Late at night clutching my pillow tight
Hoping my wishes will be granted.
I'm here again,
Staring at a streetlight
Wondering, hoping my dreams will come true
And shortly, I'll be seeing you soon -
In some distant place, far from here
At some different time, out of my cocoon.
Waiting to bust out into the clear,
While staring at the sign -
I'm just another man.

• • • •

NEAR HALL POND (2005)

You are beautiful.
One look entrances -
You are truthful.
One word is an entrance.
Nothing superficial; Nothing fake.
I cross grandstands to lakes,
Searching upon ocean and land.
But there is no better place, than my palm in your hand.

• • • •

SONGS (2004)

It's never easy to walk around with future all cloudy
Get rowdy, smoking weed and drinking can be easy to make it all gaudy.
A tease - I think I'm shoveling out while I'm truly digging in.
Talks of guns and jail, the notion unsettling,

A DAY WE MET IN LYNBROOK

To recollect I was trying to sculpt my social intellect
All those years of pain that I suppressed
Began to infect a medication I was trying to perfect.
You see, I wasn't looking to dial up, I just wanted to connect.
Conditions worsen, spraying up skulls and crossbones
The comfort zone, a long distance from home -
Songs can be heavy on the heart or they support you from the start
My hopes and dreams manifesting in room 129
To get my work done and look for my moment of sunshine.
It's never fun to be alone like the fall of 96
My friends and companions, a bunch of pinpricks
Negative words stick, but now I'm older and wiser.
They lose their alacrity and adhesiveness,
Adrenaline flowing with skies the limit.

Don't miss out!

Visit the website below and you can sign up to receive emails whenever K. Scott Fuchs publishes a new book. There's no charge and no obligation.

https://books2read.com/r/B-A-HCTAB-FAXRC

BOOKS 2 READ

Connecting independent readers to independent writers.

Did you love *A Day We Met In Lynbrook*? Then you should read *Time and Temperance*[1] by K. Scott Fuchs!

Along the canals outside of Marple, England, a despondent and lonely soul crosses paths with Temperance Lee—a woman whose beauty and elegance is matched only by her warmth, intelligence, charm, and wit. Their connection is instant, a love that defies explanation. But Temperance harbours a secret, one that shadows her every step: she is not an ordinary woman and she is not from this time.

In this electrifying split-time, dual-narrative saga that melds the Victorian era with the twenty-first century, love collides with the supernatural in a dramatic and action-filled tale of healing, redemption, and recovery. As a passionate and tumultuous romance

---

1. https://books2read.com/u/b6GXKy

2. https://books2read.com/u/b6GXKy

unfolds, two souls from different times and places find that their love does not come without challenges and troubles; challenges and troubles that they must overcome together whilst they confront their past traumas. But it will take more than just time—it will take understanding, exploration, faith, and unwavering belief in the power of love.

Read more at www.kscottfuchs.com.

Also by K. Scott Fuchs

Six Months in Wigan
Time and Temperance
Poetry From Ryecroft Hall
Mrs. Coleman of Coalbrookdale
Waiting For July
Sycamore Grove
A Day We Met In Lynbrook
The Town Upon A Hill

Watch for more at www.kscottfuchs.com.

About the Author

K. Scott Fuchs is a novelist, published poet, actor, and performer. His debut novel *Time and Temperance* was released in 2023 along with *Six Months in Wigan*, a collection of poetry. He is also the author of *Mrs. Coleman of Coalbrookdale*, (the prequel-sequel to *Time and Temperance*), *Poetry from Ryecroft Hall*, and *Sycamore Grove*, the third novel in The Miss Temperance Lee Series. A more comprehensive collection of poetry entitled *Waiting For July* has all been published and released globally in 2024.

Please visit **www.kscottfuchs.com** or contact K. Scott Fuchs at **kscottfuchs@gmail.com** to join the mailing list or for any other inquiries related to both novels and poetry releases.

Read more at www.kscottfuchs.com.